Woman's Sigh, Wolf's Song

Kathryn Madison

Windstorm Creative
Port Orchard ❂ Seattle ❂ Tahuya

Woman's Sigh, Wolf's Song

published by Windstorm Creative

ISBN 1-59092-130-5
First Edition July 2005
9 8 7 6 5 4 3 2

Cover by Buster Blue of Blue Artisans Design.
Author photograph by Daniel Herron Photography of Mountain View, California.

Quote from *Shades of Gray* by Renee Askins; Intimate Nature, the Bond Between Women and Animals; Random House.

Quote from *The Greatest Salesman in the World* by Og Mandino. Random House.

Lyrics for "Ten Thousand Pine Trees," author unknown, used by permission.

The staff of Windstorm Creative wish to thank Elsie B. Emond. Without Mrs. Emond's faith in Windstorm, the incredible works of Kathryn Madison may never have found a home with us.

Windstorm Creative is a multiple division, international organization involved in publishing books in all genres, including electronic publications; producing games, videos and audio cassettes as well as producing theatre, film and visual arts events. The wind with the flame center was designed by Buster Blue of Blue Artisans Design and is a trademark of Windstorm Creative.

Windstorm Creative
Post Office Box 28
Port Orchard, WA 98366
wolfsong@windstormcreative.com
www.windstormcreative.com
360-769-7174 ph.fx

Windstorm Creative is a member of the Orchard Creative Group Ltd.

Library of Congress Cataloging-in-Publication data available.

Dedication

To my husband, Michael, who removed every obstacle, provided every tool, encouraged with his words, and sustained with his love.

To my mother, who refused to let my dream fade.

And to Celeste, the future.
May she one day hear the howl of the wolf in Yellowstone, and recognize a kindred spirit.

Acknowledgments

No novel leaps fully-formed from the author's mind to the bookstore shelf, and I owe a great debt of gratitude to the following people for their help and support.

While this is solely a work of fiction, the author is grateful to the following wildlife biologists and professionals for their meticulous documentation of wolf behavior and society: L. David Mech, Renee Askins, Diane Boyd, Mike Phillips, Barry Lopez, R. D. Lawrence, Lois Crisler, and Rick Bass. Where Patriarch's pack moves and breathes convincingly, it is due to their diligence; any misinterpretations of their observations are mine alone.

I also appreciate the assistance of the following wildlife organizations, who worked to bring the wolves back to Yellowstone National Park: The Wolf Fund, Defenders of Wildlife, National Wildlife Federation, Yellowstone Wolf Project, National Resources Defense Council.

Without the opportunity to see wolves in the flesh, and be allowed to watch them interacting within their environment, it would be difficult to truly paint them with words. I am indebted to the following organizations who allowed me this privilege: Wolf Haven, in Tenino, Washington; Bronx Zoo, New York City, New York; Denver Zoo, Denver, Colorado; and especially the staff of Mission:Wolf, and their canine ambassadors, Sila and Merlin.

For walking me through the intricacies of veterinary medicine, I extend my appreciation to Drs. Peter and Amy Hosein, and their staff.

I am grateful to the Yellowstone staff of the National Park Service, the guides of the Seattle Underground Tour, and the biologists and docents of the Monterey Bay Aquarium for their assistance.

The staff and writers of the Squaw Valley Community of Writers have my deep appreciation, for it was during their conferences that I was first called a writer, and this book first drew professional criticism and encouragement. I am especially grateful to my workshop leaders, Sands Hall, and Pam Houston.

I also appreciate the advise and counsel of M. J. Bogatin, a lawyer with his heart in the arts.

I am especially thankful for the dear friends who read early drafts of this work: Laurie Woodfill, whose tears made my heart sing, Dan, Eileen, and Amy Noble, Debbie Frincke, and Sara Madison. Among my friends are two talented editors, and this work lives today because Penny Marquez and Erin Rand boldly took red pencil in hand.

I am grateful to Vic and Kathy Hopner, who offered their mountain home for my writing efforts in the earliest days of this novel.

To my parents, Andy and Wilma Anderson, and my sister, Vicky, who shared the early events that imprinted my passion for animals, my deepest appreciation for their love and support. My first stories were born during childhood outings in Kodiak, Alaska, where the bond of family was taught by example.

Most important, I thank my husband, Michael, who accepted his role as remover of obstacles and provider of tools, when my dream was in its infancy. His loving support and encouragement over the years continues, unwavering. Simply, without him, there would be no book.

All the effort and loving support previously mentioned would have been fruitless were it not for the professional attention of the staff at Windstorm Creative, including my editor, Sue Hogan, and especially Jennifer and Cris DiMarco, Windstorm's chief executive officer and senior editor, respectively. Their patient guidance through all aspects of the publishing process brought this story to life, and the courtesy and respect they extend to their writers sets a high standard.

Finally, thank you, Chinook and Nikita, you were the inspiration.

Kathryn Madison

Kathryn Madison

Woman's Sigh, Wolf's Song

Kathryn Madison

"…A deep, profound truth still resonates in us;
by some grace our souls still whisper to us,
our wildness still calls us…
Instinctively we know that what we do to the wolf,
we do to ourselves.
And what we do for the wolf, we do for ourselves."

—Renee Askins, "Shades of Gray"
Intimate Nature, the Bond Between Women and Animals

Chapter One

Rain in Seattle, what a cliché. A bone-chilling, flesh-numbing cliché that pelted through Sean Denny's uniform as wet and cold as on bare skin. The police Sergeant was soaked from collar to socks before he'd run half a block. His flashlight spotted a bushy tail as it vanished around a brick building and he grinned. His partner was much better equipped for the weather.

Rain rolled off the brandy and black German Shepherd without notice, a downy undercoat kept Rommel warm and dry, and only muzzle and feet sensed the wet. Huge paws splashed water as he dashed into the dark alley.

After a murderer.

Twice as many feet propelled Rommel twice as fast, and Sean was panting after three blocks, sweat blending with rain on soggy navy wool. Rommel's long-striding pace demanded a human sprint just to keep him in sight, and Sean was awed by his partner's abilities to disregard the elements.

Sergeant Denny loved that dog as much as he would have a human partner, maybe more.

Stray human hairs and dislodged skin cells were all Rommel needed to track, and rain only dampened the game. He had paced the murder scene, sniffed the victims and identified death by pools of coagulating blood and cooling human skin temperature. But he made no value judgement. Rommel lived to find people... missing people... injured people... people who didn't want to be found. And he was very good at it.

Rommel burst from the alley into Pioneer Square, dimly lit by old style gaslights. The usual contingent of winos and panhandlers had vacated their regular habitat for drier ground and only the pigeons squabbled over real estate under the opaque glass canopy.

Rommel paused momentarily, sniffed the ground, scanned the air, and bolted through the park and across the next street to a metal fire door on a derelict building. The padlock on the door was still locked, but the hasp had been recently pried from the crumbling brick. The scent on the metal was sharp and fresh and tingled sensitive olfactory cells. Rommel lunged against the door, barking with excitement, but smart as he was, opening it required an opposing thumb, so he waited for his partner who had one.

"Oh shit, Rommel, not down there!" Sean muttered, "I hate the underground!" The agitated dog barked and bounced. "Rommel, down!" But prey was too close, he couldn't sit still. Sean hauled him back by the collar, but when he opened the door Rommel dashed down the shaky stairs and vanished into the darkness.

Sean keyed his radio, "2210, requesting backup at Seattle underground fire door #8. Repeat. Perp's gone into the underground."

"2210, this is control, ten-four."

Sean took a deep breath—the last clean air he'd taste for a while—and followed Rommel down the rickety steps. Twenty-two feet down and a century and a half back in time. To the tunnels of old Seattle. The first Seattle. And to the restless ghosts of its first citizens.

Two miles north a cab pulled to a stop and an attractive blonde rushed into the lobby of the Westin Hotel. She paused at a large mirror, touched up her lipstick, tugged a crooked earring back into position, and smoothed the front of her scarlet Valentino original. Transformation complete. Alex Davidson Verazzano, DVM, was now Alexandra Verazzano, lawyer's wife.

"Late again," she muttered to the reflection, "for another gathering of the beads and sequins."

Shoulders back, smile glued on, she grasped the enormous brass door handle. Her posture and the set of her jaw screamed battle ready, and camouflaged shaky nerves and a queasy stomach. Swinging the giant door open, she drifted gracefully into the ballroom. Hating every high-heeled step.

Two hundred pairs of eyes followed her to the vacant

seat next to her husband and a brief glance confirmed the frown she had expected. She responded with a tiny 'sorry, I-couldn't-help-it' shrug and faced the front of the room.

Alex, she thought to herself, *you are still a goldfish in this tank full of sharks.*

The evening's host picked up where he'd left off. "As I was saying, tonight's speaker brings with him twenty years of experience working with inner city children. I believe his cause is worthy of our consideration."

Light applause seated the host, and ushered the speaker to the podium. Alex glanced around the room, noticed the same faces draped in couture's latest greatest, and sighed. Middle-class Alex had realized early in her marriage that charity banquets weren't really about charities. Yes, money was donated, frequently large, tax-deductible sums. But here the city's ambitious and powerful mingled and postured while their trophy wives, coifed and primped, displayed the family jewels. Quiet, but binding deals—and people—were made or broken. This was the arena for sophisticated political games, subtle games you really couldn't learn unless you were born into them. Alex wasn't, and she still didn't know the rules.

Alex, veterinarian, disguised as Alexandra, wealthy wife, parked her handbag in her lap, settled a lawyer wife's smile on her face, and prepared to endure the evening.

Watching her rain-stained shoes dry.

The same storm buffeting Seattle stretched north and east a thousand miles, where temperatures plummeted and snow fell instead of rain. It blanketed a large wolf, coating the soft fur of her muzzle, lodging in her eyelashes. But she was oblivious to it.

Winter-hardened claws scraped away snow, then scratched the earth's skin in earnest, forelegs assaulting the shoulder of the hillside with single-minded focus. Huge paws threw mud, then dry dirt behind her in a staccato rhythm that kept time with her relentless drive to prepare for her unborn young. Four feet into the east-facing hill she angled her tunnel upward, creating a rise that guaranteed a dry den.

Cub-bearer, alpha female, attacked the hillside with no tangible blueprint, save the absolute design dictated by centuries of instinct.

The three yearlings of last winter's joining romped in the slushy leavings of her work. Canine teenagers, they were an awkward age, large in body, small in wisdom and experience. Slate gray Cunning batted her tan brother in the face and Jester rolled backwards down the hill, too clumsy to break his fall. Gentle, a carbon copy of her mother's rich red hues, cowered instantly before her sister, shrinking beyond reach. Her gentle spirit had no stomach for Cunning's brash aggression. Bored with her siblings, Cunning stuck her head in the tunnel in time to get a face full of dirt. She growled, but not loud enough for her mother to hear. Dominating her siblings was one thing, challenging the adults was something else.

Gentle and Jester spied their uncle, Guardian, asleep under a fir tree and pounced on the large gray male. Guardian wrestled the two cubs, at one point pinning Jester down, the yearling's entire head in his mouth. Jester had never been safer.

The adult wolves had fought and killed to feed the yearlings and keep them safe, but soon parental care would be abruptly terminated. For twelve months they had been nurtured, now they would become the nurturing.

Ominous silence greeted Sergeant Denny when he reached the bottom step. Rommel was out of sight and sound. A wooden walkway led left and right into the darkness and in the filth on the plywood Sean found a large pawprint. Rommel had turned left—south—at the bottom of the stairs.

Sean's limited human senses restricted him to a pace much slower than the dog's, and the musty air and thick silence of the underground raised the hairs on the back of his neck. He had no idea how far Rommel was ahead of him and the pitiful spot cast by his service flashlight brought little comfort. Glowing pairs of eyes hovered in the darkness and small feet scurried through the dirt on either side of the walkway, then skittered across the plywood behind him.

"Rats", he muttered. "Perfect!"

Sean unbuckled the safety strap on his revolver.

"Rommel, where are you, boy? This place gives me the creeps." Sean Denny had proven his bravery many times since joining the force, but this place reeked of a little boy's nightmares, and the ghosts that haunted him here would not die with a bullet.

Tensed by every rustle and rat scratch, Sean's imagination resurrected Seattle's colorful past, attended by the ramshackled junk around him. Spider webs draped old wooden crates, rusty ancient tools, and leather strapping. Hollowed-out logs mounted end to end hung along the wall, Seattle's first sewer system.

Charred timbers loomed out of the darkness to Sean's left, glaring reminders of the fire of 1899. Raging fast and hot through lumber mills, feeding on piles of sawdust, it had leveled most of the existing city. After the smoke cleared many merchants decided to build higher, solving tidal flooding problems. Using the old first floor as a foundation, they relocated their business entrance on the new second floor.

Over the years the spaces in and around the old lower floors were filled in and fell into disuse as businesses vacated. Stairways and doorways to those subterranean ruins were boarded up, built over, and forgotten by everyone except the rats.

It was along those recently excavated streets that Sean followed Rommel.

He prowled down the eerie old sidewalk, past a print shop, then the remains of a blacksmith shop, next to some sort of accounting enterprise. Grateful for the dirt-covered plywood trail that made tracking the dog easier, he audibly sighed every time he saw the German Shepherd's paw print. Sean had no idea where he was in relation to the city above him. He keyed his radio, "2210, to control, over." Only static responded.

"Control, this is 2210, over." More static.

"I sure hope someone's tracking me like I'm following you, Rommel-dog."

Beyond sunset and into the evening Cub-bearer labored, pushing dirt to the opening, then outside, packing the floor with her paws and smoothing the walls with each pass of her body. Human eyes would notice and forget the two-foot hole, but when she exited the tunnel late that night Cub-bearer had completed her cozy natal nest, three feet in diameter, nine feet into the hillside.

Panting, she gazed at her family, four sleeping mounds of fur in the snow. Except one. Patriarch watched as she climbed to him, her fatigue visible in each step.

Nothing interrupted the black of Patriarch's coat, so dark he virtually disappeared on moonless nights. Even after the trials of winter he carried over 120 lbs. on his large frame and the footprint he left in the snow measured five inches in length. He evinced the wisdom of six winters survived, and leadership's mantle rested easily on his strong shoulders.

Patriarch cared for his offspring, but his affection was tempered by the weight of responsibility, and merely a look from his golden eyes could freeze an underling in fear. Little effort was required to believe the cunning and clever brain behind those eyes was capable of some semblance of logic. The pack fed or starved by his wits.

He was Patriarch. Alpha. And he demanded absolute respect.

Cub-bearer collapsed in the snow, exhausted, and he dropped next to her. Their valley stretched below them, blanketed in new snow, moonlit from end to end. A surging river roared a lone reminder of the glacial ice that had chiseled lowland from mountain a millennium ago. This valley of the wolves breathed a virginal wildness, pure and untouched. In its isolation it was timeless.

☪☪☪

Sean turned a corner and froze. Every hair on his body leaped to attention.

"What the hell...?"

A soft purple light quivered and danced on the plywood trail ahead of him like some century-old spirit, trapped and trying to escape the underground. Rommel's pawprint seemed to shift in the eerie glow with a life of its own. Sean pulled his revolver and stalked up to the apparition. Then looked up. He shook his head and grinned. A halogen streetlight from the current century above cast powerful beams through an ancient skylight of thick glass, tinted purple with age.

"I don't believe in ghosts," he mumbled, "but if I were going to consider the concept, this would sure be the place to start." Several deep breaths and the sound of his own voice calmed him, but he still had no idea how far Rommel was ahead of him.

Minutes later Rommel's tracks turned sharply and entered what looked like an old theater through a gaping crack in the wall. Sean crawled through the hole and heard bipedal footsteps across plywood and, in pursuit, the reassuring sound of claws tapping a canine gait. Rommel was closing in on his prey.

Shining his flashlight around, Sean could see the room was not large by today's theater standards, but it was at least two hundred feet to the other end. Barking and growling erupted from what would be the backstage area and he sprinted down the ancient center aisle.

Seconds later he found the dog leaping up and snarling at a hole in the ceiling, an opening to the floor above.

"Rommel, down!" The dog glanced at him and obeyed reluctantly. Sean pointed his light up into the darkness, and a gunshot whizzed by his head.

Rommel leaped up, putting his seventy-five pound frame between the two humans and the next bullet hit him squarely. He collapsed and Sean aimed at the dark hole, letting off four rounds. A human dropped through the ceiling and hit the ground next to the dog, bleeding and unconscious.

Sean kicked the gun from the sniper's hand and immediately turned to Rommel. He heard footsteps and yelled for his backup.

Rommel was so still Sean's stomach knotted, and when he knelt next to him canine blood seeped into his pants from under the dog.

"Oh, God, no," he groaned. Sergeant Denny tasted real fear for the first time that night.

But when Sean stroked his head, Rommel opened his eyes and whined softly. Sean exhaled, his partner was still alive.

In his flashlight's glow he concluded the shell was still in the dog's thigh so he pressed his hand over the entrance wound, applying pressure to slow the bleeding.

"We gotta get you out of this rat-trap, partner, you could catch the plague down here." A lump in his throat swelled to keep company with the knot in his stomach while he stroked the dog's head with his free hand. "Hang in there, Rommel, you stay with me, pal."

Not one thought passed through Sean's head for the condition of the killer next to Rommel.

The silent pager vibrated inside her evening bag, rudely summoning Alex to consciousness. She checked the number and made eye contact with Stephen, who nodded, lips pursed. Arrived late and leaving early. But now she didn't care. In the hotel lobby she pulled out her cell phone and dialed her message service.

"This is Dr. Verazzano, you have a 911 for me?" The lethargy and boredom of the evening vanished.

"Yes, have them take him to the clinic, then call Tony. I'll be there in ten minutes." She hung up without waiting for a response and caught the eye of the concierge who had been watching her.

"Cab, please?"

"Yes ma'am, right this way."

Dr. Alex Verazzano wrapped her satin coat around her shoulders, marched briskly across the marble lobby and stepped into the waiting cab.

A very special patient had been shot.

Chapter Two

Seven minutes later Alex opened the car door and red satin heels struck pavement before the taxi rolled to a complete stop. Her technician's orange Volkswagen bug was flanked by two Seattle police cars, parked at odd angles, blue and red lights hypnotically probing the darkness.

"Rommel, how are you, boy?"

The veterinarian had cared for Rommel since his qualification with the department four years earlier and her first words conveyed a familiar affection. Rommel was conscious and his eyes followed her approach, unblinking. When she was close enough to touch him, he raised a bushy tail and flopped it once against the vinyl seat. He easily recognized his caregiver beneath the rustling satin.

"Looks like you made somebody pretty angry tonight."

She stroked him between the ears with one hand and inched the other along the length of his body to the wound in his thigh. He flinched.

"Easy Rommel, I'm not going to hurt you."

Alex performed her initial triage, her soothing voice ministering to Rommel's spirit as her hands worked over his body. There was a lot of blood dried in his fur, and fresh blood oozed slowly from the wound itself.

"The second the perp fired at me he leaped between us and took the next round!" Sean's pride and affection for the dog was obvious. "He's gonna be okay, right?"

Alex looked up and noticed the large bloodstain on his shirt.

"How far did you have to carry him?"

"Hard to guess, there aren't any street signs in the underground. At least half a mile, maybe more." She nodded.

"Tony, take Rommel to the surgery."

Her technician, nervously pacing beyond the perimeter of uniforms, started toward the dog, but before he could pick him up Sergeant Denny stepped in front of him.

"I'll carry him." Sean's voice communicated authority equal to his uniform.

"Yes, of course." Tony stammered and backed away. "This way, please." Sean, with Rommel cradled like a large hairy baby, followed Tony to the stainless steel table in the surgery. Two other officers completed the parade.

Alex tossed her evening bag on her desk and kicked her ruined shoes into a corner of her office.

"Start two IV's of Ringer's, Tony," she called, "front legs." But he already had one needle inserted and lactated Ringers solution flowing before she verbalized the task.

"What's that for?" Sean's demanding voice made Tony jump. Alex answered from her office while she slipped into a pair of worn Reeboks.

"Sean, we can't let Rommel get dehydrated, he'll lose electrolytes. The Ringer's will keep his fluids up during surgery and while he is unconscious." Tony handed the two IV bags to Sean to hold while he retrieved stands, and the other two officers took their moral support to the waiting room. The antiseptic smell of surgery made them as nervous as they made Tony. Sean, however, remained firmly planted next to Rommel's table. Tony reached around him to insert a rectal thermometer, while he counted Rommel's respiration.

"Vital's, Tony?"

"Temp is 99.7, respiration is low." Alex made entries on Rommel's chart.

"Sounds shocky. We can't operate until he's stable, so let's give him dexamethasone."

"What's that?" Sean's interrogating tone was starting to annoy Alex.

"It's a steroid to stabilize him." She reached around Sean to tape contacts to Rommel's chest and then plugged the contacts into the EKG. Sean watched the two professionals and felt as useless as a piece of broken furniture. Alex and Tony shuffled around him as if he were. Finally, Alex tired of the ballet.

"Sean, you'll have to wait outside. As you can see, there isn't a lot of room in here, and Tony and I have our own dance routine for getting around."

"I'd like to stay. If you think the blood will bother me, it won't."

"That's not the point." Alex spoke with as much authority in her jurisdiction as he had in his.

"I'm in the way?"

"You read my mind, Sergeant." He stroked Rommel's head and reluctantly joined his fellow officers, amidst the pet magazines and pamphlets on heartworm and parvo-virus.

"X-ray his left rear, Tony, and I'll prep the anesthesia." She calculated the dosage for the large canine—1 cc. of 4% thiamylal sodium per five pounds of body weight—and they worked in silence for fifteen minutes.

"How's he doing now?"

"Pulse and temp normal and stable for the last three minutes."

"Good, let's go ahead." Within minutes of the injection Rommel was breathing deeply in his drug-induced slumber.

"'Trach tube now."

Working together, they inserted an endo-tracheal tube down the canine's throat to insure a clear airway and administer the general anesthesia during surgery, and Alex tied Rommel's muzzle closed with gauze, to keep him from chewing on it. Then Tony passed Alex a hypodermic of atropine, and she administered the subcutaneous injection to check his salivation.

While Tony shaved Rommel's left rear, Alex studied the x-rays, noting the position of the slug.

"This is good, didn't nick the femur. Tony, what conclusion could you draw from the amount of blood loss he exhibited?"

The tech thought briefly and then said, "The bullet didn't hit the femoral artery either. Not enough blood." Alex smiled.

"Right. It looked like a lot of blood to Sean, but it was already coagulating when they got here." She pointed to the X-ray, "This is one lucky dog, it's sitting in the fleshiest part of his thigh."

Tony shaved and washed the surgical area generously with betadine and Alex started the flow of 2% halothane through the endo-tracheal tube. For two minutes she watched the system of tubing to and from the canine, through the rebreathing bag and into the flutter valves that visibly counted the dog's respiration.

Rommel was one of the brightest dogs she had ever encountered, and a hard-working member of the Seattle Police Department. She recalled watching him climb a ladder with the agility of a cat, and walk across a two-by-four, half as wide as his body. He had been tested repeatedly for the number of times he would return to an assailant that had caused him pain and he never cowered.

But it was the other side of Rommel that touched Alex. He was six years old, yet he retained a puppy-like curiosity. More than once he had received a nasty swat from Sheba, the clinic's cat, when his nose drifted within striking distance.

His stillness on the stainless steel table was out of character.

When all was functioning smoothly she and Tony scrubbed for surgery with the same care as if their patient was human. They masked, covered their hair, and gloved. Tony stepped behind her to cover the Valentino gown with a well-washed green cotton smock and Alex stepped into it without a second thought. The incongruity of the image was striking, a beautifully coifed woman in worn Reeboks and red satin, gloved and masked for surgery.

"Okay, Tony, let's do it."

The sun's first rays were bathing the hillside in gold when Cub-bearer entered the den to stay. She did not eat and silently kept her own counsel, awake and waiting. Outside, the pack stationed itself around the entrance to the subterranean nursery.

No sound escaped the den as Cub-bearer panted through her labor, each contraction more intense than the previous one, but she suffered her whelping in silence and darkness.

She gave birth to her first cub as sunlight touched the valley floor. With the same teeth that could crush a moose's leg, she bit into his embryonic sac and drew him out, licking away all traces of birthing matter. Then Cub-bearer nuzzled Red-cub, a male, to her side to nurse while she delivered his sibling.

The next cubs were born together, a pair of gray females, First-twin and Second-twin. Their coincidental birth kept the shewolf busy cleaning and licking, and she worked quickly, massive teeth gently tearing away the slimy film. They risked suffocation inside the fetal sac if she didn't release them within seconds.

The fourth cub to make his appearance was another male, Black-cub. Cub-bearer cleaned and nudged him next to his siblings and closed her eyes to rest until the next contractions started. When they came, they were the strongest yet, but the exhausted bitch bore them in silence.

Tony retrieved the sealed pack of surgical instruments and opened it over the sterile environment of the table. Alex slowly probed the wound, following the path of the bullet. It had entered Rommel's thigh front to back, stopping just short of the femur.

When she felt the probe strike metal she nodded at Tony and in one smooth exchange, he took the probe and handed her the electro-cautery. As Alex sliced the skin, it simultaneously cauterized the incision to reduce the bleeding, and keep the surgical field clear. The odor of burning flesh assaulted her, familiar, expected, and repulsive. Alex never got used to it.

Then she took the scalpel with a deftness born of experience and cut into the muscle only as far as necessary to extract the bullet.

"Hemostats, Tony."

She paused to glance at the x-rays on the wall, verifying the bullet's orientation, then she extracted the long forceps, and the deadly slug clanked into the tray near Rommel's head.

Alex irrigated the opening generously with aqueous penicillin while Tony prepared the sutures. With smooth movements she closed the muscles internally with Dexon, changing to Braunamid to suture the thick external skin.

She examined the surgical site and, satisfied, began the methodical shutdown of the systems that had sustained the dog. The halothane was turned off before the two caregivers transferred Rommel to a recovery table. As soon as Rommel showed a swallowing reflex they removed the trach tube, but the IV's would be left in place until he regained consciousness. Alex left Tony cleaning the surgery to give Rommel's friends his prognosis.

"Sean? Officers?"

"How'd it go?" Sean stood up and Alex smiled.

"He's going to be fine. That dog leads a charmed life, gentlemen, the bullet lodged in the largest muscle of his thigh and there was no bone damage."

The men exhaled in unison and the release of tension was palpable.

"That's great, Doc, can I see him now?"

"Yes, for a few minutes, but he's unconscious and I'll keep him sedated for the rest of the night."

Sean's two friends left the clinic and he followed Alex into the surgery. She understood his need to see Rommel himself. Surgery holds a primal fear that can only be dispelled by personal touch. When Tony saw the police officer coming, he moved away so Sean could get closer to the dog. Sean's eyes drifted from the needles and tubing in Rommel's front legs to the stitches in his shaved thigh.

"How you doin', pal?"

His voice was quiet and the gentleness with which he stroked the sleeping dog dissolved the toughness of his station.

"He's really going to be okay, Sean. He should be fully

conscious tomorrow, why don't you come back in the morning?"

"Okay, Doc. And thanks for everything." He glanced at Tony but the vet tech was loading surgical instruments into the autoclave on the opposite counter. Obviously he didn't think Sean's gratitude included him.

"Thanks to both of you."

At that Tony turned around and nodded his head at Sean without meeting his eyes. Alex wondered if it was Sean's uniform or the strength of his personality that unhinged her technician.

She walked Sean to the door of the clinic, and when she returned, Tony was checking Rommel's vital signs. He was unaware of her observation and she was struck by the contrast of his confidence and skill with the animals and his gawky nervousness around people. Alex smiled. She recognized much of herself in the sensitive, but unfinished young man.

"Tony, I'll finish up here, go on home."

"That's alright, I'll stay with Rommel tonight."

"No, we have a full schedule in the morning and I'll need you rested and alert. Go home and get some sleep."

"Okay." Tony patted Rommel one last time and left the clinic.

Unattended paperwork beckoned so Alex made a pot of coffee, switched on her portable office radio and returned to the room where Rommel lie still and quiet. There were no other patients overnighting so the silence was only broken by deep sighs from the tranquilized dog and faint music from her office.

The largest of Patriarch and Cub-bearer's litter was born last. White-cub was absolutely white except for a black nose and black slits that defined his unopened eyes. Cub-bearer cleaned him as she had his four littermates and nuzzled him to her side, unaware of any world beyond their underground nursery.

Cub-bearer sensed her time of delivery was complete. Satisfied her cubs were clean and safe, she curled her body around them and rested her nose across the litter, hiding them with her tail. The exhausted mother slept.

Outside, the northern lights shimmered across a moonless sky to the howls of a wolfen chorus. From her underground nest Cub-bearer listened as the voices of her family harmonized with the rhythmic suckling of her cubs.

A large black wolf sat motionless on the hill above the den. Lifting his nose skyward, Patriarch sent his haunting song spinning through the night.

Rommel woofed softly in his sleep and Alex rested her hand on the dog's head until he quieted. For the first time since arriving at the clinic she became conscious of the designer gown under her surgical smock. It was spotted with blood and the satin showed wet circles where some liquid had spilled and dried. She smiled weakly, her drycleaner was used to odd spots on her clothes. But not on Valentino. She picked up the mail.

"Hey, a letter from Greg," she mumbled to the walls.

Her eyes recognized her college friend's handwriting and reached for the large manila envelope. A flashy pamphlet fell out with a Post-it note attached.

"Alex,

The enclosed information is about an international conference on biodiversity we are organizing for this fall in Calgary. Please read and consider chairing the session on the restoration of endangered species. I know this is something you feel strongly about from our conversations in the past. It's a hot topic, Alex, and we could sure use your cool head, emotions are running high on this issue. I know how busy you are, but please consider it. And, as usual, I need your answer yesterday.

As always, Greg"

Alex devoured all the information and then read it again. Every fiber of her being said she had already decided to participate, but she knew Stephen was not going to be excited about this opportunity. Lately he had become critical of how she managed her time.

It had been so long since she had been involved in any wildlife activity—since she opened her clinic—and with each reading the conference appealed to her more.

This will require serious negotiation with Stephen, she thought, *but it'll be worth it if I can go. After all, I haven't been away by myself since our wedding, and this was what I studied in college. I've got to convince him...*

Rommel returned to his dreams, and Alex to her coffee, and they passed the night together.

Chapter Three

The huge wolf swung his head around and stared at Alex. She held her breath. His ears pricked forward, then he padded softly over and stretched his neck until his nose hovered four inches from hers. She froze, no breathing, no blinking. Blood pounded in her ears. Amber eyes studied blue and held her gaze as firmly as a human's might. Alex felt naked under his scrutiny.

Does he think I'm prey? Thoughts exploded and images plunged over the cliff of her mind, as mental chaos competed with physical stillness.

He leaned closer. Two inches. One. His nostrils twitched. Then his breath feathered across her face as he inhaled her woman scent.

Time stopped, then reversed. Centuries evaporated as the ancient and primeval loomed contemporary and familiar. Behind Alex shadow demons cavorted on cave walls and she saw herself—ragged and filthy—kneel to warm callused hands, hardly recognizable as hers, over an open fire. Golden eyes stared as she ripped a hunk of meat from a charred carcass and stuffed half in her mouth, untroubled by the grease dripping down her chin. The wolf snapped up the rest when she offered it, and swallowed it whole, then licked her hand and flopped a sinewy foreleg across her thigh. Her bare thigh.

What?

The present jerked Alex back and she shook her head.

What the hell was that?

Logic and rational thought groped their way back into her brain as the wolf drifted away, curiosity sated. Alex inhaled for the first time in—centuries?—and felt her fright-flight response relax. Nothing is six years of veterinary practice had prepared her for the wolf's raw physical presence. Wild power draped him as naturally as silver guard hairs caped his back. This animal had killed, and killed easily.

The moment passed but Alex could not shake off the

effect of wolfen eyes scrutinizing her own. A cogent creature had entered her mind with authority, as easily as his canine nose had learned her scent. The event passed to memory and clung to Alex. It did not fade as she left the encounter room.

Matt was waiting in the hallway.
"So you still think they're just big dogs?" His familiar voice stopped her. Alex shook her head, the surreal nature of the experience still clouding her brain.

Nose to nose with a wolf in the Doubletree Hotel?

"No, that was clearly not a dog. Even my most intelligent police dogs don't have that presence, and there was no submission in those eyes."

"Now my ol' lab partner's getting it." They moved down the hall into the hotel lobby. Alex's friendship with Matt Kramer had taken root in freshman biology, when their common passion for animals had drawn them together. The years since college had only strengthened the friendship that was now surviving his career as a wildlife biologist, hers as a veterinarian, and her high profile marriage to a leading Seattle attorney.

"In their eyes we humans never rank higher that equal." His eyes sparkled. "The only time a wolf submits, it's to another wolf."

Should I tell him about my—what was it?—daydream? vision? Don't think so.

"So, let me buy you a drink and you can tell me what you felt when you met my pal, Nakiska."

Settled on a stool in the hotel bar, Alex thought for a minute.

"The first thing that struck me was his size. Everything about him was huge! His head was larger than mine." Drinks arrived and the Merlot warmed.

"But what did you feel?"

"When he first looked at me? Fear. In spite of my experience with big animals—even aggressive canines—and in spite of knowing THAT wolf was not a threat, I felt fear. It was visceral." She studied her wine, "but the fear faded..." The primitive vision returned and she shook her head and changed the subject.

"Greg sent me a note—the advisory board wants me to chair a session on reintroduction at the Calgary wildlife conference next fall."

Matt chuckled, "Oh, Stephen'll love that!"

"What do you mean?" Defending her husband to Matt was a familiar chore.

"Alex, think about it. Who does his law firm represent?"

She knew where this was going and didn't respond.

"Large mining and timber companies. He's not going to be thrilled with you publicly working for the enemy."

"That's not fair, he's always supported my work with animals."

"As long as that work didn't interfere with his agenda. Why do you think he was eager to put up the money for your vet clinic?" His eyes held hers as the wolf's had earlier. "Because he didn't want you to follow your wildlife major. Come on, Alex, are you so naïve to think that the house—excuse me, compound—and the horses, and the rest of your sweet life comes without a price?"

She'd heard this before too, but it still annoyed her.

Matt paused, and his voice softened, "Don't you get it? Alexandra Verazzano, you're Stephen's trophy wife, just like the Picasso in his study, and the Waterford crystal he sips his aged cognac from. I don't think he'll tolerate losing any of his trophies."

She had not heard this before. Outside lightning and thunder brewed up a storm, and so did she.

"You paint a pretty ugly picture of my husband. Marriages take compromise, Matt." She glared at him. "What do you know about marriage anyway?" She regretted the words before they cleared her lips, spotlighting his shattered engagement stung him deeply and he winced.

"I guess I deserved that." He finished his beer and the

rain started right on cue. "I hope I'm wrong about Stephen, you'd be perfect for that session. It will get confrontational and that compromising head of yours would be a real asset."

Alex sighed and reached across the table and squeezed his arm, "I'm looking forward to leading it," their eyes met and she smiled. "Guess I'd better get home and close this with Stephen."

They sprinted for their cars and left the hotel to the wolves.

Sibling rivalry set in from the beginning as the sightless cubs wrestled among themselves for the most generous teats, and their tiny baby growls hinted at events to come. Abundant food for Cub-bearer meant there was always milk to fill their bellies, and their weight doubled in their first two weeks of life.

Twelve days after their birth the skin covering their eyes parted slowly, the slits widening over hours, allowing the cubs their first blurry views of the world. On that day they all had the same dark eyes, but at four weeks of age, each cub took the unique shade of amber or gold he would wear for life. Only one in ten thousand wolves is born with blue eyes, and as time marked those first days White-cub's eyes did not turn brown, or hazel, or gold, as his littermate's. His eyes grew pale, lighter and lighter, until ice blue glowed from his white face, eyes to haunt the nightmares of those who crossed his trail.

White-cub had never considered that his subterranean home was not the whole world. He never questioned where his mother went when she left, or where the other shadowy beings were, when they weren't with him in the den. So he was alarmed when his mother gently, persistently, nudged him beyond the boundaries of the dark nursery.

White-cub's limited experience included dirt, roots, and earth smells, mingled with those of wolf, so his heart raced with fright when he saw the light from the den opening below. Terrified, he turned to bolt back to the warmth of his littermates, but Cub-bearer would not allow retreat. Her powerful nose pushed him forward, toward the light and he panted with fear, short legs quivering with each tentative step. The tunnel seemed endless, but Cub-bearer coaxed him down, until he cowered, trembling, at the den opening.

And then it happened.

Suddenly every wolfen sense sprang to attention, bombarded with new information. A million scents overpowered his nose, eyes darted to capture shapes, and ears twitched to catch and identify each new sound. He had never felt a breeze, and now this invisible thing ruffled his fur. His brain worked frantically to file and categorize all he was experiencing, and an insatiable curiosity drew its first breath.

White-cub took one shaky step. Then another. Then another. He felt the warmth of the sun on his face, saw his parent's clear forms for the first time, heard a squirrel scold from a nearby tree, and saw the shadow of a hawk track across the ground.

He wobbled to his father and sat in his shadow, white touching black. Patriarch licked his son's face, his huge tongue washing the cub in one stroke, and White-cub's fear evaporated. He mimicked the alpha, raising his head proudly, trying to point floppy ears that refused to stand up. For a second White-cub's eyes reflected the instinctive cunning and graceful bearing of a thousand generations of wolves.

Before sunset all five young wolves had seen their parents and each other clearly for the first time outside the den. They responded in kind with heart-stopping terror followed by exuberant curiosity, exhilarated by their sensual overload.

Every fragment of matter required keen sensory investigation. Each item was sniffed, licked, then paraded around the den site with great flourish, as if that cub was the first planetary being to discover a rock, or a pine cone, or a dead bug. Their minute attention spans shifted constantly, as infant brains processed each bit of new information, filing and sorting in the priority of wolfen thoughts and needs.

Is it alive?

Will it hurt me?

Can I eat it?

Each breath of wind carried a different story, a bird's scent, or the recent passing of some large animal, still unknown.

That day they became aware of their older brother and sisters and learned that while their care was a high priority, they were definitely last in the hierarchy of the pack. Gentle and Jester were patient in their chiding of the cubs, but Cunning did not veil her disdain for them. When they crossed her path the snarl was terrifying. Patriarch also allowed no offense to go unnoticed, and discipline was swift and frightening. Respect was a difficult concept, and the cubs suffered repeatedly for their inability to grasp it.

These days, while they were no taller than the weeds and grasses they explored, were the most dangerous of their lives. In the den they were isolated, easy to protect. But the world lay before them, seductive and enticing, a world full of enemies with generations of historical animosity for the canines. Tiny nursing teeth would be no match for a hungry lynx or wolverine.

That first day was so demanding that they collapsed in an exhausted heap in the den. Cub-bearer licked each cub thoroughly and they slept.

Alex still felt a twinge of embarrassment every time she drove through the wrought iron gates to her house. Embarrassed that she should live in such a blatant expression of wealth and power, and embarrassed that her blue-collar background even thought of the place as a house. By anyone's standards, it was an estate. Seven acres of prime real estate on Mercer Island with manicured lawns and gardens that sloped gently into Lake Washington, extended to the boathouse and dock, and encircled the guesthouse. The brick driveway coiled around a fountain featuring a life-size bronze stallion reared on his back legs, nostrils flared, pawing the air.

Not exactly subtle.

The main house was appropriate to the property, eleven

thousand square feet divided among three stories of turreted gray stone and leaded windows, built to impress and intimidate. It did both. It intimidated Alex, even though Stephen had it built for her as a wedding present.

Two garage slots were empty, Stephen was still at work. She parked her Jeep Grand Cherokee, and heard Alpha and Omega barking before she was out of the car. The exuberant Huskies occupied a large fenced run (more square footage than her parent's house, Alex had noted early on) and lived for the time her attention was focused on them.

"Hi guys!" she called, and a hundred pounds of rambunctious affection slammed into her. They raced out across the driveway and into the yard. She picked up two tennis balls and both dogs froze, ears perked, eyes glued on her hands. When she let them fly, the dogs exploded onto the grass, legs pounding, tongues flopping. Alpha and Omega lived to run, and most afternoons required at least forty minutes of tennis ball tosses to exhaust them. She was always tired of throwing before they were tired of chasing. The last act of their play was a human-canine lovefest, Alex wrestling with the strong dogs, scratching their stomachs and behind their ears.

Stephen had commented that the gardener was not thrilled about the condition of the grass after a few weeks of Husky wrestling matches, but Alex ignored him. It looked too much like a golf course for her taste, anyway.

Her work uniform—Levi's, a work shirt, and Reeboks—always seemed out of place when she walked through the mansion's imposing double doors, especially when her uniform smelled distinctly of dog.

If Alex was embarrassed by the estate where she lived, she was even more so by the staff Stephen employed to keep it. And nowhere was there more staff present than at dinner. Since their first day in the house he had insisted on formal dinners every night, even when it was just the two of them eating. Alex would've been happy with TV trays in the den, but she learned quickly that image meant everything to her husband. So when they were in town, dinner was served to them at opposite ends of a massive dining room table by uniformed help. They practically had to shout at each other past the ten brocade-covered chairs, and intimate conversation did not occur at dinner.

In the five years since she'd married into the wealthy family of lawyers, she'd realized that her ambitious spouse battled the looming specter of his father's reputation. Alex thought it was ridiculous. And she also thought Stephen was not winning.

"Mrs. Verazzano, will there be only you and Mr. Verazzano for dinner?" Carmen's gentle voice floated over her shoulder.

"Yes, Carmen, just Stephen and me." *Thank God for that*, she thought, as she watched the pretty Hispanic disappear toward the dining room.

Two hours later her teal jumpsuit rustled as she walked down the spiral staircase and chuckled softly.

Someday I am going to slide down this banister...

Stephen walked through the front door as she reached the bottom step and smiled appraisingly.

"You look lovely, Alexandra." He hugged her at the foot of the stairs, and she felt the familiar warmth spread from her stomach outward. Her husband moved her.

"Thank you. How was your day?"

"Prepping for this tax evasion case is getting tedious. It's clear that our client, shall we say, overlooked, some taxable income, so my defense is going to require an extra bit of creativity." Arm in arm they drifted into the study.

"Would you like a drink before dinner?"

"Yes, there's something I want to talk to you about." Stephen poured himself a Scotch and Alex a glass of Cabernet.

"Well, let's hear it. My beautiful wife has my undivided attention."

Alex was struck again by how handsome he was, even after a long workday.

She took a deep breath. "I've been asked to participate in

a conference on wildlife diversity this summer." Stephen sat behind his desk, she tucked a leg beneath her on the couch. "I'm seriously considering it. I haven't had much opportunity to work with wildlife issues since the clinic opened. What do you think?"

"I think you have quite a lot on your plate right now. Don't you agree?" Stephen's green eyes drilled into hers. She felt her cheeks flush.

"Stephen, the clinic is going well, and I could schedule the week ahead of time, and get someone to fill in for me without much trouble."

"I wasn't just thinking of the clinic. We have a lot of social commitments coming up this summer, the symphony ball, and the hospital benefit, and the rest. I need you there with me, Alexandra."

She felt her temper rising and tried to stifle it. "You don't need me at those events and this is an opportunity to make a real contribution to something I care about. He wants me to chair a session on wildlife restoration. Like bringing buffalo back to the plains, and wolves back to Yellowstone." Stephen's smile vaporized and his demeanor stiffened.

"Who's sponsoring this conference?" Alex was sure witnesses had heard the same interrogating tone.

"Several national and international wildlife organizations. They're all quite reputable. Why?"

Stephen left his chair and stood over her. Towered over her. She tried to stretch her legs out, but he was standing too close to the couch.

"Don't you listen to anything I tell you? My family's firm represents forestry and mining interests that spend a great deal of money trying to control zealous environmental groups that are hell-bent on destroying their companies."

He sipped his drink, shook his head, and chuckled. "There's no way my wife is going to get involved with the organizations that cause such litigious problems for my clients. How could you think I would approve of this?"

"First, I wasn't aware I was asking your permission. This

was my course of study before we met, and I still care about these issues." She stood up, forcing him back from the couch, invading his space.

"And second, what difference would my chairing one session of a three-day conference in Calgary, Alberta make to your clients? I'm not their lawyer, you are!"

"Yes, I am, and that's something you should keep in mind, Alexandra. Representing those clients pays the bills around here, and I won't have my wife personally running some strategy at counter purposes to mine. Period."

Several seconds passed as they glared at each other.

"Are you *forbidding* me to do this?" she asked, incredulous.

Stephen realized an edict would be gas on the fire. He took a deep breath, and softened his voice. The voice that always grabbed her gut and everything south of it. "No, I'm asking you to support me by not aligning yourself publicly against some of my clients. Will you do that for me?"

"I don't know if I can. Until now, I have gone along with everything, the social hobnobbing and the parties and the dinners. But this is something I want to do, that was part of me before I ever met you. I think you exaggerate the potential fallout."

It wasn't the response Stephen expected and beneath his polished control, he seethed. He'd always been able to manipulate her before.

"Dinner is served, sir," Carmen announced from the doorway, and a silent truce was called. After all, you can't be late for dinner with all that staff waiting.

Chapter Four

Cub-bearer weaned the cubs when they were six weeks old. Needle sharp teeth and lengthening claws rhythmically scratching her belly motivated her, and White-cub and his brothers and sisters tasted meat for the first time.

The older wolves ranged many miles from the den in their search for food. After a successful hunt, they gorged on the kill, as much as fifteen to twenty pounds of meat apiece. Upon returning, they were mobbed by the cubs, licking and nipping their mouths frantically until they regurgitated their precious cargo. A free-for-all ensued. The scent of meat and blood was one of their oldest memories, and now they were as excited by it as the adults. Their swelling appetites always exceeded what the pack could provide.

The cubs delighted in hide-and-seek, wolf style, and became proficient at silently stalking each other around the pines and bushes. Discovery triggered a wrestling match, and all body parts were fair game for sharp young teeth. Intense scuffling was accompanied by very serious puppy growls and they learned which pranks were tolerated, and which ignited genuine anger.

Gentle and Jester became objects for climbing and hiding, the grown wolfs' reclining bulk quite sufficient to conceal a cub. The older wolves accepted this mauling with stoic forbearance, even participating in the fun on occasion. But when the annoyance became too much, a frustrated adult simply trotted out of range. Only Cunning avoided social interaction with the five pups. She was as aloof toward them, as she had been to her own littermates, and White-cub and his siblings feared her more than any other wolf in their family.

White-cub was sabotaged by his exploding growth. Tender bones developed so fast that they demanded the lion's share of nutrients, causing his skin to dry and his coat to lose its earlier shine. He gained inches as well as weight, so yesterday's legs were today longer and less stable. The chubby, bow-legged cub was transforming into a lean, lanky wolf—still uncoordinated and clumsy, but taller. Body parts matured at different speeds, often out of proportion, and ears and paws too large by any scale added no dignity to his image. The easy grace and rhythmic gait of the adult wolves eluded White-cub and his four littermates.

"He acted like it was a trivial request. He even laughed!" Alex's voice drifted around her mustang, Viento. In the next stall Danielle brushed Kiowa, then tossed the saddlepad over his back.

"Alex, in his mind it is trivial. You've never done anything that was against his wishes so why should he think you will now?"

"That's not true!"

"Name one time you did anything that didn't have his stamp of approval. He's been pulling your strings since you started dating, and you know it."

"Viento, stand still!" The frisky mustang danced around the stall while Alex buckled the girth. "Pulling my strings? What's that supposed to mean?"

"You weren't going to open a vet clinic when you started college, right?"

"Well, yes, but that worked out. I love my clinic."

"Not the point, sis. It was a concession you made to marry Stephen. You've never tested your marital boundaries, and now, after five years, he doesn't expect you to." Danni mounted the roan and cantered toward the trailhead. A few minutes later Alex followed her. Gray sky threatened rain, but like most Seattlelites, the sisters had learned long ago that if you canceled plans for potential rain, you'd never leave the house.

Blonde and brown hair flew with manes and tails when they gave Viento and Kiowa their heads to gallop down the soft trail. Cedar and Douglas fir towered on either side and the Christmas-sweet smell of damp evergreens hung in the air. After ten minutes they reined to a walk.

"So you think if I force this issue he won't give in?"

"Has he ever? From the second we met him, he's been a control freak. He was measuring you up from the get go, Alex. You always agreed to his ideas, and went along with his plans. Not that his plans weren't easy to agree to ...dinner in his favorite Italian restaurant—in Rome ...shopping for new clothes—in Paris ...and then there's that cozy little lakeside hut he built for you. Mother Teresa wouldn't be able to resist."

Danni chuckled. "That plus a good disposition, tolerable looks, and the fact that you hardly ever spill your food, made you quite appropriate."

"Tolerable looks? Thanks alot!"

"Tolerable is the best you get from a sibling."

Alex thought for a minute, "Appropriate for what?"

"Stephen had a pretty clear picture of what the next generation Mrs. Verazzano should be, and you're it. With a healthy application of money, he probably figured he could keep you happy and under control. Case in point, your clinic. Bought and paid for by him, right? Or how 'bout these fine mounts? You got Viento for a wedding gift, and he gave me Kiowa for my birthday—I'm sure, so I could keep you company on these little Saturday outings."

"You paint my husband as a very calculating man."

"Have you ever doubted it? I think a calculating nature is a prerequisite to being a good lawyer."

"Well," Alex got quieter, "It's true, he is much more comfortable expressing his affection with gifts than anything requiring serious emotional investment."

Danni searched her sister's face, "Doesn't that hurt?" she whispered.

Alex shrugged. "I've learned to ignore it. I don't doubt that he loves me, and shows it the best way he can. A lot of men are not expressive, Danni. And like you said, I'm not exactly leading an abused life."

Danni chuckled, "I can name a dozen women who would kill to be so abused. Closet space most women fantasize about, and an allowance to keep it full. A clinic to practice your vet stuff, and a gorgeous husband. It could be a lot worse."

"Absolutely." Alex stroked Viento's warm neck. "But that still doesn't tell me what to do about the conference."

"How is Stephen when he loses a case?"

Alex rolled her eyes, "Not a pretty sight."

"Then I think you better circle the wagons if you intend to force the issue. But be sure you want to do this, you may see a whole new side of Stephen," she clucked at the roan and he lunged to a canter, "... a very unpleasant side of Stephen," she muttered out of earshot.

Their conversation was getting dangerously close to giving advice, and she didn't want any responsibility for Alex's decision. Not one atom of responsibility.

Daily skirmishes shattered the peace around the den. The time had come for the cubs to determine the hierarchy within their litter and brawls, predominately among the three males, raged for several days. First-twin and Second-twin bowed to them early and were content to watch the males from the safety of their mothers' side.

The twin females were growing into personalities as similar as their physical traits. Matching gray bodies showed the promise of Cub-bearer's sleek lines, and their early nurturing instincts reflected her gentle disposition. They wrestled together, but it lacked the intense competition roiling between their brothers.

White-cub, Red-cub, and Black-cub sparred without interruption, and from their raised hackles and growling, one would have thought serious blood was about to be shed. But it never happened, and the older wolves did not interfere. This was a test of intangibles—courage and stamina, more than strength. The cubs' hierarchy would be determined long before they were strong enough to do each other serious injury.

Their competition was intensely significant, the drive for dominance genetic. Tooth and claw events usually started as three individuals, but ended with Red-cub and Black-cub uniting forces against White-cub, so much larger was the white whelp. He fought Black-cub and Red-cub individually or as a team, and as a result he became a better fighter, faster. Their dual challenge improved his coordination more quickly than theirs, and after a few days the skirmishes faded. Competition finally ended when White-cub stopped Red-cub with just a growl, and after that day his dominant position in the litter was unquestioned. Pack life resumed its peaceful flow.

No physical scars marked the cubs, but this time of trial had sharpened and defined emerging personalities. Black-cub and Red-cub became inseparable. White-cub walked taller and began to spend his resting time close to Patriarch, a situation that did not pass unnoticed by his jealous older sister, Cunning.

The black alpha regarded his white son with an affection he held for none of his other offspring. After hunting he offered him choice bones, and this intensified Cunning's jealousy. She missed no opportunity to intimidate the young canine.

Wolfen politics and the structure of power were not optional lessons. White-cub and his siblings learned to keep their disputes under control, asserting themselves without directing their full potential for violence on one another. Cub-bearer's second litter went through their rite of passage, absorbing the complex socialization imperative to the survival of their species.

Stephen's arm snaked around Alex's waist from behind as the darkened elevator left the ground. The lights of Seattle fell away through the window and when he kissed the nape of her neck, the sweet spot south of her navel and north of her crotch warmed. Stephen didn't just know how to push her buttons, he played them like a concert pianist a familiar Steinway. The elevator's rise matched her heat and her face flushed. Stephen was irresistible when he was affectionate and attentive.

Unfortunately, Alex had yet to realize it happened almost exclusively when he won a case. Tonight's dinner in the Emerald Room of the Space Needle was to celebrate winning his tax evasion case and Alex hoped his mood would hold through her announcement.

"Mr. and Mrs. Verazzano, it's so nice to see you again. We have a nice window booth ready."

Their booth faced out the window, elevated a few feet above the floor so nothing blocked their view as the restaurant revolved.

"May I get you something to drink?"

"Yes, a bottle of Dom Perignon, '76, please, Tina."

"Oh, a celebration!"

Stephen put his fingers to his lips, "A quiet one, we hope."

"Yes, of course." She left them to their menus and the view. A rare clear night offered up a postcard perfect panorama that circled every hour. The sun, just setting behind the Olympics, cast a neon pink glow across Puget Sound and into Elliott Bay. Ferries to Bremerton and Bainbridge Island left glittering chevrons in their wakes.

"What did your father say about the case? He must have been impressed."

Stephen smiled and nodded. "Yes, and he was happy we got it over with so quickly and quietly. This was not the kind of case we like to do, but a client on retainer gets the full service, and this guy is a big client." The champagne arrived, he tasted, and both glasses were filled. "I'm just glad to be back working on the corporate side of the house."

They ordered dinner and Alex considered how to open her discussion of the conference. For weeks she had struggled to find the perfect argument—the no-holes justification—that Stephen would not be able to disagree with. It was time to present her case and she had no case.

Stephen rubbed her thigh under the table, "You seem quiet tonight, Alexandra, is something wrong?"

Not yet, she thought. "No, nothing's wrong, but there is something I want to talk to you about. I didn't want to disturb you while you were working on that case, but maybe now we can discuss my attending the conference?" She took a deep breath. Stephen removed his hand from her leg and his eyes, appreciative seconds before, now pierced.

"I thought that issue was closed. I do not want you involved with radical environmentalists, Alexandra."

"They're not radical environmentalists." Another deep breath. *Stay calm, Alex. If you lose your temper, you lose the war...* "Why did you marry me?"

"What?"

"Why did you marry me, Stephen? What criteria elevated me above the other women you had dated?"

He fidgeted, uncertain where this was going, but willing to play her game. "Criteria? Like I was buying a car, or something? Well, you're beautiful, of course, and a good skier." He smiled and warmed to the topic. "You had such a passionate curiosity about things. And you seemed unaffected by my money."

Her voice was very soft. "Stephen, I'm still passionately curious. And I need to feed that curiosity and stretch my mind. I just don't see why my participating in that conference is such a bad thing. Is it the trip itself? You travel often, for weeks at a time, and I don't complain."

"First, I travel on legitimate business, Alex, that brings the money in that pays for your nice clothes, your car, and your horse. I don't consider this conference legitimate business. If you were going to a conference on veterinary medicine, that would be legitimate. But the bigger issue is that I told you the groups running that conference are particular opponents of several of my big clients." Dinner arrived and the silence hovered in the air, heavier than the steam rising from their plates.

"I really didn't think you would defy me like this, Alexandra."

Alex's intense voice sliced the silence like steel. "How dare you sit in omnipotent judgement of what is legitimate business for me! I was studying wildlife biology before I ever met you, and only committed to the clinic when we decided to get married. The last time I checked I was running a *very* successful clinic to service very valuable animals, for which their owners pay quite dearly. I was under the impression those funds contributed to the family budget, so I don't need to hear about how you are paying all the bills, Stephen. That sounds like an argument your father used on your mother. Don't use it on me."

"Your clinic barely breaks even. All the state-of-the-art equipment you bought won't be paid off for another year." He took a breath, having an argument in whispers was draining. "So, as far as you're concerned, I do pay the bills."

They both picked at their dinners, but the salmon Alex ordered sat on her tongue like sawdust.

"You exaggerate the impact of this conference on your clients. Frankly, unless they take the daily paper from Calgary, they won't even know about it, and I doubt whether a conference of science and biology types will be big news, even there."

She put down her fork and looked him directly in the eye. "But just so I understand the rules here, I'm not supposed to pursue any interests that aren't politically in line with the family business. Is that it, Stephen?"

Keep it quiet, she told herself, *or we'll be reading about this argument in the Times tomorrow.*

Stephen's jaw clamped firmly beneath his green eyes, strikingly reptilian. He almost hissed, "Alexandra, you married into a wealthy, powerful family with old ties to several large corporations. Your failure to understand the seriousness of that concerns me greatly. I do not want to hear about my wife's antics in Canada from my father."

The waiter appeared and filled their champagne glasses.

"Well, then let's hope your father doesn't read the Calgary paper, because I am going to do this." She inhaled and let her breath out slowly. There. Done. Alex knew she had drawn a line in the sand.

"I will try not to embarrass you or your family, but it would be a waste of my education not to participate. I really hope you will find a way to understand and accept it. Other husbands would be proud their wives were even considered to chair a session at an international conference."

"I'm not other husbands!" Alex suddenly saw the other side of Stephen and it frightened her. His controlling attitude, which she had never seen before—or chosen to never see before—made her stomach knot. The bird who had never believed she was caged now struggled to fly.

"I'm not asking for anything other than the right to exercise my intelligence and contribute to society. It frightens me to think that you cannot support me in this, and that you consider your clients' possible discomfort a higher priority than my personal goals."

Alex didn't remember finishing her dinner and neither spoke during the drive home. The air was almost too thick to breathe. Instead of parking his Mercedes in the garage, Stephen pulled around the drive to the front door.

"I'll drop you off here, I'm going out for awhile." He didn't even wait until she was inside before he put the car in gear and sped away. Alex watched his taillights disappear, and glanced up at the mansion. Her home.

It looked like a prison.

Her heart thumped in her chest. Reluctant to go in, she visited Alpha and Omega, and they wagged their tails, sniffed her clothes, and nuzzled her hands, devouring every scent morsel of her dinner, leaving white hair firmly lodged on tailored black silk. Their tails beat a rhythm of pure devotion and Alex embraced their open affection and tried to swallow the lump in her throat.

She shivered and gazed at the stone building, "Oh, what have I started here, guys?"

Chapter Five

Patriarch and Cub-bearer hid the litter in the den and led the rest of the pack away. Predawn darkness, when other animals dozed, wolves hunted.

The cubs were still sleeping hours later when the first strange noises awakened them. Grunts and snorts and scraping sounds drifted up the tunnel, and a new gamy smell invaded their untrained noses. Musky and unfamiliar, it carried overtones of carrion and death. It frightened them.

They had never experienced a grizzly bear, by sight or scent. Yet at some deep primal level where the collective memories of a race are stored in genes and passed on as instinct, the infant wolves knew this was a danger to be feared. They huddled together and backed into the farthest recesses of the den, scared of this menace with no name seeking violent entry to their home.

Fear multiplied and exploded into terror, but White-cub and his siblings uttered no sound, drawing comfort from each other. Competition forgotten, they closed together, flesh upon flesh.

The old grizzly made short work of the narrow hole at the mouth of the den. Five-inch claws and the muscles that drove them formed powerful tools, and the wolf cubs he smelled would be a far more substantial meal than the insects those tools had unearthed recently.

The bear had entered the wolves' valley after losing a territorial fight with a younger, more agile male. Infected gashes on his shoulder and rear oozed puss and he was delirious in his pain. Naturally poor eyesight had become useless in his advanced years, and the septic injuries made hunting impossible. The old bear was in agony. And he was hungry.

He labored through the hot afternoon to enlarge the narrow tunnel, huge paws ripping into the packed dirt. His head and shoulders were deep into the hillside when Patriarch and the rest of the pack caught his scent on their way home with food for the cubs.

Wind carried the grizzly's spoor to canine noses a quarter of a mile away and the wolves accelerated, leaping over boulders and crashing through the undergrowth. Agility and speed powered them, muscles compressed and extended, paws barely touched the ground. Hackles raised, fangs bared, Patriarch's family raced home, poised for war.

Cub-bearer erupted through the brush and dove at the hairy giant first. She sank two-inch fangs into a hind leg, dug her claws into the dirt for leverage, and jerked her head back repeatedly to rip muscles and tendons. The bear roared with surprise, and as he backed out of the tunnel, Patriarch and Guardian grabbed his throat. The grizzly tried to stand on his hind legs to crush them in a death squeeze, or disembowel them, but he never got the chance.

In a flash of gray, Cunning leaped at his face, burying her teeth into his nose. None of the previous wolf strikes delivered the excruciating pain of her fangs locked onto his snout. He shook his head side to side, jerking Cunning through the air like a stuffed toy shaken by an angry child. But her grip held firm, tearing the tender flesh on the carnivore's nose.

The wolves moved with rhythm and coordination. As one lost his grip another rushed in, allowing the grizzly no relief. Cub-bearer dashed under him and attacked his soft belly. With Cunning's body covering his face, the bear could not see, but sensitive nerve endings communicated this new injury to his brain and the forest shook with his thunderous cry. Guardian released the bear's throat and darted to his rear, biting at his hamstrings with Gentle and Jester. The bear kicked out, first one leg, then the other, but the three wolves dodged each strike.

Ursine roars were answered by canine snarls as the battle was joined in earnest. The wolves' collective rage was translated into grinding teeth and strong jaws, hundreds of pounds of pressure gaining purchase and slicing into the bear's hide. They attacked his most vulnerable places with precision.

The bear broke Cunning's grip with a violent jerk of his head and sent the yearling bitch flying through the air, her fall cushioned by a blueberry bush. He rose on his hind legs and turned to face the rest of the pack, a looming giant over eleven feet tall. He raked the air with his front paws and the earth shook with each step.

Patriarch dashed in to attack his exposed abdomen, bleeding from Cub-bearer's assault and the grizzly swung a massive paw at him. But the graceful alpha dodged the strike. The rest of the pack circled, teeth snapping in frenzied rage.

The bear realized he was in no condition to win this fight, but he was unable to extricate himself. The wolves sashayed so fast in their macabre ballet he rarely saw attacks before he felt them. He would have given a better showing of himself in his early years, but with his previous injuries he was powerless to respond offensively. After several minutes his only desire was to be anywhere else.

Patriarch directed the fight down the hill away from the den and the wolves widened their circle. When the alpha sensed the grizzly's resignation he pulled back, allowing his escape. The bear dashed into the river and the wolves followed, snarling and snapping at his hind legs until he had entered the dense forest on the opposite shore.

Once the bear was out of sight Patriarch turned away, drawing the wolves back to the den, where five terrified cubs huddled in the far corner of their subterranean nest. It was several minutes before Cub-bearer could coax them out. Grown wolves pawed and nuzzled the cubs and each other under a starlit sky, reaffirming the family structure that had served them so well in battle.

Danielle rolled over and smiled. If she was smelling pancakes it must be Sunday. Living at home with her parents to finish her doctorate had not come without cost, but it did have its advantages. Saturday pancakes were definitely an advantage.

She put on her robe and slippers and trudged out to the kitchen.

"Good morning, sweetheart!" Her mother was in the same spot she'd occupied every Saturday that Danni could remember.

"Is it? Oh, yes, it is morning..." she mumbled.

"How late were you up last night?" Her dad was in his assigned seat also, newspaper in front of his face.

"About 2:00, I guess. I was hoping to get those papers graded before I went to sleep. But that didn't happen." While she waited to hear on various job opportunities, Danni had taken an assistant teaching job at the university. First year Zoology.

"Were the papers bad?"

Well, they seem to have a decent grasp of the material, but I fear for the native tongue." She rubbed her eyes. "I think some of them missed a few English classes, like basic grammar and sentence structure. I spent most of the night deciphering, instead of correcting." She poured herself coffee and sat at the table.

"I sure hope one of those research jobs comes through soon, it's clear to me I'm not teaching material." Her mother put a plate of pancakes in front of her and sat down.

"Are you riding with Alex this morning?"

"No, she postponed 'til this afternoon. Had something to do at the clinic."

Her father put down his paper. "How is Alexandra? We haven't seen her in a few months." Her father had christened them with heavyweight names, in the hopes they would grow into them. He insisted on using them, even though the sisters were never more than Alex and Danni to each other.

"Well, I think she and Stephen may be approaching a new, um, level of understanding."

Her mother put down her fork. "What do you mean?"

"As long as they've been together Alex has never challenged him. And now she's been asked to chair a session at an international wildlife conference—a prestigious opportunity she's more than qualified for—and Stephen is adamantly against her attending at all."

"Her father looked up. "What's his reason?"

"He said their law firm has some corporate clients—mining and logging mostly—who would be very upset to hear that his wife is participating in a wildlife conference sponsored by some of the organizations that bring litigation against them."

"I can understand his concern. Your sister should probably back away from this." Danni gaped at her father. To him the issue was closed.

"Why do you say that?"

"Because it could threaten Stephen's career."

"What about Alex's career?" Danni was stunned by her father's uncharacteristic support of Stephen.

"Her career is the clinic. Stephen brings in the big money and has the larger responsibility."

"Why is his career so much more important than hers? He sure didn't work any harder to get where he is than she did—probably much less, since daddy owns the law firm."

"Danielle, Stephen's career is much more public than Alexandra's. And probably more vulnerable to problems with public perception."

"So, Alex's career goals are not to be considered if they conflict with the family platform? I can't believe you're saying this, dad! You know how hard she worked! I don't think Stephen mucked out horse stalls to pay HIS college tuition!"

"Danielle, calm down. I'm sure other opportunities will come up for Alexandra."

"Not where she's asked to chair a session at an international conference. This is exactly what she was working for when she met Stephen, the clinic was his idea." She drank her coffee and stared at her father like she was seeing him for the first time.

"That has to be the most sexist thing I've ever heard you say. Where's the dad that told us to be independent and not afraid to challenge the good ol' boy network? Both Alex and I had to fight that attitude, and here you are using it to defend

Stephen. I sure hope you stow it somewhere when you see Alex. She thinks you support her."

"I do support her, but she needs to be realistic."

"Do you think she'll go to this conference?" Her mother was concerned, she didn't like unrest, and this sounded like a very large serving of unrest.

"Yes, I think she will. And since we all know how flexible Stephen can be once he's taken a stand on something, I think she's gonna need our support. She's got mine." Danni put her plate in the dishwasher and glared at her dad.

"I will never marry somebody who can't think of me as an equal, intellectually, as well as emotionally. No matter how much money and influence his family has." She started for her room.

"Oh, Danielle, wait. Here's your mail from yesterday."

She rushed to grab it and checked the return addresses. "How long were you going to wait to give it to me, mom? 'Til next Saturday?"

"Danielle, your sarcasm isn't attractive."

"Neither is your Alzheimer's, mom," she chuckled. One business envelope caught her eye.

"Okay, let's see what New Orleans said." She ripped it open and her face fell. She looked from one parent to the other.

"Guess I won't quit my day job just yet. The Aquarium of the Americas seems to have all the marine biologists they need."

She wandered down the hall, "Well, back to the classroom..."

Husband and wife looked at each other across the table.

She said, "You didn't really mean that, did you?"

He shook his head and sighed. "No, I didn't. Alexandra was pretty naive when they got married and overwhelmed by all the money and privilege. Hell, we all bought his 'prince charming' act."

He drank his coffee. "Now she's feeling the need to be the headstrong firstborn we know and love, and I don't think she's considered the possible repercussions. Stephen does not strike me as someone accustomed to being challenged."

He nodded down the hall. "But I didn't want Danielle running off to her sister telling her that we think she should do this. She has to take that step on her own because she will have to live with the consequences."

He lowered his voice. "I suspect Stephen has a real mean streak under all the polish, and I would hate to see it leveled at Alexandra when she steps out of her place."

"You're thinking about how he treats their help?"

He nodded. "You remember that scene with little Carmen, too? I could not believe the way he spoke to her in front of all of us. He took her apart for breaking a wine glass, for God's sake!"

Ron and Gloria Davidson pondered their daughter's future.

He shook his head and gulped down the last of his coffee. "There's no question that I support her, Glo', I'm even a little proud, but I'm afraid our Cinderella may have discovered her castle's a gilded cage."

Patriarch and Cub-bearer collected the cubs one morning and headed for the meadow as they had on previous days. This outing, however, did not stop in the grass, but continued on toward the river. Guardian was in his usual spot at the rear of the parade, nudging the straggling cubs who dawdled over every distraction. Gentle and Jester accompanied them as well, but Cunning left the pack at the water's edge.

The cubs had never been close to water, it was unlike anything else in their experience. While they had a healthy curiosity about this flowing creature that bubbled and roared, they were learning to be wary of new things in their world.

The five older wolves waded into the water, leaving the cubs on the bank, whining and crying and pacing back and forth. Ignored, they howled louder in the hot sun while Patriarch and Cub-bearer romped in the chest-deep water. Gentle and Jester chased each other through the shallows, splashing the cubs as they galloped past.

Seeing his father midstream, White-cub finally stepped tentatively into the water. It felt cool, and on this hot day, pleasant. He lifted each foot high, unable to comprehend this strange stuff that did not support his weight or break under it. The specific qualities of liquids and solids were undefined, and the characteristics of this oozing wetness confused him.

The other four cubs continued to howl, and only after White-cub had all fours thoroughly wet and was prancing about in the shallows did they join him. Within minutes, all five cubs were frolicking near the sandy edge of the river. They splashed and fell, and rose to fall again. The rocks in the bottom were slippery and uneven, so the young canines were surprised when one paw settled much lower than the others. An invisible current pulled their feet from the rocks and surged around them. Coordination vanished.

The water cooled the tongue and refreshed sun-warmed skin and they played rowdier, romping with total abandon. Occasionally they foundered and sank below the water's surface, but chubby buoyant bodies popped up quickly amidst much sputtering and shaking.

Gentle and Jester nipped and nudged the cubs into deeper water and Guardian pushed Red-cub and Black-cub with his nose. First-twin and Second-twin were the last to test the depths, but they soon overcame their fear, paddling with oversized paws. By late afternoon the litter had joined the older wolves on the opposite side of the river.

They each selected a spot of sweet grass and stretched out, physically spent. The warm sun worked its magic on the exhausted wolves and their sleep deepened as the temperature rose.

Alex sat at her desk in the clinic and pondered her life and how the decision she was making would affect it. That there would be repercussions was obvious. She considered the uglier side of Stephen that she could no longer ignore.

Why didn't I see him like that earlier? Do Mom and Dad think about Stephen like Danni does?

That embarrassed her, like when she brought home a C in Mathematics. Her parents had been satisfied, but she had seen in their eyes that they knew she hadn't done her best. With all his money and charm, maybe in choosing Stephen, she hadn't done her best.

What am I in his life? We share a bed, and an address, but am I just what Danni said? Just appropriate? God, what a thought. He seems to love me, we're good to each other—vertically and horizontally. She smiled. *Just thinking about his hands gets me hot.*

But he hasn't even kissed me since the argument.

What is the worst thing that could happen if I do this conference? Her mind drew a blank because she had no experience of challenging Stephen to draw upon.

Her eyes fell on her degrees framed on the wall.

One thing is certain. If I walk away from this, something else will come up with the same problem. So, do I deal with it now, or hold off the battle for later?

A framed snapshot of her and Danni on horseback as children reminded her about their riding date.

She grabbed the phone and dialed.

"Hi Greg, it's Alex. Yes, I got it, and I'm very excited about participating..."

The whump, whump of powerful wings and Second-twin's terrified screams shattered the peace and the wolves looked up in time to see a large bald eagle grip Second-twin's back in vise-like talons and snatch her off the ground. Patriarch and the other wolves leaped up, but too late to save her.

The powerful rhythm of the eagle's broad wings was pure strength against gravity. Three-foot wings flexed and pulled, each stroke gaining lift.

Patriarch and Cub-bearer raced after the huge raptor, leaping again and again to snatch back their daughter, without success. In moments the white-headed predator flew over the river, caught an updraft and rose above the valley with his cargo.

Leaving the pack to deal with its first loss.

Guardian and Gentle huddled the remaining cubs, trying to quiet their piercing cries.

Cub-bearer bolted into the water after the eagle, and stopped midstream where they had played just hours before, and her howls echoed through the valley.

Patriarch lifted his nose in the air and snarled. The proud alpha who fought a grizzly to protect his young, had lost a daughter while he slept.

Cub-bearer had never lost a cub and this searing hurt that did not bleed was new to her. She howled and clawed the ground, with an intensity that frightened her offspring.

Shadows lengthened and the pack returned to the den. None of the wolves felt Second-twin's absence like the small gray female that had lost her sister. First-twin and Second-twin had bonded even before birth, and now she felt truly alone. She trudged down the trail, head down, tail dragging, and seemed to shrink with each step.

Patriarch led the pack home with his hackles up and his nose pointed to the sky moving from side to side, to catch a glimpse or scent of the winged monster that had taken his daughter. There was no outlet for his wrath and the other wolves distanced themselves from him, unwilling to be a target for his anger.

When they were about halfway down the trail, White-cub crept next to his father, and only when Patriarch looked down and saw his son did his anger subside. He still had young to care for and a pack to lead. He was still alpha, so he filed this memory, a hard lesson learned.

That night all the wolves howled but two voices stood out, the mournful voice of a mother grieving for her lost young, and a small voice crying for her sister.

Chapter Six

First-twin was inconsolable. She turned away from the food brought to her and the shine left her eyes. She spent her days alone in the forest or sleeping in the den, but no place brought her comfort. Her behavior confused the other wolves and none of their efforts at play revived her. She grew thinner and weaker each day.

Cunning watched her from the day Second-twin was taken and the cold-hearted bitch began to warm. When it appeared First-twin was near death, Cunning went to her. The older yearling licked her younger sister with an affection she had never shown another wolf, and she joined First-twin in the den that night, wrapping her body around the thin cub, cradling her near her own warm belly. Cunning did not sleep that night, but licked First-twin constantly, stimulating her to live.

Sunrise found a bright-eyed First-twin, and when Cunning gave her meat she ate ravenously. From that day, Cunning taught First-twin her clever ways and in return First-twin warmed the shewolf's heart.

Danni was waiting when Alex stepped off the elevator, and the change in her appearance was startling. There were circles under her eyes that makeup could not hide from a sister's scrutiny, and it looked like she had lost weight. Only the smallest hint of a smile answered her own.

"You sounded like you were going to erupt on the phone. This must be important if you're paying for lunch." When they hugged Danni felt bones under Alex's sweater that she hadn't felt before.

"Very funny. Wait 'til we're seated and I'll tell you." She nodded at the hostess and they were led to a booth overlooking the marina.

Alex was glad Danni had invited her to Sunday brunch, she definitely had no other commitments. In fact, she hadn't had any family commitments since she told Stephen she would be participating in the conference. Most mornings he was gone when she got up and their paths rarely crossed. It was easy to avoid interaction in their house. When they did happen to have dinner together, a dark cloud formed and hovered between the massive candlesticks at the center of the table. Alex had attempted to get through the storm front, asking about Stephen's work and activities, but nothing warmed him. He was civil and polite, but her questions solicited only single syllable responses. After several attempts, she quit trying.

Others in the seafood restaurant noticed the two women, men performing a more detailed investigation than women. Alex and Danni had been blessed with fine Scandinavian genes, and their long legs and slender builds did justice to the well-fitting jeans and sweaters. That they were sisters was subtly evident, but not because of physical similarities. Danni's dark hair and brown eyes played autumn to Alex's spring blue-eyed blonde features. Their sibling relationship expressed itself in their personalities, the raising of an eyebrow, how they both ran a hand through their hair when they spoke, and the way both mouths curved easily into identical smiles that blossomed into laughter. That they loved each other was obvious.

"Well?" Alex hated it when Danni toyed with her. "What's your news?"

"You are now dining with the newest marine biologist employed by the Monterey Bay Research Institute!"

Alex lit up, "That's great, sis!" She reached across the table and squeezed Danni's hand. "What a great opportunity! When do you start?"

"They want me as soon as I can get my toys packed and my truck on the road. I'm thinking I'll leave next weekend."

"Next weekend?! That's so soon..." Alex voice drifted off. *Danni's leaving next weekend?!*

"I'm going to miss you, kiddo. I'm proud of you, and happy for you, but I'm really going to miss you!" They grasped hands across the table, eyes locked.

"Thanks, Alex. It's going to be strange not having you closeby. You know—to help me with my homework." They both chuckled. It was a well-worn family joke.

A waiter took their orders and vanished.

"Guess I'd better get all the salmon I can before Friday, God only know what I'll find in California..."

"What did Mom and Dad say?"

"Mom freaked when she heard I was leaving so soon, but Dad 'bout burst his buttons. I think he thought he'd be stuck with me forever. Maybe he was happy because he finally gets his den back. He said some words about both his daughters making him proud, and Mom cried. You know."

Alex nodded. "It's going to be hard on them with us both gone."

"I don't know about that. They were talking about going on another cruise when I left today, I think the adjustment took about ten seconds. They really are quite happy together without us, Alex."

"I envy their relationship."

A heavy minute hung in the air then plopped without grace to the floor. Danni didn't know how to ask, Alex knew she wanted to, and sarcasm won the moment.

"So... speaking of wedded bliss, how are things?"

Alex's half-hearted smile told her. "Let's just say things have been real quiet. Like living in a casket." She sighed. "I know that I'm not doing anything wrong, but in his eyes I see accusation and in knee-jerk response, I feel guilty."

Mimosas arrived and Danni sipped hers. This was an important conversation for them both, and she didn't want to blow it.

"You've been programmed for five years, Alex, don't you see? Nothing bad is ever Stephen's fault. How do you think it will end?"

"Well, when I get back from the conference and he realizes I haven't single-handedly destroyed his career and the family practice, I think he'll relax. Then we'll talk." The lump in her throat threatened to choke her, so she changed the subject. "I'm really gonna to miss our Sunday rides. What are you going to do with Kiowa?"

"I figure I'll let you and Stephen decide that. He was a gift from Stephen."

"Right. A gift. He's yours, Danni."

"Well, maybe you'd look after him, ride him once in a while, until I can figure out if I can keep him down there."

"You got it."

They ate in silence, memorizing each other for later.

The cubs were now large enough that the den was no longer necessary, so Patriarch's pack resumed its nomadic lifestyle. More important lessons loomed ahead.

The cubs' acute senses, no longer tools for play, took on increased importance as Patriarch led the pack up and out of the valley. Immature noses learned to recognize not only what kind of animal had shared their trail, but how much earlier it had passed, and whether it was young or old, healthy or sick. White-cub and his littermates watched the sky for signs of changing weather and learned to sense falling barometric pressure in their inner ear, then use their surroundings for cover during the storms that followed.

Four months had passed since they first glimpsed the world beyond their den. Their bodies had transformed from round fuzzy pups to sleek adolescent wolves. Dense, hard bone replaced the soft bones of infancy, and muscles previously well-padded with baby fat, were now sinewy and strong. Stubby noses used for nursing extended and puppy teeth were pushed out by sharp canines, carnassials, and molars. Downy fur disappeared under the overlapping capes of coarse guard hair, and the muted colorings of their youth deepened to rich grays and reds and browns. The playful eyes of Cub-bearer's newest offspring became keen and watchful, very little escaped their attention.

The older wolves gradually decreased the food they

provided the cubs to stimulate their interest in the hunt and White-cub and his siblings experienced gnawing hunger for the first time. But hunger sharpens a predator's senses and the cubs began to see the creatures of their valley in a new light, no longer curious neighbors and playmates. Sharply divided by an inviolate line, all forest inhabitants were segregated into two groups, prey or competing predator.

Mice and squirrels were caught by the older wolves and dropped, still alive, in front of the cubs to entice them, but the cubs were pathetically uncoordinated. So significant was their ignorance of the movement patterns of other animals, that many of the intended martyrs brought to this deadly game escaped handily.

Hunger is a great motivator and soon behaviors learned wrestling brothers and sisters outside the den surfaced with new drive and purpose. Canine minds and bodies recalled their play, and began to anticipate the movements of their dainty prey. White-cub took more than his share of rodent prizes. Forgotten were the carefree days of play around the den when their hunger was sated on demand, and the cubs learned the grim reality that hunting was hard work and often unsuccessful. Many nights White-cub fell asleep with an empty belly, too exhausted to continue his pursuit.

Frequently the older wolves split off with one or two of the cubs in search of food. The groups kept in contact by howling and their eerie music echoed through the trees.

Large prey animals were not difficult to find that fall. Learning to bring them down successfully was the challenge that faced White-cub, as Patriarch and Cub-bearer led him to a broad grassy clearing, many times larger than the meadow near the den.

Several mule deer grazed in the open field, females with their young and immature bucks and does. White-cub shot past his father and into the cluster of animals, scattering them immediately. Patriarch and Cub-bearer found a shady spot on a small knoll and waited for their son to exhaust himself.

White-cub bounded from one deer to another through the morning, never getting closer than six feet before the animals sprang easily away. Many exhausting dashes finally convinced the cub what his parents already knew. He could not run as fast as the deer, and he would never catch one by chasing it.

But none of the deer left the meadow. Once the white cub gave up on a particular animal, it would stop, drop his head, and begin to graze. As long as Patriarch and Cub-bearer maintained their reclining positions away from the game, the deer exhibited no fear. Finally, however, the large alpha wearied of his son's hopeless pursuits.

He and Cub-bearer rose and started for the deer.

Instantly the mood on the meadow changed. The two wolves trotted in a fluid gait toward the deer, all now fully alert. White-cub watched his parents and his brain registered their energy-conserving pace, as they glided toward a young fawn that shuffled with an irregular step.

Patriarch and Cub-bearer flowed through the grass unhurried, and precise, circling the deer in opposite directions. It was impossible for White-cub to watch both of them at the same time, a deadly dilemma for the fawn. They paced themselves and arrived at the doe with the chosen fawn simultaneously, Patriarch from the front and Cub-bearer from the rear. Abruptly they dashed for the fawn, cutting her from the rest of the herd.

Patriarch sank his fangs into the fawn's nose as Cub-bearer grabbed her rear leg and pulled her to the ground. Although its mother kicked at Cub-bearer to defend her offspring, the futility of her situation forced her to leave her offspring to its fate. The young mule deer's deformed leg made escape impossible. It was over in seconds and the two wolves began to eat.

White-cub's own hunger drove him flying down the knoll towards his parents, and his next meal. Forgetting protocol, he stuck his nose into the kill and had started feeding when Patriarch snarled and rolled him hard on his back, fangs poised around his white throat. White-cub was more frightened than hurt, and struggled to free himself from his father's jaws. The alpha growled with unveiled menace and did not release his son until he quit fighting. Pack hierarchy, and his subordinate position in it, must never be forgotten.

White-cub humbled himself, tail between his legs, head down and ears back, and begged food from his parents, as he had seen the yearlings do. After a few minutes of feeding alone the alphas consented, and White-cub satisfied his hunger. He would never eat first until he was alpha of his own pack.

Chapter Seven

"Ladies and gentlemen, please! You cannot all speak at once!" Alex felt impotent in front of the audience as she watched confrontations flare up between individuals. She couldn't hear the words, but anger permeated the air like skunk musk. Across the crowded hall where fate had seated people of opposing ideas next to one another, faces were red and animated with emotion. And they all ignored her.

"My family's grazed our cattle on that land for five generations! Who are you to tell us we have to tolerate wolves takin' our cows?" shouted one irate attendee. Before he took his seat several people jumped up and started speaking at once. Only one longhaired environmentalist was loud enough to be heard, yelling over the din.

"It's NOT your land! That land belongs to the people of the United States, and you've been squatting on it long enough!"

"We pay to lease that land, mister!" responded the rancher, taking large steps in his worn cowboy boots toward the longhair.

"A fraction of what it's worth, and nowhere near what you'd pay me if it was my land!" A woman's voice joined the fray from across the room. The rancher turned to identify the female antagonist.

"Who cares about your goddamned cows?" A tall man in the third row rose slowly, his huge belly draping over a brass belt buckle shaped like a pistol. National Rifle Association patches on his camouflage jacket caught the house lights like military medals, as his deep drawl and slow delivery rumbled through the ambient noise like thunder through a rainstorm.

"We have a constitutional right to hunt outside the National Forest and wolves'll kill off all the game! We pay a lot of money for licenses to hunt there!"

"Can't you bloodthirsty morons find a more civilized hobby?" The longhaired environmentalist was shaking, his face crimson with rage. He was quite out of control and his passion was frightening those around him. And Alex.

"La-dies, and, gen-tle-men, *please*!" Alex enunciated each syllable, and as she leaned into the microphone she could see two of the three speakers on the platform to her right fidgeting in their seats. Their anxiety mirrored her own, as the audience hostility mushroomed by the minute.

Alex had lost control of the packed hall.

To quiet the crowd she thumped the microphone firmly with a fingernail and the public address system blasted out the amplified booms like cannonfire.

She raised her voice again, "Ladies and gentlemen, I must ask you to sit down and be quiet, or I will be forced to close this session."

In desperation she picked up her water glass, held it next to the microphone and struck it repeatedly with her pen. Hard. The brain-jarring noise reverberated through the hall with immediate effect. Voices dropped to a murmur and people slowly returned to their seats. Alex took a deep breath while she waited for quiet.

The sessions that had preceded hers at the environmental conference ranged from frightening to hopeful and for two days Alex listened to biologists and ecologists present their field work. The number of reputable scientists involved in environmental issues encouraged her. Without their meticulous work and the data it produced, there could be no ammunition to stimulate change by governments and powerful corporations.

Her session was scheduled for the last morning of the conference and the clouds threatened Calgary with the snow already falling in the Rockies to the west. The weather seemed appropriate. Wildlife restoration was contentious because it always involved sacrifice by human beings at some level, and the most painful sacrifices were invariably tied to money.

Tom Graycloud, representing a coalition of Native

American Indian tribes, discussed efforts to return the buffalo to the reservations on the great plains of the United States, and bring the Indian way of life back to an economy based on hunting, instead of farming. The cattle industry saw the increase in buffalo meat products as a threat to their market.

Karen McDonald, a marine biologist, documented the urgent need to return the sea otter to the Pacific waters off the coast of Southern California. Armies of sea urchins were systematically decimating the kelp forests that were home to thousands of fish, including many commercial species. As they grazed through the kelp beds, they left huge swaths of barren ocean in their wake, useless and unprotected. The otters' natural appetite for sea urchins could return the biological balance and save the kelp. Opponents believed the local shellfish industry would suffer from an increase in otter population.

But the most emotional arguments centered on the return of the gray wolf to Yellowstone National Park. When her friend, Matt Kramer, presented his work, Alex discovered that this was the single most volatile restoration issue. At its core was the value of one apex predator against another—wolf against man. Emotions flowed as hot as lava.

Alex stood silently behind the podium while the people in the audience that had seats returned to them. The conference planners had anticipated an audience of 400. Now, with every chair filled there were still about fifty people leaning against the walls. T-shirts and buttons represented popular wildlife causes, and those people with opposing views could be identified by their determined scowls.

"Thank you. We will respond to your questions and comments in an orderly manner, one at a time. Please." The vocal rancher raised his hand and stood when Alex acknowledged him. His face was still flushed with anger.

"I represent several ranchers that live around Yellowstone and we do not want wolves preying on our cattle. Our parents remember what it was like when wolves ran free.

Lady, when I was little my folks wouldn't even let me play alone outside! Even today there are reports of 'em maulin' kids. You fancy scientists don't know what you're dealin' with. These animals are vermin and they *should* be extinct!" Satisfied with his speech, he sat.

Alex turned to the speaker nearest her on the stage, the only one not fidgeting.

"Matt, would you like to respond?" He rose and she returned to her chair, relieved to vacate the podium.

The six-foot tall biologist removed the microphone from the podium and walked to the front of the platform. He looked unaccustomed to his gray suit, but moved cat-like inside it.

He made eye contact with the rancher and held his gaze, unintimidated by the older man's outburst. Matt waited for silence like a man with no commitments, and he was not uncomfortable waiting.

Alex knew Matt's first job at a wolf sanctuary had set his career path, and he achieved respect at a young age for his extensive and thorough studies of wild wolf behavior. He spent much of his time alone in Alaska's Denali National Park, and similar remote locations across Canada, studying the wolf in his own environment. Matt understood them better than most, and his respect for them was well documented.

"Let me respond to the issues you raised with the most current data we have on wolf behavior." His eyes left the rancher and roamed the room.

"In 1989 a female timber wolf moved south from Canada into the Ninemile valley outside Marion, Montana. She was observed, even video taped, by the two brothers that owned the pasture from the first day she took up residence. Within weeks she delivered her cubs in a hollow tree stump, and even though there were cows birthing within fifty feet of that stump, she continued to travel miles from the ranch to kill deer for herself and her young. This is not an isolated case. When wolves hunt they follow a "search image", pursuing the same type of game they were taught to hunt when they were young. The wolves restored to Yellowstone would be wild, with "search images" for elk and other species that are now over-populating the park. They would be classified experimental, so we could destroy any that habituate on livestock." His eyes found the rancher again.

"And for any isolated renegade attacks on livestock, you ranchers have already been offered compensation for each loss." Matt paused momentarily, and the rancher looked away, uncomfortable under the younger man's scrutiny. It was obvious who Matt was addressing.

"As for wolf attacks on children, there have been no documented cases of a healthy wolf attacking a human in North America as long as they have been keeping track of such information. Please note I said, healthy wolf. Lately it has become fashionable to own wolf-dog hybrids as pets. All reported cases of attack in recent years have been by such crossbreeds. The nature of the wild wolf is not a mystery, we know they are shy, intensely loyal to their pack, and caring parents to their young. And we know they instinctively avoid humans. But when you breed this creature with a domestic dog, the product is unpredictable and dangerous. These are the animals that attack children, and the hysteria and fear caused by such stories is inaccurately attributed to the wolf."

Matt's peripheral vision caught the hunter as he leaped to his feet, eager to be the next speaker. He did not wait to be acknowledged.

"That's just great! They won't attack livestock and kids, but they'll wipe out the deer and elk we have a right to hunt! The game'll vanish, sure as shit!" Alex watched Matt level his amber eyes at the hunter in a look that reminded her of her wolf encounter, the way that wolf had dominated her with just his eyes. Both stares were unsettling in their naked dominance. Matt took a deep breath before responding.

"On Isle Royale in Minnesota—a geographically isolated environment—populations of wolf and moose, the canine's prey species, have been tracked for more than thirty years. During that time both predator and prey numbers rose and fell together.

When food was plentiful for the moose they bred easily and the wolf populations reflected the increase in the size of their litters. In bad years, when moose numbers fell, the wolves did not reproduce, naturally reducing the population of predators. The ratio has followed this cycle, and neither species decimated the other. The balance of nature isn't just a nice phrase we all learned as kids. It exists and is quite efficient when allowed to function without human tampering." Matt paused and his eyes narrowed slightly and drilled through the NRA member.

"There is one effect the wolves will have on your hunting activities, though. The presence of predators in the National Forest will make the game species much more wary and cautious. But I'm sure you and your friends will appreciate the challenge of tracking more elusive game, won't you, sir?" Alex wondered if the rest of the audience heard the sarcasm. During the rest of the public session no questions were directed to Alex's other two speakers. They didn't appear disappointed. The cloud of controversy that formed in the room that morning settled over Matt, and did not dissipate.

Alex's gut-wrenching tension was in total contrast to Matt's strong sense of calm. He fielded questions and comments with courtesy, and met each verbal assault with cool confidence. His voice was warm with as much concern for the people that shared their habitat, as he had for the wolves.

Alex closed the session after three hours, physically and emotionally drained. She thanked Karen and Tom for their presentations, and when she shook each of their hands she noticed the relief on their faces. She approached Matt as the other two left the platform.

"You were very calm under that pressure, I don't know how you do it."

"Thanks, but it's not the first time I've heard any of those comments. This was actually pretty civilized compared to some meetings I've pitched. In Montana ranchers show up with guns." He latched his briefcase and faced her, smiling. "Loaded guns. What bothers me is I always hear the same arguments, and they come from folks who I don't think represent the majority of the population. I believe most Americans want the wolves in Yellowstone for their kids to hear someday." Alex reached for her notes.

"That guy from the NRA was a piece of work, wasn't he?"

Matt nodded and chuckled in agreement. "He was a clown, and I don't believe he was representing anybody but himself. The NRA moves with more dignity than that and honestly, Alex, I have fewer problems with them than other groups. Let's face it, if the wildlife disappear, their fun's over. Lately they have seen the value in policing their own. They've even been responsible for the arrest of several poachers in the Pacific Northwest. I think the NRA will not be amused by their representative today when they see him on TV. They work hard to wipe out that 'good ol' boy' image."

The room was almost vacant. Matt looked at the empty plastic chairs and the trash on the floor.

"These meetings do one thing for me, though. They really make me appreciate my time in the wild. Sometimes I'm convinced the wolves are more civilized than we are."

"Don't you ever get lonely out there?"

"No," his eyes held hers, "the wilderness has a strange way of level-setting my priorities. It's hard to explain, but the important things really rise to the top when I fall asleep looking at the stars."

He paused while packing his slides. "You look exhausted, Alex, could I buy you a late lunch somewhere?" She noticed how the blonde streaks in his sandy hair highlighted the gold flecks in his eyes.

She shook her head and looked away. "No, but thanks anyway. I'm going to try to catch an afternoon flight and go home today instead of tomorrow. I think I've had about all the conference I can handle." When she looked up, she knew his eyes hadn't left her face. It was disarming.

"I'm surprised that Stephen agreed to you doing this—

surprised and pleased. He's a bigger man than I thought he was."

"Well, he wasn't thrilled..." She fiddled with her wedding ring, and the knot in her stomach that had briefly relaxed, cramped tight. She wasn't brave enough to tell Matt he'd been right.

"You did well, you should be pleased. Have a good flight home, Alex." The softness when he said her name made her pleasantly uncomfortable.

"'Bye, Matt, and watch out for those armed ranchers!" She heard him chuckle as she turned and left the hall.

When she reached her hotel room she called Stephen's office.

"Law offices, Stephen Verazzano's office, may I help you?"

"Hello, Sheryl, this is Alex, is Stephen available?"

"No, Mrs. Verazzano, he's in conference with a client, would you like to leave a message?"

"No thanks, I'll try later." Alex was weary of her brief exchanges with Stephen's secretary. She had left three messages over the last three days, each of which Stephen carefully returned during the following day, calling her hotel room when he knew she would be attending the conference. Alex recognized his avoidance routine—she'd seen him use it on troublesome clients.

She hung up the phone and rubbed her neck, the tension had returned full force. By defying Stephen to participate in the conference she had pushed him away, and his emotional absence over the weeks had become a gnawing pain.

She phoned the airline and changed her return reservation, then packed and checked out of the hotel.

The storm that had threatened all day, exploded over downtown Calgary while she drove to the airport. Worn windshield wipers struggled to sweep away the snow and Alex struggled to sweep away her growing anxiety.

☪☪☪

The wolves were a team, rehearsed, prepared. They knew the terrain and they knew the ebb and flow of the animals they pursued. As the prey darted and turned, the wolves shadowed them, pivot then bolt ahead, sidestep and race forward, waiting for the stumble or missed step that marked their next victim. With each stride, they grew more determined, closing the distance between hunter and quarry inch by inch. It was dance on a grand scale, predator and prey, partners performing their moves with flawless precision to music neither could ignore.

Competition between the cubs was intense. Who would be the first in this litter to make the kill? Would it be White-cub with his superior strength and speed? Or First-twin, crafty understudy to her sister, Cunning? Or Red-cub and Black-cub, the teamwork of their den days now matured into a coordinated threat?

Who would draw first blood?

Fall was retreating, the first snow had dusted the ground, when the scent of returning caribou crossed Patriarch's nose. These migrating ruminants constituted a large percentage of the wolves' winter diet, and Patriarch's past success hunting them had kept the pack alive.

Hunting the caribou became Patriarch's singular goal, and these chases surpassed anything the cubs had experienced with deer and elk. Caribou spent their summer months under the constant threat of arctic wolves, openly visible to the migrating herds. Challenges and parries between wolf and caribou occurred each day.

But the caribou were not defenseless. The same sense of smell that could find food under several inches of snow could detect a wolf half a mile away, and sharp eyesight noticed the smallest movement against the backdrop of winter white. Sure-footed and agile on ice, they made Patriarch's pack work hard before sacrificing a victim to their hunger.

White-cub, Red-cub, and Black-cub set out with their parents, and the rest of the wolves formed a second group and followed Guardian. The air was so cold White-cub's exhaled breath formed small clouds before his nose.

After a few hours Patriarch scented caribou, at least one cow and calf not far ahead of them. When the cubs caught the scent they drew up to the Patriarch and Cub-bearer, nuzzling each other with excitement. The hunt was on.

They branched out, travelling downwind, circling the unsuspecting animals, and when Patriarch was sure his family was ready, he burst from the trees. Chaos erupted. In their flight, calves were separated from mothers, as the wolf pack dashed to isolate a victim before they all could reach top speed and bolt away.

White-cub caught a tiny movement behind a bush and whirled towards a terrified calf, with Black-cub racing behind him. White-cub sprang after the fleeing caribou, catching his hind leg, slowing it enough for Black-cub to run alongside and leap at the young animal's throat. The brothers held firm as the young caribou struggled to free himself and it took all their collective muscle just to hang on.

The calf was still fighting when his enraged mother exploded from the trees behind Black-cub, and before he could react, she reared up and rammed both front hooves down on his exposed body. Only one short yelp escaped the black cub before he collapsed, silent and still.

His cry summoned Patriarch and Cub-bearer, who made short work of the calf. Faced with the rest of the pack, the calf's mother retreated, leaving the wolves to feed. And mourn.

Black-cub's lifeless body lay close to the body of the calf. In seconds, the eternal chase had ended both lives. Cub-bearer nuzzled her son's quiet form, trying in vain to raise him. The pain of losing Second-twin was revisited on the large bitch and her howling summoned Guardian and the rest of the pack. Red-cub whined and pawed at his brother, and licked the blood flowing from the gash where his back had been broken.

The wolves fed quietly, bickering and snarling silenced by their sibling's lifeless form. The dark cub was already growing cool, and his absolute stillness imprinted his death on the pack. As night descended Black-cub's family silently left him, the blood of wolf and caribou mingling on the frozen ground.

Thousands of miles away a phone rang.

"Law offices, Stephen Verrazano's office, may I help you?" She paused, then with much greater respect, "Yes, sir, Mr. Truette, I'll put you right though."

In the spacious office behind the woman, Stephen picked up the phone, and before he could utter a syllable heard,

"Can you explain to me why I'm watching your wife on TV at a wildlife conference with a bunch of wacko environmentalists, Stephen?"

While he groped for an answer, Stephen seethed.

Chapter Eight

The plane lurched and shook, awakening sleeping passengers and heads popped up, anxiety etched on each face.

"May I have your attention, this is the captain. Evidently we're in for a little rough weather, so please stay in your seats with your seatbelts securely fastened. We'll try to get around this storm as soon as possible. Thank you."

"Perfect," Alex muttered, "I don't even like flying in good weather."

Sheet lightning flashed and streaks of rain slashed diagonally across her window. She thought the captain was extremely optimistic about flying around this storm, it had all the earmarks of a Seattle monsoon.

"Could I offer you something to drink?" The flight attendant appeared unaffected by the weather.

What class in flight attendant school covers that, Alex wondered?

"Yes, could I get a sparkling water, please?"

"Of course." Her Miss America smile was radiant.

Another flash of lightning cast a blue pall over the young woman's face. She didn't even flinch.

Amazing, thought Alex.

The uniformed woman's perky demeanor was in marked contrast to Alex's. Her stomach was beginning to respond to the turbulence outside with a turbulence of its own.

She sipped her Calistoga water and rested her head against the seat. Behind closed eyes the situation with Stephen escaped its locked cell and loomed on her mind's horizon. She thought of the Canadian Rockies passing beneath the plane, of Banff in winter, and six-year old memories folded around her like a well-worn bathrobe.

"Alex, would you please hurry up? Half of Canada will have tracked the snow before we get out there!"

"Relax, Danni, I can't find my other glove. Mom, have you seen it?" Alex foraged through the mound of ski gear drying in the middle of living room floor.

"Yes, it's under your dad's boot bag."

"Alex, please! Let's go!" Danni knelt to help her sister look through the pile of neon-colored Goretex and Supplex.

"Did I ever tell you how much I appreciate your patience? Honestly, Danni, it's one of your best things." Her relaxed voice offset the strident urgency in her sister's.

"Here it is. Thanks, mom." She clipped both gloves together and collected the rest of her gear. "Aren't you and dad skiing today?" Danni rolled her eyes in frustration at her sister's question. More time to wait for an answer.

"Oh yes, as soon as he gets showered and ready." Gloria glanced beyond the condo's picture window to the slopes. "We got some new snow last night, and it looks like it'll be a perfect day. Don't forget your sunblock."

"If we don't get out there soon it won't be a problem," Danni muttered, "it'll be dark!"

"Oh c'mon, let's go." Alex started for the door then paused and looked at her sister. "You know, I really hate waiting for you all the time." Danni slapped her arm with a pair of padded ski gloves.

In spite of Alex's misplaced glove the girls arrived at the base chair at Lake Louise before it was running, and there were only a few people in line ahead of them. Muffled explosions rumbled as the resort crew set off dynamite to control avalanche danger. The lift started up when the blasting stopped.

Blinding sunshine reflecting off virgin snow greeted them on the mountaintop. No wind chilled muscles and joints, and the weekday crowd was still far below them. Conditions were perfect. Boots snapped into bindings and they glided to the trailhead, Alex savoring the shoosh of her skis against packed snow, and within minutes the dense forest gave way to a huge bowl, nearly a half mile across and unmarked.

"Virgin powder, Alex, this is ecstacy!" The sisters gazed

at the untouched white.

"Let's sign it before the masses arrive."

"After you." They tightened their boots, adjusted their goggles, and glided into the great concave of white. Alex and Danni sailed through the fresh powder, knees flexing and weight shifting subtly from one leg to another. Hips swayed as they left hourglass traces in the snow. The girls skied as instinctively as most people walk, exhilarating in the rise and fall of each turn.

They flew through the snow without conscious effort and their graceful forms attracted a solitary observer. Dark eyes followed their sleek spots of color from the chair lift overhead, watching them raise giant rooster tails of powder until they had completed their run through the bowl.

"That was great! Alex, this place is Heaven, just let me die here!"

"Amen." Alex caught her breath in the thin air. "Where to next? It looks like the herd has caught up with us." Both girls looked back at their symmetrical tracks in the snow. Skiers were now racing down the bowl behind them.

"Well—" Danni looked at her sister with raised eyebrows, "how 'bout something a bit more challenging? That is, if my old sister is up to it." Heavy emphasis on the word, old.

"I can keep up with you, on my worst day." Alex drove her poles into the packed snow and shooshed off for more remote black diamond runs.

The hidden eyes that had watched their flight down the bowl, followed them on skis. Undetected.

They traversed the resort to the expert trails on the backside of the mountain where the chutes were steep and narrow. Trees lining either side tolerated no errors in judgement.

"Oh, now this is more like it! What d'ya think, Alex?"

"I think you have death wish." But the thrill was rising with her adrenaline as she gazed down the unfamiliar run, dropping away nearly vertical. The bottom was not visible from where they stood.

"I bet the air's thicker down there—looks like about sea

level." Danni's eyes challenged her sister. Alex took a deep breath, already calculating her first few turns down the steep chute.

"I sure hope someone knows where to send the bodies. I'll go first, Danni, but let me get to the bottom before you start. I don't want you crashing into me when you fall."

"When I fall? Not likely, sister!"

Alex leaned confidently into the hill, mentally stimulated by the risk. Here, the rhythm of the snowdance was much faster, pole plant, bend knees, rise, turn in mid air, opposite pole poised for next pivot point. Her turns came fast to control the speed of descent, and she pointed her shoulders straight down the fall line to maintain her balance.

Her lower body spent the energy conserved by her torso. Thigh and calf muscles burned, and hips and knees took the brunt of each jump turn. Unlike the smooth bowl, this face demanded that Alex plant each pole and edge hard into the hill. If she missed one turn, her fall would not end until she reached the bottom. Mind and muscle worked the run and her skis defied gravity, pulling her out of the snow, to reverse direction, blissfully airborne.

Courage as much as skill was tested, and Alex and Danni pushed each other to the limit.

They moved from one steep chute to another and through the day they were observed in silence from the trees. He followed them down each run, behind them in lift lines, intrigued by the graceful women.

When they called it a day late that afternoon their thighs tingled with the warmth of an intense workout, and the winter sun had added its own glow to their cheeks.

The warmth of the lounge was inviting, twinkling white lights blinked Christmas greetings through pine boughs draped over the bar, and the scent of mulled wine mingled with that of wet wool and warm bodies. Other skiers were filling the room so Alex quickly took the last vacant table near the windows while Danni waded through a human sea to the bar.

☪☪☪

Alex shed her jacket and gloves and looked at the slopes, tinted pink in the setting sun. She shook out her long blonde hair from its captivity under her hat, and the unintentionally erotic movement sparked genuine interest in the voyeur sitting alone at the corner of the bar. He lifted his beer and watched her over the edge of the glass, amazed that they were as interesting off the slope as on.

He studied Alex and her sister for several minutes, the women lost in their conversation and unaware of his scrutiny. The physical resemblance between them was subtle, but it was their comfortable relationship that convinced him they were sisters. He envied their sibling bond and the affection that flowed between them, the absence of a brother or sister had left a tangible void in his life, and the many advantages of his wealthy childhood did not make up for it.

He wanted to meet Alex. Her freshness was unique among the sophisticated women he usually dated. He motioned the waitress when the girls had finished their drinks and ordered them another round. Not an original idea, but he was confident it would produce the desired response. It always had before. Stephen was the kind of handsome that mothers warn their daughters about, and fathers never trust. And he was fully aware of his effect on women. He stared at Alex's face as the waitress pointed him out to the girls, anxious to see her first expression when she acknowledged him.

When Alex raised her head and their eyes met the effect of her simple nod and smile shocked him. His body remained still but his pulse quickened. Arousal was immediate. He had not been so moved by a woman since the onset of puberty. No word had passed between them, and he felt momentarily lost for a response, behind in a game he had initiated. Finding his feet and his tongue, he strolled to the girl's table. His eyes never strayed from Alex's face.

"Hello, my name's Stephen Verazzano." The girls exchanged glances. The name was not unfamiliar to them, it was a lawyer name, a newspaper name, a money name.

"Hi. Thanks for the drinks." Both girls voiced their appreciation, but he only heard Alex.

"I'm Alex Davidson and this is my sister, Danni." Stephen's charm oozed like honey and he shook Danni's hand first, then lingered momentarily before releasing Alex's.

"Would you like to join us?" A few uncomfortable seconds of silence passed before Alex voiced her invitation. She was more familiar with animal mating rituals than human, and his Italian looks were more than a little distracting. He even smelled rich.

"Thank you. How are you girls enjoying the snow?" He tried to speak to them both, but his eyes were already memorizing the angles of Alex's face.

"It's absolutely incredible! Much better than what we have at home!" Danni gushed, but Stephen did not notice.

"And where is home?" He looked into Alex's blue eyes, hoping she would respond before her sister. She did.

"Seattle. We grew up skiing in the Cascades."

"No kidding? So did I. I was born and raised there." Another slice of silence. Alex fiddled with the cinnamon stick, stirring the whipped cream floating on her hot cider.

"Do you still live in Seattle, Stephen?"

"Yes, I'm an attorney." The girls made eye contact. *Oh, THAT Verazzano.* "What about you two, how do you fill your hours, when you're not skiing, that is?"

"I'm finishing a degree in wildlife biology and vet medicine and Danni's just starting college." He nodded.

"A veterinarian? I hear that's about as tough as law school."

"I don't know about that, but it was enough of a challenge for me." The conversation gradually came easier, a trickle of words turning to a stream. Stephen showed interest in both women and put them at ease, orchestrating the scene with a practiced hand. Alex and Danni opened up to him, powerless before his charm.

His eyes and voice stroked something warm and deep inside Alex that no other man had touched. While they labored at the awkward beginning of their future, Danni saw her sister's face glow like she'd never seen it before. She saw the same look on Stephen's face.

"Do you plan to open your vet practice in Seattle?"

"Actually, I want to use my vet skills to work with wildlife in the field. Then maybe start a practice later. I've thought about a clinic specializing in caring for highly trained, valuable animals like police dogs, seeing eye dogs, and companion dogs for the disabled. These animals are valuable for their training and the service they provide, and I think I could make a good living offering care several notches above the annual vet visit for rabies shots." She smiled, "But first the wild ones."

"That sounds creative and original." Stephen immediately appreciated the good fortune of meeting a beautiful woman with a brain and ambition.

That night after dinner with her family, Alex met Stephen at one of the clubs in Banff, and as they danced their bodies learned each other, the feel of Stephen's skin beneath her fingers, the smell of Alex's hair against his face when he held her close. At the end of each song they held each other a second longer than the music, afraid their growing passion would fade with the last chord.

During a break in the music, outside on the heated balcony, they quietly traded bits and pieces of their lives. They told the easy stories first and kept the sharing in the shallows.

Stephen took off his jacket and put it around her shoulders, smoothly turning her to face him. He saw the apprehension in her eyes and softly touched her face to relieve it. He pulled her close.

"I'd like to hear a lot more about your ideas, Alexandra." His lips hovered near hers, tempting, anticipating, and she waited for their touch without breathing. Then Alex lost herself in that first kiss, riding the waves of pleasure rolling through her body. Reticence and anxiety drowned in them.

Alex recalled how easily they had fit together then. And then she recalled that only after they were married, did Stephen admit that he'd followed her and Danni that first day while they skied. The memory did not sit well.

Why does that bother me now, when it didn't then? How much of him have I just never looked deep enough to see?

"Please fasten your seatbelts in preparation for our arrival in Seattle." The present burst into her reverie and as the plane rolled to the gate she renewed her determination to resolve this problem with Stephen. Tonight. She missed the marriage that was born in Banff.

Chapter Nine

Weary passengers exited the plane and merged into the stream drifting through Sea-Tac Airport toward their luggage. Deserted ticket counters and shops and concessions lining the terminal were dark. Even the cocktail lounge was vacant and the bartender fought sleep watching an old movie on the television suspended from the ceiling. It was after midnight and the drawn faces of the passengers bore witness to their unpleasant flight.

The baggage carousel jerked to life, and duffel bags and suitcases slid down the chute and revolved in front of the waiting passengers. Alex retrieved hers and walked quickly to the elevator, anxious for the familiar comfort of her car.

The air smelled clean and fresh, and the bracing chill aroused her from her jet lag. Traffic was light, and the CD player in her Jeep Cherokee pumped out Earl Klugh's soothing sounds.

Alex never tired of Seattle's skyline. The storm had washed the queen city, now it sparkled in the moonlight, welcoming her home. The Space Needle faded from her rearview mirror as she turned east, passing through the University of Washington onto the Evergreen Point floating bridge. The wind had died, the lake was calm, and moonlight on the water illuminated her way.

The house was completely dark when Alex pulled into the driveway. It was only one-o'clock, and she had hoped Stephen would still be awake. The confrontation she had prepared for would have to wait, there would be no resolution tonight. Exhausted, she left her Jeep parked by the front door and her luggage in the back.

Alpha and Omega whined from their run, but they knew better than to bark at this hour, or whenever Stephen was home. They had identified her car long before it stopped, ears alert, tails wagging; they anxiously waited for her. She stroked each of them and they jumped back to their favorite sleeping spots—not in their doghouses, but on top of them, as is the way of huskies.

Alex silently unlocked the door, crossing the entryway and climbing the staircase to the master bedroom in the dark. She only turned on the hall light outside their bedroom to hang up her coat.

Her world was upright and functional as her hand turned the knob and opened the bedroom door, but it slipped its axis and shattered a second later.

Aroused by the sound of the door, two heads popped up from the bed, caught in the light from the hallway. Alex gasped at the faces of Stephen and his secretary, Sheryl.

"Stephen? Oh, my God—!"

Instantly every brutal detail was burned into her mind. The empty champagne bottle and used glasses on the nightstand. A woman's overnight bag that was not her own. Clothes strewn all over the floor. Her nose caught the unmistakable odor of sex, ripe and hot, and Alex exhaled hard like she had been punched in the stomach.

She froze for a small eternity and then bolted down the stairs to her car. The driver's seat was still warm.

Immediate shock kept the tears at bay until she reached the street, but then a wrenching sob, deep and visceral, erupted.

"No! Oh no, Stephen, not this..." She drove without direction, and the city that had welcomed her home from Canada embraced her again. She crossed the floating bridge and entered the heart of Seattle, roaming without conscious thought. The streets were mercifully empty as the hysterical woman covered aimless mile after mile. Sometime before her Jeep ran out of gas, she parked in front of her clinic.

Alex unlocked the door and collapsed on the couch in her office. Great wrenching sobs racked her body and she let the pain swallow her. She reached for the phone and dialed her sister in Monterey, aching for her familiar voice, but when the number connected, pain overwhelmed her. She couldn't speak.

"Hello?" A sleepy Danni answered. When she heard the crying on the other end, she jerked awake instantly.

"Alex, is that you? What's wrong? Is it Mom and Dad?"

"No", a heavy sob caught in her throat; "it's Stephen."

"What happened? It's 3:00 in the morning." Alex tried to compose herself.

"I came home from the conference early and when I got home I caught him and his—his secretary in bed." She whispered the last few words and then couldn't say anything. In the gentlest voice she could summon, Danni reached out to her sister.

"Alex, try to calm down, you'll make yourself sick. Take deep breaths—listen to me—deep breaths. Don't try to talk just now. That's it, slow deep breaths. Let me talk." The crying steadied to regular sobs and sniffing.

"Did you have any idea this was going on?"

"No. I thought the only problem was the conference, and I came home early to try to work it out."

Danni weighed her words carefully. "Do you remember when we met Stephen? All the gossip columns talked about him and all those women?"

Choking sobs filled her phone. "So I have an unfaithful husband and he has a fool for a wife, is that it?"

"You just don't have the suspicious nature most of us do, Alex. That's no crime. You sound exhausted, why don't you go to Mom and Dad's and get some sleep."

"I don't want to involve them in this yet, it's bad enough I woke you up."

"It's in the job description, sisters are for waking up in the middle of the night. Where are you gonna sleep?"

"Right here at the clinic, I've done it before. I've got a comfortable couch right here and it's really—nice—and—quiet." Her voice faded away and the phone slipped from her hand to the floor as she drifted off to sleep.

"Alex? Hang up the phone first... Alex?" Danni hung up. She was wide-awake and seething in the dark a thousand miles away. Stephen had a notorious reputation as a lady's man before he met Alex, but after they married he played the role of consummate husband. Now Danni remembered his out-of-town trips and late nights that never raised the slightest hint of suspicion in her sister.

Danni's stomach knotted up, "This is only gonna get worse," she muttered to herself. In that primal mind where women weigh words and deeds, she knew Stephen had been cheating on Alex for a long time. To the extent that she loved her sister, she hated him.

She turned on the light and went to the kitchen to fix some hot chocolate. And ponder committing a major felony.

"I could kill that son of a bitch for this! *And* I lose a night's sleep!"

Alex's sleep brought her no rest, interrupted by the picture of Stephen and Sheryl's faces. Over and over the scene played in her mind and she tossed and turned on the couch until the nightmare finally woke her just before dawn. The reality struck her hard in the gut. Fresh pain. Fresh tears.

She made a pot of coffee and took a cup to her waiting room with its picture window facing Puget Sound and the Olympics. The sun was rising behind her, and the mountains radiated orange, as if the first rays set the snow on fire. The view revived her optimistic spirit and she felt comforted by the mountains' presence.

"I know we can work this out, Stephen, I know we can fix this..."

She waited until 8:00 to drive back to the house. She wanted it vacant when she arrived, and by that time Stephen and Sheryl would have to be gone. She knew he had a deposition that morning. After locking the clinic she merged into the morning rush hour traffic, for once grateful for the delay. Unfortunately, it gave her time to review the past, a dangerous place for her fragile mind to play. Memories of Stephen's business trips and late nights at the office made her feel foolish.

"I have been so naive." Her courage withered at the thought of confronting him.

"But I know he still loves me," she muttered, "I'm sure

he does." She sounded like she was trying to convince herself.

The more she dredged up the past, the more potential infidelity reared its head. Stephen had hundreds of opportunities and Alex ached to have back the ones she'd given him.

All at once she wasn't sure of anything anymore.

The house did not welcome her when she turned into the drive. The Verazzano name, the power, the influence all dwarfed her. The stone building loomed dark and threatening, a cloistered asylum of secrets that everyone knew but her. Alex's stomach knotted.

She unlocked the door and tiptoed slowly through the house like a stranger, seeing each room and piece of furniture as if for the first time. She passed the study without entering, it was Stephen's favorite room and she remembered making love on the thick rug in front of the fireplace. She backed away from the doorway as if struck.

Her own office welcomed, the one spot in the whole house that was hers alone. Her haven. She collapsed in her chair and gazed at Lake Washington through the french doors. The walls were decorated with prints of rare birds, and her most treasured piece still stood in its place of honor on her desk. She ran her hand over the cool Baccarat crystal horse, felt its flying mane, slid her fingers over its smooth flank. Stephen's mother had given Alex the horse on her first birthday as Stephen's wife. She loved to watch its different moods as it caught and split the light, casting prisms on the wall.

Her knees were weak as she climbed the spiral staircase to their bedroom, working up the courage to open the door.

What she saw made her question her own sanity.

Not one thing was out of place. The bed was made and all traces of the previous night had vanished. She didn't know what she expected to see, but this wasn't it.

Alex suddenly realized if she had come back today, as scheduled, she still would not know about Stephen's infidelity.

The invisible knife turned a little deeper into her heart and she sank onto the bed, unable to hold back the tears. She didn't know how long she'd been there when she heard Stephen's voice.

"Alexandra, where are you?"

"Up here." She quickly wiped away her tears and took a couple deep breaths, the only preparation she would get. He walked through the door and she stood up, but didn't move to him automatically, as she would have in the past. He didn't reach for her. They looked at one another across the room.

"I never wanted you to find out like this, but now that you know, I think the best thing is to put this all behind us."

"I agree." Her voice was that of a frail child, but the woman's mind noted the lack of any apology.

"We're both bright adults and I think we should be able to work this out without a lot of trouble."

"I'm glad to hear that, Stephen. I know I made you angry by attending the conference, and if that's what this is about, we can talk it out. We have built too much together to not find a solution to this."

"I don't think you understand, the conference isn't the issue, I've been wanting to end this marriage for quite awhile, I think this is the time to do it."

"You want a divorce?" Alex looked at him, incredulous. "Just like that, you're ready to throw five years away?"

"For the sake of the rest of our lives, yes. I haven't been happy in this marriage for a long time, Alexandra, surely you must know that. We're not the same kind of people and we don't fit into each other's worlds."

"I though we fit pretty well, up until now." She heard herself begging for a future with the man who had lied to her at the most intimate level.

"Stephen, we can make changes. I'll make changes, I'll be a better wife. Just don't throw our marriage away like this!"

"I don't want you to make changes. You've been very clear, you have your own goals and they don't fit into my life." He paused, considering his next words. "The fact is that I just don't love you anymore."

Alex sank back onto the bed whimpering, and he made no move to comfort her. His voice got quieter, but he continued his emotional attack.

"Sheryl and I have a lot in common, our families have known each other for years, and we really want to be together. She knows what I need in a wife. Alexandra, I'm going to start divorce proceedings, and I hope you won't fight me on this." She groped for a response, her mind numb, her body one searing pain.

Fight him? I can hardly breathe.

"I'm sure you don't want a long drawn out divorce, so I'm going to get one overseas, neither of us needs any ugly publicity. Don't worry, I'll be very generous to you, I owe you that much, I know."

She stared at him, her mind reeling.

This is a nightmare! I'm going to wake up and this will all disappear.

The room had no gravity and there was nothing to support her but the bed.

"What about my clinic?" She whispered the words.

"Of course you can keep your clinic, it's your career, and I know how much it means to you. I want this house, though, so you'll need to move out as soon as you can find another place."

"When will all this happen?"

"I'm flying out tomorrow and it should be final in a week. It'll be quicker and cleaner this way, Alexandra. Trust me."

Why do men always say, "trust me", when they're the least trustworthy?

He left her without even saying goodbye.

She buried her face in her hands and let the monstrous sobs wash over her. There was no more reason not to.

Alex realized that in the counting of things, she was as disposable as the other toys in her rich husband's life.

Chapter Ten

The snow came to stay a week after Black-cub's death. Large white flakes blanketed the ground while the pack slept, unnoticed for two hours, until White-cub stirred to shake himself and adjust his sleeping position. Flakes landed on his nose and eyelashes, and the lanky cub shook his head vigorously to dislodge them. His rustling awakened Red-cub and First-twin.

Their world of green and brown had been transformed into a moonlit fantasy of blue-white. The circular spots their bodies had occupied, the only naked earth still visible, were filling with snow before their eyes. They licked the cold fluff and were surprised by the way it disappeared when it touched their tongues. It lodged on paws and faces, but fell so gently that the cubs had no sense of it lighting upon them.

Not a breath of wind disturbed the descent of the mysterious icy down, and the complete silence alarmed the young canines. Eyes darted and ears twitched but nothing broke the stillness.

The steady respirations of their world—the footfalls of nocturnal hunters, the stirring of slumbering animals, and the constant rustling of trees and grasses had vanished. The forest held its breath and waited.

The older wolves did not share the cubs' curiosity, at least one winter marked their days and they knew what their world anticipated. It paused to evaluate this year's young. Which would measure up against nature's greatest challenge? The earth settled into a period of hibernation, prepared to claim the bodies of those who failed, to wrap them in shrouds of white.

Cub-bearer's soft "woof" recalled the cubs to the thicket. Each curled a bushy tail across a cold nose and dropped off to sleep.

The snow continued to fall.

They awoke the next morning before the rest of the pack to a cloudless sky. The air had a fresh bite, icy and clean, and sunlight sparkled off the snow. After the first apprehensive steps, White-cub and his littermates chased one another through the drifts, slipping, falling, disappearing beneath mounds of feathery white, to pop up shaking and sputtering.

Patriarch watched the cubs and glanced at his mate and his brother. Cub-bearer returned his gaze and the three adults nuzzled one another. They had endured the hardships of too many winters to share their offspring's enthusiasm.

Even the yearlings, now full-grown, did not join in the frivolity. Cunning, Gentle, and Jester remembered the hungry days of last winter, when their education had been put to the test and successful hunting had been the gauge of their mortality.

On this glorious winter day White-cub and his siblings did not understand that they would be tested to the full measure of their skill as predators, and if they failed this test, they would die.

The cubs met the dark side of winter just days after that first snowfall. Their playland fantasy became a nightmare of heavy gray skies and howling winds and the once gentle snow attacked, burning their eyes in gusts that blew it horizontally.

Other species that shared their mountains disappeared overnight. Animals driven to pass this time in hibernation vanished from the land and only the raven and eagle filled the sky. The raven's raucous scream grew louder and more desperate each week as their metabolism shifted to its winter diet of meat. Hunger intensified.

Patriarch drove the pack daily after the faintest scent, usually without success, and they survived off old kills, devouring what little had been left by the scavengers. The wind played cruel games, snatching the scent of food from their noses, and the returning caribou disappeared into the trees like shadows. Playfulness was forgotten and the cubs matured quickly under winter's heavy hand.

Greater energy was required to just keep canine hearts beating and blood circulating. With each breath, lungs sucked in icy air that cooled their blood, forcing large arteries and tiny capillaries to work even harder. Fat reserves from the bountiful feedings of weeks before vanished.

The pack underwent subtle changes. Gone was the light-hearted behavior of the summer months, and in its place was a tribal determination to survive. The wolf cubs of White-cub's litter reached their peak of physical development in the early weeks of winter. Thick warm coats covered lean muscle that worked smoothly over tempered skeletons of steel-hard bone. Icy trails sharpened claws and toughened the pads of their feet until they were impervious to the cold. Hunger made them alert, keen to forest sounds and animal movements that in easier times would have been ignored.

White-cub and his siblings became efficient before winter's challenge, learning to squint to protect their eyes from icy snow and high winds. They discovered that snow worked as a blanket, trapping body heat in their dense pelage. Even during sleep, the snow rarely touched their skin.

The pack looked to Patriarch to find prey and he reaffirmed why he was alpha. On those occasions when they were victorious, the hierarchical structure of the pack was enforced absolutely. Patriarch and Cub-bearer always ate first, the rest of the wolves prostrating themselves before the two alphas. Each wolf occupied a position in the pecking order of the pack, and at no other season was it more obvious.

The snow deepened and White-cub's family ranged farther into the wilderness, nomads traveling hundreds of miles from the den of their birth. The prehistoric instinct that called dire wolf to hunt mastodon in the beforetimes, beckoned nine wolfen souls.

Chapter Eleven

White-cub's first winter intensified, and its fury surpassed any the older wolves had experienced. Hunger was no longer the exception, but a constant companion, and wolfen stamina drove them thirty or forty miles each day in pursuit of food. Their ability to go long periods of time between eating became their singular hope for survival.

The previous winters of Patriarch's life had been unremarkable in their sameness, and with each spring's arrival, the alpha's confidence grew stronger. But this year his search was more difficult and less rewarding. He led the pack farther than he'd ever gone before, far beyond the mountains of his marked territory.

He had no technical comprehension of meteorology, of wind velocities and blizzard conditions, Patriarch simply recognized it as the worst winter of his life. The determined alpha defied the elements with resolute tenacity.

White-cub was now bigger and heavier than the yearlings. Red-cub, while smaller, was equally coordinated, and First-twin had matured into a copy of her older sister, Cunning. The yearlings had matured as well, and were now adults. Jester outgrew his clumsiness. Gentle, as loyal as ever to Cub-bearer, was now quite comfortable to be alone from time to time. Cunning retained her aloof demeanor around all members of the pack except First-twin.

And they all were hungry.

Eleven sunsets had passed since their last kill, and if food was not found soon, they would start to weaken. For Patriarch's pack this was a critical turning point. It was imperative they maintain enough strength to be able to mount a chase when game was found. Their search became a race against time, and time was marked in strides, and breaths, and heartbeats.

Hunger stressed the pack structure, and nasty bickering

flared between pack members who were normally cordial. Alliances and animosities born in warmer days surfaced with new clarity. Red-cub and Jester snapped at each other for some long-forgotten misdemeanor and even sociable Gentle was ill-tempered and disagreeable.

The worst infighting erupted between Cunning and White-cub. Her jealousy of Patriarch's affection for his white son, born months before, had taken root and matured into full-fledged loathing, mean and venomous. Any attention White-cub received from his father fed her rage.

During those remote times when food was available Cunning invariably placed herself in a position to steal the large cub's share. If that wasn't possible she would simply growl at him maliciously while he ate. But the jealous bitch failed to notice that each time she intimidated White-cub it took her longer to force him into submission. At the last few feedings he had responded to her growling with snarls of his own, and forfeited no food.

During a break between storms, Patriarch aroused his pack and in two loosely organized groups they set out to hunt. All three yearlings, with First-twin close behind Cunning, set out with Guardian. White-cub and Red-cub followed Patriarch and Cub-bearer.

Patriarch led his group down what was left of the trail, now just a depression in a five foot deep snowdrift. After an hour the four wolves left the trail and fanned out through the dense forest to pick up any possible scent, and soon they lost sight and sound of one another. White-cub was flanked far left of Patriarch's group and, had it not been for their scent, he would not have known there were other wolves among the trees.

They made slow progress. Every ten or twenty strides each wolf paused to sniff the wind, listen, and look in all directions, receptive to the forest's constant song. After three hours of tedious travel White-cub caught the scent of elk, fatigued and sweating, after an arduous run. He came around a stand of cedar and saw the female ungulate. She was upwind, stripping and eating the fissured bark from an Alpine fir.

He froze the moment he saw her, one front paw suspended mid-step. She seemed unaware of his presence and continued to work her way around the thick trunk. When she finished stripping that tree she moved to another, closer to White-cub. She looked up nervously while she chewed, sometimes directly at him, yet did not flee. This puzzled him because he could clearly see her. Every time she looked up, he was sure she would see him and bolt away.

He drew shallow breaths, motionless, as she moved closer, one tree at a time. The rest of the wolves were too far away to assist and White-cub's own hunger nearly drove him mad. Waiting. For once the wind remained constant, blowing his scent away from the elk, and although she continued to glance in his direction, she failed to make out his form.

As long as he remained still and the wind carried no hint of his presence, the cow could not see him, white fur against white snow.

Tree by tree, the elk inched through the snow until she stood within a few feet of White-cub. As she reached high up on the trunk, he launched his attack. Springing from his frozen position, he grabbed her throat, biting down with all his might. Warm blood spurted into his mouth.

The elk was strong and shook her head vigorously, locked in a fight for her life. With each swing of her head, she jerked White-cub off his feet, but adrenaline pumped and he refused to let go. Each jerk drove his fangs deeper into her throat. She rose up on her hind legs to dislodge him and White-cub's claws scratched her chest. She tried to kick him, but he had not forgotten the lesson of Black-cub's broken back, and he leaned beyond the reach of her hooves.

The noise of the fight attracted Patriarch and Cub-bearer and they raced to the clearing and grabbed the elk's back legs to bring her down.

White-cub had his first kill, and there was food for the pack.

It did not take long for the rest of the pack to assemble, and the starving wolves paced and snarled at one another. Family affection was totally absent as they waited for Patriarch and Cub-bearer to eat first, and only when homage had been paid did the alphas allow the rest of the pack to feed. Chaos broke out, and the yearlings muscled their way to the best positions, hoarding meat from the younger cubs. Generally this behavior was quietly tolerated by White-cub and his siblings.

But not today.

With the same speed that had brought down the elk on which they fed, White-cub charged between Patriarch and Cunning, to eat next to his father. Cunning slammed her full weight into the cub, to throw him off balance and regain her position next to Patriarch, but White-cub tolerated none of it. He planted himself solidly in the snow next to his father and met Cunning's assault with teeth bared and hackles raised.

Faster than any being could have moved to prevent it, white male and gray bitch—brother and sister—were fighting in the snow like enemies. The animosity that had been brewing for months exploded and Patriarch made no move to stop it. This was no small altercation between two of his offspring, but a full-scale battle between two dominant wolves for the one thing that carried weight in the pack.

Respect.

White-cub met the bitch muscle for muscle, adrenaline still flowing from the success of his first kill. They rolled, clenched in combat and the snow darkened, stained with blood—elk's blood—still wet and warm from their coats. Bitter snarls rang through the sterile silence of the forest and the rest of the pack paused to watch the fight.

White-cub yelped as his sister caught his right rear leg, but White-cub spun his body unexpectedly to the left, freeing her grip on his leg and bringing his face around to her exposed throat. He sank his teeth into her steel gray fur and instantly Cunning went limp and began to whine in his grasp.

Blood spotted the snow below Cunning's neck, but

White-cub did not kill her. He held her down for several seconds, growling his dominance before he relaxed his grip on her throat. Although he relieved the pressure, he still did not free her until it was clear to all the pack that he was the victor. When she had humbled herself sufficiently, White-cub released her.

Cunning immediately put her tail between her legs and rolled on her back, exposing her belly and White-cub stood over her and snarled.

With that the conflict was over, and the pack hierarchy was changed forever. From now on he would humble himself to no wolves but the three adults.

They both returned to the elk, Cunning to feed with the cubs and yearlings, and White-cub to stand next to his father.

When the blood-stained white wolf returned to his kill there was new pride in his carriage and icy fire in his cerulean eyes.

Chapter Twelve

Alex was surprised to see a patrol car parked in front of the clinic when she arrived early for work. None of the police animals were scheduled for an appointment, and she hadn't been paged for an emergency. Her apprehension grew when one of Stephen's law partners got out of the car with an officer she did not recognize. The lawyer was serious and his expression did not improve when she greeted him.

"Hello, David, what can I do for you?"

"Hi, Alex. I'm afraid I'm here on some unpleasant business." The police officer moved around the car closer to her, as David opened his briefcase and Alex's heart raced.

God, it's not over...

The fear and anxiety of the previous weeks, bubbling and simmering in the shadows, came screaming back to center stage. She held her breath, afraid to hear his words. The lawyer cleared his throat nervously; his discomfort hung on him like his expensive suit.

"Alex, I wish like hell, I didn't have to do this."

Why do men always deliver bad news with the softest voice you'll ever hear?

"As Stephen's attorney it is my responsibility to notify you that he is closing your clinic. As you know, he financed your practice, and now he wishes to divest himself of this property. Immediately. This is your official notification to vacate the premises within thirty days."

There were still words coming out of his mouth, but she didn't hear them. Mentally, physically, emotionally, Alex shut down. In her mind she only heard a crystal horse, rare and priceless, shatter against the ground.

Although blood continued to flow through her veins, Alex Davidson Verazzano's life was over.

Chapter Thirteen

Three days after winter solstice Patriarch aroused the pack and led them through the pre-dawn darkness. They climbed steadily toward a lake high in the mountains, a secluded place where he had hunted successfully with Guardian during their bachelorhood. Overnight temperatures plunged below freezing, creating a firm crust over the deep snowbase that supported their weight, so the pack trotted along briskly behind the alpha and his mate.

Ice crystals trapped in the thin air and the rising elevation of the mountains made breathing difficult, but Patriarch was unwavering in his climb, drawing on geographical and topical memories from years before. The sun climbed slowly to its winter zenith just above the horizon, a pitiful source of light. It offered no warmth. A sundog appeared, reflecting the sun's own light against the icy air, and the parhelion glowed no warmer than the original.

Near noon, with the sun as high as it would rise, they reached the crest to view their destination a thousand feet below them. The long, narrow lake was rimmed with dense fir, and its shoreline, steep and rocky. Nature was still constructing this place of jagged granite and rough unfinished landscapes, and there was no gentleness in its wild beauty. Where cliffs did not mark the lake's boundary, heavy forests descended through the rocks to its edge. On this day, however, evergreens extended to the edge of thick snow-covered ice. The lake had been frozen solid since before the autumnal equinox.

Cautious as they reached the place where cliffs shadowed ice, Patriarch sniffed the air and stared into the forest on the opposite shore. Behind the adults, the yearlings and cubs scratched the ground and sniffed the bushes for the scent of prey. Excitement mounted, tails wagged and the pack clustered together. This remote area was rich in the right scents of prey and barren of the wrong scents, those of other wolves. Patriarch was far outside his marked territory and he had no appetite for war with another pack.

Patriarch focused on the trees across the lake and within a few minutes his scrutiny was rewarded. Three caribou cows and their calves hesitantly ventured onto the lake, oblivious to the wolves presence. Once on the ice they moved steadily towards the shoreline just below the pack.

All the wolves saw their intended prey and froze. No sound. No movement. White-cub stood next to his father and Cub-bearer was flanked by Gentle. The rest of the pack hid in the shadows behind them. Not an ear twitched, not an eye blinked as they waited for the caribou to slowly move closer.

But a simple crossing was not their intention. When they were near the center of the ice they turned east, traveling away from the wolves down the length of the lake. Patriarch immediately sprang off the rocks onto the ice with the rest of his pack close behind him, and they closed much of the distance before the caribou detected them. Once the ungulates realized they were being chased, they bolted to top speed, and the race took off in earnest.

So intent was Patriarch on his prey, that at first he did not notice the faint buzzing. It sounded like a bee or a deerfly, nothing that would have caused the alpha a conscious thought, even if he had been idly resting. Now, with all his attention on the pursuit ahead, he was clearly not stirred by the noise. But as the animals continued to run the steady hum grew louder, until finally Patriarch looked over his shoulder.

What he saw was outside his wolfen comprehension. Flying towards them was the largest bird he had ever seen, and by then it sounded like a swarm of bees, a large swarm of angry bees. It flew low, directly toward the canines, and as it got closer and louder, the wolves broke off their pursuit of the caribou and turned to face the unknown winged beast.

Patriarch's family fanned out across the ice and the roaring creature dropped even lower, aiming for them like an eagle targeting a trout. The wolves recognized its attack posture and faced it as they would any other predator, hackles raised, teeth bared.

As long as wolves had run wild and free, their response to attack had been to stand and fight, and this is what Patriarch's family prepared to do with this gigantic bird.

Explosions erupted from the huge bird as it roared over them and instantly Gentle dropped to the ground, her life extinguished in one heartbeat. The deafening noise of the plane and the instant stillness of the kind-hearted bitch caused panic among the pack and they scattered across the ice. Beyond their youthful days in the den, fear was not a common experience, and they had no learned response for it.

They had never been another predator's prey.

So they ran.

The phantom passed over the lake and banked to come around again. The smell of gasoline and engine exhaust blended with the scent of Gentle's blood and the wolves' terror was complete. They raced without order for the safety of the trees and only Patriarch stood his ground, braced to fight the monster. He coiled against the on-coming plane, hackles up, scratching at the ice and snarling.

Patriarch's noble courage was lost on the inhabitants of the plane, who saw the black wolf silhouetted against the white ice and considered themselves fortunate. They had no specific target this day, only idle hours to fill with diversion. This was a contest of pride, not a life-sustaining search for meat, and these wolves were a bonus beyond their wildest fantasies. With bellies full of alcohol, and hearts full of conceit, they had no need for food. Their motivation was one of arrogance and the empty thrill of killing a defenseless animal. They did not intend to take back any of their victims, their plane was not equipped to land on the ice. They were worshipers at the altar of grand sport, and on this day, wolves would be the sacrifice they'd make to that god.

The rest of the pack reached the trees and turned to watch their leader—father, brother, mate—fall to the fiery explosions from the giant bird. The alpha leaped at the plane as it passed over him, and in his last gesture of attack, Patriarch received his deathblow in midair, falling lifeless to the ice. In his ignorance Patriarch made the only incorrect decision of his life as alpha. He had never faced the enemy called man, so he could not possibly understand the opponent now in front of him could only win.

Since the lake was clear of living targets, the predator of the air rose and disappeared over the mountains leaving the bodies of Patriarch and Gentle bleeding on the ice. A shroud of silence descended over the lake.

Man had come to this place of the wolves.

Nothing stirred for long minutes, as if every living creature held its breath. Guardian was the first to move onto the lake towards his brother, followed closely by Cub-bearer. None of Patriarch's offspring joined them, so consuming was their fear.

Guardian reached the body of his fallen brother and stared at him for several seconds, waiting for Patriarch to wake up. Unable to recall a moment in time when the form in front of him had not been part of his life, in the way of wolves, Guardian grieved. They had shared all the hours since their first fetal heartbeats and the gray wolf felt a piece of himself stilled.

Cub-bearer's grief was more poignant. She licked the wound from which Patriarch's lifeblood flowed and whined softly. She nuzzled his face with tenderness and gently touched him with her paw, willing the great alpha to lift his head and lick her face as he had during their bonding play. Her whining screamed a universal pain. Nature never intended her to keep walking without Patriarch, and Cub-bearer lifted her nose to the sky and howled for the loss of her mate.

Guardian watched the bitch and memories of good feelings shared between the three of them, in the days before the cubs, returned to the gray male. Guardian had led a contented life with Patriarch and Cub-bearer, and now that life was changed forever.

With Guardian attending, Patriarch's spirit passed from this world to the next, and the mantle of leadership passed from one brother to the other. After a few minutes Guardian lifted his head slowly and all who saw him knew a change had taken place. The large gray male with the laughing face now contemplated the world through the eyes of Fenryr, legendary spirit wolf, strong and willing to lead. His were the eyes of his fallen brother. They were the eyes of an alpha.

The next wolf to find his courage was White-cub. He did not approach his father hesitantly, but walked head up, proud and dignified. When he came to the spot where Patriarch lay he stopped, and with a delicacy out of character, he pawed his father's muzzle and nipped his face as when he had begged food as a cub.

Below the surface brewed a confused anger. He remembered Black-cub and recognized the stillness of death. But he puzzled over the monster that killed without touching its victim. Frozen in White-cub's brain were the scents of gasoline and gunpowder and the growling roar of engine noise. And just as his uncle could recall the sweet feelings of his years with Patriarch, so Patriarch's son would store these sensations bound up with his fear and grief.

He walked slowly to Gentle's still body. Emotion for his affectionate older sister returned and he felt her lost kinship. Next to her body, White-cub found something for which his index of learning had no entry. On the ice, still smoldering, was a small white tube. It carried a scent like singed brush after a lightning strike, and although it was warm, there were no flames. Cigarettes, so much a part of man's world, were a mystery to the white wolf.

He sniffed it, nostrils trembling, almost touching the strange object. Then another smell invaded his sensitive olfactory nerves. This scent was new, but familiar, a unique addition to an existing type, and it triggered an intelligence trained to recognize animal scents. This was the smell of a predator. An eater of meat.

A competitor for food. A rival.

It was the essence of man.

White-cub's confusion vanished. Patriarch's white son affixed this predator's signature scent to the events of the day. The great flying monster was now a real animal of flesh and blood. And just as he had learned months before to identify and recall the smell of rabbit and deer, White-cub filed away this scent in his mind. If it ever crossed his path again, Patriarch's son would recognize it and recall this day's pain.

The rest of the pack finally ventured timidly onto the ice. Jester tried every trick he could remember to raise his sweet-tempered sister, unwilling to accept her stillness. Cunning straddled Patriarch's body for several seconds, and the hackles rose along her back. She lifted her head and a frightening snarl that started deep in her chest exploded across the ice.

Cub-bearer responded to ancient instinct and placed her fangs gently around Patriarch's throat for the last time, and slowly dragged his bleeding body across the ice in jerking steps. Jester's last gesture to his sister was the same, and the two wolves backed up, step by step, with their heavy burdens until they reached the trees along the lake's edge. They made slow but determined progress, as if by some wolfen code they were forbidden to leave their fallen kinsmen undignified and vulnerable on the ice. The gods had ordained that this silent animal of the shadows should take his final rest there.

Darkness veiled their mourning and the wolves returned to the safety of the trees. A full moon illuminated the clear winter night, casting an eerie blue light over two large spots of blood, frozen into the lake ice.

The wolves howled as they kept their vigil and their plaintive song soared over the trees, floating on the wind for miles. As the moon set, the aurora borealis danced across the night, and its shimmering northern lights guided two wolf spirits to their last hunt.

One star shone brighter than all others. In the world of humans the coming day was the greatest of significant days. For twenty centuries this star had recorded the birth of their highest alpha. As the hours passed the Christmas star kept watch over the wolves as they sang their haunting song for the safe passage of two canine souls.

Chapter Fourteen

The next morning, while the wolves quietly fed on one of the migrating caribou, the sound of another airplane dropped over the lake and the wolves scattered immediately. They reached the trees before the plane was more than a speck in the sky. These bright canines, whose survival depended on learning quickly the lessons of each day, had learned this one in an instant. They vanished into the trees near Patriarch and Gentle's bodies and turned to watch.

A different plane, one fitted with runners, passed over the length of the lake then rose and banked, slower and closer to the ice. Guardian and the rest of the pack watched this strange bird touch down with its unusual feet and skid slowly to a stop near the spots of blood left by the two dead wolves. Protected in the trees, their curiosity overpowered their fear, so they studied this new beast as they would any new animal in their territory.

A door opened and two men clamored out of the plane. They were bundled in thick parkas of animal hides and presented bizarre forms as they shuffled across the ice, and the wolves noted their clumsy gait. The men conversed with each other, and although they were fifty yards away the wolves caught the unusual sound easily across the ice. Seven pairs of canine ears and eyes focused on the two creatures lumbering upright across the lake.

"Well, I'll be damned, look at this," said one, pointing at the smears of blood along the ice.

"Where the hell did they go?" asked the other. "I didn't know wolves had any enemies."

"Every animal has enemies, mister. But no enemy did this." The bush pilot fingered the handgun at his side and looked nervously around them as they followed the blood smears toward the edge of the lake.

"What are you talking about, what else but another animal would do this?" This voice was different than that of the pilot; it held authority and belonged to a man accustomed to instant response from his hired help. Educated at the finest schools, this successful man was a commander of business, a collector of vast sums of money.

"Well sir," said the local, "I've been hunting and flying over twenty years and my guess is we'll find the carcasses up ahead in those trees. Sometimes wolves drag off their dead. And sometimes they hang around for awhile too, so I advise we get this over with, and get the hell outa here."

The men reached the place where Cub-bearer and Jester had left Patriarch and Gentle. The wolves backed deeper into the shadows.

"What did I tell ya, see, here they are," said the old-timer.

"Well, I'll be damned. And look how big that black one is. He sure didn't look that big when I shot him."

"Yeah, he was probably their leader," the old-timer's voice grew perceptibly quieter as he gazed down on Patriarch's body.

"Yeah, well, he'll look great in my office, stuffed and facing the door." The tycoon laughed at the thought of his associates' reaction to the black wolf, mounted and snarling, when they entered his office.

"He'll be good for business." Again he laughed, comfortable with this trophy he had only flexed a forefinger to earn.

"Yeah, sure. Look, you drag that other one over here and I'll get started on this big feller." With that, the old pilot pulled a sharp, but well-used skinning knife from his belt and grabbed Patriarch by the head.

"Never mind the other one, it's nothing to look at, I only want this big black bastard," said the leader of commerce.

"Fine with me, mister, but you're gonna have to help me here, he weighs a ton an' he's frozen solid. Here, hold his head up. No, not like that, like this, you always cut 'em from the neck through the belly, then they're cleaner to stuff." With that he placed the point of his blade under Patriarch's jaw and cut the canine lengthwise. Then he carefully caped the wolf, taking the head and skin, leaving that which the taxidermist couldn't use in a pile at their feet.

The wolves watched this procedure in silence, comprehending in wolfen terms that this new upright enemy fed off their kills like themselves. The men returned to the winged beast and White-cub watched as the bloody carcass of his father was tossed into the plane. Within minutes the engine roared to life, the flying monster turned and glided across the ice, increasing speed. Then the rigid-winged creature rose into the sky and disappeared.

Guardian led the pack to the place where Patriarch had been gutted and they sniffed the area thoroughly. Cub-bearer scratched the ground and whined, confused by what had happened. But in their confusion all the wolves memorized the scent of this new predator and grew wiser.

This was an animal to be avoided at all cost.

They returned to the caribou and continued to feed. That night, after they were rested, Guardian led the pack away from the lake. They traveled through the freezing clear night by moonlight, up and out of the mountains towards their own territory, a place Guardian must now mark as his own.

As frigid weeks continued, Patriarch's brother proved worthy of his alpha status. Guardian had his instinct for finding prey and the pack sustained no other losses that winter.

The loss of Patriarch and Gentle profoundly affected the wolves, and the manner in which they died left a new and permanent mark of fear on the pack. Red-cub and Jester formed a close bond in Gentle's absence, and First-twin never left Cunning's side. Cub-bearer's female alpha status went unchallenged, but when her time for joining came weeks later she turned Guardian away, there would be no new cubs this year.

White-cub walked quietly and there was a new depth in

his blue eyes. When something caught his interest, he did not simply glance at it as his littermates might, he studied it. But the greatest change was his relationships with the rest of the wolves. White-cub locked away the affection he'd given his father and, although he was sociable to all the other wolves, he formed no strong bonds with any of them. His size and clever stalking ability made him the second ranking male in the pack, even before Jester, who was a year older. None of the wolves crossed him, he had earned their complete respect.

White-cub had risen from the gene pool of his birth, the best of the dominant and recessive code that defines wolf. The white wolf was sentient, aware of himself and his place in the world. Fleeting shadows of an alpha followed White-cub like the spirit of Fenryr had followed his father.

Chapter Fifteen

"Hi, Danni, it sure looks like California agrees with you."

The apparition that greeted Danni had all the familiar features of her sister, but the months following the divorce had exacted a visible toll. Dark circles shadowed blue eyes dulled by months of pain. Her skin was drawn and tight, and new lines mapped the course of her misery. Danni had talked to Alex almost daily, but those conversations had not prepared her for the physical damage. They hugged.

"It's good to have you home. Real good." Alex's voice was soft, almost fragile.

"It's good to be home... and it was SO nice of you to arrange this rainy weather, I don't know if I'd recognize Seattle if the sun was shining." Her sarcasm masked her concern. Beneath Alex's thick coat, Danni felt unfamiliar edges and angles. Alex was a skeletal effigy of her former self.

"I knew you'd need some rain after all that disgusting California sunshine."

Danni refused to give Alex her bag, and they walked unhurried through the airport.

The months that took one sister to the threshold of a promising career had shattered the other's dreams. The younger was now the stronger. Danni considered the change in their positions, and while it intrigued her, she was not comfortable with it. The person walking next to her was a victim, a refugee of some war of hearts, not the confident older sister she'd known all her life.

"How's it been, living with Mom and Dad again?" The conversation trickled like the rain on the windshield.

"They've been great through—well—everything. I think they like having a daughter back in the house."

"Poor ol' dad is never gonna get his den back. Must be strange, sleeping in that house after your other one."

"Actually, it's kind of nice," Alex checked the rearview mirror then glanced briefly at her sister, "lots of good memories in this house." Danni smiled.

"Oh yes, and the decorations are so classy too." This comment brought the second hint of a smile to Alex's face. Their mother's affinity for hanging every crayon masterpiece from their childhood on the walls of the family home had been an ongoing source of amusement.

Danni glanced at her sister as she drove. Each motion was deliberate and mechanical, as if Alex consciously considered each insignificant gesture before performing it. It raised the hair on Danni's neck.

The radio offered up the electronic smooth of Manneheim Steamroller and she waited until the song ended to broach her next question. "So, sis, how are you doing? I mean how are you REALLY doing?"

Alex sighed heavily before answering. "I'm okay." She caught Danni's skeptical look across the car. "Really, Danni, I'm doing alright. Not great, but all right. Listen, I want to hear all about your new job and California and everything. It must be really exciting." Danni accepted Alex's move to change the subject and dropped her questions.

Both parents greeted their younger offspring with easy affection, her dad's bear hugs still warm and strong. The same familiar blend of smells that had identified her family home when she was young, eased her mood when she walked in the door. Both parents fired questions at the same time while she unpacked. Alex withdrew with the newspaper to let them catch up.

Suddenly, without a word, she dropped the paper, grabbed her keys and hurried out of the house. Her car was out of the driveway before anyone could say anything. Danni heard her leave.

"What was that about?"

"I don't know, honey." Both parents shook their heads, they'd seen it before.

"Does she do this often?"

"Yes, but I don't understand her leaving just after your arrival. She was really looking forward to you coming." Gloria handed her second daughter a cup of coffee.

"Thanks, Mom. Where does she go?"

"We don't know for sure," Ron said, "but we think she goes riding. Her car always smells like it's been to the stable."

"That's what I'd do. She really loves that horse." Then sarcastically, "I'm surprised Stephen didn't take him back too."

Gloria's face hardened, "He probably would've if he thought he could make money selling him."

"What happened to her dogs?" Danni suddenly remembered the two huskies. "Does he still have them?"

"Yes, Stephen said he'd keep Alpha and Omega at the house until she gets herself situated. We'd take them here, but without a fenced-in yard Alex worries they would run." Ron paused, then added, "I don't think she's in any condition to take care of them now, anyway."

"How bad has it been since the divorce? She looks awful and acts like a—a zombie."

Ron nodded. "It's like someone just cut the heart right out of her. At first she cried for weeks, sometimes every night. When that finally stopped we thought she was getting over it, but this," he threw up his hands, "this is worse."

"Did you push her to get help? Professional, I mean."

"Would you talk to a stranger about this if it were you, Danielle?" Her father knew the answer before he asked.

"No, I s'pose I wouldn't."

"Well, Alex's only a little less stubborn than you are. We convinced her to see someone a few times, but she finally said, no more. He prescribed some tranquilizers and mood control stuff, Prozac, I think. After that, she said she would handle it herself."

Danni sipped her coffee and sat in the chair Alex had vacated. "She's so different! I feel like I'm looking at a stranger. Every little move seems," she groped for the right word, "calculated—it's creepy!"

"It's her way of maintaining self-control. At least that's what the doctor told your father and me."

"You went to a shrink?"

"Psychiatrist, Danni. The one Alex went to. We thought we should at least know what to expect. And we hoped he could give us some advice."

"What did he say?"

"He said to expect this, that she's trying to get her world under control. If she can control her emotions, then she can control her life." Danni searched her parents' faces and noticed new lines and wrinkles. Alex's struggle had etched itself there also.

"Her mood never changes, it's very flat, no highs or lows. And while she fights to control her emotions she completely disregards her body. Sometimes I have to remind her to shower, and comb her hair, and eat—I'm sure you noticed how much weight she's lost." Her mother shook her head.

"It's like she has no will to live." Ron's voice cracked with father-love and Danni watched him open and close his hand in a fist over and over. "She just can't seem to get her feet back under her."

"How long can this last?"

Gloria shrugged. "No idea. The doctor said some of the personality changes may be permanent, especially the longer it goes unresolved."

"Great!"

"And now she refuses to talk to us about anything related to the divorce. Says we've beaten that dead horse enough. Your sister is not coming out of this, Danni. I'm sure you'll see what we mean after a few days around her. Stephen closing the clinic broke her. When I think of that guy I get so angry..."

"Gloria, let it go, that won't help Alex." Ron's voice was edgy and Danni had the feeling he'd said those words before. But she could identify with her mother's anger, her own was rearing its head. She picked up the paper from where Alex had dropped it.

"Shit! This is probably why Alex bolted out of here!" She folded the paper around an article accompanied by a photograph of a man and woman.

"Listen '...a large traditional church wedding is planned for May 12th for Sheryl Aiello, daughter of Mr. and Mrs. Anthony Aiello, and Stephen Verazzano, son of Mr. and Mrs. Robert Verazzano. Both families are overjoyed about this union of two old Seattle families. Stephen has achieved success as a full partner in the family's legal firm of Verazzano and Verazzano, where he met Sheryl who was working as a legal secretary. The newlyweds plan a two-month honeymoon trip through Europe before taking up residence in Mr. Verazzano's Lake Washington home.' Oh, Alex *really* needed to see this! It's like their marriage never existed! And he's taking her to Europe just like he did Alex."

Gloria took the paper from her daughter. "And then they're going to live in the same house—no wonder she took off."

Danni's eyes took on an iciness her parents remembered from her youth. They were not pleasant memories. "Have either of you spoken to Stephen since all this happened? You know, asked why he closed her clinic after telling Alex he wouldn't?"

"No, of course not, what would we say? He holds all the cards here, Danni. The clinic was built with his money, and he owned it outright, you know that."

"Well, maybe somebody should have talked to him." She stood up and grabbed her jacket. "Could I borrow your car for awhile?"

"Danni, don't do this. There's nothing to be gained from antagonizing him. He's rich and powerful and we're better off not stirring things up." She glared at her father silently until he dropped the car keys in her outstretched hand.

"You're probably right, Dad, but I vaguely remember my parents teaching my sister and me to stick up for each other. Rich and powerful or not, Stephen should not have closed her clinic. He took away everything, even her self-respect. He didn't own that, but he destroyed it just the same." She retrieved the newspaper from her mother's hand. "I'll be back later."

Ron and Gloria exchanged looks. Now they had two daughters to worry about.

The three men occupying the elevator scanned the tall woman's reflection in the mirrored walls to avoid looking at her directly. Something in her eyes did not invite interaction. Black leather boots added three inches to her height, clearly taller than any of them, and her demeanor suggested that she was quite comfortable with that fact. A black leather jacket hinted at what tight jeans revealed, a firm youthful body from neck to ankle. Femininity was not absent, but strength dominated the image as she waited impatiently for the elevator to reach the top of the towering building. If she noticed how out of place her attire was for the marble and glass structure, she did not appear to care.

The elevator's other occupants were gone by the time it opened on the top floor. Her boots tapped across marble to imposing double oak doors. She did not break stride when she turned the brass knob, rolling through the reception area and past a beautiful secretary like a tidal wave.

"I'm sorry ma'am, Mr. Verazzano is in confer—"

"His conference is about to end!" She pushed an office door open abruptly and stood in the doorway, glaring at the room's primary occupant.

"Danielle!" It took Stephen only a fraction of a second to perceive her anger, like looking at a volcano a moment before eruption. He addressed the other man in the room. "John, let's get back to this later, alright?" The paralegal exited the office with noticeable haste.

Danni entered and closed the door behind her with a firmness just this side of slamming. She tossed the newspaper on his desk and it slid across the polished wood and stopped in front of him. Stephen looked down at his own likeness.

"Why didn't you just put a bullet in her head, Stephen,

or do you get some sick satisfaction out of watching her die a little at a time?" The volcano erupted. Danni's face was flushed, but she was quite in control. Rage fueled by adrenaline quickened her mind to deliver venomous words with spitfire precision.

"Danielle, please sit down." She didn't flex a muscle. "Of course, I don't enjoy hurting Alex, but some things can't be helped." He returned to his chair hoping it would convince her to sit. It didn't. She strode across the room and faced him over the intimidating desk. Manicured nails rested on the polished teak and she leaned toward him, inches from his face. Danni had the dominant position and Stephen realized his error seconds too late.

"Danni, let me explain—"

"Shut up, Stephen! There is nothing you can say that could possibly explain why you closed Alex's clinic after you promised she could keep it." He tried to speak again, but she cut him off in a voice growing quieter, but more intense. "Don't talk, counselor, just sit there and listen, I have a few things to say to you."

Stephen had defended too many passionate females not to recognize the sincerity of her wrath. He briefly wondered if she was armed, the leather jacket didn't confirm or deny the possibility. Wisely, he decided not to respond to her anger in kind. The office door opened behind them.

"Is there a problem, son?" Verazzano senior filled the doorway with his considerable bulk, although Stephen couldn't see him with Danni's body dominating his view. Danni didn't take her eyes off Stephen.

"No, dad. We're just talking." Black eyes under the silver hair moved from Danni to his son and back to Danni. Then, with a nod he left, closing the door behind him more quietly than she had.

"You are scum, Stephen!" Danni hissed before he could utter a word. "With that fancy education did you receive any lessons on ethics, or morals, or compassion? Or was there just not enough time for such trivialities?" She was so close to his face he could feel the heat coming off her body. Under other circumstances he would have found it erotic.

"Well, counselor, my education may not have been so gilded, but you know what I learned? In every environment there is a balance among all the creatures that dwell there, from the bottom of the food chain to the top. When the predators take more prey than can be replaced and their food supply diminishes, they starve and die. That's you, Stephen, the predator." She glared at him unblinking, jaws tight.

"In simple terms, counselor, what goes around comes around, and you will get yours for what you have done to Alex! Maybe not this year, or the next, or even in the next decade, but this," she slapped the newspaper hard with her palm, "will be answered." He flinched, unable to control the reflex. "Maybe something awful will happen to your new wife, or a future child, but rest assured, Stephen, it will happen. I only hope God allows Alex to be there when it does, maybe then she'll begin to regain the self-respect you destroyed."

"Are you threatening me, Danielle?" He found his lawyer voice and attempted to sound as strong as possible. The circumstances did not lend support to his position, and he still couldn't tell if she was armed. Discretion kept him under control.

"God no, counselor, I'm not that stupid. This will all sort itself out without any participation on my part. You see, people like you attract each other, and when there's no longer prey to feed on, you'll feed on each other. Your selfish greed and cruelty are passed on like some deformed gene of inbreeding. It will return to you, count on it! I do!"

Her last words hit him with naked contempt and before he could rise she turned on one heel and stormed out of the office. This time she slammed the door. Hard. Stephen was still sitting at his desk when she drove out of the basement parking garage.

Danni's verbal skills were only exceeded by her passion and he did not doubt she wanted him dead. She had caught him off guard and his rapid heartrate and shallow breathing exposed a fear that embarrassed him. And angered him.

He waited a few minutes before calling his assistant back into his office, a conscious effort to put Danni's recrimination behind him. But like some harbinger of hell it revisited him during the next days, hateful words returning to reverberate through his mind when he least expected it.

Alex's car was still not in the driveway but both parents were waiting when Danni got home. Ron's voice was sharp. "Well, do you feel better now?"

"Yes, as a matter of fact, I do." She returned her dad's glare. Like father, like daughter.

"You didn't do a damn thing for Alex by hassling Stephen, and I doubt he repented because you verbally attacked him."

"That's not the point, dad. Stephen is a vulture, and unless you stand up and wave your arms around a bit people like him will keep feeding off you. It stroked his ego knowing how much control he had over Alex's life and how easily he could destroy her without a word from anyone. I didn't expect to accomplish anything beyond showing him that even we lower humans are capable of family loyalty. If my sister can't speak for herself, then I will speak for her."

The anger drained from his face and he hugged her. His voice softened, quieter, a voice from her little-girl days, "You humble me, kiddo. Your mother and I wanted you two girls to take care of each other. I guess that lesson stuck."

"Lots of the others did too, Dad."

Gloria spoke up, "Now maybe you can use that sharp mind of yours to figure out a way to help your sister out of her depression."

"Well, I do have an idea, but you'll need to help out," she raised her eyebrows, "with the financial end."

"You know we will. What's your idea?"

"I think Alex should come back to California. A change of scene would do her good, so would a little sunshine for that matter. This rain would depress Mother Teresa. I can trade some days and take her diving, maybe spark that fire in her again."

"That's a great idea, but you'll have trouble convincing her to go. I can't even get her to go shopping with me."

"Oh, I'll convince her to go, leave that to me." She checked her watch. "How late does she usually stay out, anyway?"

"She's always back before dark."

Cooking smells were drifting through the house when Alex entered the bedroom. Danni was sitting on the edge of the bed looking through an old family album, waiting for her.

"Boy, I'd forgotten about these old pictures." She giggled. "They're great!"

Alex looked over her shoulder, "Oh! Those awful perms mom gave us! We should burn those."

"Amen to that!" She turned a couple pages. "Look at these from when you took me on my first dive. I had to try on my new dry suit for the folks, remember? God, I thought I'd faint from heat prostration before I could get the thing off!" This brought a faint smile to Alex's face that Danni didn't fail to see. "Have you been down lately?"

"No," Alex's heavy sigh spoke volumes. "I haven't really had a dive partner, you know?"

"Don't you miss it? Seems like that world would be kinda inviting after what you've been through in this one."

"I miss a lot of things, Danni."

"Well, I have a great idea. I think you should come back to California with me and I'll show you some great dive sites." She held her breath.

"No, I don't think so," Alex looked at her hands in her lap, "I just don't feel like travelling now."

"Alex, this is your sister talking, and from what I've seen you don't feel like doing much of anything. I think a change in scenery would do you good and the last time I checked, your dance card was free. How 'bout it?"

Alex looked her sister in the eye for the first time, "You aren't going to give up on this, are you?"

"Like a dog with a good bone, so you might as well say yes now and save us both some time."

"I'm not up for an argument. Okay, yes, I'll go back to Monterey with you. I could use some sun, if nothing else."

The girls spent the rest of the evening discussing the trip, but Alex's indifference saddened Danni. The only reason she ever certified as a scuba diver was because of the fantastic things her older sister told her about the undersea world. Alex's enthusiasm had been contagious, even after she married Stephen. Now it raised only casual interest and Danni felt the loss.

Chapter Sixteen

"You live here?" Alex was impressed with the gabled scrollwork of the three-story Victorian. Danni laughed.

"On my salary? Not quite. I rent the guest cottage in the back. It's much more humble."

They grabbed luggage and followed the sidewalk around the house onto a manicured lawn. Past a gazebo and a couple dozen trees, in the farthest corner, nestled the guest cottage. Danni wasn't exaggerating, humble was the appropriate word, but what it lacked in space it made up in charm. It looked like a gingerbread house.

Clean white walls trimmed in royal and sky blue mirrored the ornate construction of the main house. The front door—the only door—faced away from its parent structure and overlooked Monterey Bay from the highest bluff in Pacific Grove. Bougainvillea climbed over the roof and cascaded down the front of the structure, a magenta floral embrace. Two patio chairs crowded the dainty porch.

"How did you ever find this place?"

"In the paper. The owner is a widow who's very particular about her tenants. She wanted prompt rent and peace and quiet, and I wanted her garage to store my gear. She no longer drives and I'm no party-animal, so it was a perfect fit.

"It looks like a dollhouse."

"Yeah, and just about as big. Actually, it was built for her daughter when she was a little girl. You know, a rich kid's playhouse. Now she rents it out to, let's see, how did she phrase it, to 'serious-minded, single, career women'. It only has one room and a tiny kitchen and bath—I can almost do the dishes sitting on the couch."

There was actually a third small area that functioned as a closet, but by the time they had unloaded all the luggage, it was jammed. Dry suit, BC, regulator, and other scuba paraphernalia took up temporary residence in the tub.

"I bet you don't have many overnight guests."

"Only sequentially. Be glad that couch is a hide-a-bed, or you'd be sleeping in the truck. How 'bout a glass of wine? The sunset from my porch is worth a month's rent."

Everyday burgundy appeared in cheap wine glasses and they retreated to the blue and white striped lawn chairs on Danni's porch. To their left the sun melted into the Pacific, spreading golden light across Monterey Bay like butter oozing across a hot skillet. The scent of eucalyptus and gardenia blended and swirled in the evening air. Bradford Marsalis' light jazz came through the open door to softly accompany the sunset and the sisters relaxed in each others company.

Alex leaned back in her chair and let the music soothe. Gold light washed her face as she stared at the bay. Suddenly she squeezed her eyes tight against an unexpected memory she once welcomed.

Danni saw it all and a wave of compassion rose from an uncharted place in the abrasive younger sister. Tender, intimate, and unfamiliar. She squeezed Alex's hand, willing her own strength to support her sibling, and planned the days ahead to breathe life into Alex's stagnant dreams.

"Welcome to California, sis." It was almost a whisper and two sisters locked eyes and smiled. More words would have crowded the moment.

"Alex, wake up, it's almost time for lunch." Danni was making enough noise in the cubbyhole of a kitchen to awaken all of Monterey.

"Who could sleep with your racket? Is that noise producing any coffee?"

Danni passed a steaming mug to her sister. "Fold up that couch or we won't be able to get dressed." Alex surveyed the room, now a wall-to-wall expanse of rumpled sheets and blankets. With the hide-a-bed extended there was no room to walk between it and Danni's bed in the corner and had they needed to leave, they couldn't. The end of the foldaway blocked the door. She wondered how Danni had managed to get from her bed to the kitchen.

The restaurant inside the Monterey Bay Aquarium was a perfect place to begin her tour and Danni was pleased to get a window table overlooking the bay.

"This is a great view." Alex settled into her chair and noticed a group of kayakers gliding through the kelp beds below them. "Aren't they worried about getting run over by some power boat?"

Danni chuckled. "Oh, no. That kelp canopy is incredibly dense, over ten feet thick in spots... very nasty to any propeller-driven craft. You can kill a whole afternoon untangling that stuff. People don't run power boats in here more than once."

Large brown pelicans, once nearly extinct in California, flew in formation at eye level, reminding Alex of ancient pterodactyls. She easily visualized them soaring from the same rocks eons ago on bat-like wings to draw their food from the bay.

The waitress took their order and disappeared.

"This seems to be a rich marine environment, lots of life."

"You're looking at just a piece of the Monterey Bay National Marine Sanctuary. It's incredible. Beneath Monterey Bay is an ocean trench over a mile deep and about as big as the Grand Canyon. So close to land like this, it offers easy access for deep-water study that can normally only be done far out in the ocean. We've discovered several new species in the trench."

The waitress returned with glasses of wine and Alex heard Danni's passion in each word. "There are more different species of life between this table and that buoy out there than in any other body of water the same size anywhere. I swear I could drop to the bottom and spend a whole tank of air without moving from that spot." She paused and they watched an adolescent harbor seal try to push a much larger one from his sunning rock below. Her voice sounded wistful and faraway. "I love this place. It will take a lifetime to answer all my questions."

Experience and intellect had replaced youthful enthusiasm, and Alex recognized in her sister an enthusiasm she once felt. Danni spoke with zeal, in a voice of confident authority, relaxed in her knowledge. In contrast, Alex felt the absence of purpose in her own life.

Lunch arrived and the subject changed. Danni glanced at her sister.

"What are you gonna do with your dogs? I wouldn't leave them with Stephen too long, he might remember they are AKC-registered and worth some money."

"Yeah, I know. But I don't know what I'm going to do yet, so I really don't have much of a choice."

"What if I brought them down here on my next run home and kept them until you get settled?"

"You think your landlady would go for that?"

"I think I can convince her. She might think they'd make good watch dogs." Both women laughed at the idea, familiar with huskies' long-standing love affair with humans. All humans.

"Anyway, the yard's large and fenced-in, and the climate's pretty mild. They'd be a big hit when I run 'em on the beach." Danni finished her wine. "I'm driving back up in a couple months. You could call Stephen tonight and arrange it."

Alex considered the idea and nodded. "Are you sure you want to do this? They can be pretty demanding."

"I could use the company." Danni smiled mischievously, "Who knows? Maybe they'll help me find Mister Right. Dogs are great conversation openers."

"Well, I'm convinced, if you're sure." Alex took a deep breath. "I'll call Stephen tonight." They ate and relished the view. Then Danni returned to the day's plan.

"I'm going to take you behind the scenes of this place after lunch. I want you to meet a couple of my friends and see my work. I think you'll find it interesting."

Alex saw her sister in a new light, a serious professional, intellect and emotion focused in the same direction. Their relationship had changed, they were equals, and their conversation became a discussion between colleagues. Alex found a new respect for Danni, the woman, the biologist.

After lunch they entered the public exhibit area of the aquarium but quickly entered a door marked "employees only".

"This is the part of the aquarium the public rarely sees. Most of the research is done across the bay at the Institute, but much of the work back here results in the great exhibits out front."

Danni led Alex across the room and through a door into a huge area with several round tanks each thirty feet across and surrounded by short gated enclosures. Creature sounds came from the enclosures, but Alex couldn't see anything.

"Here's my home away from home." Danni brightened. "Come and meet my friends." Behind the three-foot gate Alex heard a scurry of feet across the cement floor. Small feet, with claws.

"Brace yourself, they're very friendly." Alex followed Danni through the gate and immediately she felt whiskers and a wet cold nose against the back of her bare leg.

"Oh!" She turned abruptly and looked down into soft brown otter eyes, inquisitive and fearless. She bent over then paused, "Can I pet him?" The whiskers moved up her leg as far as the otter could reach, sniffing and tickling her warm skin.

"Oh yeah, but HER name is Madonna." Alex dropped to her knees and Madonna scurried over, instinctively stretching to smell her face. Across the cement, her roommate playfully mauled Danni.

"How old is she?"

"Three. This is Elvis and he's about four. They've both been here since they were rescued as orphaned pups. This is the only home they've ever known and their ease around humans makes them less stressful subjects for study. They think the monitors I put on them are all part of a game." She ran across the flat area next to the pool, stopped and crouched as Elvis body-tackled her, his sixty well-muscled pounds slamming into her back. It was obviously a game they had played before. Danni laughed and embraced the animal, and woman and otter wrestled on the floor.

While Alex watched her sister, Madonna discovered a way under her tank top. The touch of her cold nose against Alex's chest gave her a start.

"Whoa, there!" Danni laughed as Alex tried to disengage the animal, now thoroughly tangled up in her shirt.

"She really likes the touch of bare flesh," said Danni between giggles.

"Right. Okay, Madonna, just settle down here." Alex finally withdrew the squirming otter. "Oh, great! I smell like fish!" She stroked the thick fur and Madonna quieted and curled up in her lap. "They're really strong, aren't they?"

"Yes, that's part of my research project. I monitor their metabolism during dives, sometimes as long as four minutes—you know: heartrate, body temp, stuff like that. I'm trying to understand how they retain their strength underwater. They're able to wrench an abalone off a rock at fifty feet while holding their breath, humans need an ab iron."

"They're so affectionate."

"Otters are very social by nature and since we are the only family these two have ever known, we all try to give them as much playtime attention as we can spare."

"So what have you learned so far?"

Danni stroked Elvis and thought for a minute. "That it's going to take a long time to answer all my questions."

Danni showed Alex the other research projects going on in the backstage area of the aquarium, and as the crowds started to leave they drifted into the public area.

"It's almost closing time. I wanted you to see this place without the masses, it's really quite amazing. We'll start in the Outer Bay."

Alex turned into a vast room, facing the largest unbroken window into the largest aquarium tank in the world. The Outer Bay. Standing next to the window she was dizzied by the effect of the tank with no limits, no boundaries. Clever design gave the illusion of open ocean. Not one edge or angle broke the spacious blue through which yellowfin tuna and barracuda schooled, and large mola molas drifted.

"This is breath-taking," she murmured.

Danni nodded. Minutes glided by as slowly as a giant sea turtle crossed their view.

"The rest of the place is empty, Alex, let's go back downstairs." They were alone when they reached the main floor of the aquarium, and the silence of the large open areas was eerie.

"Tomorrow you'll see the kelp forest yourself, but this is better than any words I could use to describe it." They stepped around a corner and suddenly rising in front of them was the tallest tank Alex had ever seen.

"Incredible!" Behind thick glass, giant living kelp rose three stories, swaying with the surge, like a terrestrial forest bending to the wind. Alex sat on one of the benches to watch. The Plexiglas walls curved around the viewing area and she felt like she was in the tank.

Bright orange garibaldis swam through the yellow-green leaves and larger species, perch and lingcod, occupied the lower levels between the gigantic stalks and their holdfasts at the sandy bottom of the tank. Danni watched Alex watch the tank.

"This is wonderful, Danni," she said without taking her eyes off the tank.

"When my work isn't going very well I come out here and sit for awhile. It helps put a bad day in perspective." She took a deep breath before continuing. Then softly, very softly, she said, "What about you, sis? What are you going to do with yourself?"

Alex met her gaze and dropped her eyes, then looked again at the tank. "I don't know. I have to do something, but I feel paralyzed when it comes to making a plan and acting on it."

"You know that every minute you play the victim is one more minute Stephen owns you. Alex, it fed his ego to destroy your life. Are you going to let him take away even your career, your love of animals? That was part of you long before he was." Alex didn't respond, concentrating on the flashing silver and orange beyond the Plexiglas.

"Where's the older sister who told me to find something I care about and give my heart to it? Where is she?"

"She's trying to remember how to breathe, trying to just get from one minute to the next." Alex looked at Danni, "I don't know that I have anything left to give, I've never felt so weak and empty. It still hurts too much."

"You need to find something else that makes you angry, or moves you, or needs your touch. Find something, Alex, or the world will have a big hole where your contribution should've been."

Danni stood behind Alex and hugged her sister, supporting. She felt a sob rise, deep and painful.

"I love you, Alex, and I can't just sit and watch your life slip away because you married an asshole. What attracted him to you was your independence and ambition and intelligence, and I know all that is still there. But it means nothing if you don't use it."

"I know. God knows I'm not the first or the last woman to marry the wrong guy. What I don't know is how to get past it."

"One step at a time, I should think. One step at a time." Danni sat next to Alex, keeping one arm draped around her shoulder for physical, as well as emotional support. "Have you considered any options at all?"

Alex sighed twice, big gasping sighs, to stop the tears. "Yes. I've gotten offers to join other vet practices, but after owning my own place, I'm not eager to be a partner. And there are a couple of wildlife opportunities, too. There's an opening in Yosemite, but the crowds would drive me nuts. And I've even thought about teaching. It would give me time to do some research of my own."

"And a place to hide?"

Alex met Danni's gaze. "Maybe. The one opportunity I keep thinking about is with the Canadian Wildlife Service. Matt Kramer wrote to me about it last month. They want to add more area to Jasper National Park and need fieldwork done to justify it. I'd live there for a year or so, take data, and build a case for them."

"Sounds pretty remote."

"Yeah, well, there wouldn't be a lot of neighbors—at least not the human kind."

A silvery school of jack mackerel flashed, then pivoted in unison and swam the opposite direction. A moray eel rose from his hole to investigate, beady eyes peering into the water. Finding no reason to stay, he backed into his shadowy home.

"Well, whatever you decide, Alex, I'm behind you. I miss the sister who taught me to love this world," she nodded toward the massive tank, "and I want her back."

They sat shoulder to shoulder in silence and the kelp forest slowly swayed back and forth, back and forth.

Chapter Seventeen

Guardian sniffed the alien track in the snow and the unfamiliar urine that marked his scentpost. The scent surged past his nostrils through vomero-nasal passages, until it impacted on sensors in his brain. Identity complete.

Large wolf, mature male. Rogue.

This spoor implied a challenge, so he searched the trees beyond the scentpost and growled whisper-soft. The charcoal alpha covered the rogue's urine with his own, but not before the whole pack had smelled it. And learned it. Then Guardian turned his rear to the scentpost and scratched the ground, slamming snow and trail muck against the old Douglas fir. Some of it stuck to the gnarled bark. Hair rose across his saddle and lips drew back revealing fangs, poised and ready. Guardian prepared to answer this threat.

He started off at a trot, following the stranger's scent, and behind him the rest of the pack joined the pursuit. They ran for six miles through dense pine forests, along trails worn and familiar. But in the slush near the river the rogue's essence mingled with those of other animals and vanished. Guardian stood over the last indentation in the snow and stared into the trees... then along the river... Was the stranger just passing through his valley? Guardian looked across the water and turned away. Other concerns.

Hunger.

Snow was still deep in the Canadian high country and although lengthening days foreshadowed spring, finding food continued to be Guardian's highest priority. So he filed away the stranger's scent and lifted his nose to taste the wind. For deer. Or moose. Or elk. He took several steps along the river's edge and repeatedly sniffed the air. The pack milled around behind him, all except White-cub and Cunning.

Brother and sister had left the pack at the scentpost, loping in the opposite direction through the slush until they reached a narrow ice bridge connecting the two riverbanks. They looked at the ice span, but Cunning turned away, uneasy. Only White-cub stepped onto it, one cautious step after another, confidence growing with each gently placed paw. He stopped and turned into the wind, tasting the air that rode the river beneath him.

Patriarch's white son had not yet challenged Guardian's position as alpha, but his independence was as strong at nine months of age as Cunning at two years. He was at ease alone, and if the pack's structure remained unchanged, the challenge would come. He had inherited Patriarch's size and intelligence, all he lacked was the wisdom to use it, the wisdom hard-won through experience. Each day filled his head with new information. Fresh lessons. More knowledge.

He lowered his head to read the air swirling above the water. Nostrils trembled. It was there, barely perceptible. White-cub closed his eyes. The faintest smell of meat teased his nose, then was snatched away by the wind, only to return, subtle, elusive.

Elk!

The drifting air gradually fleshed out the information like nuances of color filling a black and white outline. There were more than one—two, maybe three—all dead.

White-cub also caught the scent of another presence, one he had smelled before, but never encountered in the flesh. Musky and warm. He knew by the way the scents mingled that this one was alive and with the meat.

White-cub looked up and down the river's edge for his pack, but the wolves were out of sight. Even Cunning. So he raised his nose and uttered one long sonorous howl. The opening pitch was low and quiet, but as the tones modulated, the volume increased, rising through two octaves, then falling away. The sound was not painful to the ear, but it cut the winter silence, sharp and solitary. Buoyed on the air, it rolled over the water, and the wolves heard it.

White-cub crossed the bridge as the last echo faded. He

did not wait for his family, any second the wind might snatch away the meat-scent, so he trotted briskly along the shore, head bobbing up and down, left and right.

More than once he stopped and waded into the icy water where the breeze was unbroken to recapture the elk's spoor. Air swirled around him and turned back on itself like the river did between his legs. The emptiness in his belly dominated all other signals to his brain, the frigid water went unnoticed. With a fresh sense of direction he returned to the slushy ground, where he could make faster progress.

White-cub realized, as the scent of elk grew stronger, so did the smell of the other.

Guardian and Cub-bearer heard his howl, so did Cunning, and they converged on the ice bridge where they picked up his trail and loped after him. Although White-cub was several minutes ahead of them, time was unimportant as long as air and ground held the white wolf's spoor.

The meat-scent floated more easily through the trees the closer White-cub got to it, and when it was very strong he left the shoreline, turning into the trees. For the last quarter mile he knew exactly which direction to go and raced ahead. He expected many animals to do the same, winter carrion usually attracted a myriad of hungry beasts, but only the musky presence shared the air.

The creature he did not know.

His paws made no sound as they touched the snow. Morning sun had softened the hard crust that might have crunched beneath his weight. Fallen trees and the tops of boulders were exposed so he negotiated slag and undergrowth gracefully. When the scent was irresistible, he stopped. Cautiously, he glided through the trees, a white shadow drifting against a white background. He stayed downwind of the elk. And the other.

Camouflaged by the trees, White-cub saw the elk laid out as a feast for the wolves. Four stands of hemlock formed the corners of a small clearing and in the snow between the trees three elk had collapsed, emaciated victims of the season. Shabby fur coats draped bony skeletons like canvas over tent poles, their gaunt bodies silent witnesses to the season's heavy hand. Each hair was sheathed in ice, evidence of an arduous river crossing. Their last challenge. No living creature had brought them down, exhaustion and hunger were the enemies that defeated them.

White-cub's nose and eyes located the origin of the musky scent, but its form was unfamiliar. It looked like a small brown bear, well-furred, but smelled like a skunk, and the blonde stripes down its sides and thick bushy tail added to his confusion.

What was it?

White-cub held back in the trees and watched the animal rip hunks of meat, stiff and near frozen, from one carcass. Long claws sliced smoothly through the elk's hide and strong jaws crunched through bones. The unrecognized predator tore large chunks of bloody meat, each piece much larger than it could swallow in one bite, but it gnawed and chewed until each was devoured. It snapped a rib bone with a loud crack and White-cub salivated.

Hunger finally overruled his prudence and the female wolverine responded in rage the moment he stepped into the clearing. Fearless, she climbed over the elk and charged him, head on, snarling in wheezing, hissing growls. Sharp claws shot out at his face, slashing the air and he jerked his head back, to dodge her blow. He crouched and backed up quickly, as swing after swing whizzed past his face. Raging black eyes stared into his and promised pain if claws connected.

Face to face, the wolverine backed him to the trees, and only when there was enough distance between White-cub and the carcass, did she return to her meal. Her ferocity and complete lack of fear surprised him, few animals challenged his presence. Her black eyes watched him over the elk's body, but he did not pursue her. White-cub waited for the pack and watched. Hungry and perplexed.

The wolverine had recently broken her solitary lifestyle to mate and carried the sperm suspended in her body, delaying impregnation until conditions were right. Now she was ravenously feeding and caching food against the pending birth of her litter. Generally unsociable, she was as mean and possessive of meat on this day as any other in her life.

White-cub's confrontation with the wolverine was only a preamble to what happened when the rest of the pack arrived. Crazed with hunger, the pack dove toward the elk without hesitation and her rage increased proportionally. A snarling whirlwind of teeth and claws, she raced from one carcass to the next, crouching to mark them with her musk.

Guardian and Cub-bearer had encountered this creature before, and even Cunning recognized the mean-spirited mustelid, so they kept their distance. The older wolves snatched chunks of meat while her attention was diverted, dashing away to eat.

Jester and Red-cub, however, were totally ignorant of the wolverine's fearlessness and when she came after them they crouched, poised to attack. Hackles raised, fangs bared, White-cub's brothers lowered their heads and leaped to the fight. Shoulder to shoulder they cornered the wolverine against the gutted elk's abdomen.

She rose on her haunches and snarled once before rushing the canines, an assault they had not expected. Again, rapier claws sliced the air, inches from their faces. Their offense evaporated into defense with her charge, and they backed away from the carcass. The wolverine followed them, step for step, lashing out and growling.

Suddenly Red-cub slipped and fell, and the wolverine leaped on him, raking her claws along his sides, biting his back. Red-cub scratched the icy ground, but it offered him no foothold. The wolverine pinned him down and rode him, biting and tearing through his fur. Canine claws finally gained purchase and Red-cub pushed off with a single foreleg and they rolled in the slush, locked together. Growls and snarls rang through the cold silence. The rest of the pack approached, but there was nothing they could contribute to Red-cub's defense.

The wolverine was ruthless and fast. Her claws found their mark more times than not, and Red-cub yelped. This was pain unlike any in his experience, but it triggered his greatest strength. He found his feet, shook her free and turned to face his enemy. But she had fought before and instantly charged head-on, launching on powerful back legs to drive her claws into his chest. Red-cub sank his fangs into her neck through fur as thick as his own, and bit down, enraged. The power shifted suddenly, her growls turned to a scream. She now fought to escape.

As quickly as she had charged, the wolverine untangled herself. Immediately Guardian and Cunning sprang between the combatants and turned the pregnant mustelid away with snapping teeth and snarls. Their challenge and the number of wolves behind them convinced the wolverine she had lost the advantage. Slowly she limped off, turning only once to watch the pack fall on the elk in a feeding frenzy.

Red-cub bolted for the trees the second she disengaged, where he collapsed, panting. Blood spread in the snow beneath him, but his stomach was also empty, so after a short rest he staggered unsteadily to the elk, hunger dominating pain.

Although he had fought for their meal the wolves did not wait for him. The feeding frenzy was at its peak, pack hierarchy obvious. The red wolf shook himself and drops of blood landed on the other wolves and the elk carcass. The wolverine had bit his back and throat, and scratches marked his face and both front legs. But the four deep gashes in his chest were the worst injury, and warm blood from them melted the snow where it landed. Suddenly light-headed, he moved away and collapsed again, weak from blood loss.

Jester approached, nuzzled him a couple times and began to clean his wounds. After a few minutes hunger again forced Red-cub to his feet and he joined the rest of the pack sating their hunger on the elk.

Veiled by the wolverine's cloying musk, the rogue wolf's scent lay undetected on the meat and alien paw prints Guardian would've now recognized had vanished in the fight. The rogue had discovered the elk first, and eaten his fill before the wolverine chased him away.

The pack slept near the elk that night, to discourage other predators. Red-cub slept fitfully and at sunrise he rose, stiff and sore. Again Jester attended to him, his pink tongue rhythmically cleaning each open wound.

Red-cub had proven himself in battle, but not without a price. Muscles would've healed and blood lost would've been replenished, save the four deep puncture wounds Jester's administrations could not penetrate.

Clostridium tetani was the enemy waging unseen war on the red wolf. Transferred to him from the rotting flesh on the wolverine's claws, the tenacious bacteria found a perfect breeding ground in the warm muscle tissue beyond the reach of Jester's tongue.

Vaccinations against tetanus did not exist for the wild ones.

The bacteria spread, lodging in his spinal column where it obeyed its own genetic orders, blocking the signals from brain to muscle.

Red-cub's deterioration was gradual, but within days the effects of his infection became obvious to the rest of the pack. He twitched intermittently, and stopped eating when he couldn't open his mouth. The slightest physical stimulation—Jester's tongue on a wound, or White-cub's rowdy body contact—caused uncontrollable muscle spasms. The jerking became constant and the red wolf found no rest.

None of the wolves had ever seen an animal afflicted with lockjaw and his family was confused by his unnatural movements and lack of coordination. There was no bloody injury left to clean, they were closed and forgotten. In their canine society where the slightest change in facial expression spoke volumes, Red-cub's behavior was abnormal and his twitching made them nervous. As the spasms became convulsions, their nervousness became fear, so, while they did not abandon him, they withdrew whenever he approached. Even Jester avoided physical contact. When Red-cub finally succumbed to tetanus he fell in the snow and died while his family looked on, from a distance.

They watched his convulsions slow, then stop, and when he was finally still they turned away and left him.

The pack had matured and wolf-death was no longer a mystery.

Chapter Eighteen

Warm fingers outlined the contours of Alex's face, gently tracing her lips, then down, under her chin, to close around her neck. They rested there, feeling the pulse of carotid blood surging below her ears. Moving again, the hands feathered along her collarbone cupping both breasts, skin cradling skin. The caresses were slow, painfully slow and gentle, and she ached for a harder touch. Index fingers brushed her nipples, playing and teasing, until she arched her back, rising into the hands, wanting more, faster. The strokes grew in strength and their gentle petting became a squeeze. Thumb and index finger closed around her nipples, then released... closed... released.

Deep breathing became shallow, near panting, and her heat rose to match that of the hands playing across her body. A mouth found her earlobe and sucked in and out, for a second, then the familiar tongue licked a trail along her jaw, past her throat, settling over one breast. Lips closed and the tongue circled around and around in lazy turns until the captive nipple swelled hard in response. The hand traced her body's centerline into the blonde down of her crotch, and skilled fingers triggered the raging appetite residing there. Her body responded without thought, each molecule waiting for the final touch that would release her. Set her free. Let her fly. But that touch would not be rushed.

Lust rose with each pass of hot finger over her flushed red center, and female hips began their mating dance in pulsing rhythm, ancient and primal. She begged with her body for what her body wanted. Teeth closed around first one nipple, then the other, gentle bites bringing exquisite pleasure-pain.

Then, at the summit of all she could feel, Alex's orgasm exploded and she cried out, "Stephen!"

Instantly the spell was broken. Awakened by the sound of her own voice, in a darkened room she did not recognize, Alex groaned, consciousness a pain as raw as her orgasm. It lingered no longer than the dream, and her breathing returned to normal.

"Alex, are you alright?" Her sister's voice brought her back to the gingerbread house in Monterey.

"Um, yeah. What time is it?"

"Almost three, we need to get up at six." Unasked questions hung in the air, but Danni had heard her call Stephen's name, and for this intimate pain she had no comfort. Alex heard her sister roll over and minutes later Danni's breathing slowed, then deepened. She was asleep.

Alex stared into the darkness, sleep for her now a lost cause. With no place to focus, the images she could banish during daylight flashed helter-skelter, unbidden, overwhelming her. She suffered this night like she had all the long ones that preceded it. No better, no worse. A line from F. Scott Fitzgerald joined the parade through her brain, "In the dark night of the soul it's always 3:00 in the morning." He was right.

The twenty-foot Zodiac slid off the boat trailer and into the water with a splash. "Secure the tanks in those Velcro straps on the floor. I'll park the truck and be right back."

"Okay." No mention of Alex's nighttime outburst had passed between the sisters that morning as they prepared for their dive trip. If Danni remembered it, she was acting like she didn't, and for that Alex was grateful. The situation made her more vulnerable than ever. She brushed it from her mind and concentrated on the four scuba tanks in front of her.

Before Alex strapped the tanks down she removed the rubber dust cover, the plug protecting the valve and O-ring. She took a minute to examine the O-ring for cracks before replacing the plug and cover, and then repeated the drill three times on the other tanks. She was just finishing the fourth tank when Danni stepped into the boat.

"I replaced those O-rings last night, so they should be okay. I also have extras." She pointed to a pocket on the side of the boat.

"I should've known."

"Why don't you put the food in that cooler near the bow?" Alex looked forward, confused. When she didn't move Danni looked up and saw her puzzled expression. She chuckled. "The box marked 'SPECIMENS', Alex."

"Oh, right. Hope it's empty." She lifted the lid and sandwiches, fruit, sodas, and Danni's requisite Oreos disappeared into the insulated box and she glanced around the boat. Straps and canvas pockets had been permanently sewn to the inside rigging of the inflatable, and each appeared to have a specific purpose.

"You've fixed this thing up pretty nice."

"Yeah, I bet Mom never imagined this when she was teaching us to sew. I have a place for everything a diver needs plus some personal luxuries. Wait 'til you see what I designed for when it gets hot and we have to sit out decompression time between dives."

Marine biology became a consuming passion for Danni her final year in high school. The years of college classwork didn't dull her enthusiasm and now the gray inflatable was her most prized possession. There were more miles on it than her truck.

"Have you planned our dives?"

"Uh-huh." Danni finished strapping their buoyancy control vests to a spot on the port side. "The Pinnacles are two seamounts about a quarter of a mile apart, close to the Carmel Trench. The water rising from the trench is colder than the bay, but more clear, and rich in nutrients and plankton. So the diversity of species on and around the peaks is pretty spectacular."

"How deep will we go?"

"First dive will be along the shore side peak and the area between the two, to about fifty feet. We'll have a leisurely lunch, then we'll dive the ocean side to about seventy feet. You'll notice a marked difference in the two locations." Danni checked the consoles connected to the second stages of their regulators for cracks. "How's that sound?"

"You're the one that knows the site. Just be sure you worked out the decompression profile since the deeper dive is second."

"Yeah, yeah, I know. A case of the bends will spoil your whole day."

Alex gazed at the gray overcast sky. "If this was Seattle, I'd bet on rain."

"Me too, but this is pretty typical for February mornings around here. The sun will break through by 9:00 and it'll be hot by noon."

They stripped off their jeans and sweatshirts, and jammed them into waterproof bags. Underneath they wore simple one-piece swimsuits. And panty hose.

Alex learned the hard reality of cold water diving on her first open water class dive into the icy waters of Puget Sound. Bone-numbing water rushed into her ill-fitting wet suit from all openings, and settled in the spaces between flesh and neoprene. It circulated continually through the suit with each movement of arm or leg, or turn of the head, at the ambient temperature of the ocean—about forty degrees. Within minutes her skin was numb and by the end of the dive, coordination and reflexes were measurably diminished by the cold. Hypothermia was a real threat each time she went down. But the freezing water did not dampen Alex's enthusiasm, so after her certification she looked for warmer alternatives.

The option to a wet suit was a 'dry' suit and the theory behind its ability to warm the body made sense to her. A one-piece garment like a jumpsuit, it has soft seals at all body openings, and a waterproof zipper so frigid water never touches the body. Air trapped in the suit warms quickly to body temperature—and stays warm. When Alex learned they were rated for ice diving, she immediately ordered hers and Danni did the same a few years later. Neither woman regretted the additional expense.

Alex turned her suit inside out and started putting it on,

feet first, rolling the quarter-inch neoprene up her body.

"I'm still not sure these panty hose help."

"Have you ever put it on without them? You'd notice the difference." Alex stood up and tugged and yanked on reluctant neoprene, inching the awkward suit past her buttocks, then they both blew air into the mouthpiece dangling from their shoulders. The air inside the suit warmed and they stopped shivering.

"I think we're ready." Danni moved to the rear of the Zodiac. "Release the line and push me off." She jerked the powerful Yamaha outboard alive and its roar shattered the morning silence. Alex released the line and jumped into the inflatable as Danni turned the bow towards open water outside the kelp bed.

The first buoy passed them on the port side as Alex settled herself near the bow. They cleared the breakwater and she felt the craft gently rise beneath her as Danni opened the throttle. Alex was literally airborne, flying over the water as the motor's propeller ground through the water of Monterey Bay. She liked the feeling.

In minutes they passed the aquarium. The wind was icy, but Alex let it blow directly into her face, grabbing her hair, banishing her night terror with its cold. The noise of the engine made conversation impossible and the two sisters were lost in their own thoughts for the duration of the trip.

The sun was slowly lighting the sky behind them as they rounded the point at Pacific Grove and entered the rougher waters of the ocean. The Zodiac bounced across the chop like a horse bucking against the first touch of a saddle. Alex devoured all the sensations, feeling more alive than she had in months.

Danni cleared Cypress Point and turned southwest, staying as close to the shore as safety allowed. While her Zodiac was a durable craft for calm water like today, it was no sea-worthy ocean vessel, and she had healthy respect for its limitations. A gentle breeze lifted very little surf and she smiled. It was a perfect day for diving the pinnacles.

When she sighted the Castle House, a pink landmark

used by divers to locate this dive site, she positioned the Zodiac about three-quarters of a mile offshore between Cypress Point and Pescadero Point. While she could not see it, Danni knew from experience she was directly over the outer of the two submerged peaks. She slowed the craft looking in all directions, then cut the engine completely. The inflatable drifted slowly into the kelp.

"Grab the 'divers down' flag in the pocket under your left leg and stick it in the slot right there. Let folks know we're here."

"Will there be other boats out here?"

"Probably. Because of the trench, this is a prime fishing spot. And there is nothing more annoying than getting caught in some fisherman's line at fifty feet. Trying to get yourself unhooked while some eager sportsman is reeling you in can be very unpleasant." A small anchor splashed overboard and she fed out line until it hit the bottom.

They both opened Velcro compartments and unloaded their gear, settling into a familiar routine. Watching each other, they performed the set up they had both done countless times. Tanks strapped into BC's. Regulators connected. Air on, pressure gauge checked. Both second stage mouthpieces tested—blue one familiar to the lips, airflow on demand, orange emergency second stage good, airflow also on demand. Dive computers strapped to wrists. Remaining first stage port connected to BC for buoyancy control. Push button control checked.

Danni and Alex had logged hundreds of dives together in the murky cold waters of Puget Sound. Underwater they would be each other's best chance to survive any mishap, and the sisters watched each other's set up, not from lack of confidence, but out of visceral concern for a sibling's welfare. They were each other's favorite dive partner.

"We'll surface at 300 psi. No less, okay?"

"Why save so much air?"

"Divers have drowned in this kelp only a few feet from the surface because they sucked their tank dry at the bottom and tried to surface on their last breath. It's very easy to get tangled up in that stuff. Also, watch how I enter the water. If you do a backward roll instead of jumping in, you start out less tangled."

"Okay." Danni dropped the ladder off the stern. They'd use it to climb aboard after the dive.

Hoods on. Knife sheaths strapped to their legs. Fins over dive boots. BC's strapped on.

"I'm ready, how 'bout you?" Danni eyes sparkled with the rush of anticipation. She felt it every time she went down, it was as intoxicating as a drug.

"I'm good. Let's do it." They were sitting side by side on the edge of the boat. Regulators in the mouth. Masks lowered to position. Eyes met, they nodded and backward rolled into the kelp bed.

The instant cold on their faces was shocking. Long leaves of kelp flowed and danced around them, blocking their view of each other briefly. Then the familiar silence welcomed them like an old friend, and only the sound of their own respiration, measured and relaxed, was audible. Soon the water and the kelp settled and they made eye contact. Danni gave the thumbs down signal to descend and Alex nodded. She felt good. Very good. She followed her sister head first, towards the bottom, equalizing the pressure in her ears and mask.

They dropped below the kelp canopy, to clear water. Here the tangle of foliage took on specific form. A primitive forest of vine-like trees reached for sunlight from root-like holdfasts anchoring them to the ocean floor. Relaxed strokes brought her closer and she saw its intricate structure. Inch-thick stalks coiled around each other, held upright by gas-filled bladders the size of onions

The top plateau of the outer seamount was directly below her and it was literally carpeted with color. Quarter-sized red corynactus anemones, the underwater groundcover, waved pink tentacles in unison. Interspersed among them, white plumed Metridium anemones rose eight inches above their daintier cousins, feathery tentacles swaying in the gentle current to strain food from the rich soup of the Carmel Trench. Occasionally a large green anemone would find a foothold, its thicker lavender tentacles competing for the rich plankton broth. In one arm's length Alex counted six different species of iridescent nudibranchs creeping slug-like over the anemones. Orange-fringed gills identified the blue spanish shawl grazing the same algae-covered spot with opalescent tritons. Small red crabs bounced on the current without direction, over the top of their stationary invertebrate relatives, picking at any speck for food value. The living garden was so densely encrusted on the peak's surface that no rock was visible at all. The population of each square inch had reached maximum capacity.

Alex was so visually overwhelmed that Danni had to gently urge her forward to keep her from lingering too long, or stopping altogether for each new specimen. They wove through the kelp forest toward the deeper water between the peaks.

Danni rapped her knife against her tank, and Alex turned in time to see a huge medusa jellyfish slowly pulsing up from the depths. Its magenta-striped dome was a foot in diameter and, drifting on the surge, its pulsing movements reminded Alex of a mammal's respiration rhythm. The pulses were as regular as heartbeats. From a gap in the rocky surface a wolf eel watched the women, his beady eyes undersized for head and jaw. They gave him wide berth.

Suddenly, they had company.

Dark shapes jetted past them, and around them, and at first they moved so fast Alex could not identify them. She thought immediately of shark, and just as her pulse quickened a whiskered face popped up, directly in front of her mask, so close, so fast, that it startled her and she jerked her head back. But it did not move and looked directly into her mask, eye to eye. Then she smiled. Obviously she was not the first diver this otter had ever seen, and as she reached out her hand he dashed away. A flurry of tiny air bubbles streamed from his dense coat leaving a trail behind him. She caught Danni watching her, and even though she could not see her face she knew her sister was laughing.

Danni continued down the gentle incline of the shore side slope to about fifty feet. Here the kelp was sparse, not clustered like the massive canopy, but individual trees with open water between them. Shafts of light knifed from the surface exactly like it does through a pine forest, and Alex knew the sun had burned off the overcast just as Danni predicted. The visual effect was breath-taking, a million blues and greens and yellows competed for her eye.

The women paused frequently, hovering over a dense collection of invertebrates, studying the diversity of life within a few square feet. So caught up were they in their investigation that they did not notice the slow gathering of larger creatures around them.

Rising from the trench, drawn by the smell of blood the sisters could not perceive, sharks silently converged near the surface.

Danni and Alex only glanced up when a nine-foot long blue shark swam over them, momentarily blocking out the sunlight.

What they saw took their breath away.

In the fifty feet of water between them and the surface over forty sharks dashed and spun, darted and rushed. Danni and Alex had observed the relaxed cruising of sharks many times. This was not it. Intense darting and quick dodges signaled feeding.

Danni and Alex instinctively drew closer to each other. Neither panicked, but the rate of their breathing increased proportional to their heartrate, and they watched their own air bubbles rise through the swirling mass of predators.

In seconds their pleasant dive took on measurable seriousness.

Danni looked at her console. Only 420 psi. Alex grabbed her own console—430 psi. They each had only minutes of air left, but rising through the tangled kelp was now the least of their worries.

Chapter Nineteen

Sunlight sliced through the water and played off the sleek bodies, white underbellies contrasting blue-gray topsides as they dashed and rolled. Sickle-shaped tails and pointed pectoral fins provided thrust and maneuverability beyond any a human could match, and the speed of their dance froze the sisters. Sharks twisted and spun over them, silhouetted against the bright surface, crescent mouths open and expressionless black eyes hunting. Alex and Danni knew they could not surface through the frenzied predators unnoticed. Like demons released from Hell, more drifted up from the abyss, inches from the women.

A rhythmic drumming joined the sound of their own racing heartbeats, and within minutes a large hull passed over them and stopped. Dark spots appeared around the forty-foot vessel and the sharks' excitement intensified. Danni and Alex recognized the chunky liquid falling into the ocean. Chum. The bloody remains of dead fish, gory heads and tails and guts. Shark bait.

The diesel idled in position. Where scattered drops of blood had earlier hit the surface, now buckets of chum darkened the water as it swirled and dissolved.

The sharks responded as they had since the Triassic period when their efficient form ceased evolving. Shooting through the blood-scented water, mouths gaped open, prepared to close around anything, they hit one another in the confusion, snapping at their own pelagic relatives.

Alex and Danni recognized the feeding frenzy. Their eyes met and, sharing their fear, the two women hovered neutrally buoyant, inches above the seamount's surface. Heads continuously pivoted in a hopeless effort to see every animal zooming over, or jetting past them. Masks limited their peripheral vision, and the women intimately felt their vulnerability. They did not move. They tried to relax. Slow their breathing. Conserve their air.

Alex identified three species of shark. The largest and most numerous were the blues. Lean and long, they were the most graceful, parting the water with untapped power. Smooth-cruising and patient, they were in no hurry for what was to come. They had waited for centuries.

The makos were shorter and stockier, but more frightening. Larger gills supported a faster, warmer metabolism, and they swam with quick jerking turns and thrusts. Open mouths revealed long teeth, curved inward, inescapable for its prey. Lunate tails and thick caudal keels generated greater speed than their cousins.

And they brought their ominous reputation. Makos have fed on human flesh.

Last to arrive were the threshers. Tail fins, nearly as high as their bodies were long, arced like scimitars raised in threat. They looked more ancient than the others, and paralyzing fear pulsed through two warm-blooded women trapped beneath them.

Blood and guts clouded the water. Faster and faster sharks dashed around them, intoxicated by the blood, and Danni and Alex were unable to watch each individual. Tails and fins mingled and merged in the melee. Danni held the console with her pressure and depth gauges in front of them both, eye level, and tried to stay calm. Alex saw the pressure gauge. 210 psi. Hers was similar. Dropping fast.

They were running out of time.

Suddenly one thresher was jerked off its course and dragged head first toward the surface. Humans in the boat had dropped hooks and lines, and all that had passed before was preamble. Now the real frenzy began.

The hooked shark rose, thrashing in panic, jerking and twisting. His requiem cousins responded instinctively and attacked him with unbridled violence. Before he broke the surface, a mako ripped a large chunk of flesh from his abdomen. Then a blue moved in for his share and the mako turned on him, defending its meal. Other sharks joined in and as one tore living meat from its victim, it too became a victim. A thresher locked teeth around a hunk of mako flesh and jerked back and forth to tear it loose, even as it, also, was disemboweled. No sight in their experience had prepared Alex and Danni for this carnage.

Other sharks were hooked and yanked out of the water with amazing speed. But when the first carcass splashed back seconds later, missing its pectoral and dorsal fins, Alex looked at her sister, puzzled.

Danni's eyes were hard with anger, rage equal to her fear. Alex looked up and one after another of the sharks hooked and landed, splashed back into the water. Alive and jerking. All missing their fins.

The fear those animals first aroused, eased, replaced by pity and disgust as the women watched them helplessly thrash and roll, unable to swim with only their tails. Their open wounds attracted healthy sharks to this easiest meal, and more blood and bits of meat filled the water. All they could do was watch. And wait.

The most eerie element of the macabre event, as frightening as the killing itself, was the total silence. No cry escaped the wounded to hammer on the eardrums of the two women. Not even the mutilated bodies splashing into the water from above created sound waves audible to them. This silent slaughter was only a visible event for Danni and Alex. No scent. No sound. Only the regular rush of their exhaled air bubbles interrupted the sea's silence. Counting down their remaining breaths.

The diesel engine increased power and slowly chugged off, away from the carnage and gore drifting in the water. The surviving sharks, appetites sated on their cousins started back to the depths.

Danni's pressure gauge read 70 psi. She tapped Alex, pointed in the direction of their boat, a spot they could not even see. The women slowly eased away with cautious strokes, to attract no interest from the carnivores.

They tried to breathe conservatively, inhaling and exhaling slowly and steadily. Alex grabbed the anchor line and started her measured ascent behind her sister. She savored each breath, expecting it to be the last, and she fought the strong desire to shoot to the surface.

But her mind functioned clearly. The risk of the bends loomed larger than at any other moment of their dive, so hand over hand they climbed the chain to ten feet from the surface and stopped. Back to back, they waited out a safe decompression stop that seemed endless, flushing excess nitrogen from their blood.

Finally, with her last breath of air, Danni surfaced and threw her fins into the boat in one smooth movement. Alex's fins flew past her as she rolled onto the plywood deck, spit out her regulator, and sucked great gulps of fresh air. Alex dashed up the ladder, and collapsed next to her sister. Side by side, unable to talk, they filled their lungs in huge gasps, as much from physical need as emotional release.

Danni removed her mask and hood and looked at her sister.

"Are you alright?"

Alex took two deep breaths before responding. "Yeah, how 'bout you?"

"I'm okay." She searched the horizon for the fishing boat and located it, now just a speck in the distance. "Get in that pocket behind you and pull out my binoculars, will you? I want this bastard."

"What were they doing?" Alex shook her head, "that was obscene."

Danni put the binoculars to her eyes and pointed them towards the distant craft. "You like Chinese food? Maybe a little shark fin soup? Well, you just saw how they harvest them. This must be a small local operation, usually they use large processing boats. I'd love to ID that guy and call the Coast Guard." She focused on the diesel, now nearly out of view to Alex's naked eye.

"Shit! There's no way I can catch him, he's too far and

moving too fast. He probably saw our diving flag at the last minute and thought he'd better beat feet with witnesses down below."

She put down the binoculars, took a deep breath, and looked at her sister. A radiant smile abruptly filled her face, "I told you it would be a breath-taking dive, right?" Alex smiled, then chuckled, then burst out laughing, releasing her tension. Soon both sisters were caught up in spasms of nervous laughter.

"So, let's have the food, I'm starved."

Alex shook her head, "We kiss the grim reaper at fifty feet and you're hungry! I draw comfort from the fact that some things never change."

"The thrill stimulates my appetite. And don't tell me it doesn't do that to you, Alex. I know better."

Danni glimpsed an old contentment in her sister's eyes. And then the tiniest nod, yes, the fear fed her too.

"So, I s'pose you want to call it a day and head back, right?" she raised her eyebrows, "after all the danger and excitement, I mean."

Alex shook her head. "What could possibly be worse?" She popped open a soda. "And you're right, it felt good."

"Survival usually does, I hear. Pass me a sandwich—*and* the Oreos."

Chapter Twenty

The girls unzipped their suits and dropped them to their waists. Then Danni began unpacking something from one of the Zodiac's storage compartments.

"What are you doing?"

"You're gonna love this." A roll of lightweight nylon fabric and several fiberglass rods piled up on the plywood floor.

"That looks like your old dome tent."

"It is," she grinned, "with a few little modifications." She unrolled the bright yellow ripstop and unfolded the jointed 1/4 inch fiberglass rods creating three equal rods about twelve feet long. Handing one to Alex she said, "Here, feed this through the flap at that end."

Alex slid the fiberglass through the pocket and smiled at her sister's ingenuity. Looking along the sides of the boat canvas she spotted the fittings.

"This is very clever, your Home-Ec teacher would be proud."

"I needed something to protect me from the sun on hot days, and this works pretty well. I wouldn't use it in high winds, but it does the job on a calm day like this."

They finished installing the rods and working together, fastened the ends into the appropriate fittings in the canvas, resurrecting a horseshoe-shaped awning that spanned the rear half of the Zodiac. Lightweight lines secured it fore and aft.

"It looks like a giant tennis shoe, the old lace up kind." Alex giggled.

"Thanks a lot! You won't be laughing later when it gets hot. We get a nice little breeze through this thing." She crawled under the arched nylon, which was high enough for them to sit up. Alex joined her and they split a soda. Just like when they were kids. Easy laughter filled the remnant of the dome tent.

Conversation slowed and gave way to silence. The sisters reclined in the shade against the sides of the inflated boat and a light breeze played across their bodies and through their drying hair. The ocean rolled easy beneath them.

Neither woman felt compelled to fill the quiet with talk, and the slapping of the water against the rubber boat lulled them. Minds drifted through the shared space and time, content in each other's company. Danni checked her watch occasionally and crawled beyond the awning to view the ocean around the boat. She had her back to Alex when she heard,

"He fucked her in my bed. Did you know that?" Danni turned and looked hard at her sister. She had never heard Alex use that word. Or any other profanity, for that matter.

"Yeah, mom told me."

"Did she also tell you that Sheryl had clothes stored in my house?" Danni shook her head, hardly believing Stephen's gall.

"...in his study—where I never looked because I respected his privacy. How could a woman be so gullible?"

Danni thought for a moment and then said, "How long are you going to beat yourself up with this, Alex? I think the only people who are never taken advantage of are dead. And from where I sit this self-recrimination is an empty purse." She moved back into the shade next to Alex.

"I know, but I need to understand how it happened so I can be sure it won't happen again."

"Oh, is that what this is about? You think you can guarantee it won't happen again? I don't think that's possible, not if you want to live in a world populated by people. We all get 'done unto' once in awhile, sometimes repeatedly, and one real nasty round doesn't excuse you from the game. At least not in my experience." She took the red and white can from her sister and took a long drink. "We're not allowed to see the object that takes us down as anything BUT seductive, so we become totally vulnerable, every time. It's some kind of cosmic law, I think."

"Well, you may be right, but at this moment I can't imagine the next time..."

Danni checked her watch. "We should do the next dive

now so we're out before the tide changes. On the ocean side the surge can get pretty rough."

The sun's reflection on the water was painfully sharp, like the fire of a million diamonds burning into their eyes. So when they dropped below the surface the world that presented itself was not the one they had encountered that morning. The seamount glimmered and sparkled in the diffused sunlight, and colors, muted and dark earlier, were now vivid and bright. The top sides of fish were mottled with lines of shimmering light that rippled constantly from head to tail.

And there was peace. No evidence of the morning's violence littered the tranquil environment. To the marine beings passing through now, it never happened. Water previously clouded with blood and drifting bits of flesh was clean-washed and vacant of death.

Alex rediscovered the natural rhythm of her stride underwater. Muscle memory retrieved the skill and she welcomed the current's pressure against her body, moving her as easily as the giant kelp. For a few minutes she gave herself up to that power, drifting over the seamount. Toward Australia… or Japan… or Hawaii.

No color was unrepresented on the seamount. Lavender, orange, yellow, and pink seastars challenged the seaslugs—yellow sea lemons, red sea hares, black and yellow narvanaxes, and neon blue and orange spanish shawls—for beauty. As they crawled through their landscape the spectrum of hues shifted like oil on water, continually rearranging into new patterns.

A glint of light caught Alex's eye and she reached for a discarded beer can, its shiny aluminum unaffected by the salt water. She grabbed it to store in her nylon dive bag for disposal later. As she fumbled with the drawstring, a baby octopus burst from the pop-tab opening and affixed itself to the nearest stationary object. Her mask.

Alex's slow drift stopped instantly. She knelt and put her hands to her mask to dislodge the tiny cephalopod. He walked across the glass with fluid grace, oozing, one slender limb coiling over another. As his four-inch legs moved over her face, she could see the dainty tentacles grab and release the glass. His indignation was obvious, colors rippled across his body in waves—brick red—dark brown—bone white, in a feeble attempt to frighten off this monster that had uprooted his home. But Alex had no fear of this animal as she carefully removed him from her mask to her glove for better observation.

He was fully formed, a minute replica of his parents, and he lithely climbed from finger to finger and hand to hand. The canary-sized beak opened as it brushed her glove and Alex smiled. This infant was still learning what elements of his world were edible. In only weeks he would know with certainty the textures that meant food.

She recalled her dives with the giant octopi of Puget Sound, eight-foot legs whose embrace could rattle the calm of the most confident diver. As she watched that dainty mouth open and taste neoprene, the wonder that once drove her to vet school drew a refreshing breath.

Before she was ready for him to leave, the octopus vanished in a spurt of purple ink.

The seamount's plateau ended abruptly and they cruised over the edge, a sheer cliff that disappeared into the blue black beyond their eyesight. They descended slowly, feet first, in a lazy fall that never hit bottom.

They inflated their buoyancy control vests gradually, tapping on the button to draw air from their tanks and leveled off at sixty-five feet. Slowly they began their investigation of the vertical wall. Here larger species of game fish, yellowtail and seabass, shared habitat with silver schools of jack mackerel and sardines.

The area of the pinnacles Danni had chosen for their second dive was humbling in its scope. With their backs to the wall nothing but ocean filled their masks. Alex had the feeling she was hovering on the very edge of North America, resting her back against the continental shelf, and were she to swim west, no land mass would rise in front of her for thousands of miles.

Around a large rock outcropping they discovered a six-foot sandy ledge, running horizontally along the wall for forty feet. There were no invertebrates rooted here and its barrenness radically contrasted the rest of the cliff. Perhaps some unique current flow kept all plankton from this ledge. Alex's mind worked on the puzzle like it hadn't reasoned in months. Questions to consider, a situation to understand. The process felt good.

Alex was close to Danni when she touched the ledge so they were equally startled when it came to life, a four-foot section rising beneath her hand like a sandy flying carpet. In seconds the sand fell away and they watched a very healthy bat ray glide off, unhurried. His pectoral fins, long ago evolved into underwater wings, undulated slowly up and down with as much grace as any bird. Alex ached to move like that.

When she turned back to follow Danni something felt out of place. Her sister had paused and was waiting for her with the same puzzled look on her face. Then Alex noticed all the larger fish had vanished. Only the stationary invertebrates, who had no choice, remained on the wall. She caught her sibling's eye and Danni shrugged her shoulders and held her palm out flat, hold position. There was no fear in this feeling, just curious anticipation. They hovered in place, as if anchored to the rock behind them like the invertebrates.

Slowly a large spot, darker than the water around it, began to take shape. And grow. Larger, much larger. Before it was identifiable it filled their masks. A huge black torpedo-shaped head, scarred and scratched, came into focus and Danni and Alex both released the breath they had been holding in an uncontrolled gush of air bubbles.

A full grown California gray whale glided by less than thirty feet in front of them. Aware of their presence, she gave them no more attention than a human would give a falling leaf. Sixty-five feet of whale passed them and Alex had the sensation of watching a train pass, the barnacle-studded head faded from view to their right before the large tail flukes became visible from the left. There was no discernable muscle action, but no human could have matched her speed. The enormous cetacean seemed to cruise unpropelled by any obvious power.

In all her dive trips along the California coast, Danni had never seen a California Gray, but it was late February and perhaps this one was late beginning her migration back to Alaska from their wintering ground in Mexico. When she saw Alex's head jerk hard to the left the situation became instantly clear.

Less than twenty feet from where they hovered against the wall, a baby gray whale swam between his mother and the women, struggling to keep up. He passed so close that Alex and Danni could clearly see his large eye focus on them, a curious new lifeform in his world. His first humans. This was not the cold black eye of a shark, this eye was connected to a brain, and the women knew they were being inspected with as much curiosity as they had for him. His jet-black skin was smooth and unscarred by the barnacles and lampreys that would mark him later. Although he was big by human standards, there was a delicacy about him, so much smaller was he than his mother. He was fifteen feet long, and the rise and fall of his tail flukes was clearly visible. As he passed it caused a small pressure current that gently pushed Alex and her sister back against the rock.

As quickly as they appeared, the whales were gone.

For Alex and Danni the amount of air left in their tanks was irrelevant, nothing they could possibly see in the remaining minutes of bottom time could come close to the last few seconds. They looked at one another, Alex gave the thumbs up to surface and Danni nodded. This dive was over.

They did not talk much as they took down the awning and packed the Zodiac for the trip back. Maybe they had no words, or maybe they didn't want to lose one second of the experience in the sharing of it, before it was forever fixed in their memories. Only after they had returned to Danni's house, showered and were relaxing on the porch did the words come.

"Penny for your thoughts." Danni handed her sister a glass of wine.

"I'm not sure what I think. I can't find words that don't diminish it." The Cabernet warmed her throat. "Maybe this isn't a 'think' kind of thing, so much as a 'feel' kind of thing."

"Then how do you feel?"

"Words aren't leaping to my mind in that category either. What about you?"

Danni shook her head. "Just old cliches. You may be right." They sipped their wine pensively.

"I feel like the first time I saw a horse foal. You know—privileged to be there."

"Yeah, that fits. Like getting a present that you really wanted, on a day that's not your birthday."

"...and the present far exceeded your expectations."

Danni nodded and they sat quietly, freezing forever the memory of the whales' passing.

"I'm going to take that job in Canada." Danni searched her sister's face and saw fresh determination. "I know what I've become since the divorce. I see it in your face, and Mom and Dad's, and I *do* know, Danni. I need to find out what's left of the woman I was before Stephen. Living alone in the woods would force me to look at her. I have to be good company for myself before I can really trust other people."

"Sounds like pretty drastic therapy to me. I don't suppose you could do this self-analysis a bit closer to civilization?"

"Do you think I can't make it out in the wilds, alone?"

"No. I know you know the "how-to's" of living in the boonies, and I know you don't make dumb mistakes in the woods. What worries me, sis, is the living alone part. I think you should have a few people around."

"I'll get a clear view of who I am if I'm alone. Stephen was such a consummate part of my life that I'm not sure how much of me he took with him when he left. This is one sure way to find out. It's meaningful work and they're having trouble finding someone to do it."

"Why does that not surprise me?" Danni shook her head.

"Mom and Dad are gonna love this..."

In the days that followed, the two sisters drew closer, the common wonder of the whales binding their hearts and loosening their tongues. Their talk was quiet and strong, logical and loving.

They dove often in the next week, and explored Monterey and Carmel. The younger sibling supported the older, and Alex found clarity where there had been confusion. Daily wonders, on a smaller scale than the whales, re-ignited her need to question, and learn, to examine, to know both the world and her place in it.

Danni's pickup stopped in front of the curb at the airport. "Are you sure you don't want me to park and help with the luggage?"

"Yes. You know how I hate long goodbyes. Just toss me out and drive on."

"Okay, but before I do, I have something for you." She reached behind her seat and pulled out a package wrapped in brown paper. "Don't open it until you're settled in your place up there, okay?"

"Don't do this to me!"

"I mean it, not until Viento's in his stall and you're in your, um, well, whatever it is you're gonna be in."

"Okay."

Danni helped unload the bags for the skycap and hugged her sister. She looked her right in the eye and said, "Be careful up there, Alex. Don't get careless or anything, it's not Disneyland, you know. They can't just call over the PA system for anyone that's lost a blonde veterinarian..."

"Don't worry so much, that's Mom's job."

"Yeah, and this scheme's gonna keep her real busy."

"'Bye, sis." One last hug and Alex turned away and walked into the terminal, to avoid the threatening tears. From inside the window she waved as the black Toyota pickup pulled away from the curb.

Chapter Twenty-one

Spring equinox heralded a new phenomenon to alter the valley of the wolves. Winter's snowfall would remain for weeks, but beneath huge drifts the melt had begun. Drops of water joined as trickles, trickles mated and gave birth to rivulets, and all obeyed gravity's pull. The heavy runoff transformed the friendly river into a violent entity. It swelled beyond its appointed boundary until, powerful and unpredictable, it spread over the valley, submerging all in its path. This was not a problem for the wolves and they avoided it easily, but for the smaller members of the forest community the flood was a disaster.

These were the den days, the days of mating and birth and even without a new litter, the pack responded to their code of behavior and relaxed from their nomadic life.

Cunning had always found this annual lethargy tedious, but this year her frustration was intense. She was two years old, a full-grown bitch, and the urge to mate swelled in her for the first time, as powerful as any that had moved her before. She did not challenge Cub-bearer for her alpha position, something kept her from that fight. But to relieve her tension she avoided the den, following her wanderlust down mile after mile of trail, racing through unmarked territory. Hormonal changes triggered a craving for which she found no relief. Passionate as she was strong, this hunger drove her away from her family.

On these forays Cunning discovered fresh signs of the rogue, but she did not communicate this information to her pack.

Instead, she began to track him.

She refused to allow First-twin to accompany her and her younger sister was confused by the rejection. The young female did not understand, but in her hard-edged style Cunning made it painfully clear First-twin was no longer welcome. The strong bitch snapped at her viciously and snarled whenever First-twin followed her. Finally, Cunning grabbed the young female by the scruff of the neck and jerked her to the ground. The pain and indignity made her point clear, First-twin never tried to follow her again.

For a week Cunning ranged miles from the den, but she found only old spoor around killsites, and faint traces of the rogue's urine on scentposts. Cunning was one of the best trackers in the pack, only Guardian and White-cub were more skilled, and the longer she pursued the rogue without success, the more determined she was to find him.

These were the opening days of her sexual need, the rising of an ebb and flow that would grow stronger.

But Cunning's skill at tracking was no match for her quarry. The gray bitch had inherited Patriarch's skill as a hunter, but she did not possess his calculating mind. She never played the games of puppyhood, like hide and seek with her littermates, so she never learned that, in the turn of a head, or a look, or a growl, the hunter can become the prey.

Yellow eyes watched her as she left the den area and the alien trail she followed was laid a second time, wolfprints over her own. The rogue sniffed the mark of her heat, drops of blood in her urine and on the trail where she paused, and his own craving intensified. The red-gold rogue was seven years old, and he had the experience of those years to weave a trap for the gray bitch as subtle as a spider's web. His motivation for attracting her was stronger than her sexual need to find him.

Cast out by his birth pack after a bitter challenge against the alpha, the rogue had struggled through the winter, alone. He had no territory, no familiar place to rest, and no old kills to ease his hunger. Each sunrise found him entering another predator's territory—cougar, bear, wolf—and those confrontations had taken their toll.

On another day the rogue would have fought for the gray bitch, and shown himself well in the contest, but now he was in no condition for a fight. His last meal had been the elk, fourteen sunrises earlier, and then he had barely escaped the wolverine. The rogue was weak and thin, scarred and hungry, and he needed a hunting partner. A companion. A mate.

When he was sure Cunning was following him, he laid a trail to entice and intrigue the two-year old bitch. He drew her farther from the den with a scent that was each day easier for her to find than the day before. As she tracked him, he pursued her.

The rising sun edged the predawn clouds with gold. It was the fifth morning of her search and the air was charged and electric, all the animals felt the late storm building energy. Cunning trotted through the familiar forest until she picked up the rogue's trail near the river. Nose to the ground, she became excited. Her tail swayed gently as she scoured the earth in ever widening circles. This scentmark was very fresh. Then she found a fallen pine where the bark was wet with his urine. It was still warm! So close! Sniffing the wind she loped along the riverbank, eager for the joining her body craved.

At a great turn in the river, where the trees thinned abruptly, she spotted him. The ground rose gently from the river to a small bluff and there he stood, a red-gold silhouette against the churning sky. He stared at her. Intent. Still. Waiting. The rogue was hungry and thin but his pride ruled the moment of their meeting.

The cold wind that had blown steadily, stopped. A raven screamed once from a nearby tree, and was silent. Cunning did not race to the rogue's side, but stood her ground, nostrils trembling to catch every shade of his scent. She, too, was unwilling to show submission.

She lowered her head, keeping her eyes on the rogue and neither moved for several seconds. Tails remained high, a wolfen test of wills, but her heat had reached its peak, and mating's lust drove her forward.

The hair rose along the bitch's back and, with her first stiff-legged step, she growled softly. If she must walk to him, she would do it with a show of strength. Her pride forbid any other response.

Two long minutes passed while Cunning climbed the slope, moving regally, pausing every few steps. During the whole time the rogue stood his ground. Motionless. The wind came up again, stronger, and the only movement besides Cunning's cautious steps was the rogue's red-gold winter coat, swirling around him. It filled out his gaunt body, granting him a bulk greater than he could rightfully claim. He was starving, but his age and experience demanded a posture of pride, regardless of the gnawing in his belly.

Cunning stopped two feet from him. Face to face. Only windblown fur moved. Yellow eyes fixed on hazel and not even the thunder rumbling overhead distracted them. The boiling clouds that had hinted a great storm, now signaled its arrival.

Without so much as a friendly lick or wag of the tail, the rogue lunged and grabbed her muzzle in his mouth. Cunning jerked away and sank her teeth into the fur near his throat. She snarled and although he tried to pull away, Cunning held on. There was no affection in their first touch.

The rogue escaped her grasp and quickly jumped on her broadside, huge paws across her back, weight on her spine. She tried to move out from under him, but his teeth solidly gripped the back of her neck and they danced their mating ritual over the snow. Growls charged the moment as the first strike of lightning charged the air.

Cunning broke loose and swung her full weight into the rogue, crashing her chest against his flank. Their wrestling had taken them to the edge of a draw, a seven-foot gash in the hillside where the water-laden earth had slid away. Her blow was unexpected and the rogue lost his footing at the edge and slipped into the muddy scree, rolling over and over until he reached the bottom. He collected himself quickly and charged up the dirt slide after Cunning.

Without hesitation he grabbed Cunning's throat and pulled her head down, a large front paw on her neck. Every ounce of energy was required to hold the struggling, snarling bitch, but he pushed her down, hard. Finally, when his strength was nearly spent, Cunning's front legs buckled and her chest hit the ground. Even then he did not release her.

The rogue had bested the gray bitch. Her growls became whimpers and she lowered her rear end. Of her own will. Only when she made an effort to roll on her back, to submit completely, did he release her. He straddled her while she licked his face, his mouth, and eyes, lying on her back. Finally he stepped back and allowed her to rise.

Ritual complete, the rogue mounted Cunning and mated the proud bitch for the first time. Thunder rolled through the mountains and lightning illuminated their coupling on the hillside overlooking the raging river.

Cunning killed two rabbits in the hours that followed and fed her mate. If she noticed his weakness and hunger, it was no longer significant. After their meal they left the valley, bonded.

In her loneliness First-twin turned to Jester for companionship and he was receptive, socializing with her as he had Gentle and Red-cub. First-twin learned from Jester how to play for the sake of play, an activity Cunning had never practiced. They romped through the slush and rolled in the mud, and she enjoyed his close physical contact. He showed her an affection that was beyond Cunning's personality, licking her face and bumping her shoulder when they ran side by side. This was new to First-twin and she enjoyed it. Jester took the toughness out of the hunter Cunning had trained, and soon First-twin did not miss her sister.

The birthday of Patriarch and Cub-bearer's second litter dawned and departed without notice. The year had not been kind to the pack. Black-cub, Second-twin, and Red-cub had died at the hands of nature, and Patriarch and Gentle had died at the hands of man. Of the five cubs, only White-cub and First-twin survived their first year.

An owl's attack disturbed the night with a near silent

rush of wings and the scream of its rabbit victim awakened Guardian with a start. His senses searched the darkness. The rabbit screamed once more, then silence resumed.

Six nights had passed since Guardian found Cunning's mating smell mingled with the rogue's, and he knew she would not return. The alpha stood and yawned, shook himself from nose to tail, and surveyed his pack sprawled out across the den area.

Cub-bearer. Jester. White-cub. First-twin. Now they were five.

Chapter Twenty-two

Alex's Jeep lurched and bumped over the unused fire road for over an hour. First one wheel dropped into a hole on the left and climbed out, then both right wheels hit the bottom of a ditch on the other side. Only her seatbelt restrained her head from slamming into the roof of the cab. She listened to tires spin, then dig into a new hunk of mud and was grateful for four-wheel drive. The topographical map in the passenger seat offered little reassurance that this road was, at some level of human understanding, fit for mechanized vehicles.

In her rearview mirror Alex watched Viento's head bob up and down and side to side. The horse was trying bravely to brace himself inside his trailer. He wasn't having much more success on four legs than Alex was having on four wheels. The two-way radio clicked.

"Alex, how are you doing?"

"I'm okay, but Viento is having a tough time. I think I should stop and let him walk alongside the trailer. How much farther is it?"

"About three miles."

"Then let's pull over, he's really getting bounced back there."

Both vehicles stopped and Matt helped Alex drop the tailgate of the horse trailer. Viento required no encouragement to back out of it. He tossed his head and stamped his feet, obviously relieved to feel terra firma beneath hoof. Alex walked him in circles for a few minutes to stretch his legs and work out any cramps.

She stroked Viento's neck and her soothing words conveyed a comfortable intimacy with the animal that was not lost on Matt.

"No, that wasn't a very pleasant ride was it, V.?"

Matt watched graceful fingers rub Viento's velvety

muzzle and in response the horse brushed the side of his head up and down against Alex's cheek. Lucky horse, he thought, observing the affection between woman and mustang, how blonde hair flowed in the breeze just like Viento's mane and tail. Worn jeans, bulky fisherman-knit sweater, boots. He smiled, the image was perfect.

Alex tied Viento on a long lead to the trailer and they continued their slow progress down the road, toward her new home.

Ancient pines rising over a hundred feet perpetually shaded the dirt trail, barely more than a glorified animal track. Their branches formed such a dense mass of dark green that only a thin sliver of sky was visible, directly overhead. At this moment it was blue and still daylight. Dirty snowdrifts, axle-high and covered with pine needles, hunched beneath the trees and along the road like sleeping polar bears. Sunlight had little opportunity to melt them, only summer temperatures would reduce their mass, and that, only slowly. Freezing nights would follow warming days, and weeks would pass before they vanished.

No fanfare heralded the arrival of spring here. Winter-weary bark on a few deciduous branches split, and offered minute glimpses of green buds. In small patches of ground where sunlight had melted the snow, slivers of new grass sprouted, harbingers of renewal. Winter gave up its hold on this land with great reluctance.

Click.

"Are you keeping track of the mileage?"

"Yes, let's see... 18.6 miles since we left pavement, on road 203c, right?"

"That's it." Click. In areas this remote roads often had numbers instead of names, and those numbers corresponded to map coordinates. Alex smiled, it was the same in Washington. Coffee-stained topographical maps of Mt. Rainier, Mt. Baker, the Cascades, and the Olympics, were packed somewhere in the boxes and clutter jamming the rear of her Jeep. Forgotten days with Search and Rescue—cold, rainy trips on horseback looking for lost kids, or injured hikers—were non-threatening memories and Alex welcomed their company.

Viento walked comfortably behind the trailer. Nostrils flared and his head bobbed side to side, absorbing the identity scent of this forest. Moisture from melting snow amplified the smell of fir, cedar, spruce and groundcover. Even the dirt beneath his hooves offered up an unfamiliar smell. Each was similar, but not identical to those he had learned in the Cascades, and his mustang brain catalogued each nuance like Alex tracked mileage and road numbers. He saw the direction shadows fell, found the sun, and oriented himself in his new environment.

Ten minutes later the forest thinned and the road climbed in earnest along the side of a valley. Here the trees were older and stood alone, windbent and solitary. Mountains towered above them on the right, and a steep cliff disappeared over the left edge of the road. The view across the valley to the peaks that formed the opposite wall was unbroken.

Click.

"The cabin's just ahead, Alex. Pull around the left side, the stable and corral are in the back."

Alex's first view of her home for the next year made her seriously reconsider her decision to take this job. The original part of the building was an old log cabin, foot-thick logs, notched and joined at the corners like a giant's Lego set. Jutting out to the left was an addition of more contemporary style and behind it she saw the corral. Attached to the backside of the cabin like an afterthought was the stable and garage. They too were frame and board construction, easily fifty years younger than the cabin itself. Two stalls opened to a large corral through dutch-doors. Matt came into view as she set the emergency brake.

"Well, here it is, home sweet home! What do you think?"

Alex looked at the ancient cabin dubiously, "I may move into the stable with Viento." Matt chuckled.

"Don't be fooled by appearances, this cabin has been

here for decades. It's cool in the summer, warm in the winter, and very solid when the wind blows. You'll appreciate it later, believe me."

Alex untied Viento and walked him in circles, changing direction to evaluate his gait for injuries from the trailer ride. Matt watched her with as much interest as she was showing the horse.

He fumbled at any conversation about her divorce, choosing to discuss the work instead, safer ground for them both. But watching her now he began to see the toll her marriage had taken. She was still attractive – as always – but thinner, her eyes darted to avoid eye contact, and she rarely smiled. He found himself watching intently for one of her smiles. A pale band of flesh on her left ring finger, previously hidden by her wedding ring, marked her like a brand on livestock.

Her voice grew louder, she was talking to him,

"...and he's not a high-strung horse, quite even-tempered actually, but long trips in a trailer really tighten him up."

"Make me ride all the way from Seattle in that thing and I might tighten up, too."

"Oh, I didn't trailer him in this thing all the way! A horse hauler brought him up with some rodeo horses in a much larger rig, with air conditioning, and everything." She casually combed her fingers through Viento's mane. "A Cadillac compared to this. I picked him up in Calgary." After a few minutes she unclipped the lead and turned him loose in the corral.

"I'll leave him here for awhile to get some fresh air. That road was pretty awful."

"Yeah, I'd forgotten how bad it can be after a heavy winter. You could lose a bear in some of those potholes."

They walked around the cabin to the front door, "It's been four years since I stayed here," he chuckled, "and you'll be happy to know they've made a few improvements since then."

While he talked, Alex surveyed her new home. The door

was centered in the middle of the front wall, log walls stretched about twenty feet on either side of it. Wooden shutters covered two windows, one on either side of the door. Matt opened them.

"If you're going to be away overnight be sure to close these, glass won't slow down a wolverine once he smells your food." Alex noted the claw marks on the shutters, deep claw marks.

"They won't come around while you're here, but don't leave the place open when you're gone."

The front door was heavy and Alex wondered if it was as old as the cabin. Matt unlocked both the deadbolt and the key lock and it swung open easily, well-balanced, in spite of its weight. Sunlight through the doorway and windows illuminated a single room, about twenty feet deep with windows in all four walls. The addition jutting to the left was more modern, a kitchen/bathroom area.

Matt flipped a switch near the door and lights came on.

"Electricity?" Alex was surprised. "Tom didn't mention that in his letter. I assumed I'd be really roughing it."

"All the comforts of home!" He saw her raised eyebrows.

"Well, the necessities, anyway. There's a generator out back for the 'fridge and the lights. It runs on diesel, I'll show you how to start it in case it dies. The propane tank is for the water heater and the stove. It was just filled so you shouldn't have any problem with that. For room heat you have that beautiful antique in the corner." Alex followed his gaze to a wood-burning stove in the far corner, positioned to face the center of the room.

"It's ugly but a real efficient heat source. If you bank the fire at night it's easy to start in the morning. Looks like about four cords of wood split and stacked against the side of the house."

To her immediate right against the front wall was the bed, to her left, under the window was a small table and two chairs. A large two-way radio sat on the table.

"Do you know how to use that thing?" Matt asked.

"Yes." They both examined it.

"Yeah, that's the right frequency for the park service. When you use it, remember that most locals monitor it, so watch your conversation."

On the left wall was an old two-door wardrobe and a dresser, then the kitchen-bath addition. With both of them in the small alcove it was cramped.

"The plumbing's pretty basic, you need to connect this hose," he pointed to a thick black hose draped over the shower rod, "to the sink over here when you want to shower or take a bath. The water heater is behind that door." He nodded to a narrow closet door.

The kitchen fixtures were all undersized; tiny sink, a petite refrigerator, two dainty burners on a gas stove with an oven about the size of a breadbox. There was a tub beneath the shower, an old porcelain affair with brass feet, standing solidly beneath a hanging pink shower curtain, so new it still smelled like plastic. She smiled and wondered if Matt had installed it.

On the back wall of the cabin, between the kitchen alcove and the living area, was the door to the stable, and the familiar smell of hay and leather greeted her when Matt opened the door. A bare light bulb hung from the ceiling over two stalls on the left, another one hung over the stall and tack area to the right. A door on the right wall led to the garage, and the two stalls on the left opened into the corral through dutch-doors.

"This is pretty cozy."

"Yeah, it wasn't here when I used the cabin. The Park Service added it a couple years ago when they brought up horses to work the backcountry." She smiled.

"Viento will be comfortable in here."

"The park service had hay and grain delivered last week."

Alex nodded and wandered back into the cabin. She noticed a long workbench to her left built into the back wall, running from the doorway to the wood-burning stove. The window over the workbench looked out on the corral and beyond it, to a clearing rising into the mountainside. Clusters of trees dotted the hillside.

"This will be a nice work area. Are there electrical outlets around here?"

"I think so." Matt crouched to look under the bench. "Yeah, there are two down here."

"Good, I brought a microscope and a computer, but I wasn't sure I'd be able to use them." Matt stood and looked at her.

"A computer?" It was his turn to be surprised.

"Yes, it's the laptop I used in my clinic for data entry, now I'll be able to re-charge the batteries."

"Do you use it in the field?"

"I haven't yet, but I will." He shook his head.

"What were you going to do if there was no electricity?"

"I have a quick-charger that plugs into the cigarette lighter in my car."

"Incredible!" Matt shook his head and thought of the dozens of shirtpocket-sized spiral notebooks, water-stained and wrinkled, that chronologged his career. The presence of high-tech in his wilderness made him uncomfortable.

"Well, I think that's the tour," he looked around the cabin, "have any questions?"

"I don't think so. We better get my stuff unpacked so you can get out of here before dark. That road looks like it would be a real challenge at night."

"Actually, I got pretty used to it while I lived here. You will too. It's only heart-stopping the first few times you drive it."

Alex disconnected the horse trailer and backed her Grand Cherokee close to the front door. There was little conversation as the two of them carried in her boxes and luggage. A heap grew in the center of the floor; books, clothes, camping gear, backpack, vet equipment and medications, a box marked "fragile" containing the microscope and computer, a small CD-cassette tape player, and her guitar. It saddened Alex to see how small a pile her remaining earthly possessions formed, and how little time it took the two of them to create it. No Valentino gowns here.

Matt's eyes followed Alex from truck to cabin, and back again, like he would observe a new animal, and his curiosity was only partially sated. As much as he knew about her, their years together in school, he still wondered what her life had been like with Stephen. And he regretted the times he had forced her to defend him. To leave that world for this must be major culture shock. He would never have admitted it to anyone, but when she accepted this job he went out of his way to greet her arrival.

Matt considered most of the women he met shallow and self-involved. Even worse, he thought they all talked too much. He understood that his work gave him a different perspective on the mating game, but the women that attracted most men did not appeal to him. Because Alex didn't clutter silence with empty chatter, he was interested in what she had to say.

Alex was unaware of his observation as she strode from Jeep to house, and he caught glimpses of her vulnerability, nervous eyes, and a heavy sigh. She was a wounded animal, bearing her pain, enduring from one minute to the next. Surviving. Matt hoped the emotional wounds that went with the white skin around her finger would heal as fast as the summer sun would tan the pale flesh.

"Looks like that's it, unless there's more stuff in the trailer?" He looked at her expectantly.

Alex shook her head. "Just Viento's tack, I'll get that later."

Matt sauntered to the kitchen and Alex noticed how quiet he was on his feet. Definitely not a city creature. He opened a cupboard. "Let's see, there were glasses in one of these cupboards... yeah, here they are." He pulled out two heavy tumblers and rinsed them out.

"What are those for?"

"You'll see, I'll be right back." While he walked to his

truck Matt considered his next move, and the wisdom of it. Actually, he'd considered it all the way to the cabin. Too late now. Alex watched him from the window as he grabbed a bottle and returned. He held it out to her.

"To wish you success, Alex." It was the soft voice of a friend and his easy access to that vulnerable place she protected so diligently, unnerved her. She tentatively took the bottle.

"This is, uh, very nice, Matt." Silence. The moment was awkward, they both felt it, and Matt instantly regretted bringing the wine. He watched her face, but she masked her feelings well. She pulled her keys from her jacket pocket, attached to them was a Swiss Army knife.

"I think there's a cork screw on this thing somewhere." Her voice was artificially light, but it broke the tension of the moment. Matt still couldn't read her response, but he appreciated her gracious recovery.

"Here, allow me." He took the knife, pulled out the corkscrew, and opened the bottle. An inch of rosy wine darkened each glass.

"It's a Gamay from British Columbia, hope you like it." He passed her a glass and raised his. "Here's to your work." Her responding smile snuggled into a permanent niche in his memory.

"Thanks, Matt," she looked at the floor, "this is nice." They sat in the two overstuffed chairs facing the ancient stove. Matt opened the cast-iron door and laid a fire, tinder and dry wood from the bin on the floor.

"This place sure brings back memories."

"How long did you stay here?"

"Over a year. Most of my early wolf studies were done out of this cabin. I spent days and nights tracking the pack that lived in a neighboring valley four years ago, documenting their behavior. Although I didn't have a computer." He struck a match and tinder ignited, and his eyes sparkled above another great smile. She heard the tease in his words, but looked away when their eyes met.

"Are there a lot of wolves around here?"

"There were then," the larger wood popped and ignited. "I don't know now. You'll have to let me know."

He left the stove door open and returned to his chair. They both gazed into the flames. His voice was colored with quiet respect.

"They're amazing creatures, Alex. I remember each of them as distinctly as the members of my family. I hope you get to see one while you're here."

"Get to see one? Are they that elusive?"

"Worse. You'll find tracks and scat and an old kill once in a while, but it's rare to catch a glimpse of them. Yet they'll know you're here by the time this smoke drifts a thousand yards." He looked at her. "Spooky, huh?"

"Yes." The fire crackled and through the small door they watched sparks shoot around inside the iron chamber.

"What are you working on now?" Alex's voice broke their reverie.

"Well, tomorrow I'm off to Alaska. They're still trying to justify a major wolf hunt to increase the caribou population. To bring in tourism." The sarcasm in his voice was unmistakable.

"I thought that issue was dead years ago."

"It keeps coming up because predator/prey populations constantly fluctuate. Some people think when the predator population rises it should be reduced immediately rather than letting it happen naturally. Predator populations usually shift in response to changes in prey populations, but it takes a few years. Nature's actually more a pendulum than a balance. And there are other elements in the system that can decimate either predator or prey."

He leaned forward, resting his elbows on his knees, and swirled the wine in his glass. "But the worst element of the equation is man, we are the most deadly addition to any habitat. If there's a buck to be made, you can bet we'll exploit anything to feed the greed."

"You don't have a very high opinion of human beings."

"No. I don't." Alex started to say something, then stopped. She wasn't prepared to argue the virtues of human beings at this point in her life.

"Sorry. You get me going on this wolf hunt thing and I get kind of crazy. Just when I think reasonable people are making the decisions, they decide to do it again." He poured more wine in both glasses. "Oh, I almost forgot, what kind of gun did you bring? I didn't see one when we unloaded your car."

"I don't own a gun. It's not exactly a tool of my trade."

"Alex, it was on the list of things you should bring."

"I can't imagine a situation where I would kill an animal with a gun. There are other more humane methods of accomplishing that, and I'm quite qualified to administer them." It was the first assertive tone he'd heard from her since they arrived. "And anyway, I don't know the first thing about using one."

"It's not just the animals you need to worry about. I'm more concerned about poachers. Last year there were eleven arrested in these mountains. These people are seriously unpleasant, Alex, and would kill you in a heartbeat to protect themselves." He rubbed his face with both hands, thinking. "I want you to take the .38 I have in my truck."

Alex stood up and looked at him. "And then what? I could throw it at them, right? Matt, you're not going to teach me to use a gun in an hour, and I wouldn't use it if you did." Her voice was rising. "Frankly, it doesn't sound like such a risk to me. Eleven arrests in a year. Over how many square miles? Several hundred?"

"That's just the ones they caught." He stood up to face her and noticed she was even more beautiful when provoked. Her cheeks flushed and reflected firelight sparkled in her eyes. Memorable.

"You're being stubborn and naive, Alex." She picked up the glasses and took them to the sink, a clear signal Matt's visit was over.

"Maybe so. It wouldn't be the first time." She returned and faced him, eye-to-eye. "But I'm not taking your gun." He shook his head and reached for his jacket.

"It's your decision."

"Exactly."

They walked to the door, and the silence was awkward again, but for a different reason. Their disagreement hung heavy in the room.

Outside, the night sky glittered, diamonds against black velvet. Matt tossed his jacket in the truck and stretched to relieve cramps that didn't exist. To kill time. Seconds crawled by and silence crowded the space between them, but Alex did not miss the sight of strong arm muscles flexing under the rolled up sleeves of his workshirt. More silence. Matt took a deep breath and the frosty air chilled his lungs.

"I'm sorry I came down on you like that, but I still think you should have some kind of weapon up here." He looked her in the eyes, "but since you won't, I'll just have to worry about you."

That soft voice touched Alex again and she smiled. "Well, I can think of worse things."

"There's a bar in town called the Knotty Pine, the owner is a friend of mine named Softouch. He's a bear-sized American who came up here after he got out of the service. I told him you're out here, so if you get into trouble, use the radio, he monitors it all the time. He's also the best pilot I know, a good friend to have in these mountains."

"A 'bear of a man' named Softouch?"

Matt chuckled, "Ask him when you meet him. He's got some rough edges, but a good guy, Alex. Promise you'll call him if you have any trouble?" His concern was genuine.

"I promise." Alex looked up. "What an incredible sky!" The Milky Way spread across the sky like diamonds on black velvet.

"I bet you never got a view like this in the city." Tension broken, he was suddenly reluctant to leave her, a new sensation in his experience. Seizing the moment, he grabbed her hand and squeezed it—quickly—and released it before she could respond. Or reject.

"You're going to love it here, Alex. Good luck on your work." He got into his pickup and shut the door between them, unsure of the next move. Or if there was a next move.

"Thanks again for helping me move in. Drive carefully, Viento and I don't want to have to come rescue you."

He chuckled and started the pickup. The sudden growl of the engine offended the black silence. Taillights disappeared around the bend and the dark quiet that engulfed Alex was absolute. No cars, no phones, no TV. Just the Canadian high country settling in for the night.

Her shoulders sagged in fatigue as the exhaustion of the previous few days caught up with her. She bedded Viento in one of the stalls and fed him quickly. By the time she had banked the fire, locked up, and changed for bed she could hardly keep her eyes open. Across the room she saw the outline of Danni's package on the table. It would wait until tomorrow.

Her last memory before falling asleep was a distant howl, perhaps more dream than reality.

Chapter Twenty-three

Bracing mountain air awakened Alex the next morning just after sunrise. Her bed was warm and she was not anxious to leave it, so she glanced around the cabin, noticing details that had escaped her the previous day. While the walls were ancient, the glass windows were insulated and double-paned, ingenuity from two centuries. Spread across the hardwood floor were four hand-braided rugs. Softened by wear, they invited the foot. The wood stove sat on the low hearth of an old stone fireplace, whose chimney now exhausted the stove's smoke.

Pencil drawings by some unknown artist—local wildlife scenes—broke the horizontal monotony of the log walls. They weren't fine, but matted and framed, they did not offend the eye. The scratched and dented dresser looked like a leftover from some long forgotten garage sale, the piece that wouldn't sell at any price.

I bet the drawers stick when I open them. And those chairs!

Two over-stuffed chairs faced the wood stove and looked like they came from the same garage sale. They had once been green, but Alex wasn't sure what to call their present color.

Her eyes moved to the pile of her belongings in the middle of the floor, and she groaned. Time to get up and move in. She was anxious to get out of the cabin and explore, but this chore demanded her first attention. She also felt a strong need to make the cabin her home, hang her clothes in the wardrobe, arrange her books on the shelf. Nest. The clock on the small night table motivated her to move... 7:12.

Even though she was mentally prepared for it, the icy air took her breath away when she lifted the covers.

"First item of business, Alex, is to get that fire going." Her toes curled against the cold when her feet touched the floor. She laid tinder against the coals and blew on it very gently. Warm black embers glowed faint orange and brightened with each breath until they ignited. Alex shivered and dressed quickly, a sweater over her shirt, jeans, and thick socks inside her boots. When the fire was blazing she foraged through kitchen cupboards for coffee fixings. Beyond the back wall she could hear Viento shifting restlessly in his stall.

His ears pricked and eyes focused on the door when she opened it. He tossed his head and whinnied.

"So, what do you think of this place, boy?" She patted his neck, "Think we're gonna be happy here?" Alex wondered how the horse assimilated the events of the past few days. His surroundings had changed dramatically from the well-kept Seattle boarding stable where he'd spent the last five years. Alex ran her hands over his body, and down each leg, checking again for any injuries from the rough trailer trip. Viento welcomed her touch and beneath human fingers horseflesh quivered. Not only were there no scratches or swelling, his friskiness convinced her that he was content in his new home. The inviting smell of coffee drifted through the door, so she released him into the corral and returned to the kitchen.

Alex filled a large mug and walked out the front door, ambling past her Jeep, to the far edge of the road where the mountain dropped away into a steep gorge. Her view was unmarred by any sign of humanity. Steam rising from the mug joined her own breath, and curled up and away in a small cloud. Alex surveyed her wilderness while the mug warmed her hands, and each sip warmed her inside.

The gorge ran north and south and formed a rugged "V", whose walls joined in a sharp angle at the bottom. Across the chasm, the opposite wall dropped away even more steeply than where her cabin stood, no long-term structure would survive its incline. White and brown spots drifted across the rock face, mountain goats and big-horned sheep owned the vertical environment.

Alex scaled the mountainside with her eyes, getting acquainted with this neighbor. Deep vertical gouges in the granite, as large as boxcars and skyscrapers, sheltered masses of snow in their shadows. As the sun slowly rose, it illuminated the jagged wall in a wave of light that spread from top to bottom, altering the mood of the rocky incline. Bright areas faded to dark, shadows grew light, and the cliff came to life, an animated face of granite.

Suddenly, a huge boulder, larger than a bus, broke loose high above the tree line and started to roll. It gained momentum then collided with a tall granite outcropping, shattering it, and ricocheting into the air, bouncing in great arching strides. Alex was so far from the event that the sound of each pulverizing impact failed to reach her ear. Dropping below the tree line, it toppled several giant pines like a bowling ball mowing down ten pins. When the dust settled the boulder looked like it had been nestled amidst the broken trees for centuries.

Water in the valley floor caught the sunlight's reflection and exploded into a sparkling, glittering chain, but its distance from Alex was so great that she couldn't tell if it was a small stream or a raging river. The grand magnitude of her surroundings offered no point of reference.

And so it was with everything in her line of sight. Higher, bigger, farther away. These mountains clearly towered above those of her youth and the view was dizzying. Nowhere in the Pacific Northwest had she seen such jagged peaks, sheer cliffs, and massive crags of granite—knife-sharp wilderness carved by the hand of some ancient god, to stand forever. The vastness overwhelmed, and Alex felt sublimely insignificant.

Man had visited these mountains for decades, and survived, even profited, but he had never mastered them. The power of this place allowed him to compete, but never win. Alex knew there were areas less remote, that were logged off as bald as clearcuts in the Cascades, stripped naked, but they were miles from where she stood. Man's mark, if he left one, was not evident here.

Alex suddenly realized that hers were the only human eyes that had witnessed the boulder's crashing plunge down the cliff and her absolute isolation suddenly loomed in front of her, threatening and ominous. A hundred disasters paraded through her mind—accidents, injury, illness, each image more perilous for her solitary situation. If she screamed or yelled, no human ear would catch the sound.

She was alone.

What she felt at that moment was not fear, but an alarming sense of reality. She took a deep breath to clear her head, mentally distancing the potential disasters as far beyond consciousness as possible. She was accomplished at this. In recent months she had buried many events and memories in the pitch-black recesses of her mind.

The remaining coffee in her mug was cold when she finally turned back to the cabin. She took one step, looked up, and gasped. Her mug hit the ground with a dull thud.

Standing directly in front of her, halfway to her front door, was a bull elk, larger than any she had ever seen. He was grazing across what could be called her front yard, and her movement and noise brought his head up instantly.

The bull outweighed her by seven hundred pounds, although they stood eye-to-eye. His growing rack of antlers was already three feet across, and his well-muscled body suggested he was accustomed to its weight. He showed no fear, and if he was surprised by her, his posture didn't reveal it. His demeanor communicated years of experience in his environment. He had survived many winters.

Face to face they stood, unmoving; him, curious about this new two-legged creature in his domain, her, amazed by his stately bearing and fearlessness. Only a few yards separated them and Alex could see the varied shades of tan and fawn, gray and sepia, that made up his coat, as well as the rich chocolate brown of his mane. Fuzzy velvet still sheathed the points of his antlers and, as large as they were, Alex knew their greatest growth was yet to come. This old bull would be magnificent by fall.

She watched the elk investigate her. He inhaled her scent with a loud snort, nostrils flared, and ears twitched, focusing on her. The spark of light in his large brown eyes drifted up and down as he studied her body. Constant chewing—an action that was both vertical and horizontal—accompanied this inspection.

A forgotten childhood feeling returned to Alex, and she was instantly aware of how long it had been absent from her life. But she clearly remembered the first day she felt it, standing with her dad on Hurricane Ridge, watching Olympic elk race through an alpine meadow. They had flown across the new grass, antlers high, touching the earth for only an instant before defying gravity in another arcing leap. The feeling was very old. A tingling at the base of the neck, breath held, pulse quickening. Wonder? Discovery? Yes, all of that, plus a sense of privilege, to be a human present at a great non-human moment. The old memory was so strong it raised goosebumps on her arms. And it abolished the anxiety of the previous hour.

When the old bull's curiosity was satisfied, he turned and stalked into the trees. Unhurried, he left her as silently as he had come.

Chapter Twenty-four

The dresser drawers did stick when Alex tried to open them, but after she rubbed soap on the tracks they slid smoothly. Including this chore it still took her less than an hour to unpack her clothes. Organizing her work area—books, maps, computer, and microscope—on the workbench along the back wall consumed more time. When she paused to look at her new home, bits and pieces of her life looked back, safe mementos of friends and family.

Pre-Stephen.

Viento watched her intently as she carried his tack from the trailer and stored it in the stable. He tossed his head and whinnied when he recognized the sight and smell of his own things.

"Want to go for a ride, boy?" He trotted back and forth along the fence, tail up, head high.

"Okay, give me a couple minutes to finish up and we'll check out the neighborhood."

Binoculars, maps, and a water bottle joined her jacket hastily jammed into the saddlebags, and Viento skittered around like a colt while she tried to saddle him. He felt the same exhilaration that buoyed her.

Matt had pointed out two trailheads leading away from the cabin that intersected a shifting network of smaller animal tracks and pathways. One followed the line of the road, continuing laterally along the side of the valley. The elk had taken this trail.

The second entered the forest behind the cabin, at the edge of the clearing visible from her back window. This was a challenging three-hour hike to the summit, but Matt told her the view from the top would help her get oriented in the mountains, so this was the direction Alex chose. Horse and rider set out just after noon. The sky was clear blue and where sunshine touched her, it was warm.

Viento trotted through the clearing, itching for a full gallop, but Alex held him in check. Pine needles camouflaged fallen tree branches and squirrel holes, nasty traps for a galloping horse. Viento snorted his displeasure and tossed his head, eager to run.

"Whoa, boy, not here." He pranced and chomped on the bit, pressing her beyond a trot.

"Viento, slow down." Her firm hand and voice ruled the moment, and by the time they entered the trees he had drawn up to a brisk walk.

Animal sounds floated through the trees, some sharp, some muffled. A small creature scurried away, low to the ground. A sudden thrashing jerked a bush, then was silent. Alex looked hard each time in the direction of the noise, but saw nothing. Her eyesight was perfect, but she felt blind under the dark green canopy. She envied Viento. These were wild sounds, uncommon to a city dweller, but the horse responded to each with a different level of interest, as if he knew what they were.

The mustang, to a greater degree than Alex, received and evaluated each scent and sound. Bark skittered to the ground as a squirrel raced up a tree... Pine needles crunched beneath his hooves, releasing their pungent smell... A jay screamed his rage at their trespassing... And from somewhere nearby, the scent of fresh deer droppings awakened an old memory. Alex watched his ears scan like radar, thirteen pairs of muscles moving each one independently, forward and back, to the side, then forward again.

Viento was born on the open prairie of Wyoming, and in his first year of life saw no man or barn. The diet of his parents—rough buffalo grass and spring water supplemented by minerals licked from the ground—filled his belly after his dam weaned him. It made him tough. Sharp senses of hearing and smell kept him alive, and he learned early to detect predators or find water miles away. At eighteen months of age he was more clever than any domestic horse would be, fully grown. The first time Alex saw him he was racing a group of colts across flat prairie, easily dodging their playful bites, always in the lead. Viento flew over the ground like the wind, and in the tongue of his Spanish ancestors, wind is what she named him.

The trail climbed modestly steep, easier for horse than human. Trees thinned after a couple hours and forest sounds faded away until they broke out into open space. They were above the tree line and the backbone of the mountain rose directly ahead. There was a strong breeze and from the looks of the leaning shrubs around them, it blew constantly.

Alex dismounted and Viento dawdled behind her, performing his own investigation, nose to the ground. But there was no graze here, just chips and chunks of granite in all sizes. She hiked the last few hundred feet to the highest point and climbed on a boulder to take in the view.

Sunlight sliced through the gathering clouds in isolated shafts, spotlighting particular peaks and valleys. Alex faced west, and, while there were a few mountains higher than eye-level, she was very close to the top of the world. Although hundreds of miles stretched before her, she imagined the Pacific Ocean just beyond the farthest summit.

Time and distance lost their meaning from her stone perch. What value were minutes in a place that marked its age in centuries? Or miles, when your mind's eye could embrace both edges of the continent?

The afternoon drifted lazily by as she studied her maps and found landmark peaks and valleys, orienting herself within the geography. Her spirit also settled, content, at peace.

Only when the wind came up did she notice the time. Almost 5:00, the sun was setting fast and it would be dark in minutes.

She was three hours from the cabin.

She whistled for Viento and when he cantered up she put on her windbreaker, checking the pockets for gloves. There were none.

"How could I have been so stupid?" she muttered. Viento's ears twitched at the sound of her voice. "And I didn't even bring a flashlight!" She mounted and turned the horse toward the trail.

Dusk softened the shadows as they dropped back into the trees and the temperature fell as fast as the sunlight vanished. 40 degrees... 35 degrees... 30 degrees...

Below-freezing cold. Dry, clear, bone-numbing cold.

Alex had only the clothes she was wearing. No gloves. No light to read the trail map in her saddlebags. Her mind raced.

Damn, there was only a quarter moon last night, not much help, even if the clouds break. And how many animal trails did we pass that intersected ours? Seven? Eight?

Plenty of opportunity to get lost.

Lost! The word blasted into her brain, foreign and frightening. Alex didn't *get* lost, she searched for other people who were lost. She exhaled slowly, to control her rising alarm.

"I think I have a little problem here, V."

In her haste to explore her new home Alex had been careless, and now her heartbeat accelerated, keeping time with her anxiety.

"You might be okay spending a night out here, my friend, but I'm not exactly dressed for it." She took a deep breath and icy air frosted her lungs. The next breath was slow and shallow.

"We have to get back to the cabin, boy." She was barely whispering, but the horse heard shivering in her words and fear between them.

She leaned forward and rested icy palms on his muscled neck for a full minute, considering her options. There were few. Alex knew with clinical certainty that this cold could kill.

"I think I really screwed up here, V." She frowned. "Do you remember the way back?" She shook her head, not optimistic the mustang had retained his wild instincts.

I have no choice.

So Alex relaxed her grip on the reins and gave Viento his

head. He had never demonstrated the instincts she now had to trust, and releasing control to him compounded her anxiety.

Viento was confused when the reins fell loose, unsure without her firm hand. She clucked to him and he took one hesitant step, then another, eventually settling into a slow walk. Alex's eyesight was useless, she couldn't see past the mustang's cloud of exhaled breath, and she had no sense of direction in the dark. The absolute blackness of the forest created a unique claustrophobia, trees closed in, branches slapped her face.

I don't remember branches at eye-level on the way up...

Alex was shivering when indigo faded to black, and thirty minutes later her shaking was constant and uncontrollable. Fumbling fingers unrolled the heavy turtleneck of her sweater up past her nose, but breathing through the wool only made the cold air condense into ice crystals, freezing the knit into a gooey mass around her mouth. The lightweight jacket stopped the wind, but offered no warmth. Her Levi's wicked away what little body heat she generated, and the stiff denim rubbing against her bare legs felt like ice.

Without gloves her fingers grew numb and cramped in position, gripping the reins. Then she couldn't move her toes. All unprotected flesh—nose, ears, eyelids, fingers—ached, then went numb. Alex had been cold before, but nothing compared to this, and it frightened her.

The possibility of frostbite compounded the fear that she was lost, and Alex tasted her own panic, bile rising in her throat.

How much time's passed since we left the summit? The ride up took about three hours, maybe we're close... if we're on the right trail. She brought her watch close to her face to read the glowing hands on the small dial. 6:05! Only an hour! How could it get so dark, and so cold, so fast?

"Damn!" Viento stopped in his tracks, and his head came up abruptly. "Sorry, boy, not you." She clucked again and he settled back into his careful walk.

He should be getting hungry, that might help him find the cabin. In Seattle Mom and Dad are sitting down to dinner about now...

Viento felt her shivering, smelled her fear, and, confused by her lack of control, tensed. Alex was barely aware of his muscles tightening and collecting. Ready to run.

Well, some of his instincts are still strong.

Slivered moonlight appeared intermittently between the shifting clouds, teasing her with a flash of light, only to disappear again. Each time the darkness that followed seemed blacker. Alex hunched down over Viento's withers, hands pulled up inside stretched-out sweater sleeves and tucked close to her stomach.

Her eyes watered and her teeth chattered.

The cold forced her into the nearest thing to a fetal position that she could form and stay in the saddle. If Viento bolted now, he would leave her in the trail behind him.

Ominous night sounds replaced day sounds and Alex remembered that most large predators were nocturnal. Owls hooted overhead and the thrashing in the bushes that was interesting hours earlier, terrified her now.

Creatures died in that sound.

Every wind-rustled bush became a lynx, or a cougar, or a bear. Or one of their victims.

"Alex, this is a great way to begin a new career! Lose a few fingers to frostbite! Oh yes, Danni will love this!" She feigned boldness, but her voice rang hollow.

She stopped talking. Viento's ears were focused on her, listening to her babble, instead of concentrating on the trail. Distracting him was not wise, and even she could hear the fear in her voice. Like a terrified child whistling in the dark.

Suddenly a cougar screamed, ripping the darkness behind her. The shriek slammed against human eardrums already tensed for any threat. Alex's stomach knotted, then cramped, and she squeezed her eyes shut against a new wave of panic, desperate to find some mental calm. Not possible.

The lion's scream shattered the last vestige of mental control, and bloody images of animal attacks and gruesome deaths tumbled through her mind, a new dimension to her fear.

Have I ever heard of a cougar attacking a horse and rider? Has THAT cougar ever seen a horse and rider? How many large predators inhabit this mountain, and how hungry are they?

The irony of her situation might have been amusing under other circumstances—that was exactly what she was sent here to find out.

She exhaled the breath she had been holding (how long she couldn't remember) and tried to breathe calmly.

Get control, Alex!

She thought it like a mantra, over and over. *Control, Alex, control.*

Then the howling started.

Closer than the lion. Much, much closer. First one wolf, then another. Then others joined the first two, until she lost count. At least four. And the haunting sound was not stationary, it floated and darted, each canine voice never heard twice from the same direction. The cacophony swept through the trees, over and around her, driving ahead, advancing. Branches swished closeby with a rhythm of bodies passing.

Toward her.

The rustling came closer, grew louder until she could hear their panting. No howls now, only short, soft cough-barks signaling to each other, wolfen echolocation. Twigs snapped under their weight on both sides of the trail and, in brief moonlit moments, Alex caught glimpses of fur among the branches.

Matt's words from the previous day that might have relieved her fear were buried in a part of her brain she was not occupying at that moment.

Alex inhaled, and held her breath again. Sweat appeared on her numb skin and she trembled, a primal response to her fear, like shivering against the cold. An occasional growl interrupted the panting, pinpointing a single wolf's proximity. That predatory voice terrified her as it would any prey.

This nightmare walked and breathed, had shape and form, was clever and organized. And it, too, had a brain.

When moonlight illuminated a pair of glowing eyes

floating in the darkness a few feet away, terror paralyzed Alex. Her pulse throbbed and pounded in her brain like a jungle drum, light years beyond cognitive reason and rational thought. Like a deer in the headlights, her fear froze all movement.

Oh God, this is worse than being lost! Or trusting V.! Or even frostbite!

Alex squeezed her eyes shut to keep from crying and kept them closed for a long time. If Viento could smell her fear, so could the wolves.

She slumped over the saddlehorn, pressed her face into the horse's mane, and started making deals with God.

"If you get us out of this..."

Chapter Twenty-five

Viento demonstrated less alarm than Alex. He was tense and his ears twitched, but there was no panic in his stride. His pace increased to a brisk walk, but he did not bolt.

The wild instinct of his ancestors identified the wolves' presence less like a chase, than an escort.

But Alex failed to notice his reaction so it brought her no relief.

Minutes ticked by as slow as centuries. When Viento finally stopped in front of the corral, the wolves had vanished and the woman on his back was not the same woman that rode out with him that afternoon. A quivering mass of terror straddled the mustang, and what little confidence she brought to the mountains, was left on the trail that night.

Alex Davidson had been changed.

She slid out of the saddle and when her boots touched the ground her knees buckled. Stiff cold legs could not support her weight and she fell. Shaking, she pulled herself up the fence hand over hand, until she reached the top crossbar. Numb fingers, cold useless appendages, refused to respond to mental direction and struggled to work the simple latch to open the gate.

Not once did Alex look behind her. Her terror forbid it.

So she never saw the white wolf leap into the clearing and stop, a blue-gray phantom against the trees. He watched the woman-horse creature separate into two beings. Incomprehensible. White nose slightly raised, nostrils twitching, he tasted their merging scents, then bounded away.

Viento followed Alex through the dutch-door like a devoted puppy, head down from his own tense exhaustion. He ambled into his stall while Alex shuffled across the room to the light switch where she collapsed against the wall, hitting the switch with her elbow. Welcome light flooded the stable. Trembling, she rested there for several minutes, eyes closed, an attempt to banish the demons.

She gasped when she looked at her hands. Her fingers were white, deathly white, and hard to the touch. They didn't even feel like flesh. In stark contrast, the palms of her hands were pink and a sharp line defined where the blood has stopped flowing to her fingers. She was bleeding from a gash in her right hand, an injury she could not feel or recall.

Alex Davidson, veterinarian, recognized frostbite and realized in an instant the true dimensions of her carelessness. She began to whimper.

Viento stood patiently as her shaking fingers fumbled with his girth, unable to loosen the familiar knot. Liquid brown eyes looked around at her, puzzled by the delay.

"I can't undo it, boy," she whispered, then leaned her forehead against his flank.

"But I can't leave you like this," she tugged again at the knot, "not after you got us home." She tried repeatedly to make her fingers grip the stiff leather as the sweat on Viento's coat began to dry. Unsuccessful.

"Damn!" Frustrated, she pulled her keys out of her pocket and put the Swiss Army knife near her mouth. Gripping the cold edge of the largest blade in her teeth, she opened it. With both hands wrapped around the knife, she sliced through the girth just below the buckle. Alex put her shoulder against the saddle and shoved it off the mustang into the straw, leaving it where it landed. Manipulating the knife she managed to unbuckle Viento's bridle and it, too, landed on the floor. Immediately Viento stuck his nose in his water bucket, but jerked it back.

"What's the matter, V.?" Alex looked into the bucket and saw her own reflection in the ice that had frozen over his water. "It's even below freezing in here." She spotted a scrap of wood, a chunk of 2x4, against the wall of the adjacent stall. Wrapping both arms around it she smashed the ice in Viento's bucket and he instantly began sucking and gurgling great swallows of water. It was a comforting sound. No howling wolves or screaming cougars inside these walls, just Viento's sloppy drinking.

The tears came slowly at first, then in great wrenching sobs Alex released her pent-up terror. She flopped one arm over Viento's neck and cried, her tears mingling with his sweat.

"Viento," she whimpered, "what are we doing here? I almost got us killed!" She looked at her hands, "and now this!" He raised his head to grab hay from the hanging rack above him and looked around at her, jaws working a mouthful of food. Ears twitched, rotated, then centered on the only human he had ever trusted, confused by her alarm. They were home now, safe, there was food and water, and they would soon be warm, what more was there to fear? She touched his face and he whickered in response, a deep, gentle, chest sound, like a mare comforting her foal. Alex grabbed his blanket and tossed it over the mustang's sweaty sides, unable to brush him out properly.

About that moment the numbness in her limbs started to wear off, and a dull ache gradually took over arms and legs. Alex grimaced as she staggered into the cabin, anticipating the pins-and-needles sensation of returning bloodflow. The pain of taking her boots off took her breath away, but she knew the worst was still ahead.

Tears of fear gave way to tears of throbbing pain as feet and hands burned and tingled back to life. It was all she could do to put fresh wood in the stove and ignite it before she collapsed into one of the chairs. Desperate for warmth, she leaned towards the stove, palms facing the fire, and rocked her body back and forth. She groaned through the rising pain and tried to remember the proper treatment for frostbite.

Re-warm quickly? Yes, that's right. What else? Do not rub. Okay, I won't rub. There's something else... What is it?

Events of the day ricocheted inside the doctor's mind. *How could I be so naive to think I could live out here by myself? What a fool! I didn't even last one day!* A sob made it past her lips, the only sound inside the log walls.

Stabbing pain in her hands and feet intensified with each pulse of fresh blood into icy flesh. The throbbing was rhythmic, and it took all her will not to rub her hands together.

Alex stared into the cast-iron box at the dancing flames and old nightmares rose to dance with them...

Stephen in bed with Sheryl...

losing her clinic...

the divorce...

the doctors...

Each memory overlaid the previous one, mounting failures and vulnerability, heaping inadequacies and fear, the ashes of her life collected like a pile of black cinders beneath the stove.

New images joined them. From the caged inferno a pair a wild eyes—unblinking wolf eyes—stared at Alex and she was caught in their hypnotic spell, a mirage of her pain and terror. The images began to shift and merge until she saw Stephen, with wolf eyes, laughing at her helplessness. In that moment all the frightening and hurtful events blended into one oozing lava flow that threatened to destroy the last fragment of Alex Davidson.

"Leave me alone," she whispered, "please!" She jumped out of the chair to clear her mind and pain exploded in her feet.

"Oh God!"

Light-headed, she leaned on the chair for support and her eyes fell on the radio on the table, but she knew help could not reach her tonight.

Push warm liquids. Yes! That's the other thing for frostbite! I'll make tea. Just have to heat some water. I can do this. I... can... do... this.

On partially numb feet she hobbled to the kitchen, bent at the knees, hunched over like a woman three times her age, broken in body as much as spirit. While she waited for the small gas stove to heat the water, she washed out the gash in her hand. Even the most routine act required her complete concentration and she struggled to open her medical bag. She applied antiseptic clumsily, but a bandage was beyond possible. Then her eyes fell on the other things in the bag. Drugs. Animal drugs. And her drugs.

I have to get some rest. I need to sleep tonight. I'll only take a couple.

She stared at the Valium bottle on the counter next to the mug and tea bag for several seconds. Then, with the same hammer she had used that morning to hang pictures of her family, she smashed the plastic bottle, knowing she would never get the child-proof cap off. Pills scattered across the counter with shards of amber plastic, and at that moment the teakettle whistled, an alarm signaling yet one more wrong decision.

She quickly filled the mug with water and dragged the tea bag up and down until it was the same amber as the pill bottle. One club-like hand scooped several pills into the other, and then into her mouth. The first swallow of tea washed them down. With both hands she carried the mug back to the chair in front of the stove, covered herself with the blankets from her bed, and curled up in a fetal position.

Only a few pills. Not too many. I can't overdose on Valium and die, anyway. Not possible.

The pack had vanished when White-cub returned to the trail. He hesitated only a moment before turning away and, nose to the ground, retraced the steps of the woman-horse creature. Canine curiosity was triggered by an old memory... something long ago... something very bad... that hovered at the edge of his mind. Beyond recall.

The scent was easy to follow, but it puzzled him. Sometimes the smell of horse dominated human. It was new, with no history to draw upon. He typed the animal as a grazer, ungulate, potential food. Non-predator. Like deer, but not deer. In other places the human scent was stronger, and at those locations the white wolf paused, nostrils hovering over the smell, to summon the memory that drifted without clear form in his brain. Almost familiar.

White-cub reached the mountaintop where Alex had

stopped and he canvassed the area, nose to ground, for every nuance of the new creature. He found fresh horse droppings, a shrub that had been munched, and then he came to the boulder.

Alex's scent was strongest where she had rested, and when White-cub reached it he inhaled the sharp odor for several seconds, but only fuzzy images of snow and ice and moonlight returned to him. And a quickening of the pulse. The wolf's brain stretched into the mist of his before-time, but found no match. No reason for the apprehension racing through his blood.

He leaped off the boulder and returned to his family, the new mystery buried under his more immediate hunger and the familiar scent of the pack's fresh kill. Warm meat. A full belly.

While he ate, barometric pressure dropped, clouds collided, and spring's only large storm exploded over the mountains. Thunder, lightning, and pelting rain demanded his immediate attention.

Chapter Twenty-six

Alex was right, she couldn't die of an overdose of Valium, but awakening from the drug-induced sleep was its own punishment. Grogginess held her mind captive for several minutes and there was an awful taste in her mouth. Her hair was matted against her scalp and her clothes from the previous day were stuck to her skin and reeked. Muscles and bones ached from sleeping in a knotted position, and for a full minute she wondered where she was.

Brutal awareness hit her when her left foot touched the floor. Pain screamed from ankle across instep to sole, from arch to toes and heel. She gasped and looked down. A bright red club of flesh with five swollen sausage toes rested on the braided rug. She didn't recognize it as her own foot. She pulled the other one from under the blanket with the same nerve-jangling reaction and put it next to the left. They matched, but looked foreign connected to her leg.

All this was a major challenge to a mind struggling to regain consciousness. But the jolt of pain brought recollection, and the previous night came rushing back. She groaned, as much from the memory, as the pain, which settled to a constant throbbing level, the maximum she could handle without screaming.

I need a bath. And food. I need to feed Viento.

She withdrew one arm from the blankets and winced from the pain in her hand. She could reach fresh wood from the chair so she tossed it into the stove, a move that brought supreme agony to the top half of her body.

Come on, catch fire, damn it!

As if it heard her thoughts, the large split of wood ignited. She leaned back in the chair.

Thank God! And I need to go home.

She looked around the room and depression replaced the elation of the previous day. Like a black pestilence, it murdered yesterday's good intentions. An eternity had passed since she woke feeling so right about her presence in the mountains.

Outside rain fell steadily, the conclusion to last night's storm, and the light was subdued, already afternoon. She looked briefly at the radio, to call for help, but thoughts marched to more immediate concerns. Like walking.

I can do this. I have to do this. I can't sit in this chair forever. Let's see, hands and knees?

She slid out of the chair until her knees rested on the rug. The pain was intense, but tolerable. She crawled on her knees and forearms back to the kitchen.

Connecting the water hose at the sink was a supreme challenge, and the effort almost defeated her when she became light-headed standing on one foot leaning against the counter. But she succeeded in screwing on the hose and staying conscious, and hot water filled the old porcelain tub. Her clothes landed in a heap and she eased her battered body into the water.

Warm water on hands and feet brought a new shade to her palette of pain, but it subsided. Or maybe her tolerance was growing stronger. She inspected her body inch by inch, clinically, and was amazed at the bruises and scratches she had acquired in just twenty-four hours. In addition to those on her face, there were purple bruises on both knees and her forearms were equally marked. The frostbite had reached the swollen stage, stretched red skin, painful to the touch, unrecognizable as part of her body. She knew red indicated perhaps the damage wasn't permanent and she might not lose fingers and toes. And she knew only time would tell.

But her nakedness in the water did not reveal the greatest injury. Alex had never known fear like the previous night's terror, and it scarred her spirit as surely as frostbite now marked her body.

Wilderness, the one place she had always felt competent and safe, no longer welcomed her.

She kept adding hot water to the tub and after a long soak was able to move more easily. Her joints weren't so stiff, even though her extremities still throbbed.

From the tub her eyes caught the shattered pill bottle on the counter and a measure of guilt joined her broken mental state. Alex's spirit had suffered defeat at every level and while she soaked away the sweat and filth of her ordeal, the depression of it took root. This she could not wash away.

She heated a can of tomato soup after her bath and settled into her chair, wrapped in a large warm bathrobe. The familiar smell calmed her nerves.

She saw Danni's package on the table and shuffled across the room to retrieve it.

Two books fell into her lap when she tore open the brown paper, a thin paperback and a large old hardcover book she recognized immediately. Her Bible. The one she had dutifully memorized verses out of as a child and challenged as an adult.

I know what to expect here, this can wait.

A note was on top of the books—

"Alex, I still think this 'find yourself in the woods' plan is a bad idea, but since your mind's made up, and since I won't be there to complain and whine, (read bitch and nag) I've sent a few friends to do it for me.

I love you, sis, but I think you took a lot of unfinished business to the mountains with you. Emotional business, if you know what I mean. You will have to work out your problems by yourself, and I think you're gonna learn a new definition for 'alone' up there in the boonies. There's good stuff in these books, yes, even the Bible you left at Mom and Dad's years ago. Listen to them, Alex.

I know you'll do great work and make us all proud. Just remember to take care and stay safe. Your sister loves you." It was signed simply, "Danni".

Make you proud? Stay safe? Oh, I've done very well in my first couple days, Danni, you'd be VERY proud.

Alex's sarcasm was as sharp as her pain.

The paperback was unfamiliar, and the book lover in her

would not let it go unexamined. It took her completely by surprise. "The Greatest Salesman in the World", by somebody named Og Mandino.

Danni, you really got me this time, 'greatest salesman'? What is this? Og Mandino? That can't be his real name.

The cover talked of ten ancient scrolls and how they could change your life.

Right.

She opened the thin book near the middle and read, "I was not delivered into this world in defeat, nor does failure course in my veins... I will persist until I succeed. Always I will take another step," Alex looked at her swollen feet. "...In truth one step at a time is not too difficult."

It was dark and her soup was cold when she put the book down, consumed cover to cover. Eyes focused on her swollen hands and feet, while thoughts focused on unexamined territory, the dangerous and unexplored terrain of her own life. Silent minutes passed, sweet memories were recalled and embraced, bitter ones endured, and discarded, events weighed and tallied. Then Alex took a deep breath and, in a whisper barely audible to herself, said,

"I will not run away from another home. I will survive. I will stay here and do my job because I gave my word. And I will not run. I... will... not... run! This... is... my... home!"

It was not high drama, just the first step in a new direction for a battered soul.

Alex never radioed for help, stubborn pride kept her silent. But it also kept her there. She spent the days of her recuperation studying field guides until she could identify the local plants, and the different tracks and signs of indigenous wildlife.

For ten days Alex suffered the uncertainty of her frostbite, but the uncertainty about her future dissolved with winter's melting snow. The unfinished emotional business she brought with her was still there, now keeping close company with a new dark terror that ran on four legs and hunted in packs.

She would face them all.

For the first time Alex Davidson acknowledged their presence, and, she could look at the wounds that bore their names without blinking.

At least for a few minutes.

Chapter Twenty-seven

The warm El Nino current in the Pacific combined with Earth's tilt to wreak havoc across North America. Annual winds that escorted moisture-laden clouds to the Canadian Rockies never crossed the Cascades and the Coast Range, so the spring rains that traditionally soaked White-cub's territory never materialized. Temperature records were broken again, 90, 95, 100 degrees. Some days sweltered even higher, and the summer solstice marked the end of a spring that never came.

Melting snow provided enough water to quench the first thirst of trees and plants breaking their dormant fast, but just enough. Thimbleberry and salmonberry blossoms dried and floated to the ground before bees could pollinate them. Alder and aspen, cascara and ash, stretched and yawned back to life, clothing themselves in delicate greens. But when roots could no longer find water, new leaves withered, browned, curled, and finally dropped.

Steadfast and vertical, evergreens alone defied the drought. Fir and spruce, pine and cedar recorded centuries not seasons, and dark patches of earth beneath them provided the only shade.

Remote water sources, mountain ponds and feeder creeks, dried up in the blazing sun. But the madness that comes to thirsty mammals would not be ignored so, with the variety of Noah's ark, animals congregated at the river that would not have done so before the drought. Cougar and bear muddied the same water, while deer and moose sated their thirst within kill range. A tenuous truce prevailed along the river and the wolves joined this congregation of survival.

Animals with the capacity to sweat cooled rising body temperatures quickly, but the spiraling heat tormented the wolves. Panting brought only limited relief and they moved slowly or not at all during the scorching midday hours. Sides heaving, tongues hanging out, they rested in the shade and waited for sundown.

Thick fur that had protected them against winter's freeze threatened to suffocate. Scratching and shaking and squirming fish-like on their backs released the undercoat, tufts and clumps at a time. The rabbit-soft fluff drifted on the sultry air until captured by some naked twig or branch, flora and fauna joined in an unholy union, wolf fur sprouting where leaves should be. During the shedding process the wolves' mangy appearance contributed nothing to their dignity, but in a fortnight it was over and only stiff guard hairs covered canine skin.

The shed cooled their bodies but also exposed them to new enemies. Armies of voracious insects attacked without mercy, deer flies and botflies feasted on the easy blood in ear tips and tender nose flesh. Oozing bites scabbed over each night, only to be opened at sunrise by a renewed assault. Fleas and ticks also proliferated, fattened on the blood of their warm-blooded hosts. The wolves scratched and bit themselves to ease the itch but canine claws and teeth were grossly inadequate against the pinhead-size assailants. Only evening and romps in the river brought Guardian and the pack relief from the insects.

The fir tree hovered forty-five degrees between parallel and perpendicular, losing its grip on the receding riverbed one dirt clod at a time. By winter it would be horizontal, and dead. The lowest, longest branches scraped the riverbottom and gentled the rush to an eddy, creating a sheltered pool. Green needles shaded green water, cool and dark. Sunlight danced on the surface in chaotic darting flashes filtered through exposed roots and branches.

White-cub discovered the protected alcove in early summer and claimed it, marking its boundary with his urine. During the hottest hours he cooled himself, resting in the chest-deep water, hidden and alone. He had just started drinking when a foreign scream shattered the torrid day's silence.

Unfamiliar, loud and powerful, it rang exotic on White-cub's ear, an unidentifiable echo inside his brain. He lifted his head and froze, waiting. Water dripped from his chin and ripples collided with tree, and dirt, and fur, and died. The shriek came again, louder and nearer, commanding his attention, but still unrecognizable. White-cub waited behind the branches to see the creature who owned the voice.

The sound stopped and a bird, larger than any White-cub had ever seen, glided over the water without effort, casting a six-foot shadow. He cruised within inches of the surface, then abruptly splashed feet first into the water, and sank.

Seconds later the river, still churning from the plunge, released the beast. Wings pushed against water, muscle battling gravity to lift the colossal bird's wet weight. Vise-like talons held a silvery trout writhing its deathdance.

Slowly, the massive bird struggled to rise to tree height, where he landed gracefully on one foot. He pressed the fish against tree bark with the other foot, pivoting his third toe to form opposing pairs of claws. Inescapable. With a curved beak he ripped off ragged chunks of fish flesh and swallowed them.

White-cub studied the bird from his sheltered blind. Dark wings and back framed a dusty white chest and the streamlined body was easily supported on oversized blue-gray legs. Black claws, curved and sharp, gripped the branch. His white head was proportional to his body and a bold black stripe from orange eye to shoulder marked him. Between bites, he stretched his neck, ruffled his feathers, and shook, sending drops of water back into the river. Piercing eyes shifted and focused left, right, near, far out, searching the river for his next victim.

Meat consumed, the bird released the fish head and skeleton, which splashed into the river and floated slowly downstream. One more stretch and shake, then enormous wings unfolded and the flying superstructure stepped off the branch. There was no gliding on this attack, he plunged straight in, shimmering prey targeted from his perch. When he rose the wet bird did not pause to eat, but flew upstream, another flash of silver squirming in his claws. He screamed once and was gone.

White-cub had never seen an osprey. A gigantic bird that

swims. Curious.

He was still looking in the direction it had flown when the discarded fish head drifted into his alcove and canine senses investigated the bird-food. Nostrils twitched, almost touching it. He nudged the fine-boned skeleton out of the water and pawed it gently, turning it over and moving it with his nose.

Only when tongue slid across scales did canine brain identify it as meat. Food. The taste was unlike anything he'd ever eaten, but after he devoured it—bones, head, bits of skin and flesh—he wanted more. The bird had not left much on the carcass, just enough to whet the wolf's appetite. And his curiosity. Forgetting the midday heat White-cub bolted from his shelter and raced upriver after the bird.

He ran in the shallows where the traction was better and the splash cooled him. The osprey was out of sight but in the distance the strange call had resumed.

One call was answered by another and White-cub halted, mid-step. There were two of them. In his eagerness to taste the strange food again, he had not considered there might be more than one of the huge birds. With sharp beaks and claws. White-cub left the water for silent sand, no splash, no noise, and stalked cautiously around a forested bend in the river.

Ravens clustered on the gravel, hopping and cackling with excitement. They pecked the ground for bits of—what? White-cub watched the oily birds steal from each other with as little conscience as they had stolen his food when he was a cub. White-cub recognized the behavior as normal, and his eyes widened their search.

A large pine tree towered over the ravens. Clinging to one of the thickest branches was a mass of loosely woven sticks, twigs, branches, and forest litter stacked a meter high and almost a meter in diameter. The osprey's nest hovered over the river, defying the elements with the confidence of its residents. Wind and gravity should have toppled it long ago.

Canine eyes caught movement on a branch above the nest. A glint of light reflected off an orange eye. The osprey.

Then an identical striped head popped above the nest's edge. The mate. White-cub scanned the surrounding trees. Only two of them. Formidable, yes, but not life-threatening. Still cautious, he crept under the nest, immediately scattering the ravens in a noisy cloud of black. He ignored them, the smell of fish was intoxicating, and he pawed and licked the ground for any morsels. But the ravens were as thorough as they were selfish, the smell was an empty promise. No fish.

The wolf's strange behavior intrigued the ospreys and they watched him intently for several minutes. He had no talons or beak, and the shadow he cast was not large by their standards. And he could not fly. White-cub posed no threat to animals who owned the sky, so they assessed him harmless. Unaware of their scrutiny and frustrated by the absence of fish, White-cub sat down on the sandbar to sort out the bird-puzzle.

The male osprey's sudden scream ripped through the air, startling White-cub, who leapt to his feet just as the feathered beast plunged into the river in front of him. When the bird broke the surface with a fish in his grasp White-cub lunged at the trout, but his jaws snapped shut around nothing. Powerful wings slapped his face, and the creature's raging scream blasted through his skull, painfully loud. White-cub withdrew to dry ground, offended by this new insult while the osprey flew to the nest and presented his silvery offering to his mate, unruffled by the wolf's assault.

White-cub shook his head and rubbed his nose with one paw. Then he looked from water to bird, to water, and back to bird. Minutes later when the osprey dove again he remained seated, but attentive, and all afternoon he studied the bird's fishing technique as he had apprenticed under Patriarch and Cub-bearer on his first hunt.

Near dusk he waded into the stream where the osprey had hunted successfully and for several minutes he saw no fish. White-cub stood motionless—like when he analyzed a herd of hoofed prey before a chase—and slowly the fish returned, unaware of the danger hovering over them. Eager and hungry, he thrust his head beneath the water, mouth open, ready to strike. Jaws clamped shut with bone-crushing force. Around water. Failure again.

The osprey was the peak of evolutionary specialization, fish was his only food, so survival demanded the bird be well-engineered to catch them. White-cub was out of his element, and his initial attempts were pitifully uncoordinated. There was no finesse in his attack and his downward thrust often threw him off balance, dumping him in the river. White-cub's canine jaws were no match for the osprey's talons. Wrong tool, but could he make it work?

The greatest disparity between the two hunters was not weapons, but eyesight. The osprey's vision was eight times sharper than White-cub's, so he had the advantage of spotting the silvery prey from high above the water. Surprise attacks were the heavy artillery in his feathered arsenal.

Refraction also mystified White-cub. He could not understand why the fish he saw from the surface was never in that exact spot underwater. Over and over he lunged and fangs closed without success.

But while White-cub lacked the proper weapons, to his credit he had stamina and ingenuity. Without technical enlightenment, Patriarch's white son learned to move a bit left or right, forward or back, as he had learned to anticipate the movement of hoofed prey. Once he learned the trick, it was not forgotten and two days later a slippery trout failed to escape his jaws. He carried his catch to the sand where he held it down with a large paw until it stopped wiggling. Twice an iridescent tail slapped his nose when he tried to bite it, but White-cub devoured it with relish, as proud of this kill as any other. And it satisfied his hunger as much as any red meat.

White-cub spent hot days near the river feeding and cooling himself, and for the rest of the summer the drought affected him no more than it did the ospreys. He had discovered another food source. New knowledge, new experience.

Far away from the river's edge the drought rolled on and its death toll was grim. In the forest where water was only a memory, nursing does produced no milk. Teats dried and shrank; loose, useless skin offering no nourishment.

Unweaned fawns and the offspring of other parched animals died slowly, drawing one shallow breath after another. They had no defense against the oppressive heat, and those too weak to walk to shelter succumbed under the relentless sun, while their mothers watched from nearby shade.

The forest maintained an eerie silence as it grieved. Even the ravens were quiet, appropriately clad in mourning black. Moss hung from the giant evergreens like widow's rags, and no bird's song broke the oppressive stillness of the daytime hours.

Chapter Twenty-eight

Alex was aware of the summer drought, but only subliminally. She and Viento had plenty of food and water, and the thick cabin walls offered a cool refuge from the heat. And there were other issues occupying her.

Alex was frail when she arrived in the mountains, and a month later she was more so. Fear had established a beachhead, and it caged her inside the cabin as securely as a lock on the door. Self esteem and confidence seeped away and the primary thought occupying her mind was her own survival.

She did not go outside.

For four weeks Alex fed and curried Viento without glancing at the damaged saddle, and each day she released him into the paddock without gazing at the clearing. Not once. Fear whispered that the wolves were out there. Sitting in the grass. Waiting for her.

Viento grew friskier each day he went without exercise. He nuzzled her ears, a game he had played as a colt, and pranced and pivoted around her hand on his halter. It was his invitation to run and Alex recognized it.

On the twenty-ninth day she looked at the saddle. Her hands ran over the familiar leather and its smell released a floodgate of sweet memories. During her undergraduate years she had worked at a riding stable and repairing tack was part of the job. She turned the sliced leather over in her hand, running her thumb along the cut edge. As her fingers moved to the familiar task her brain wrapped itself around her fear.

Why was I so frightened by the wolves that night? Was it just being lost and cold that made them so terrifying?

Again, the ghostly canines with their glowing eyes floated through her mind.

No, they were chasing us. Matt said they wouldn't hurt us, but how would he explain the fact they were chasing us?

While she finished repairing the girth a shadowy idea,

still unformed, tickled her consciousness, then was gone. She returned the saddle to its rack.

And why does just thinking about them scare me now?

Alex was more frightened by the demons she could not see than the ones she could, and her intellect fought yet one more battle with her emotions. To leave the cabin, or not? Only Viento's impatient stomping in the paddock broke the silence. She watched him pace back and forth. Left six strides, right six strides, left, right, over and over. Guilt and pity joined the argument raging in her mind and logic fought them all. To ride, or not?

On this day reason won.

Viento felt her trembling hands as she slipped the bridle over his ears and cinched the mended girth. On another day he would've stood still and made it easy for her, but he had not been out of the corral for a month, and the need to run dominated him like an itch desperate to be scratched.

"Viento, stand still!" He high-stepped around her, scratchy and anxious. Alex's voice rose in a tone both shrill and unfamiliar to the horse. It only added to his skittishness.

"What's gotten into you? Stop it!" He playfully moved away from her. "I mean it!" Alex's chastising was lost on the restless mustang. His nostrils flared with the smells of the road and his tail swished and snapped. His species had thrived by their wits and speed, and he needed to run like she needed to breathe. Horseflesh twitched eagerly, energy to burn. Head high, ears alert. Alex saw the fire in his eyes and softened to his dance. She combed her fingers through his forelock and smiled.

"You're right, my friend, I've neglected you." She rubbed his muzzle and soft equine lips played with her fingers. "It's been awhile since we had a good run." She scratched his face and he tossed his head, "Well, let's do something about that, okay?"

Viento spun away the second he felt her foot in the stirrup, and only skill kept Alex from falling. Inertia pulled her up and into the saddle, a single action smoothed by years of repetition.

The raw power bottled up in the mustang exploded, hooves digging into the dirt road. Pent-up energy fired the combustion of piston-strong legs, launching him to a full gallop instantly. His breath came fast, lungs sucking air with the rhythm of his gait. Muscles demanded oxygen and his big heart accelerated to feed their craving. Hot blood surged into tendon and cartilage, muscle and bone, fueling an equine machine in perfect tune.

To run, and run faster.

Alex centered her weight, thighs clinging to the animal between her legs, arms relaxed, elbows close to her body, reins firmly in hand. The position was second nature and gradually her tension eased. Alex and Viento had covered hundreds of miles in such an embrace.

The mustang thundered down the road, steel-hard cannon bones driving, pounding into the ground, raising small dust clouds at each point of impact. Viento was flying in the only sky he knew, and Alex gave him his head. He stretched his neck out, each stride longer than the preceding one, and Alex realized he would not be stopped. Memories of previous rides returned to her and after a few minutes she had no desire to stop him.

His exhilaration was contagious and she was caught up in his flight. Her heart raced with his, and the wind tossed Viento's mane in her face, snapping her cabin-bound spirit back to prickly consciousness. Faster, farther. One mile... two... three... vanished beneath them. Alex let him run, he was running for both of them and she knew it. For fleeting minutes, simple joy accompanied her again, an old friend, long absent.

After several minutes she eased Viento up and he slowed to a canter, then a trot, then a walk. The familiar smell of sweating horseflesh filled her nostrils, sweet scent to the horse lover. She stroked his neck.

"Good boy! You knew better than I did, what I needed." Viento nickered and shook his head to unseat a fly on his ear. Alex saw tracks in the soft dirt of the road and dismounted to investigate.

"Well, let's see if I've learned anything... there's elk, maybe that big guy we saw grazing in the front yard that first day. And that one's a small cat, probably a bobcat, see the two-two pattern?" Viento didn't see. He'd discovered a patch of grass and was analyzing it in equine fashion.

"...and he was here after the elk, the tracks overlap." Viento looked at her quizzically, content with the tone of her voice, ignorant of its meaning.

Alex started walking back to the cabin, eyes down, caught up by the story in the dirt.

"See here, V., a rabbit started across the road. Here's his front feet, one in front of the other and the two back feet landing ahead of them, side by side. He was running when he dodged hard to the left and into the bushes over there." Viento followed her, pausing when she paused to bend over a new print in the dirt.

"I wonder what that one is... it's pretty small, maybe a weasel, or a skunk... I'll have to check..." Her voice trailed off. They walked in silence for several minutes, Alex testing her new knowledge against the tale at her feet.

Then she saw it, the one track she had dreaded finding. But she had been a vet too long not to recognize the inverted heart-shaped heel pad and four symmetrical toes of a canine. A large canine...

Wolf.

She exhaled the breath she had been holding.

"So, this is your neighborhood, too?" she whispered. Her pulse quickened, fear returned, and her brief confidence vanished.

Kneeling, she reached toward it and her hand, hovering, barely covered the pawprint. Her voice was a whisper.

"You're so big..." Terror thundered back, transforming itself into a new daytime beast, different, but just as frightening as its nighttime cousin. Alex stood and spun around quickly, nervously, searching the forest for the hidden eyes she could feel.

Where are you? Why are you frightening me like this?

Her thoughts addressed wolves that were not there, and fear screamed at her to mount Viento and dash back to the cabin. Retreat. Where it was safe. New sweat ran down her back, her breath came fast and blood roared in her ears.

Then she glanced at Viento, munching on a patch of wild clover. Tail swishing, idly swatting flies. Relaxed. Unalarmed. Alex took a deep breath.

"There is nothing here to be afraid of, and I will not give in to this!" The defiant tone of her voice startled her, but broke the fearspell. One deep breath, another. Viento looked at her, puzzled, waiting for her say something he understood.

She looked down again and found other canine tracks, similar to the first, but none as large, all moving in the same direction.

They're my neighbors, no more or less than the deer, or the rabbit, or that other animal I don't know yet... And they were here first. I'm the outsider.

Again, a vague thought hovered at the edge of her mind, but before she could focus the idea clearly, it vanished. She felt it was significant.

"Let's go, V." She resumed her walking pace, afraid that if she mounted him, she'd panic. Other tracks caught her eye and her attention, but she kept moving, caught up in the mystery of the wolves' chase.

Why did they chase us that night? There's something here... What is it I'm not seeing?

Viento nudged her shoulder, dissatisfied with her lack of attention to him. When she stroked his neck the hovering thought blasted into her head, complete.

WHY DIDN'T VIENTO BOLT THAT NIGHT?

She stopped abruptly, turning to face the horse, one hand on either side of his bridle.

"Why weren't you afraid of the wolves? You didn't even run! What did you know that I didn't?" He tossed his head, uncomfortable with her demanding tone. Had he done something wrong? Face to face they stood, as if she could read his mind by looking into his large brown eyes. Then she started to chuckle.

"...as if you could tell me, huh boy?"

If Viento wasn't scared senseless by the wolves, why was I? Her fear started to feel foolish. The memory of that night eased into a mystery that occupied her mind, and that mental activity pushed the fear back into its dark corner.

That night she poured over her field guides.

Oh, a pine marten! Right! Well, almost a weasel. She sat cross-legged in one of the overstuffed chairs and gazed into the stove's flames. Summer nights were still cold enough to require it.

Why did the wolves chase us? The answer's in Viento's response to them, but what is it?

She sipped iced tea, reluctant to form the next thought. The only way to find out is to go back up there. We'll go tomorrow. Start early so we don't get caught after dark.

The fire popped, shooting a live spark onto the floor. Alex reached for it before it could burn the rug. A wolf howled far off in the night, and his lone voice raised goosebumps on her arms, in spite of the stove's warmth.

Or maybe we'll go the next day...

Chapter Twenty-nine

Sunlight was only an optimistic gray haze outlining the mountains when Alex woke up. For several minutes she wrestled with her decision to return to the summit. No one would know if she gave in to her fear, just like no one knew she hadn't left the cabin for a month. Fear was strong the first minutes after night's retreat.

Resolve put her feet on the floor and once out of bed, she didn't question her plan again.

Let's see, I'll take a daypack this time. Extra socks, gloves, hat. Right. Maps, field guides, flashlight and batteries, matches...

The list continued to write itself and her anxiety retreated to the shadows.

While coffee brewed, she brushed and fed Viento. The mustang swished his tail with anticipation when she reached for his saddlebags.

"Binoculars... a plastic tarp... a couple cans of Sterno..." They all disappeared into the leather pouches. Alex moved rhythmically around the small barn, reciting the list of the items she should've packed the first time.

"...nylon line ...candles..."

After a quick breakfast, she filled two water bottles and a thermos of coffee, and added them to the daypack with a bag of trail mix and three apples. Two for Viento. Then she dressed in layers, tank top under a long-sleeved shirt, then packed a sweatshirt and her anorak.

Finally, she retrieved a sealed plastic pouch from the glovebox of her car and packed it on end in the left saddlebag, nestling it gently between the plastic tarp and nylon cord, away from the solid fuel. It had never been opened, and she hoped she wouldn't need to open it today.

Alex lifted the saddlebags confirming the weight was evenly distributed, then saddled Viento. The mustang sensed that this ride was not for pleasure. This ride was business.

Serious work. Like the long trips back home where they found people that smelled of sweat and fear, and sometimes blood. While she strapped and buckled, Viento stood quietly, a soldier at attention, awaiting orders. Alex's mind ran through the list again.

"Oh yes, insect repellant!" She jammed it into the day pack, mounted, and pointed Viento towards the trailhead. The only four-legged creature visible in the meadow was the horse beneath her.

Four hot weeks had wrought an environmental change that surprised Alex. Snow was long-forgotten, and under the dark green canopy the air was hot and heavy and still. Not a breeze stirred the leaves and needles above. Not even the omnipresent jays interrupted the quiet and no small animals rustled through the bushes on the forest floor. Trees shaded woman and horse from direct sunlight, but offered no relief from the eerie stillness.

Alex noticed it all, but her thoughts were on the question at hand.

If the wolves didn't intend to attack us, why stalk us? And where were we when they found us? About halfway down, I think. She shook her head, frustrated. *There is an answer here somewhere, but how am I going to find it if I don't even know where to start looking?* She patted Viento's neck absent-mindedly.

"What told you that the wolves weren't hunting us?" His ears flicked back at the sound of her voice.

"Sound, maybe, or scent?" Viento plodded on at an easy walk and Alex searched the trail and bushes for any significant sign.

Where the trail was not covered with pine needles, it was soft dark dirt, and in those bare spots animal tracks trampled each other. Some of them Alex recognized, others she didn't, but she had no illusions that wolf tracks made four weeks ago would still be visible. The answer would be something else.

Halfway to the summit, or as close to halfway as she could estimate, Alex pulled Viento up at a widened part of the trail and dismounted.

"I think this is about the place." She stood silently, listening, watching, inhaling the hot earthy green around them.

The trail was a mass of tracks, but because the ground was compost-rich soil, bits of leaves and debris cluttered underfoot, making them incomplete and difficult to identify.

"I don't know, Viento, there's been a lot of traffic here, and it's all merged and jumbled." She knelt.

"That looks like deer... and there's another one." She looked around them at the bushes and trees on either side of the trail. Broken twigs, missing leaves and slight spaces between otherwise massed brush indicated a more remote animal track. Kneeling, she pulled back branches near the ground.

"Well, hello there," she whispered as her fingers traced the outline of a bear's paw. "...and you're a mama too!" Around the large, deep pawprint, tracks of at least one bear cub circled and trampled the female ursine's mark, rambling without direction while its mother's moved along a solitary line. Typical cub behavior. Alex had met bears in the wild before, occasionally by surprise, and it was not an experience she wished to repeat.

"We'll give you plenty of room, mama," she mumbled.

The bear's print, the only one clearly distinguishable, pointed her into dense brush. Only thinning groundcover and shrubs that didn't quite overlap each other, gave evidence of the passage of large beings. Alex sensed the trail beneath her, more than saw it. No map would record it.

Less than thirty feet from the main trail a clearing opened up, a rough circle of trampled grass and wildflowers surrounded by evergreens.

Alex recognized her answer the second she saw it.

The skull and antlers of a large elk lay near the center of the clearing, all flesh and fur, and most of the bones, had been devoured. Only the skull, one chewed-up hoof, and a few small bleached bone chips marked where the ungulate fell. Scat from several predators dotted the trampled grass, and it was no longer solid, but breaking down and whitening under the hot sun.

By the condition of the scat Alex knew the elk had been dead about a month.

She knelt over the skull and her eyes took in every detail. The bone was picked clean, except for two pair of teeth marks that punctured the face. Alex picked it up, running her fingers over the bone, recalling what she already knew about canine attacks. Feral dogs attack the face, probably wolves do the same. She measured the bite by covering the four indentations with her fingers. It was so large she had to use both hands.

She set the skull down gently and sat on the ground, hugging her knees, trying to picture the scene; the terrified elk crashing through the underbrush, one wolf clamped onto his nose, others circling, snapping, lunging at his legs until he stumbled, or they dragged him down. A slow agonizing death, natural and appropriate in the scheme of wilderness, but violent beyond human experience.

And then the feeding. Snarls and growls, as wolfen egos challenged one another for the choicest morsels. They were probably eating their victim before he was dead, tempers as hot as the blood pouring onto the grass, fangs snapping at each other as they had snapped at the elk seconds earlier. She looked back toward the main trail and was not surprised she could not see it through the dense foliage.

"I'll never know for sure, V., but maybe we came by right after the kill. Intruding while they were feeding." The skull in front of her was nature's only response.

Alex recalled that night's terror again and a slow smile ripened on her face. It grew larger and turned into a giggle, then a chuckle, then she opened her mouth and laughed out loud. Viento lifted his head from the sweet grass he'd discovered, curious at her outburst. Alex's laughter carried on the still air through the trees, a foreign sound in that place. For several minutes she laughed at herself and it released her fear. She walked over to the mustang and stroked his face affectionately.

"This is what you knew, isn't it? You could smell the kill and knew the wolves didn't want us," she gazed at the skull, "they just wanted us gone." She mounted Viento and returned to the main trail, climbing to the summit.

From the same boulder where she had rested a month earlier, Alex contemplated the human psyche, that fragile engine that drives the upright animal.

Or doesn't.

In that sublime moment she mentally tiptoed across thin ice to consider her own psyche. Her own vulnerability. Rays of enlightenment filtered through that profound quiet, a silence impossible in the city, impossible to avoid in the wild. She studied her fear, turning it over and over in her mind until it was familiar, and gradually it became less threatening. She closed her eyes and willed it back to its dark hole.

Her return to the cabin was without incident and with each stride the ground offered up bits and pieces of nature's drama, a story Alex was learning to read.

In a flat area to the side of the trail where water once collected in a rain-soaked puddle, clear tracks of wolf and elk, predator and prey, had been preserved in mud. As the water evaporated, the prints dried hard. Alex remembered that last rain, and dated the tracks from it.

The night of her terrifying ride. One month ago.

Her new environment presented puzzles inside mysteries painted with wonder, and Alex exercised her mind to unravel them. She watched and listened, and embraced the mental challenge.

And she made peace with her fear.

Chapter Thirty

Bright sunlight sparkled off the mansion's windows and circling rainbird sprinklers created rainbows across the vast lawn in regimented rhythm. Danni's worn Toyota pickup was starkly out of place on the immaculate driveway. Two large portable dog kennels almost filled the bed of her truck.

She noticed immediately that the dog run had been moved from its place near the driveway, and assumed Stephen had relocated it behind the house. Out of sight. Danni knew—even if Alex didn't—that he'd always disliked her dogs. And Danni had also seen the huskies cringe and flatten their ears whenever he showed them off to guests. They weren't fond of him, either.

Three heavy raps with the large brass doorknocker summoned Carmen, and she was dwarfed by the massive oak door as it swung slowly open. Only a crack. Danni smiled to relieve the anxiety in the girl's face.

"Hi, Carmen, I'm here to pick up Alpha and Omega for Alexandra." Silence. Large brown eyes recognized her, but registered confusion.

"Maybe Stephen didn't tell you. I'm supposed to take the dogs with me. Back to California."

Deeper confusion, same silence.

"Hmm." *This isn't working.* "Is Stephen here?" The girl shook her head.

"May I come in?" Danni could almost see the thoughts circulating slowly, then the pretty face relaxed, and the door swung opened to admit her.

"Mr. Stephen not here, Miss Danielle."

"Well, that's fine." *Great, actually.* "I'm just here to get the dogs, so if you could show me where he moved the run?"

Confusion returned to the Hispanic face.

"Dogs not here, Miss Danni." The first alarm went off in Danni's brain.

"What do you mean the dogs aren't here? Stephen said he'd take care of them until I could drive up this week and get them. I heard Alex—Alexandra—arrange it with him on the phone a couple weeks ago." Danni notice that Carmen's confusion was moving closer to distress.

"Dogs went away." The Hispanic voice had diminished to a whisper.

"How long ago?" Danni struggled to keep the edge out of her voice, for fear of panicking the girl.

"A few weeks." Carmen thought hard, trying to remember. "Went before Mrs. Sheryl came to live here."

"That doesn't make sense, that was months ago." In her mind wild alarm bells clanged now, and she swallowed to control her own rising anxiety. Touching Carmen's arm gently, Danni forced her voice to be quiet and gentle. It wasn't easy, a hurricane was gathering in her stomach.

"Carmen, what do you mean, 'they went away'? They've always been kept in the run."

Oh, God. Maybe he just let them out one day. Or gave them away. Or sold them.

Carmen looked over her shoulder into the marble-floored entryway, as if someone might be listening. "One day I went outside to watch the sunset and they were just not there anymore."

Danni charted another route to the answer. "What happened just before you went outside? During that day, I mean. Was Mr. Stephen home?"

Carmen smiled, relieved to be asked a question she could answer.

"Oh yes, Miss Danielle, he was home that day, but um, he not feel good."

Not feel good? I bet. I saw that black mood often enough. She waited agonizing seconds while Carmen looked up, and scanned the ceiling, as if that ancient day's agenda was written there in the textured plaster and rich molding.

"Yes, he was home during morning, but after lunch went

to target practice. He took one of his rifles and was gone until late, told me not to fix dinner," she smiled, "and gave me the night off."

Danni's stomach knotted instantly.

Took the rifle? Target practice? Oh no, even Stephen couldn't be that ruthless!

But the horror would not be denied. The innocent girl, still ignorant of the burden of her words, continued.

"When I went outside that evening Alpha and Omega, gone." Suddenly Carmen gasped. Her eyes widened and comprehension filled the space between the two women like a deep, dark pit.

Truth lay at the bottom, and they both recognized it.

"Oh, Miss Danielle, Mr. Stephen would never do such a thing!" Carmen raced to defend her employer. Admirable loyalty, but badly misplaced. "He like the dogs. I hear him say many times they are valuable."

"Bastard!" Danni whispered, rage rising and surging with each pulse. Thoughts raced.

Where'd you do it, Stephen? Up in the mountains? That's where Alex said you used to go to shoot squirrels. When you let them go they probably ran away from you, didn't they? Gave you just what you craved, a moving target to vent your foul temper.

Long minutes joined the truth in the space between the two women and Danni weighed her next words. Carmen was an illegal alien—cheap labor—and Stephen had complete control over her. Danni recalled more than once hearing him threaten to have her deported for some insignificant transgression, and his yelling always terrified the girl. Danni even suspected that on more than a few occasions his abuse towards Carmen extended beyond the verbal. She could only imagine what Stephen would do to her if he knew about this conversation.

"Carmen, listen to me." She gripped the girl's fragile shoulders, looking her eye to eye.

"Mr. Stephen really *did* kill Alpha and Omega, do you

understand me?"

The girl's eyes filled with tears and she nodded slowly. During her first days in the huge house when her poor English made communication with people nearly impossible, she would escape to play with the dogs. Alpha and Omega always understood her words, in any language, and they had responded to her open affection in kind.

"Carmen, you must not tell Mr. Stephen that we talked about this, okay? You must promise me." Tears trickled down dark cheeks. "Do you promise?"

Carmen nodded, understanding this truth better than others.

"I need to go, now."

Danni's fury seethed just below the surface, tempered by her fear for Carmen, and she hugged the girl briefly, then closed the heavy oak door behind her.

For Danni there were no tears, only rage. It erupted, pouring out hatred until her hands shook with it, and she had to pull over to the side of the road.

"Stephen, I could kill you myself for fucking that bitch in Alex's bed. But this! Even I didn't think you were this diabolical!" Her head throbbed with the force of her anger. It dizzied her.

"God help me, I will see you pay for this! I will!" Her hands tightened into white-knuckled fists that threatened to rip the steering column out of the dashboard.

Brilliant, sweet memories flashed through her mind and fed her fury. She recalled helping her sister bottle feed the pups every few hours for weeks after their mother died. Only two of the litter of six survived, and in truth they shouldn't have. For six weeks the sisters alternated shifts feeding the helpless husky pups.

Danni realized at that moment that she loved Alpha and Omega only slightly less than Alex.

"God, you have to make this right. In your grand plan of events, don't let this go unanswered. Please!" The unorthodox prayer calmed her gradually, and she resumed the drive to her parent's house.

How am I gonna tell Alex? This will kill her! Oh God...

Days later Danni recalled her confrontation with Stephen in his office, and wondered if she had pushed him to kill the dogs. A knife through her heart could not have hurt more than the idea that she was responsible for the death of her sister's dogs.

Chapter Thirty-one

Alex's body responded to the demands of her world. Hard work defined muscles with daily exertion and soft flesh from an easier life vanished. Lithe and supple, her body machine metamorphosed into a proper beast to challenge the mountains. Strong, graceful, smooth-moving, energy-efficient. Likewise her spirit, one day at a time, cast off her sense of inadequacy. In this place, she was capable.

Sweat trickled down her neck to join the expanding wet spot on the front of her tank top. Her hair was plastered to her scalp beneath her hat and more sweat ran down her back. Alex felt each drop travel over her skin and she fidgeted in the saddle to relieve the tickling sensation. Her arms baked under multiple applications of sunblock and insect repellant and the combined smell was noxious. To her, not the insects. It was mid-morning, mid-summer, her water was gone, and Alex was miserable.

"Let's head for that stream we found last week, V. One of us really needs a drink." She clucked to the mustang and turned him toward the bottom of the ravine they were traversing.

Alex was interested in the rate of regrowth in clearcuts and this was the nearest one to her cabin. Where once mighty cedars created twenty-four hour shade, dust devils now swirled, lifting nutrient-rich top soil, blowing it around stumps and charred slash piles. Mountain winds sang the litany of man's stewardship. This was Alex's third visit, and the place always depressed her. Today, as parched and dry as her throat, it was frightening.

Sarcasm worthy of her sister shaded her thoughts.

Renewable resource? Oh yes, I can see renewal taking place everywhere I look!

A dust cloud swirled towards them faster than she could rein Viento around to avoid it. She squeezed her eyes shut and covered her nose and mouth with her hand as fine dust whirled and settled in the chemical stickiness on her arms. She wiped her face with her bandanna, leaving a line of dirt along her jawline.

The barren hillside pitched steeper as it dropped into the canyon. Viento slipped and side-stepped through the loose dirt, horse-shoes chiming each strike against buried stones. Alex let him find his own way, more sure-footed than she. And probably more thirsty.

After several minutes of descent they passed a fly-covered dead rabbit. Patches of hide were gone and small scavengers were already converting it to usable protein. The skin had collapsed against its skeletal frame, as if all soft tissue had been sucked out. Over the last weeks Alex had seen enough dehydrated young bodies to last her a lifetime, she would learn nothing new from this one. Viento put his ears back at the scent, death made both of them uncomfortable.

She swallowed and the parched raspiness made her abruptly aware of her thirst. It wasn't life-threatening, but it was worse than any she could recall.

"Come on, Viento, let's get to that stream."

The hillside flattened out at the bottom and the faint sound of water flowing over stone urged the horse forward. In a week the rushing stream had shrunk to a lazy trickle, barely a brook, and Alex shook her head. The world was drying up before her eyes.

She dismounted and both thirsty mammals went for the water, Viento lowered his head until his lips gently broke the water's surface, while Alex knelt on the rocks and scooped water with cupped hands. Viento's method was much more efficient. She had taken only one swallow, when suddenly Viento snorted and jerked his head up, startling her.

"What's wrong boy?" The horse shook his head and snorted again, refusing to drink.

"This water was good a week ago." Viento flattened his ears back and would not lower his head, in spite of his obvious thirst. Alarmed, Alex cupped both hands full of water and sniffed it, but noticed nothing. It was cool, clear, and inviting, yet she didn't drink.

"What's the problem here, my friend?" She petted his neck, leaving a hand-wide dust streak on his coat. Alex knew that horses won't drink tainted water, and for her own good, she couldn't ignore Viento's behavior.

"Alright, pal, I'm not drinking if you don't." Her throat screamed for the cool water. She splashed it on her face and neck, but the pleasing wetness on her skin did nothing to relieve her thirst.

"We'd better check out what's wrong here." She started upstream on foot, Viento following her, head hanging, tail limp, except to swat at flies. Not once did he lower his nose to water.

The stream they followed had filled a much larger riverbed in early spring and walking over the rounded stones was slow and tedious. The original course meandered around granite outcroppings and fallen trees and now, as a much smaller entity, its path was even more circuitous. Large boulders, probably submerged during spring runoff, were now major obstacles.

"What's that smell?"

Alex came around a jagged rock and her stomach lurched.

"Oh, my God!"

A bloated, rotting bear carcass blocked the stream and nothing could have prepared her for the stench and gore. The ursine had been sliced from chin to tail, and lay on its back, sprawled across the creek. Water flowed around it and over it, carrying bloody bits of decaying flesh downstream. Muscle and organ tissue had jellied, and now churned and oozed with maggots. Internal organs, exposed to the elements were infested with worms, and flies swarmed the body cavity. Alex's stomach roiled again and she covered her mouth and nose, deep breathing to calm her threatening gag reflex.

Alex had smelled bad meat before—a pound of hamburger kept too long, or an old bit of fish. But the smell of three hundred pounds of decomposing black bear was too much for her, and she dropped to her hands and knees and vomited, retching up her lunch and the last fluid in her stomach. Now her throat really burned for water. She glanced around for Viento, but he was nowhere to be seen, and she was in no condition to call him.

The nausea passed slowly and she looked at the ursine with a clinical eye, curious about his massive wound. She batted away flies and inched closer.

"No animal kills so clean and precise, this looks like an incision. And what animal can kill a bear, except another bear?" She noticed a bloody spot under the bear's right eye socket and knelt over his head, but she couldn't bring herself to touch the wound. She didn't have to.

"You just came for a drink, didn't you? Probably never even scented the man that shot you." Alex spoke to the deceased in a soft, sad voice.

"But why were you killed and then left here? This makes no sense..." She forced herself to look at the carnage, and deep-breathing fended off repeated waves of nausea. The internal organs were too far gone to be easily recognizable, but they all appeared to be there. She grabbed a stick and folded one flap of skin over the gaping laceration.

"Oh, no!" Thinned belly fur revealed swollen teats. "Where's your cub, mama? Was he closeby when...?" She closed her eyes to let another wave of nausea settle.

"This makes no sense. Why would someone shoot you and not take..." Then she noticed the bear's paws.

"No claws? You were killed for your claws?" Her dry throat allowed only a raspy whisper. She pried the bear's mouth open with the stick.

"...and your teeth!" She leaned against a large rock, overcome by the stench and saddened by the waste. Her stomach rolled again and the sour taste in her mouth returned. She needed water. Staggering upstream, a hundred yards above the bear, Alex dropped to her knees and scooped handful after handful of water, rinsing her mouth first, then drinking. When her thirst was finally quenched she splashed water on her face and neck, again and again, as if to purge the vile sight.

Trembling bushes upstream caught her eye and she braced herself. Carrion attracted hungry animals, many of them predators. Then she relaxed and smiled. Viento had found his own way to fresh water and was relieving his thirst, nose in the creek. She whistled and his head came up.

"Viento, come." Even though her voice was strong and commanding he hesitated for a minute, still thirsty. Then slowly the mustang made his way to her.

"Good boy," she stroked his dusty neck, "not too much, too fast. We don't need a case of colic, too."

Alex leaned her cheek against his large jaw, more for emotional support than physical. Then they started a slow walk back to the cabin.

They followed the brook upstream and less than two hundred yards from the bear's carcass they found the cub, as dead and dehydrated as the rabbit. He was only feet from water that might have kept him alive, but the only nourishment he'd known was his mother's milk, and water was as alien to him at that age as meat.

Alex was surprised when she lifted his small frame. Bears are heavily-muscled animals, even cubs, but he was feather light. She marveled at the tiny paws and teeth and pink tongue that would never strip a salmonberry bush or raid a beehive.

That night Alex groomed Viento longer than usual after unsaddling him, savoring his large, quiet companionship. She lingered over the spots he most enjoyed her brushing. It was a soothing activity for both of them and it gave her time to sort her thoughts.

"You know, V., I've never really been against hunting, I even like the taste of venison. But what someone did to that bear..." His liquid eyes looked around at her face, mouth working on his dinner.

"And I'm embarrassed to be from the same species. What a waste. What an incredible waste!"

Later she stood in the shower for several minutes, water cascading over her body. The skin was clean but still she felt dirty, and Alex knew if she stood there until she wrinkled, she'd never wash away her revulsion. Or her embarrassment. It was as if by seeing the evidence, she was soiled by the act. At once innocent and wise beyond her years, Alex was burdened with a knowledge of her own species she never wanted, and an uncomfortable awareness of her own naivete. The same naivete Matt had recognized immediately.

I wonder how he would've reacted today? Probably wouldn't have thrown up...

That night she stared at the latest entry in her journal. The glowing computer screen recorded the facts of the day, but there were no words for her feelings, and she silently grieved for bear tracks she would not see again.

Chapter Thirty-two

It happened every time. Male voices in easy conversation hushed faster than Alex's eyes adjusted to the dimly lit room, and the resounding silence never got comfortable. The air tasted old, as old as the log walls and hand-split bar. As old as the attitude flowing out of the clouds of cigarette smoke over each table.

That she wasn't welcome was obvious, the only question was the degree of her rejection. The Knotty Pine was a man's place, and her female foot desecrated it each time she crossed the threshold. But Softouch was here and he was her friend.

"You look kinda parched, pretty lady, could I draw you a cool one?" The smoky southern tones welcomed her as always, and she moved quickly to the stool at the end of the bar. Away from the men.

"Yes, thanks, it's stifling out there," she sipped her beer and glanced around the room, "...not at all like the chill in here." The black face across the bar grinned.

"What ever do you mean?" He mocked the obvious and Alex smiled.

"I always feel like I've been dropped into a Jack London novel when I come in here. You know, Skagway during the gold rush." Softouch chuckled.

"Your analogy does my humble establishment proud, ma'am. Thank you so much." Again she wondered just how genuine his southern accent was, but she didn't really care, it always warmed the room and welcomed her. She glanced at the assembled men who had returned to their poker and beer. Loggers, miners, lots of worn jeans and plaid shirts.

"I bet you had some hot debates on women's lib and equal rights in here." The boisterous laugh that erupted from the large black man sounded like it started in his socks.

Softouch was her first and only friend in the little town closest to her cabin. Very quickly she had realized that to the male-dominated local population she was a supreme oddity. Why would a woman choose to live alone in the woods just to watch animals? Her behavior flew in the face of tradition. Living without a man? It wasn't like she worked for the mill, or the mining company, or even waited tables at one of the restaurants here in town.

Alex's reputation was sealed one night when she brought her computer in to show Softouch. While his thick fingers played over the keyboard and they discussed hard drive size and processor speed, the old-timers stared at her like she had grown a third eye, or flew through the door on a broom.

"So what's the body count today, Doc?"

"I've lost track." She shook her head. "Actually, I haven't seen too many the last few weeks. But then I haven't seen too many live animals either."

"The old ones know where to go to escape the heat. It's the young that suffer."

The image of the mutilated bear floated in her mind. "Well, I don't know about that." She lowered her voice to a whisper and looked at him for a few seconds. "I saw something pretty awful, and it wasn't a young one, or caused by the heat."

"What?" He stopped washing glasses.

"In the creek below the clearcut there was a black bear, a nursing female. And somebody," she paused, the memory was vivid, "well, somebody sliced her open. And then just left her there."

"How do you mean, 'sliced her open'?" She noticed he wasn't surprised.

"I mean one long cut, jaw to tail. And as far as I could tell, all they took were her claws and her teeth." She looked into her beer. "And she'd been there awhile."

"Pretty ripe, was she?" Alex nodded. "Well, Doc, I'd be willing to bet they took something else." He resumed washing glasses and didn't look at her.

"What? From what I could tell she was all there, 'though I'll admit, I didn't exactly do a thorough examination."

"They took her gall bladder. The teeth and claws were a bonus."

"Her gall bladder? For what?" Alex stared at him and he put down the towel. Leaning closer to her across the bar, he whispered,

"Bear gall is worth thousands of dollars on the black market. It's small and alot easier to pack out than a whole bear." He rinsed the glasses and stood them on the bar. "Certain cultures believe it's a strong aphrodisiac. You know," he winked at her, "prescription for a limp libido. I've heard they believe it's almost as powerful as tiger penis."

"Tiger penis?" She stared at him, incredulous.

"Yeah, they dry it and in certain parlors one can fetch $25,000." He grabbed a towel and dried the glasses. "Canada doesn't have any tigers, but we have lots of bears." Shock registered on Alex's face.

"What kind of sick person would do such a thing?"

"Look around this room. Any unemployed logger or miner needing to feed his family, maybe." They both gazed at the collection of men smoking and sipping their beers. "All the men in this room have the talent, and some have the need." One of his customers waved to get his attention and signaled for another round.

"But it's such a waste to just leave it there to rot. And she was nursing! I'll bet the cub was there when they shot her."

"Probably. But I'm not sure it's such a waste. Before that meat went bad I bet there were scavengers lining up for supper, and now the carrion eaters will finish her off. By fall there'll be no trace left." His words made sense, but offended her no less.

"I understand the biology, Softouch. Surely, you don't condone this activity?" She searched his face. "Do you?" This wouldn't be the first time he'd played devil's advocate just to stimulate conversation.

"I didn't say I did. But I do hold to the truth that energy can't be destroyed. Ashes to ashes, as it were. And what's more natural for the bear, being devoured by his neighbors, or being gutted and mounted for some rich guy's wall in New York City?" He left with a tray of frothy brews and served a corner table. The well-washed apron seemed out of place draped around his large frame. Alex watched him retrieve their empties from the cards and money on the table.

Does he know who did it?

The question nagged her while he cleared two more tables and returned to the bar. He dropped the used glasses in the perpetual sink of soapy water.

"If I were unemployed and had a family to feed, I'd probably consider it. Poachers hardly ever get caught, the money's good, and remember, black bears are not an endangered species."

"I'm sure the poachers sleep better for that fact!" She scowled into her beer.

"Oh, put a smile on that pretty face, I picked up your mail." He reached under the bar and handed her three envelopes and watched as she read the return addresses; Seattle, Monterey, and... Alaska? Puzzlement crossed her face, then a smile.

"Now, that's better. I didn't even think ol' Matt knew how to write." Another big chuckle as Alex stuffed the envelopes in her back pocket.

"What? You're not going to share with your devoted friend, Softouch?"

"Sure, let's start with the one from my mother..."

"Well, that wasn't the one..."

She giggled. "No, I'm not going to share." She grabbed a pretzel from the wooden bowl on the bar and looked at her new friend. "You know my story, Softouch, tell me about yourself. How did you end up in this place? You don't exactly strike me as a native..."

"Oh, pretty lady, that's a long and boring saga that I won't burden you with now. Suffice to say that after the United States Army and I parted company, as amicably as that could be done, I needed some serious time alone." His voice got soft and quiet.

"I needed to find the southern gentleman I was before seeking my military fortune in Viet Nam. This area didn't have a pilot, I had a plane that I bought after my discharge, so it was a perfect fit."

"And who christened you, 'Softouch'? Matt wouldn't tell me." He refilled her glass, and his thick ebony hand around the heavy beer mug made it look fragile. Alex saw his face cloud over for a second and he busied himself hanging glasses over the bar to avoid her gaze. Glasses hung, composure intact, he smiled at her and continued.

"Well now, I don't want to reveal all my secrets in one sitting, do I? Leave nothing for a later visit, and you'll start patronizing my competition down the road." Alex started to protest just as the door jerked open and a huge human form blocked out most of the bright sunlight. The accompanying voice was proportionally large.

"Pour me a beer, I finally got that bastard that's been killing my hounds!" Something flew across the room and landed with a muffled thud on the stool next to Alex. Two glassy eyes looked up at her, and Softouch saw her flinch. He reached over the bar and grabbed the pelt.

"What do you have here, Bouvier?"

"The bastard wolf that's been killing my hounds! And the bounty will just about pay for a new dog. How 'bout a beer before you inspect the goods, eh?"

"Certainly, my friend, certainly. But I hate to tell you, this wolf didn't kill your dogs." Softouch draped the pelt over the bar and started to chuckle as he drew the beer.

"What d'ya mean?"

"Look at him, he has no teeth!"

Bouvier snatched the pelt and pried open the dead wolf's mouth. "Well, shit, must be that gray bitch he was runnin' with!" He dropped the wolf next to Alex and picked up his beer. "He'll get me the bounty, just the same."

Alex was drawn to the pelt, and ran her fingers slowly through the red-gold fur, caught up in her own thoughts.

Softouch was laughing at an embarrassed Bouvier, and neither of them noticed her.

"He looks like he couldn't kill a beetle! Yeah, Pierre, you got yourself a real killer there. Tell me, sir, did you see him run? Look at him, he must be ten years old, probably arthritic. And more than a mite mangy, if you'll permit me to say so." The black man guffawed at the trapper's expense and Bouvier moved away from the bar to escape him, sitting with three friends whose faces registered their own amusement. Softouch saw Alex caressing the lifeless fur.

"Really a poor quality pelt, doc."

"Would you consider this kill a waste?" She looked at him with shining eyes. He read her thoughts.

"Alex, this is a hard country, and many of these men's families fought to live here. Some of them didn't survive the experience. This environment you are so bent on protecting has taken as much from the men that made it habitable, as they have taken from it."

"Not even NEARLY as much!" She glared at him and shook the wolf skin. "This old thing couldn't kill a teddy bear. I accept a balance of give and take, Softouch, we are predators too, with a right to our share," she looked into the dead wolf's eyes.

"But we're smarter, and that makes us more responsible." Softouch thought for a few seconds, and noticed the fire in her eyes.

"I won't argue that point. But that old fella probably spent his last days in pain. Look at him. That fur is spotty and ragged, his ears are scarred and torn. Pierre probably put him out of his misery."

"Think he'll do the same to his mate?"

"He will if he can find her. Those dogs are his livelihood." She shook her head and tossed money on the bar.

"Thanks for the beer, Softouch. And, as always, the conversation was enlightening."

"Think about what I said. I bet in the city you'd put down a dog that was suffering like this gent probably was."

"It wouldn't be my first course of action." The fire had left her eyes, replaced by sadness. "I guess I'm just real tired of looking at dead animals." She walked out and drove back to the cabin in silence.

The baying hound's neck snapped easily between Cunning's jaws and she dropped him in front of her mate. The rogue's limping was now constant and feeding them both had become her responsibility. The dog was an easy kill.

Seconds later a gunshot shattered the night and the red-gold rogue collapsed over the dog. Gunfire was a brutal memory for Cunning and, terrified, she spun in a flash and raced into the trees. The gray bitch never turned back to her mate, but ran all night, toward an old home.

Toward Guardian and the pack.

Chapter Thirty-three

Merciful breezes forecast the approach of fall and all life breathed a collective sigh of relief. Cooler nights followed warm days and although dryness lingered over the land, there was a reprieve from the heat. Withered leaves that had clung so diligently to parched branches finally let go and tumbled to the ground, a blanket against the coming frost. The wolves refreshed themselves as the forest prepared for autumn's slower ebb and flow.

The pack acknowledged Cunning's return without fanfare or affection. No boisterous mingling of canine souls—wagging tails and pouncing paws, yip-yowling and cough-barking—greeted her as it would the other wolves after a separation. They simply accepted her. All felt the tease of winter, sensed the long cold and its companion, hunger, so Cunning's hunting skills gained her access where another would have been denied.

To the casual eye there was no difference in her station from before her absence, except with First-twin. The scars of Cunning's rejection were deep and permanent, and the young female resolutely ignored her older sister.

The other wolves rediscovered the joy in play that had been lost during the feverish summer and romped with abandon in the meadow. Jester and First-twin wrestled together, a 150-pound ball of gray fur rolling over and over in the dust. Even White-cub joined them in spontaneous games of tag that covered miles without purpose, crashing through bushes, bounding over deadfalls, and sprinting around boulders until they were all exhausted.

When nights were clear, the wolves coursed along trails or through parched grass into the hills beyond the river. They sprang and darted and crystal moonlight reflected off thickening coats of gray and red and white, highlighting every dash and leap, painting them with silver.

Paws pounded the earth in a cadence of sovereign power and bonded strength, and they danced nature's ballet, wilderness music choreographed for them alone. The lunar torch followed their performance like a spotlight focuses attention centerstage, gently lighting the background, illuminating the troupe.

No creature could compete with White-cub in form or speed. During those midnight runs he flew without leaving the earth. Strong legs powered him over the ground, mouth open, ears alert, as effortlessly as eagle wings ride warm thermals. Blue eyes glowed and white fur shimmered ghostly in the moonlight, like a phantom shaman enchanted to the present from his place at campfires centuries old. In his eighteenth month, Patriarch's son had achieved full growth. White-cub knew his place and occupied it proudly.

Memories of sadness and discomfort faded and blew away with the discarded leaves of summer. Food was plentiful and biting insects died in the rising chill so sleep came easily again. By the criteria a wolf would measure his days—bodily comfort, freedom of space, and the fullness of his belly—life was good. Guardian had brought his family safely through the scorching summer, and now they were content in their valley.

Nights reverberated with their howling and echoed their glory in life. Bonded by the challenges of the past, they sang with the joy of sentient beings cherishing their freedom, rejoicing in their wildness.

The faint odor of her sister's perfume drifted from the soft fleece collar brushing Alex's cheek. She wrapped the jacket closer and smiled as she stepped into the corral to retrieve Viento for the night. Danni borrowed everything.

Not even the smallest breath of wind disturbed the other hovering scents of cooling pine and earth and dry leaves, and when she inhaled, Alex recognized the air's icy edge. Fall was pacing in the wings and she welcomed its tingling briskness.

Overhead the evening sky offered an artist's palette of pink shaded with coral, lilac merging into purple, blue tinted with gold, and she was caught up in the splendor of a glorious Canadian sunset. Colors shifted and flowed, pastels darkened, high clouds blossomed neon pink with the last kiss of a sun, reluctant to surrender the sky. She took it all in, a masterpiece painted by generous gods for her alone.

Viento trotted over to her, but she hardly noticed. He stomped the ground and snorted, then tossed his head and whinnied when all else failed to solicit a response. The mustang did not understand why his mistress was staring at the sky. He got all the information he needed with just a quick glance up; a few feathery clouds—good, no wind—better yet, no smell of rain—perfect. Her rapt attention found no reason in his equine brain. Impatient, Viento nuzzled her hand for the attention he thought he deserved and she rubbed his face, chuckling at his antics.

"There is no beauty in your soul, Viento, look at this sunset!" She ran her hand through her hair and it crackled with static electricity. The crisp night was alive, and Alex's body responded like an animal, charged by the friction of earth rotating against sky, aware of the season's advance at an instinctive level beyond conscious thought.

Then she heard the first howl.

Very far away. Very faint. Alex held her breath.

Call again... please.

Silence. Viento stood quietly while her hand stroked his neck and the sky darkened to amethyst, then indigo.

Please let me hear you again... I don't want to be afraid anymore...

As if in response to her fragile courage the wolves lifted their voices as one; louder, longer, a single voice, then many. Haunting tones climbed, entwined in exotic harmonies, music as glorious as the sky it filled. Their voices stirred Alex, and for suspended seconds she glimpsed the greater mystery, the cosmic puzzle with all the pieces in place. She drank deeply of the wolves' song and their wild elixir nourished her thirsty soul.

She closed her eyes to block visual distractions and

consciously stretched her other senses for the first time, like a newborn cub just out of the den tasting his first breeze. The composite smell of the night separated into distinct scents, and she distinguished pine from cedar, moist earth from dry, crushed grass from withered leaves. Each essence swirled alone, then twisted together and blended into the wolfen aria, scent and sound one entity.

The hair on the back of her neck rose, not from fear, but heightened awareness. While ears strained to capture timbre and pitch and tone, her skin prickled and tensed, each tactile cell alert, attentive to temperature and air flow outside, her own pulse inside. And more. Her flesh sensed a spiritual presence among the physical, an ancient muse answering her question before she formed it. She stood in the corral for several minutes after the last canine voice died away, unwilling to break the spell, and watched stars assault the heavens in orderly formation.

The sensuality of the moment did not fade as she settled Viento for the night, and it lingered while she filled the tub and undressed. The full-length mirror she had previously avoided flashed with her reflection and she stopped, intrigued.

The nude woman in the glass was a stranger.

Tan skin covered a well-muscled body, a beautiful, strong, woman's body. And blonde hair, sun-streaked lighter than Alex ever remembered her own, cascaded wildly over her shoulders and around both breasts. Spellbound by this unrecognizable wild creature, Alex drew her hands slowly up her thighs, across a firm stomach, and the other woman did the same. Quadriceps flexed gracefully beneath her fingertips, and she could not take her eyes off the stranger in the glass.

Reason dictated the image must be her, but that woman's head rode high and proud, the eyes were brighter and their gaze more direct than she remembered her own. And most striking—utterly foreign—was the attitude of peaceful strength that glowed from the stranger's face.

In a radiant moment of self-discovery Alex smiled at the woman she had become.

Ursa Major swaggered through the night sky, snarling and clawing at inferior stars as he had for millennia, and beneath his glimmering lights Alex Davidson slept, content in her mountain sanctuary.

Chapter Thirty-four

Conceived behind the gates of Hell, the monster was delivered to earth by lightning's hand, and it multiplied with each blinding flash. In less than an hour thirty-two offspring drew first breath and began to feed in secluded mountain places, appetites sated on air and living carbon. Where nourishment was sparse, they withered and died, unnoticed.

But seven of Satan's children found perfect conditions and thrived. No human witnessed their birth, but their sinister presence would touch every being in their path.

The firestorms of Hell had come to the Canadian high country.

The smoldering infants caused no alarm in their first days. Smoke marked them and men christened them, names like Miner's Gulch and Sawtooth Ridge, but no human effort was expended to extinguish them. Fire was natural; it cleared, purified, stimulated, fertilized, and the winds were due any day, with their payload of rain.

Each year fire visited the mountains and each year it burned briefly and died before threatening man or beast. But for half a century fire had been an infrequent vandal, devouring a hundred, rarely more than a thousand, remote acres at a time, and the mountains had grown lush during its absence. Green life flourished and reproduced unchecked, flora crowding into every vacant niche. Foliage massed on top of foliage, greedy for earth space, blocking out the sun, a victim prime for the rape by Satan's offspring.

"You have to evacuate, Alex, that fire's moving your direction and could cut off your road." Softouch's familiar voice boomed from her radio.

"I know. The Forest Service just radioed me to leave and I'm already packing. But I don't know what to do about Viento, I didn't notice a boarding stable around town."

"Our classy little metropolis doesn't have such an establishment, but you just pack up that noble beast of yours, and I'll make some calls and find him a room."

"Thanks." She glanced around the room that had been her home for six months and suddenly grasped the seriousness of her situation. She might not return.

"...and if you get yourself down here soon, I'll fly you with me to the command center."

"Great, but I don't know how much I can help, the only fires I've ever fought were ambitious barbecues." A velvety chuckle was the response.

"I don't believe they require a college degree to make sandwiches. Now, pack and get down here, I want to leave at first light. I have a hot date with a lady up there just aching for ol' Softouch."

Alex's stomach lurched when the helicopter lifted off. The engine roar was excruciating, even with headphones covering her ears. Softouch saw her grimace and laughed.

"First time in a whirlybird, Doc?" His voice boomed into her ears and she nodded.

"Hope you ate a light breakfast." Alex's nervous stomach forbade a response as the ground plunged away beneath them. The front of the plexiglas shell curved under their feet to provide a panoramic view of the shrinking landscape between her boots. Alex did not appreciate the effect and closed her eyes.

"Don't do that, Alex. Keep you eyes open and focused ahead," he pointed out the window, "on the horizon. It'll ease the queasies." Raised eyebrows communicated her doubts that anything would calm her stomach.

Softouch reached beneath the seat and handed her a stack of white paper bags, lunch-size and wax-coated on the inside.

"...just in case..." He grinned. The bags required no explanation.

Alex's body felt gradually heavier as lift challenged gravity. Slowly the screaming engine chewed through air to free the humans from earth's grasp and she swallowed and yawned to equalize the pressure in her ears. Even when the craft leveled and moved forward, the nausea remained, aggravated by the throbbing roar of the engine overhead.

She was not enjoying the ride.

After what seemed like days to Alex, the helicopter topped a high ridge and revealed a sight that caused even Softouch to catch his breath.

"Uh-oh." One massive column of dense tan smoke spiraled in front of them, and two others, smaller by comparison, flanked it on either side. The giant cloud churned and rolled slowly, ominous even from miles away. Alex stared at it, and when she could, whispered,

"What do you mean, 'uh-oh'?"

"See how the smoke is merging into the whiter cloud above it?" She noticed the different shades of white and nodded.

"Well, this nasty lady's making her own weather." His voice was subdued. "Huh-uh, pretty lady, this is not so very fine. The fire's generating enough rising heat and humidity to create a cloud above it. That cloud is growing by the minute, sucking moisture from the ground as the fire burns." His eyes scanned the edges of the expanding, roiling gray.

"No, ma'am, we do not need this."

"Can't we just go around it?" A chuckle filled her ears.

"That beast is probably six miles high and five to ten miles across, and we're more than fifteen miles away. By the time we get there it will be even larger. No, I'm afraid going around isn't an option. This bird has the glide capacity of a brick when she runs out of juice, and an emergency landing in these li'l ol' hills will most definitely spoil your whole day."

He recovered his smiling attitude, but the jolliness was gone. Out of the corner of his eye Softouch saw Alex's hands grip the edges of her seat, white-knuckled. He rested his large hand over hers and felt cold skin.

"Now where's that spirit of adventure?" No response. Apprehension was clearly etched on her face. "Don't you worry, pretty lady, ol' Softouch always brings 'em home."

She concentrated diligently on the horizon.

"Nancy-six-one-niner, to fire command, over." Alex stared at the swelling tower of white, vaguely aware of voices in her headphones.

"This is command, go ahead Nancy-six-one-niner. Softouch, is that you?"

"Yes sir, it most certainly is. Who do I have the pleasure of addressing? Over."

"Craig Hoffman, you ol' jet jockey!" Radio discipline vanished.

"Well, long time no see, my friend! My passenger and I would like to express our sincere gratitude to you for this little greeting you so kindly sent up."

"Isn't she pretty? Wanted to be sure you could find the fire." A guffaw boomed in their ears. "Let me introduce you to Miss Sawtooth Ridge, and her daintier sisters, Miner's Gulch and Tehamma Creek. This is one hungry bitch, let me tell ya. She was grazin' pretty quiet until this mornin', then she started runnin' and hasn't slowed yet. Eatin' up the neighborhood, that's damn certain."

"Any idea how high this thing reaches?"

"Best guess is 25,000 feet, and growing. You gonna try to fly around her?

"Not possible. Any other traffic sharing my sky?"

"Nope, pattern's clear all the way in. Nothin' between you and a cold beer."

"Let's keep it that way, okay? My visibility is gonna be zip in a few minutes."

"Roger, Nancy-six-one-niner. We'll monitor your progress and you cruise careful up there. Fire command, out."

"Careful is the operative word, command. Nancy-six-one-niner, out." Only the rhythmic drumming of the rotor over their heads filled the void, and the white mass swelled and swirled larger and larger, dominating their view.

Suddenly the helicopter lunged to the left and dropped unexpectedly, and Alex's feet actually rose off the floor. Her stomach did likewise. All Softouch and Alex could see was white and the smell of smoke filled the cabin.

"Cinch up your seatbelt, Alex, as tight as you can stand it. This is gonna get rough." Her stomach knotted up as tight as her seatbelt, and the small craft galloped into the billowing white.

Alex realized full panic with the first hundred-foot free fall. She could not hold her feet down, her mouth turned to cotton, and she forgot to breathe. The paper bags slid off her lap to the floor. Her eyes found nothing to focus on, but there was no chance she would vomit, her gag reflex was as paralyzed as the rest of her.

Next to her, black fingers caressed the controls, responding to each change in pitch and yaw. There was nothing but white outside the plexiglas; ahead, to the sides, above and below. Claustrophobic, swirling white.

But as much as it unnerved Alex, it invigorated Softouch. He responded with cool concentration, flying by instinct, not sight. The tiny craft bucked and swerved on shifting air currents, as fragile as a soap bubble floating on a child's breath. But Softouch answered each blow instantly, offsetting nature's hand with his own.

Without warning, the gray around them suddenly blazed bright white, and the lightning reflected off each metal switch and glass dial.

"Son of a b—" Explosions of thunder enveloped the fragile craft.

"Shit!" Before the thunder stopped, another sheet of lightning engulfed them, then another, each blinding flash painful to the eye.

They were in the center of the storm, lightning and thunder occurred simultaneously, and the sound hit Alex like physical blows to the chest. Fingernails dug into the seat cushion and she held her breath. No noise had ever been so loud, no light so bright, and it shook her, body and soul, like the fist of some angry god.

The next flash of lightning struck the tiny craft, the engine stalled, and the bottom fell out of their sky.

Gravity reclaimed them in a slow-spinning free fall.

Softouch worked, intense and determined, his voice murmuring through her headphones, soft whispers to the equipment in his hands. He seemed unaware of Alex's presence.

"Nancy-six-one-niner, to fire command. Over." His voice was dead calm.

"Nancy-six-one-niner, go ahead." Craig Hoffman's voice was as sober as the pilot's.

"Gentlemen, we have a small problem here," his voice was lost in a deafening crash of thunder, "we've been hit, engine's stalled and we are dropping... autorotation... 16,000 feet now..."

"We have your position, Nancy-six-one-niner," Craig turned away from the radio, looked out the window and whispered to nobody, "Come on, Softouch, let's see some of your pilot magic."

Seconds crawled by. Only the seatbelt kept Alex's weightless body from rising. Her senses transmitted useless information to her brain; no up, no down, nothing but blasting thunder and flashing white light. Incoherent signals.

But not Softouch. Alex saw him smile.

He's enjoying this!

Instantly she knew this was his element, not the cozy bar on terra firma, but guiding a sick helicopter through a thunderstorm. He caught her eye and winked!

"Now, this is what I get the big bucks for, doc!" Another flash of lightning illuminated strong black fingers and the engine roared back to life. Thwomp... thwomp... thwomp, thwomp, thwomp.

"That's my girl." He wasn't talking to Alex and she knew it. The throbbing engine racket that had annoyed her earlier brought immediate comfort as the falling slowed and the craft stabilized, moving more horizontally than vertically.

Oh, I get it! 'Soft touch' on the controls!

Alex shook her head and marveled that while one half of her brain was locked in complete terror, the other half had worked out the man's nickname!

"Control, this is Nancy-six-one-niner requesting permission to land." There was a pause, and then,

"Park anywhere, Nancy-six-one-niner." The relief in Craig's voice was unmistakable.

As quickly as the white ether had sucked them in, it spit them out, and green expanse unfolded below them, broken up by trees burning orange and red, crown fires throwing off sparks like roman candles on the Fourth of July. A cluster of buildings was visible several miles ahead in untouched green. Softouch squeezed Alex's clenched fist.

"You can relax now, Doc, we're gonna make it." She took a deep breath. "I told you, I always bring 'em home!"

The helicopter drifted gently down over a large hanger, past the flight tower and windsock and hovered along a dirt runway surrounded by vintage planes and helicopters. It came to rest on a patch of grass next to what looked like barracks.

Alex exhaled, eyes closed, clenching and unclenching her cramped fists. She removed her headphones as Softouch shut down the helicopter, and sighed again. When it was quiet he looked at her. She smiled, then giggled, giddy with relief.

"Thanks for the lift!"

"Oh, my pleasure, pretty lady, my pleasure, indeed!" He took her headphones and placed them on the hook over her head.

"Feel free to sit here a few minutes, until you get your feet under you." He nodded toward the largest wooden building. "Mess hall's on the bottom floor, kitchen's in the back. Ask for Leah, she'll find something to keep you occupied. I'll check up on you later." With that he opened the door and jumped down, patting the machine affectionately before striding across the grass. Several men loped in their direction.

"'Softouch', is right!" Alex murmured, watching the men shake hands and slap each other on the back, as is their way.

Chapter Thirty-five

Smoke drifted into the valley of the wolves but among its inhabitants there was no panic. Young fawns paused in their grazing, lifted their heads and sniffed the unusual smell. Nostrils flared, ears and tails twitched nervously, and infant muscles braced for flight. But the older animals around them gave the burning smell no notice, so the adolescents relaxed and resumed feeding.

Bucks and does that had survived more than one winter knew the smell, fire was as much an element of fall as drying leaves and chilling temperatures. It visited the valley like a migratory beast, feeding, then moving on. Memories of smoke and flames and blackened timber resided on older brains, triggering no fear. Mature creatures had easily grazed ahead of its slow progress in past years, they would do so this year as well.

An event of greater magnitude dominated the valley and no resident could ignore it. Elk migrated into the meadows, females and young less than a year old first, feeding together in small groups. Primal tension increased with their numbers and hovered over the valley like the smoke. The stage was set, the audience had gathered, great drama waited in the wings.

The bulls arrived individually, former champions striding through the valley, proud and stately. Eight-, nine-, and ten-year old males sported racks six feet across, larger this year than last. Each point was rubbed smooth by weeks of testing against trees and bushes, and sunlight glinted from each dagger sharp tine, a serious challenge to any competitor.

Slow and deliberate, they promenaded into the valley, confident for each year they had survived. Chiseled, muscular bodies supported their weapons on graceful heads and, like a knight brandishes his favorite sword before the conflict, each bull flaunted his antlers, dipping and turning his head left and right. The titans of the forest advertised their strength, and the hormones that had assembled them terminated their appetites. They would not eat again.

The rut had begun.

The largest, oldest bulls staked out territory and broadcast their ownership in mournful bugling that carried for miles. They herded females into groups, prodding and biting them into submission. Then, snorting and pawing the ground against any bull who dared to approach their harem, they trumpeted their sovereignty.

Short tempers and rising testosterone triggered head-to-head combat, and thousand-pound bulls lowered their antlers to attack posture, charging full speed into one another. Racks locked and the crack echoed again and again from early morning fog into evening mist. Bulls lunged and jerked apart repeatedly, death-dealing prongs poised and ready for the next thrust.

Once engaged, brute strength, sure-footedness, and the finesse of experience determined the victor. Straining shoulder muscles and a well-timed twist of the neck drove the defeated to his knees. One parry was usually sufficient to dissuade an inexperienced young bull, eager for the mating prize. Rising slowly he would walk away, ego bruised, but unscathed.

Occasionally however, youthful passion would not bow to superior strength, and paid with its life for a challenge it could not win. When the outcome was death, the wolves paid homage to the victor, devouring his trophy.

Between triumphs the great bulls mounted indifferent females grazing nearby, and the thrusts of their mating were as powerful as those of battle. Only the fittest bulls passed their genes to the next generation, and they did so with the same raw power that won them the right.

Each day new smoke joined old. And still there was no panic.

Chapter Thirty-six

Alex heard the Lockheed C-130 long before she saw it, and the drone of its four Allison turboprops filled the noontime quiet. It appeared to hover momentarily, then touched down at the farthest end of the crude runway, roaring toward her. From the mess hall porch Alex felt the earth tremble under the plane's weight, a gentle shaking at first, then a rumbling vibration, as the 4000-horsepower engines raced past her. Glass windows rattled in their frames.

Clearly a service vehicle, the transport was unencumbered with the sleek trappings of a commercial airliner. Sunlight reflected unevenly off small dents and rectangular patches along the fuselage where the skin had been repaired. Where paint still clung to metal, it was faded and scratched.

The colossus devoured every foot of the gravel runway and finally rolled to a bumpy stop near the other planes and helicopters. They shook against their moorings as it eased closer, and its 133-foot wingspan shadowed them like a mother osprey shelters her young.

"Ah, my date has arrived!" Softouch approached Alex from behind and handed her a cup of coffee. "And isn't she beautiful?" The American flag painted on the tail of the huge plane caught her eye and triggered an unexpected twinge of homesickness.

Even before the plane had come to a complete stop, the rear loading ramp started to drop, revealing a bulldozer and crates of equipment. Uniformed men were poised to leap to the ground.

"Who are they?" Alex was intrigued by the mass of equipment visible through the opening.

"Hot shots from the good ol' U. S. Forest Service."

"Hot shots?"

"The best smokejumpers in the world. They travel in teams of fifteen to twenty, flying across the country to work the big fires like those wildfires in Malibu last year."

"What are they doing here in Canada?"

"The U. S. and Canada have had a policy of mutual aid for massive fires like this for decades. Canada lent us a hand in '88 at Yellowstone."

"Are these fires really that bad?"

"Not today, but if the wind picks up," he sighed, "yes, they could get that bad. Maybe worse." Neither of them heard Leah's quiet approach from the kitchen.

"Those men are going to need to eat, will you please help me, Alex?" Leah's gentle voice reminded Alex of water flowing over stones; graceful, but lightly sparkled with humor.

"Absolutely. Can't miss the next cholesterol binge."

Alex had just finished laying out lunch—three buffet tables of hot dogs, burgers, chili, and sandwich fixings, when boots stomped through the door and across the hardwood floor. Eighty men dropped backpacks and sauntered toward the tables. There was no obesity among them.

Boot shuffling intensified and muffled male voices assembled with their food around the tables nearest a large survey map mounted on the wall. Multi-colored pins, some sporting paper banners with names and numbers, designated various fires and their movement. There were many pins in the map.

Alex found a spot next to Softouch, leaning against the back wall. A broad-shouldered, ageless man stood near the map and his demeanor commanded respect. Squint lines near his eyes and tanned skin testified to a life spent outdoors. He waited for silence and got it quickly.

"Most of you I've already met, for those of you I don't know, I'm the incident commander for this gig, Scott Powell. Call me Scotty." Intense gray eyes made contact with those in front, and the only sound interrupting his voice was the clink of silverware.

"There are three major fires forming a loose triangle; here, here, and here." He pointed to three clusters of pins. "That nasty little cloud that greeted you boys on the way up is the Sawtooth Ridge. This monster's aiming to supplement her diet with a town or two. We need to see she doesn't get that opportunity."

"In addition to the C-130, we have two B-29's arriving in an hour. They'll drop chemicals and water. The weather's already dicey and the wind in these mountains is unpredictable. We'll try to keep you appraised, but you all know what that means." He ran his fingers through his salt and pepper hair.

"There will be maps near the door when you leave outlining pick-up sites and escape routes. Study them. Each American team will be joined by local Canadian firefighters who are jump qualified. Make sure they know your faces. They're familiar with the area and they may have to save your butts. We will also be assisted by local pilots who have volunteered their time and equipment. They'll fly reconnaissance and rescue operations in tight quarters where our heavy metal can't go."

He raised a friendly arm to Softouch and smiled for the first time. "One expatriate many of you may remember from Yellowstone has escaped the IRS by homesteading here in Canada. Since this is his backyard, he'll fly the C-130 to your drop zones." Softouch waved and several men grinned and clapped. Scotty waited for quiet and Alex pondered this new information.

Softouch didn't tell me he fought *fires at Yellowstone. Was he in the Forest Service, too?*

"...I won't fool you, gentlemen, you will be jumping in some of the steepest, most densely forested terrain God could park in one place, so watch your backs and each other. Squad leaders meet me here in twenty minutes."

The men rose as a single entity, shuffling away from the tables, except for one lanky uniform who strolled toward Alex and Softouch. His short brown hair was unruly and a line creased it where a baseball cap had rested.

"I can't believe they still give you a pilot's license, you old reprobate!" Softouch reached out his hand in warm welcome.

"Yeah, well, up here they're less particular about the questionable characters I've ferried around in the past. Look at you, Upstate! Gone and got yourself promoted to squad leader!"

"I'm not alone, so did Garth." A shorter, sharp-eyed young man joined them and his first words flowed like honey.

"Hey, Softouch! I wondered where you hightailed it to after our last little party." He smiled at Alex, "And who's this pretty lady?"

"Excuse my manners. Alex, these are old friends from the service. The tall skinny one with the New York chatter is Jarod, we call him Upstate, and the Southern gentleman is Garth, alias Georgia." Alex smiled at each of them and shook hands. "Gentlemen, this is Doctor Alex Davidson. She's from home."

Georgia turned to Upstate, "I don't remember any service docs this pretty, do you?" Upstate shook his head and swallowed the last bite of his burger.

Alex blushed, then found her voice. "Well, don't get too excited, I'm a vet."

Upstate chuckled, "Just right for this group of animals, eh, Georgia?" Garth feigned a punch at the A-squad leader, their friendship obvious.

"So what are we dealing with here, Softouch?" Garth's soft southern accent belayed the seriousness of his question. The pilot rubbed his unshaven chin and thought before responding.

"Add a nice wind, stir well, and we could have another Yellowstone." Alex watched all humor drain from their faces. The squad leader from New York shook his head.

"Oh, don't say that, man."

"The conditions are identical; dense fuel untouched by fire for about a century, a hot, dry summer, and lightning strikes nearly every day. We just haven't gotten the big winds yet. That Sawtooth Ridge fire is the one that got you guys invited. We just get one area under control and she jumps the line minutes after we leave." He lowered his voice, "And I'll tell you, working in these mountains is no picnic."

Alex looked from one sober face to the other. "You make

the fires sound like they're alive."

Upstate contemplated a second burger. "What defines alive, Alex? These beasts move under their own power, they eat, and they breathe the same air we do. Believe me, they're alive." Firefighters around them nodded.

"And you learn to respect them like another living thing, too." Georgia rubbed his eyes, "to quote a wise man, 'that your days may be long in the earth.'" They all chuckled.

"How do animals respond to big fires?"

Upstate swallowed and said, "They usually graze just ahead of it, and leave if it gets real unfriendly. Fire has always been a part of their environment. They know how to avoid it."

"Really? They don't get burned alive?"

"Huh-uh. Remember Yellowstone? Well, despite the pictures the media blasted around the world, less than a hundred large animals died in those fires. What killed them, though, was the lack of food the following winter. I don't remember the exact figure, but I think over seven thousand elk alone starved."

Scotty's voice from across the room brought them back to the present. "Squad leaders, now, please."

"It was nice meetin' you, Alex. Upstate shook her hand. "And thanks for the eats."

As they walked away, Alex heard the lanky New Yorker whisper, "I don't need this again, buddy."

"I hear you." Georgia's southern drawl was soft and troubled. Upstate grabbed two more burgers, one in each hand. Alex waited until they were out of earshot.

"They seem really unnerved about Yellowstone."

"If you ever see Upstate with his shirt off, you'll know why." Softouch looked at her thoughtfully. "They were on the same team then, green recruits. One of those firestorms sent a baseball-sized chunk of burnin' lodgepole pine right into his back like a missile. It burned through his fancy Nomex fire-resistant shirt, leaving him with third-degree burns. Georgia rolled him on the ground until the flames were out. Took months to heal."

He rubbed his face, recalling old memories. "The '88 fires in Yellowstone rewrote the rule book on firefighting. Guys got trapped fighting a line in one direction, then the wind would change suddenly and they'd be running for their lives from a fire behind them. Fist-sized cinders flew over half a mile to start new fires, and flames raced from tree to tree, sometimes as fast as fifty miles an hour. It was a miracle nobody was killed." Softouch paused, the memories still vivid. "But the worst part was the fear. Those fires were uncanny, Alex, they acted like they had a major vendetta against the human race. There was powerful hate in those flames and it unnerved a lot of brave men."

"If it was so frightening, why do they still do it?"

Softouch smiled and shook his head. "Dear lady, it's the closest thing a modern knight gets to fighting the dragon. Haven't you ever done something just because it scared you?" Black eyes bored into hers, and she wondered if he could read minds. She didn't respond.

He pointed to a large radio receiver that had appeared on a table near the fireplace. "If you want, you can monitor our radio traffic. You might find it interesting." Alex thought she'd find it frightening.

Scotty's sober voice broke through her thoughts. "Squad leaders, there are some changes in the plan." Alex watched a man shift pins on the map, and add several more.

"The Tehamma just jumped the fire line we built yesterday. She's gaining speed, and heading for the Sawtooth Ridge. If they continue on their present course they will merge on this southern face right here," he pointed at the map, "and the only place left to go is right down the valley into the town of Cascadia. This could happen as early as tomorrow afternoon, so I want you ready to go by 4:00am."

He made eye contact with Upstate and Georgia. "You will jump at first light. Georgia, your B-squad will take the crest, and build your line along this ridge of the Sawtooth. Upstate, you and A-squad will be below him a half mile doing the same thing. C- and D-squads will mirror the play on the Tehamma."

He paused for any questions. There were none.

"There's another problem. The humidity has dropped from twelve to seven percent." Alex saw Upstate and Georgia exchange glances.

"And the weather service tells us the possibility of lightning strikes tomorrow is the highest yet. Sleep well, tonight, gentlemen, tomorrow is going to be a busy day." The group broke up immediately and climbed the stairs with their backpacks, each lost in his own thoughts.

Alex finished with her evening chores and escaped outside for some fresh air. The world was radically different from the one that had greeted her that morning.

Eight large bulldozers, massive machines that construct freeways, were parked along the airstrip. Behind them several jeeps, and pick-ups, and other four-wheel drives stood ready.

Heavy plastic cargo carriers, all pistachio green and bearing the Forest Service logo were stacked near the vehicles. Those that were open revealed axes, shovels, and an odd tool that mated a hoe to an ax. Alex would learn to call it a pulanski. Large drums were stacked separately, a safe distance from the aircraft, with "gasoline" or "kerosene" stenciled on each. Near the drums a large tent had been erected and under it were tables with rows of chain saws of various sizes. Several men were fueling and sharpening them.

The C-130 had been joined by two cousins—B-29's—and forklifts hustled between cargo stacks and planes with equipment and tanks of chemicals Alex couldn't identify.

Large radio antennas and odd-looking weather equipment had sprouted from the ground, and in a tent next to them she could see Scotty Powell, headphones on, studying a monitor.

This looks like a military base! Suddenly Alex understood the magnitude of their situation.

Fire was now the enemy, and around her men were preparing for war.

Chapter Thirty-seven

"Once around the park, gentlemen, the first class tour. Eyes left or you'll miss the view." Softouch banked the C-130 circling the fire area so the jumpers could see the lay of the land. In the pre-dawn gray it was easy to see the glowing edges of the two fires.

A spotter opened the door and tossed out two weighted streamers over the drop site and, while their pink and yellow colors were indistinguishable, their near vertical coiling fall was not. The spotter smiled, no wind yet. Jumpers would fall likewise.

"Okay, boys and girls, it's game time, top of the first. Georgia, your team's first at bat. Line 'em up." Twenty uniforms stood and faced the door, rechecking straps and buckles, lowering mesh face shields.

"Ten seconds to drop." Georgia faced his team to watch each one clear the door before the next jumper leaped.

"Three, two, one, go!" A red light over the door turned green and, one after the other, uniformed men leaped out of the plane and into the stark gray of dawn, as if it was the most natural thing in the world.

Upstate was already standing behind Georgia to line up his squad. "Break a leg, man." Georgia nodded, and jumped.

"Well, sports' fans, it's the bottom of the first, and Upstate, you're up. Ninety seconds to drop zone." Softouch pulled the huge C-130 up and around, circling lower along the slope.

"Ten seconds to drop zone." Upstate looked into the eyes of the nineteen men in front of him and swallowed hard. His stomach knotted.

Now the fires are like Yellowstone.

Softouch barked, "Okay, batter up! Three, two, one, go!" Upstate tightened his helmet, leaping after his last team member.

God help me, I'm responsible for each of them.

☪☪☪

Georgia's squad drifted silently to the ground and immediately gathered their parachutes in large wads of nylon and line. Then they retrieved saws and pulanskis, gas cans and water bottles from the equipment bags dropped after them.

"Okay team, the fire will move up this back ridge, so we have to work fast. Build two lines 100 feet apart, the length of this ridge. Then we'll burn." Georgia looked at his team. "Be sure to stay on the crest, planes will be dropping chemicals on both sides of us. Does everyone know where the helicopter take-out point is from here?" Heads nodded.

"Show me." Twenty yellow-shirted arms pointed in the same direction, east and downhill. Georgia had never asked them to do that before, he was nervous, and it showed.

"Okay. Spread out and keep the next pair in sight. Listen to your radios, and if I say get out, I mean get out now. Is that clear?" Again, hardhats nodded.

"Okay, let's get to work."

Before the sun cleared the mountains to the east they had carved two parallel lines in the earth for five hundred feet. Although the thin air was still cold, B-squad was sweating. Chainsaws screamed and firefighters scraped and tore the ground, piling slag between the two lines. Swampers followed cutters in a clumsy dance, stripping the earth of anything that might burn. The lines lengthened through the morning.

Upstate monitored Georgia's instructions and turned to his own team.

"Okay people, listen up. B-squad is up on the crest. Our job is to build a second fireline across the face of this ridge. When it gets light, there will be chemical drops below us, so pay attention." He searched the sky and felt the increased dryness on his skin.

"Escape route is straight downhill, folks, along the fall line. A logging road runs along that little creek in the valley floor. It's a long, steep hike, so if I say go, no heroics, drop everything and move out. Trucks will be waiting. Stay alert, people." He ran his fingers through his hair, but the mousy brown confusion remained.

"Questions?" He glanced at them; hardhats, green wool pants and Nomex shirts – an army uniformed for war.

"Then pair up, and let's do it." His squad chose their weapons and trudged away under the weight of chainsaws and axes. Upstate keyed his radio.

"Georgia, you copy?"

"Loud and clear, Upstate. How's your neighborhood feel?"

"Dry, buddy, very dry."

"Roger that."

"Man, you watch your back up there. I don't like the way this feels."

"I hear you, Upstate. Out." Georgia fingered the gold cross his wife had given him for luck, then slid it around so it hung down his back, out of the way.

The sun came up and they all struggled in the rising heat and still air. Lungs ached for oxygen density not available at high altitude, even on a clear day, worse now with the smoke. Trees unfortunate enough to take root in the middle of the fireline fell to the saw, martyrs for the cause. Firefighters breathed smoke and chewed dirt and sawdust, and it all merged into sweaty grime on their faces. Pausing occasionally to gulp water from gallon jugs strapped to their backs, now lukewarm, they made little conversation.

B-29's roared overhead, targeting their bombing runs, zooming as close to the treetops as each pilot measured his skill. Or nerve. Or luck. Bomb bay doors opened under their bellies and pasty chemical retardant shot through the air, blanketing everything in sticky red-orange goo.

B-squad had finished their long double line by mid afternoon and thoroughly doused the area with gasoline. Georgia never would recall what made him pause and look toward the oncoming inferno before giving the order to ignite the backfire. But he did.

As he studied the blaze a breeze played across his face, then another, then another, each stronger than the preceding one. When that fresh air reached the oxygen-starved wildfire seconds later, the lethargic dragon roared into life with a whoosh that could be heard by Upstate and his team, half a mile down the front of the slope. It flared with renewed vigor and doubled its speed toward B-squad. Georgia grabbed his radio, transfixed by the holocaust racing toward him.

"B-squad, get out! Get out now! *Repeat, evacuate the area*! *Go*! *Go*! *Go*!" He dashed across the planned burn and his nostrils were assaulted by the smell of gasoline.

"Oh, my God, the gas!" Only God heard his whisper. Dolmars of kerosene and gasoline littered the area, some partially full. Most, however, were empty, their contents liberally poured over the slag.

Sweet food for the starving beast.

Georgia shook his head, there was nothing he could do about the pending nightmare, except get his squad out. To his left and right, men erupted out of the underbrush, all heading for the nearest clearing, the landing site.

"B-squad to command, the wind just hit, and the fire's running. Repeat. The fire's running. No time to burn. B-squad falling back for helicopter pickup. Out." He paused below the fireline to verify all his people were moving, but frustration overwhelmed him.

I can't see them through the smoke! Did they all get out? He waited and watched.

Behind him a wall of fire leaped and danced lapping at the crowns of tall pines. It surged and rolled up the ridge like waves on the ocean, flames rising and curving over and down, gobbling up easy fuel and charging toward him. And the gas soaked slag pile.

Scotty Powell's commanding voice from the twin-engine helicopter overhead was unmistakable, "Georgia, get out of there immediately! We can see your team moving out. Fall back, squad leader! Now!"

Finally Georgia bolted downhill.

Scotty and Softouch heard Georgia's last order to his squad. The voice was barely discernible through the crackling, crashing inferno.

"B-squad, deploy when you reach the clearing. *Repeat. Deploy. Deploy.*" Softouch called to Upstate, who was already monitoring the fire through binoculars.

"Did you copy that?"

"Roger, Softouch. The fire just cleared the crest! When it hits that gas—" The first explosion cut him off, and others followed as fifty-gallon drums of kerosene and dolmars of gas swelled to twice their size, then blew up. Each detonation blasted dirt and rocks and human-sized chunks of burning tree hundreds of feet in the air. No wartime battle could look worse.

Upstate yelled into his radio, "Georgia! You okay? Over."

Silence.

"Garth! Come in, man! Over."

Silence.

Even if Georgia hadn't dropped his radio, he wouldn't have heard his friend. The dragon pursuing him roared and snarled its insatiable hunger, and its voice blocked out all others. The squad leader's world was no longer recognizable, it glowed red as war; earth, rocks, plants, sky, everything undulated crimson, vermillion, scarlet.

Blood red.

Survival instincts dominated motor reflexes, driving Georgia beyond normal agility. He crashed through bushes and shrubs, vaulted deadfalls, veered around boulders, and kept running. Behind him the firestorm inhaled oxygen and exhaled black smoke, and with each respiration smoldering cinders struck his bare neck, and sleeves and pants. Huge embers, like flaming red and orange basketballs, whizzed past his head and crashed into trees, shattering to ignite new fires where they landed. Any one of them would've killed him.

Georgia had become the prey, and his lungs ached from the chase.

Upstate watched the uncontrolled blaze. "Softouch! Are you up there? Get your ass to that clearing and pull them out! They can't deploy in this!" He looked around at his team, wide-eyed and staring at the wildfire collecting itself at the ridge.

"Negative, Upstate. I can't get in there with this wind. They have to deploy." As if to emphasize the point, the red and white helicopter slid sideways and dropped eighty feet, taking the top off a burning fir. The A-squad leader watched the pilot recover, amazed at Scotty's voice, unruffled by their near miss.

"Upstate, get your crew out of there. Fall back to the road, trucks are on their way." The squad leader studied the fire's roiling front, now strong and organized, racing down the slope toward them.

"No time, command, it's moving too fast and the road's too far." He licked his lips and thought for a second.

"A-squad, listen up! Fall back to Widow's Cave. Repeat. *Widow's Cave*! Not the road. It's closer. Clear the entrance and deploy as far inside as you can get. Move out now! *Go*! *Go*! *Go*!" He watched several yellow backs change direction, toward the cave.

Thank God they read those maps.

Softouch muttered to himself, "Sure hope that cave's not already occupied."

Alex paced in front of the radio, running her hands through her hair, and Leah watched her new friend's intensity build. Like a cougar preparing to strike, every muscle was tight, coiled. Something was coming. Suddenly Alex grabbed a yellow shirt and hardhat and bolted for the door.

"I can't just sit here and do nothing!" The screen door slammed behind her as she raced across the airstrip toward the medical coordinator.

☪☪☪

Georgia ran faster than he had ever run in his life. Branches knocked off his hardhat and slashed his face, but he didn't notice. He refused to look back, for fear he would stumble. And afraid of what he would see.

Keep running, I gotta keep running.

Tree sap warmed, then boiled, until pines exploded from the pressure, popping and banging around him. Large burning branches, hurled through the air as by some unseen hand, flew like javelins striking the ground ahead. He leaped over them, already concentrating on his next step.

Don't fall, southern boy, do not fall!

The heat was so intense against his back that his hair began to smolder and he could smell it with the wood smoke. Fear gained a foothold and the devout southern boy started to pray,

"...even though I walk—no, Lord—*run* through the valley of the shadow of death I will fear no evil... Right, God. No fear!"

All his exposed skin began to tingle hot, then blister; face, hands, ears. Burning hands fumbled for the small yellow pouch on his belt and pulled out his emergency shelter.

Good to 1400 degrees Fahrenheit. Sure hope so.

Flames danced across the fine hair on the backs of his hands and he watched them as if they were someone else's. When he clutched them to his chest to suffocate the fire, pain screamed inside his brain, banishing all thought but survival.

Keep running, Garth, gotta keep running and stay conscious.

Lightheaded, he pressed on and the red world spun and whirled around him.

Alex saw boxes stenciled with red crosses inside a helicopter idling behind the medical tent as she approached the incident doctor. Somewhere a radio chattered with the voices in the field. The dark-haired veteran named Michael Harrison looked up when she panted up to him.

"I'm going with you, Mike."

He shook his head, "I don't think so, Alex. This could be pretty bad. Plus, you said you hate flying in these things."

Her jaw tightened and her eyes started their own blaze. "Yeah, and you don't like my chili either, but you eat it. I'll handle the flight."

"But you're a — "

"A *vet*? Look, *Doctor*, it took me as long to get my degree as it took you to get yours, and a burn is a burn. You can use my help!"

He paused only a moment, then tossed her a parachute. "Put that on, it buckles in the front. Then strap yourself in over there. Hope you enjoyed Disneyland, 'cause you're in for the E-ticket ride of your life—Doctor."

Upstate reached the cave and ducked inside, just ahead of the fire and counted his team.

They're all here! Thank God!

Nineteen dirt-covered people greeted him in silence, B-squad was on the mountain—their friends—and worry was etched in the grime on their faces. In their hands fiberglass-and-foil shelters billowed gently, like sails waiting for a special wind. All of a sudden they looked very flimsy. Upstate directed his flashlight around the cave and grimaced at the gamy smell.

"Hey, is this nice or what? A bear cave without the bear!" His team chuckled nervously.

"Okay, people, here's the situation. I figure we have about two minutes till that fire gets here, so I want everyone on their faces as far back against that rock wall as you can get." They flopped to the ground, and nineteen foil shelters billowed and settled over nineteen humans.

Outside the roar increased and Upstate had to yell,

"Don't move until I give the all clear! Breathe shallow and calm, the air will get real bad! Seal down the edges as best you can." With that he dropped to the ground and covered himself.

Seconds later Satan's grown child raged against the mouth of the cave, sucking all air from it with a rush. But there was no fuel to satisfy its gluttony, so, with a belch of black smoke, it moved on.

Georgia caught a flicker of firelight reflecting off metal and raced to join his team, already flat on the ground beneath their shelters. He spread his hands, billowing his fiberglass-and-foil sheet behind him like Batman's cape and dove for a vacant spot of grass. He secured the bottom edge to the ground with his boots and made himself as flat as humanly possible.

A fireball whizzed through the air inches above him and landed with a heavy thud...close by. Overhead trees detonated and branches rained down... crashing even closer.

The dragon invaded the clearing with a whoosh, and sucked the oxygen from the air around the prone firefighters. Georgia heard it spit and snarl at nearby trees, until they cracked and split. When all available fuel was devoured, the fire sighed—a long, moaning sigh—and noxious black smoke filled the clearing, seeping under the tiny shelters.

Sweet Jesus, the beast really breathes! Oh God, if Satan has a voice, this is it.

Georgia slipped into unconsciousness as the gold cross, given to him for luck, seared its image into his back.

Chapter Thirty-eight

The twin rotors of the large helicopter beat in uneven rhythm and everything about the ride was fast—the lift-off, the speed through the air, and the force with which the wind buffeted them. But Alex hardly noticed it, her attention was on Doctor Harrison, and his voice through her headphones.

"Here's the oxygen bottles we use, are you familiar with them?" She shook her head. "Okay, you open this valve to here," he pointed to the gauge, "and check to make sure you have a steady flow. Then you fit the mask over the face, covering both mouth and nose. Secure it with this strap around the head, and move on to the next person."

"You don't stay with them until they regain consciousness?"

"This is battlefield triage, Doctor. Find the live ones and keep them that way 'til we can get 'em to a hospital. These folks will all be airlifted to Calgary. The hospital there is already expecting us. Got any questions?"

"No, I've got it." She scanned the inside of the large helicopter, noticing the other four members of the medical team for the first time. Although they were young men and women, she knew they were seasoned veterans of fire rescue. Their faces were deadly serious and none of them made eye contact with her.

Once the helicopter cleared the fire's blazing frontline, smoke thinned and Alex could see the damage in its wake. Most of the trees were on the ground, lying the same direction, as if a raging god had blown them over. Those that stood, did so tediously, charred and black. The flames were gone, but rising smoke identified a few smoldering areas.

Then she saw them. Like discarded chewing gum wrappers, the foil shelters of B-squad reflected hazy light amidst the blackness. No movement disclosed the presence of a human being beneath each glimmering sheet.

Alex stared at the shelters, willing them to flutter, or rustle, or crumple from a living mortal's activity, but nothing moved.

Their stillness unnerved her and suddenly she was anxious to get down, rip them away, and help the person hiding underneath. Medical instincts—idle for months—returned, and she was so caught up in the moment's urgency that she only gasped when the helicopter dropped its nose and dove for the clearing. Each second was precious time they could not waste on a gentle landing. The pilot didn't.

The foil shelters rippled from the whirling blade's rotor wash, and the craft hit the ground hard. The medics leapt out immediately and fanned out across the clearing.

Silence engulfed the smoky cave and Upstate eased back the top edge of his shelter and tested the air. Acrid, but breathable. The smoke was thick and his flashlight was only effective for a few feet, outlining shadows coughing around him.

"All clear, people! All clear! Let's get out of these body bags and back to civilization!" Nineteen people disengaged themselves from wrinkled tin foil and staggered to their feet. All coughed and a few gagged and vomited.

"Count off folks so I know everyone's conscious." Voices rang out through the smoky darkness.

"One."

"Two."

"Three."

And finally, "Nineteen." Upstate sighed, grateful, and leaned against cool rock, coughing several times. When he spoke next, his voice was hoarse and strained.

"Okay, let's get out of here." He slowly felt his way to the mouth of the cave, where the smoke was only lighter in color, not thinner. He keyed his radio.

"A-squad leader to command. All accounted for. What's the current status?"

Scotty Powell's voice was a welcome sound, "Command

to A-squad, nice to hear you. The fire burned out at your fireline. Repeat, your fireline held. Ground is hot and smoldering, but you should be able to make it to the road. Any injuries, Upstate?" He glanced at the coughing group of people stumbling to the cave's opening.

"Nothing serious." He coughed and spit. "Any word on B-squad?"

"Medics on the scene now."

"Please keep me informed. Out."

"Roger that, Upstate." The New Yorker squeezed his eyes shut against memories burned into his mind, and silently offered up a prayer for his friend. Then he looked at the shaken faces in front of him.

I gotta get these people out of here.

"Okay, team, we're moving down to the road. Stay together, and share any water you have left. Keep your eyes open for widow makers, I don't want to make it this far and get killed by some falling tree, clear?" Nineteen grimy faces nodded.

"We're gonna move briskly, but slow enough for everybody. If you need to rest, sing out. This smoke is murder, and breathing isn't going to improve until we drop below our fire line. Any questions?"

No one spoke, their watering eyes said it all. He tried to smile.

"Well, people, this was really fun, but the slumber party's over. Let's move out." Slowly, coughing and gagging, Upstate led his team to safety.

Their progress down the steep incline confirmed what the squad leader had suspected; they never would've made it to the road.

Alex clamped her jaws together and lifted the first shelter away from its occupant. She didn't remember his name, but recognized him as one of the men gathered around the radio the previous night. She checked for a pulse and breathing, and sighed, relieved to find both. He was rosy-skinned, but unblistered. Shaking him gently she yelled,

"Can you hear me?" No response, unconscious. She rolled him on his back, started an oxygen bottle and strapped it to his face.

"Come on, kid, I don't want to leave you. *Wake up*!" She shook his shoulder again, and he coughed, then lurched and vomited. Alex managed to pull the mask away just in time, let him spit, then replaced it.

This one's gonna make it.

She stood up and headed for another shelter some distance from the rest, confidence high. But that confidence vanished when she knelt to pull back the foil sheet. She had to swallow hard to avoid vomiting herself.

Charred fingers gripping the foil were burned in place and hardly recognizable as fingers. She had to pry them away from the sheet. There was no skin on the hands, just burned muscle to the edge of burned shirtsleeves, and when she lifted the sheet away, she could barely recognize the cooked tissue below it as the back of a head. The hair was gone, as was most of the skin, and raw muscle was burned and littered with ash. She reached around the neck for a carotid pulse and felt the gold cross.

"Georgia! Come on, let's have a pulse, okay?" She held her breath and only found it on the third attempt. Thready and weak.

"Thank God! Now breathe for me!" She turned him gently on his side, and placed the back of her hand near his mouth and nose, to feel any respiration.

Nothing. Weak pulse, no breathing.

She pulled the discarded shelter back under his head and gently rolled him onto his back, hardly noticing the blisters and loss of all facial hair. She checked his airway, pinched his nose closed, and exhaled a strong breath into his mouth.

Then she turned her head to the side, listening for any sound that his own lungs were operating. She saw his chest fall gently and heard the quiet whoosh as he exhaled the breath she had given him, then nothing.

"Come on, Georgia, you are not going to die on me! Breathe!" Nothing.

In seconds, Alex settled into a kneeling position at his side, checked her watch, and started mouth-to-mouth resuscitation.

What's the rhythm again? Right, twelve a minute.

Every four breaths she paused to recheck his pulse and respiration, then resumed breathing into Georgia's mouth, forcing air into lungs unwilling to draw their own.

Awareness of everything around her faded, and a familiar drive, previously trained only on animals, focused the combined skill of thought and action on the man in front of her. She saw and heard nothing else.

Across the clearing the rest of B-squad had been attended to, and most were painfully regaining consciousness, coughing and spitting to discharge the smoke and ash. They would all make it, some with burns and smoke inhalation. Doctor Harrison noticed Alex and rushed to her side.

Then he recognized her patient.

"How's he doing?" Between breaths, she responded,

"Pulse is growing stronger, but no response from his lungs." Another breath.

"How long have you been at it?"

She checked her watch, "Three minutes."

"I'll get a medic and stretcher over here." She nodded. He yelled and suddenly professionals surrounded Alex and Garth with medical bags and expertise.

"When I count to three, Ray will take over, Alex. One, two, three." Smoothly the medic took over resuscitation, another applied a dry sterile bandage under Garth's head, and Doctor Harrison injected something into his arm. Alex leaned back, light-headed and exhausted.

"Let's see if that brings him around." They all paused, watching his lungs.

"Come on, Georgia, *breathe,* God damn it!" Then, slowly,

his chest rose, muscles inactive for almost five minutes resumed the work they had performed for thirty years.

"Get him on oxygen, and loaded into the chopper. The rest of the team on board?" A voice yelled in the affirmative.

"When he's on, we go." He glanced at the helicopter, filled with weary firefighters.

"Looks like a full house. Alex, you wait with Ray and Denise. Softouch will pick you up." She nodded, still watching Garth's chest to confirm he was breathing on his own. In one smooth movement four men lifted him onto a stretcher and carried him to the helicopter. She stood by the door until he was safely strapped in.

"You did a good job, Alex." The command doctor smiled at her. "I'll make sure he knows who to thank." With that, he climbed aboard and the idling rotors increased rpm's and lifted off.

Softouch landed before the first helicopter was out of sight and the two medics and Alex collapsed into seats. Within minutes they were back at the command center. Upstate rushed over when he saw her enter the dining hall.

"How is he, Alex?" She took a deep breath, searching for the right words. The sensitive, least painful words.

He grabbed her arm, "Just tell me!"

"Okay. He's in real bad shape. Third degree burns on the back of his head, neck, and hands," she coughed twice, "it may be more extensive over the rest of his body. He was unconscious and not breathing when we got there. Harrison pushed some drugs," another cough, "and we did artificial resuscitation before he started breathing on his own."

The A-squad leader collapsed in the nearest chair, aware of the significance of her words. She dropped next to him.

"He's alive, Jarod. And he will get through it just like you did." She squeezed Upstate's hand, and he returned the grip, a strong, human touch. Looking down, she couldn't distinguish his hand from her own, they were both black.

"It called his name."

She barely heard his raspy whisper. "What?"

"The beast. He heard the beast call his name," Upstate stared at her and whispered, "It's the scariest sound in the world." His words sent chills over her body.

"You need to get some rest, Jarod. Your team's already crashed, you should do the same."

He nodded, "Sound advice, Doc," and dragged himself up the stairs to a shower and a bed.

Alex grabbed a beer and walked out to the front porch where Softouch found her minutes later, lost in thought.

"Heard you did some great stuff down there, Doc. Mighty proud of you." She faced him, her haunted eyes reflecting what she had seen, and her voice was shrouded in a familiar hoarseness.

"Would it be too much to ask for you to take me home tomorrow morning? Scotty said the fire bypassed my place, so it should be safe."

"No, of course not, you don't have to stay here. But why now?"

"I want to see what's left, and," a gut-wrenching cough doubled her over, "I want to get back to work." She sipped her beer and wiped black sweat from her face with her sleeve. She coughed again after swallowing the beer.

Softouch recognized her expression, he'd seen often enough in the mirror. He knew only too well that she needed to be in her own safe reality, and she needed time to file away the horror. He put his arm around her shoulders.

"We'll leave first thing in the morning. You can pick up that fine steed of yours and be home by tomorrow night." She nodded.

"Thanks."

There were tears in her eyes when Alex climbed into the idling helicopter. She was grateful for the engine noise that hid her distress from Softouch.

The two-passenger craft that had brought them to the

command center eased gently away from the ground as the first drops of rain hit the plexiglas shell.

Neither commented on them.

They knew God had said… enough.

Chapter Thirty-nine

Denied the town of Cascadia, the Tehamma Creek Fire converged on the valley of the wolves, but its unique circular geography proved a challenge. Forward progress was checked at the mountaintop and instead of rolling immediately over the crest, the roaring blaze spread around the slopes until it ringed the valley.

Gusty updrafts along the interior slopes were strong enough to hold the fire at bay for a few hours. Beyond that natural wall, the frustrated firestorm raged and roared, and dense smoke drifted into the valley from all directions.

Beings that kept body and soul together with finely tuned senses and healthy survival instincts were tormented by the scents and sounds of this fire that did not behave as its predecessors.

The animals of White-cub's valley became alarmed for the first time.

Daylight vanished beneath the smoke and in their rising panic, wildlife congregated at the river like they had during the drought. Species from all levels of the food chain met at the water and waited, one animal's prey stood near another's predator, the hunt suspended.

Although the valley was over two miles long and almost a mile wide, it shrank that night, dwarfed in a cage of flame. Twilight deepened and a ring of orange illuminated the sky around the mountaintops.

But still the lifesaving winds blew.

White-cub and his family tracked the riverbank that night and every instinct told Guardian to lead the wolves away. But short forays down familiar trails reinforced what the alpha sensed.

The inferno circled their valley. There was no escape.

The wolves paced and lapped at the water, drinking out of nervousness, more than thirst.

Near midnight the protecting updrafts blew their last and died, and an eerie stillness reigned for several seconds, as the wildfire collected itself. Then flames topped the crest and started down into the valley, devouring all before it in a glowing ring of death. The animals at the river watched, still unbelieving, until the first screams of singed beasts drove them to action. Panic ruled the moment, larger beings trampling smaller, as all bolted without order or direction.

Trees exploded, a sound like nothing ever heard in the canyon, and sent volleys of burning wood through the air. Flames leaped from crown to crown through the forest canopy, and outran the fastest legs. Ancient trees splintered and crashed to their death, trapping helpless victims.

Each earthbound animal followed his own genetic commands for survival. Rabbits and ground squirrels raced for their burrows and were trapped by red-hot debris, beavers sought refuge on the river, only to find their lodges enflamed.

For the wolves, survival lay in speed and agility so they accelerated, running for their lives. Fear ate away the dignity and structure of the pack and they dashed in several directions, toward no particular destination.

Thick smoke blinded them twice, by scent, as well as sight. Without tear ducts they could not wash the ash from their eyes, so they ran blind, and the smell of burning trees and underbrush tinted by the ominous odor of singed fur and flesh jumbled all scents.

In the chaos the wolf pack Patriarch and Cub-bearer had created was destroyed forever.

Guardian and Cub-bearer ran for the den, more out of habit, than any knowledge their subterranean home would be safe. Jester and First-twin were last seen leaping over smoldering fallen trees into the blazing forest beyond the river. No eye saw the direction Cunning took, she simply vanished.

White-cub ran south along the river's edge. The tender grasses along the shore roiled in waves of red and orange, and victims of the inferno littered the ground, overcome by smoke before flames touched them. He covered the ground with mercurial speed, side-stepping actively burning areas by running in the shallows. His eyes burned and his lungs ached, straining to find oxygen in the dense smoke. Moving through the water was slow and difficult so he ran through the white-hot embers along the shore, searing the pads of his feet.

The instinct of 1000 generations told Patriarch's son to run, and keep running.

To his credit, the white wolf traveled farther than any of his relatives from the river where they had gathered the last time. He endured flying debris that singed his fur and burned his face and ears, but he couldn't outrun the killing monster that robbed his lungs of precious air.

When White-cub fell, the last image frozen on his retina was the osprey's nest, ablaze above the valley floor like a beacon marking the disaster.

His final steps dropped him at the riverbank and the conscious world released him from his pain.

Chapter Forty

Not a blade of grass remained to feed the forest fire's voracious appetite and an ominous stillness settled over the valley of the wolves. The silence of a tomb draped the land and it was appropriate, for what had taken centuries to create was reduced to smoking rubble in just six hours. Where thousands of animals from scores of species once walked and raced, slithered and crawled, now only their incinerated corpses littered the ruins of their habitat.

The destruction was total and complete, no life stirred between the granite peaks.

It was immediately obvious to Alex that the rain had not reached this place, and only the absence of fuel vanquished the fire. The residents of this valley had not escaped its wrath and she was deeply shaken by the unexpected scene.

Horse and rider approached the blackened remains of a large elk, antlers scorched tar black, and beyond it a smaller form, cramped and stiffened in its final agony, too charred to identify. Dead bodies dotted the ground as far as she could see.

"This is all wrong, Viento, these animals shouldn't be here." The horse stepped gingerly around the elk. "They should have had plenty of time to escape... the animals always get away..."

Alex had seen the result of fire's handiwork on human flesh, and now the gruesome death around her knotted her stomach again and volatile emotions threatened to surface. She zipped up her jacket against the coolness of gathering clouds that finally blocked out the sun. The gloom was complete, even the weather mourned.

Viento picked his way along the riverbank, frequently walking in the muddy sludge to avoid large piles of debris. On drier ground only the largest tree trunks remained vertical. Soft heartwood charred away, the hollow shells stood tenuously erect, poised for the next strong wind to topple them. Trees of finer bone that had tickled the sky days before now created a surrealistic scene, wooden skeletons cluttering the ground like a giant's pick-up-sticks. Wind had gathered some in tangled, twisted piles, scaffolds for the dead trapped in their bony fingers. There was no color here, only a monochrome in shades of black.

Shadows inside shadows.

"Easy boy," Alex said, as the skittish mustang sashayed around another carcass, "slow and steady, V." She stroked his neck, her familiar hand reassuring.

She paused occasionally in their progress to search through binoculars for any movement that might indicate life, and the mustang, usually well-behaved, did not appreciate these interruptions. He stomped his feet and snorted, anxious to leave this place that reeked of death.

Each touch of hoof to ground released small clouds of fine ash that billowed and swirled around Viento's legs. He tasted the smoky air and toyed with his bit, frothing lightly. Alex coughed at regular intervals, but it did little to clear her lungs. There was no breeze to freshen the air and smoke collected in pockets, hovering over the ground like the displaced spirits of the dead.

Viento's nervousness escalated with each step deeper into the valley, and Alex took him firmly in hand. He wanted to bolt home, and she wanted to go with him. This was an unpleasant experience for them both, and the eeriness raised the hairs on the back of her neck. Too quiet. Too still.

Her mind groped for an explanation, but the facts laid out before her resolved nothing. In a whisper she mumbled,

"They're all here except the birds, did you notice, boy? Only the birds got away. I don't understand this, why didn't these animals run?"

A war had occurred here and the casualties stretching across the razed battlefield unnerved horse and human. For Alex the accumulating desolation weighed on her, heavier with the passage of each silent minute.

She reined Viento to a stop and studied her

surroundings, trying to unravel the grisly mystery. Dismounting, she knelt over animal tracks in the ash between several charred victims and shivered, as much from what she saw in the dirt, as from the chill in the air.

"They were hysterical, V, and they trampled each other." She gazed at the corpses around her, "but why didn't they leave the valley?" Her eyes drifted to the granite peaks rising above the valley floor. She stood and slowly spun in a circle, focusing her binoculars on the rim, and saw what she would not have recognized three weeks earlier.

The burn intensity was equal and balanced down each crag, each slope, each face.

"Oh God! The fire didn't burn through the valley from one end to the other, it burned from top to bottom!" She stared again at the peaks, and whispered to the dead, "When the wind died, flames came over the top all at once, didn't they? Like a ring of fire."

The band of mountains that had guarded the secluded valley for a millennium had formed a cremating trap, and Alex closed her eyes, visualizing the victims' last minutes. Their suffering became her own, and she mounted Viento, reluctant to continue her census of death.

Despair was an old companion and it resurrected an old pain. An unseen, intimate wound bled fresh.

"You were paralyzed by fear," she mumbled to the dead, "so the fire rolled right over you. This monster was familiar to you, but you didn't know you should be afraid this time." She coughed and rubbed her eyes.

"You never had a chance..."

Alex fought for control, pent-up tears threatening.

The reins fell from her hands and her composure crumbled. She leaned forward in the saddle, resting her face against Viento's mane as familiar sadness overpowered her like the fire had overpowered its victims. The desolation around her, blended with her private anguish and sobs racked her body. Tears flowed, unchecked, leaving dark tracks in Viento's dun-colored coat.

Several minutes passed before she was calm enough to continue. When she did, the demon Alex thought she had defeated rode with them, and when he laughed at her vulnerability and sneered at her pain, his voice was Stephen's.

The gray day promised rain and the chill deepened, but she continued. Late in the afternoon she noticed a patch of sooty light fur lying in the shallows several yards ahead so she urged Viento to a canter.

Alex drew him up seconds later and stared down at the dead white wolf.

Viento's agitation intensified, nostrils flared and he tossed his head vigorously, sending flecks of saliva flying. Alex felt tense shivers travel along the animal's skin and she responded instinctively, tightening her thighs and reining him back, away from the wolf.

"Whoa, V, that big guy's in no condition to hurt you." She recognized Viento's instinctive response to the predator, who, smelling of blood and burned flesh, spoke to the horse's genetic fear. She patted his neck and rode several yards upwind of the canine, dismounted, and tied Viento to a charred stump. She stroked his face until he gentled, suddenly aware of her own weariness.

"We've certainly been to more pleasant places together, haven't we, boy?" Her eyes burned from the smoke and she coughed. "We'll get out of here soon. Promise. But I want to take a quick look at him."

Kneeling over the wolf, Alex felt along his throat for a pulse, but was not surprised to find none. The canine was lying on his side in four inches of water, only his head was on dry land, and even his blistered skin was cool to the touch.

"Well, if these burns didn't kill you, hypothermia did..." She recalled a few wolf tracks mingled with others in the ash of the valley floor, but no wolves had numbered among the dead.

Until now.

She had hoped they, like the birds, had escaped the

inferno. She dragged him out of the water.

The skills of her trade surfaced and mechanically she went through the motions of an examination. The wolf's fur was burned away in large patches and the exposed skin, was blistered and swollen.

Some areas were burned deeper, to raw muscle and oozed clear serum. The pads of all four paws were charred, and the exposed tissue was muddy and stained with blood. The outside toes on both left feet were torn away, their wounds jagged, cauterized meat. She winced at the pain he must have endured to take the final steps that dropped him in the water.

Her hand moved over his ribs and Alex gave a start.

"What?"

She held her breath until experienced fingers detected one faint heartbeat. Seconds later, another, then a third, weak and irregular. Blood still flowed through the canine's body, but slowly. She jerked her sunglasses out of her pocket and held them close to the wolf's nose.

When she saw the lenses fog up a rare smile lit her face.

"Well, you are a tough one! No wonder you gave Viento a start, you're still alive. Let's see what we can do..." She pressed her palm to the wolf's chest to monitor his heart's feeble efforts.

Minutes passed and it grew weaker. Rhythm slowed, beats came farther apart, and she clenched her teeth and shook her head. Her brief optimism vanished, Alex knew she would soon feel his last heartbeat.

She ran her free hand through her hair, frustrated, angered by what she could not control, and addressed a God she'd grown to doubt.

"Damn it, God, he's not going to make it if you don't do something. Haven't you had enough death?" There was a defiant tone in her voice, her emotions were as raw as burned flesh, as fragile as her faith.

"I'm not asking you to part the waters here, God, just a bit of your strength added to his," she took a breath, and touched the wolf's face gently, "a little leftover miracle you have lying around," then she whispered, "please? This big guy could sure use one," she rubbed her tear-stained face, "and so could I."

Only Viento's ears caught her soft voice and the words faded away through the valley of the wolves.

Chapter Forty-one

Alex lost track of time waiting for the wolf to die.

Minutes collected into an hour, and still his feeble heart beat on, weak, but persistent. Twice she thought he was gone, only to be surprised by the next frail pulse against her hand.

Darkness and cold gripped the valley, and common sense told her she should return to her Jeep. But she was reluctant to leave the only living soul she had found, seconds before his last breath. Pulling her hand away from his chest while life still existed was beyond considering, she just couldn't do it.

And she wasn't sure why.

During those slow minutes her mind wandered through its own sad landscape, recalling her afternoon tears.

Why can't I get over you, Stephen? You still seem so close, and it still hurts so bad!

The old pain surfaced with new energy.

I have to stop doing this, that part of my life is over! How will I ever get off this mental merry-go-round?

While Alex itemized her failures again, realization passed slowly from her palm to her brain.

The wolf's pulse had quickened.

Stronger heartbeats throbbed in his chest, and counting them over thirty seconds confirmed it.

"Well, you don't seem to be ready to leave this life." Alex couldn't verbalize her thanks to God, but she thought it. Then she remembered where she was.

"Now, what am I going to do with you?"

It was completely dark, she was miles from her truck, and more miles from home. Lightning flashed inside distant clouds, and Alex counted seconds to the rumble, then sighed. She was also six miles from an approaching thunder storm.

With a very sick wolf.

She stroked the soft fur between his eyes. "If this were

my clinic I would've put you down when I found you, my friend." She checked his pupils, intrigued by the blue eyes, and thought warmly of her own blue-eyed huskies, safe at home in their kennels.

"But somehow out here that decision isn't so easy."

Her professional discipline battled with her heart; wilderness life was much more challenging than she had ever imagined. Alex had observed that from bee to bear each animal's struggle to survive was a daily exercise, and she had documented the many that failed.

Battered by his environment and surrounded by death, the creature in her hands was worthy of a second chance.

"We seem to be two of a kind, don't we? Neither one of us quite in control of our own lives." Her hands moved gently under his chin, down his chest from one scorched patch of fur to the next.

"Tell you what, if you're still alive when we get to the truck, you win a trip to my cabin." She yawned. "And if you're still alive when we get home, you win the best vet care any of your domestic cousins in the Seattle Police Department ever received. How's that sound?"

She paused, as if waiting for a response, then,

"I think it's a good deal, too." Somehow talking to the wolf disarmed the teeth and claws that set him apart from the dogs she'd known. And talking to him made her feel less alone.

Another examination—as thorough as she could perform by flashlight—convinced Alex his coma was deep, he would stay unconscious for several hours.

"You need to keep sleeping, my friend, or this ride is gonna be more excitement than any of us needs tonight."

Alex carefully spread White-cub's jaws to check the color of his gums. Pink. Good. Circulation is okay. She held her breath as fingers slipped between long canine teeth and heavy-boned jaws and she recalled the bleached elk skull from the wolf kill.

Were those your teeth marks? Were you part of that pack?

When he was stable, Alex set to work on her other task,

which required less of her medical training than the Girl Scout skills she had learned in her youth.

After several minutes of stumbling around with her flashlight, she found two ten-foot long branches that had been the trunks of young pine saplings days earlier. They were stripped and charred black, but still strong. She laid them next to the wolf's back.

Then she approached Viento, who had dozed off, head down, near the stump where she tied him. His head came up and ears pricked when she tripped over a hidden tree root, and while she untangled her boot a foreign sound rustled in a large pile of debris nearby.

Her tangled foot immediately became a secondary concern, the quivering bush raised the hair on the back of her neck. But her flashlight revealed nothing. She took a deep breath.

"Napping, huh boy?" She rubbed the mustang's muzzle and gave him an apple, while probing the darkness in the direction of the noise. Her spot of light was pathetically tiny and exorcised little darkness. Viento crunched into the granny smith, and juice mixed with saliva dripped from his velvety lips.

"I'm going to need your help here, V. I know you're not thrilled about our patient over there, but he's still alive, so I'm not going to leave him. And I'm not too enthusiastic about spending the night in this, um, scenic paradise."

Again something stirred in the darkness and this time Viento heard it and shifted his ears toward the noise, then flattened them against his head.

"Neither are you, I gather." She smiled.

"So we're going to take him home, and you're going to help." The mustang nickered, comforted by her words, but deaf to their meaning. Alex retrieved blankets and twine from the saddlebags, and set about to make a travois for the wolf.

Scratching, scampering animal sounds became more frequent and kept her on edge. She had seen no life during the day, but it was easy to believe that scavengers closed in under darkness to feed off the carcasses. Their unseen presence gave her no comfort and she worked fast, fingers wrapping and tying knots naturally; double half-hitch, here, bowline there.

The spookiness she had felt earlier that day was magnified a hundred fold, and the white wolf's deathlike stillness contributed its own macabre essence to the night.

She estimated the breadth of Viento and his saddle and spread the branch ends accordingly. Then she lashed a third, smaller branch across the other two ends, securing the width of the bottom of the travois, creating a giant "U" from the scorched saplings. She tied one of her blankets between the two long branches at the bottom to form a hammock. Then came the tricky part.

Alex laid a blanket along White-cub's back and gently lifted his legs, front pair in one hand, back in the other, and rolled him over onto the blanket. This revealed the burns on the other side of his body and Alex winced at the pain her manipulations were probably causing him, even in his unconsciousness.

She whispered to him in the voice that so many domestic animals had heard before, a tone that communicated respect and trust, a voice to calm fear's racing pulse.

"I'm sorry, my friend, but this is the only way I can help you. Do you understand that?" She glanced over the burns on the other side of his body and shook her head. He had been unconscious for at least twenty-four, so in addition to his injuries, he was probably dehydrated and shocky.

Alex knew if she left him, he would be dead by morning.

She wrapped him in another blanket and, as gently as she could, slid him onto the travois and secured him with twine.

Viento balked when she backed him between the open ends of the wooden poles, and when she tied them to each side of his saddle he laid his ears back, tossed his head vigorously, and snorted. Alex couldn't tell if his response was caused by the smoke-smelling structure strapped to him, or the cargo on it, but in her fatigue, she didn't care. She mounted and firmly directed him towards the car.

They set off the way they had come at a careful walk, a trip of hours, interrupted when the travois snagged itself on a branch or boulder.

During the ride she glanced over her shoulder to confirm the wolf was still unconscious. The thought of what he would do if he woke up, trussed and bundled, gave her chills.

Midnight had come and gone when they reached her Jeep on the fire road above the valley, and she faced another obstacle. With the horse trailer attached, she could not get Viento close enough to slide the wolf into the rear of the Jeep.

How am I gonna get you into the back of the truck? I might be strong enough to lift you, but even if I could it would antagonize those burns.

After some consideration she finally resorted to the only option left, she disconnected the horse trailer and drove her truck ahead far enough to bring Viento in very close to the open hatch in the back. Then she lifted the bottom of the travois onto the rear of the car, untied the twine securing him to the branches, and slid the sleeping wolf, blankets and all, inside. Then she reversed the process, backed up the truck, and attached the trailer, each step grueling in her fatigue.

When Viento was finally loaded, she collapsed into the drivers' seat and sighed, grateful for the safety of the heavy vehicle. The creepy noises of the long ride faded. She was a vet again, with a patient who needed what only she could give.

Smells filled the Jeep. Smoke. Her own sweat, and Viento's. Burned flesh. And another smell. The essence of wild canine.

Wolf.

What have I gotten myself into here? Even if he makes it back to the cabin, he may die in the next few days. She rubbed her eyes.

And what if he doesn't?

Chapter Forty-two

Exhaustion set in during the tedious drive and Alex battled to stay awake. Thoughts of the bed she would not enjoy flitted though her mind, but she dismissed them.

With Viento settled in one of the corner stalls, she laid fresh straw in the stall farthest from the mustang. Then Alex lowered the wolf from the truck, wincing when his head banged the floor, and slid him into the stall, still wrapped in blankets.

Removing the blankets was not easy. Where his burns had drained and dried, flesh had bonded to fabric, and it took her almost an hour to cut the wool away to avoid tearing at his blisters. The fact that she was shredding two of her blankets never crossed her mind.

While coffee brewed she washed the grit and smoke grime off her face and arms, splashing her face with cold water to focus her mind on treating the wolf.

The fact that she brought the wolf home already screamed that her judgement was clouded, but she side-stepped that thought.

Let's see, he's no different than a severely burned dog at this point—or any mammal for that matter—so treating his burns will be no different than, well, a firefighter. At least until he becomes conscious. Infection and dehydration are the major issues. And I need to figure out some way to keep him off his feet until they heal. That's a problem.

Alex collected the equipment and medications she would require, two pairs of clean socks, and filled a thermos with steaming coffee before returning to the barn.

Only the quiet rustling of Viento shifting his weight from side to side in his sleep broke the cozy silence. Evidently the scent of his predatory stable-mate did not keep the exhausted horse from sleeping.

Alex paused when she stepped into the wolf's stall. Glaring light from the naked bulb overhead defined an animal much larger than he had appeared in her car. She had imagined wolves to be the size of German Shepherds, but her new patient was much larger than Rommel and his peers. Paws almost as large as her hand, and canine teeth easily two inches long caught her breath. His head was not wide, but the skull and jaws were dense-boned and tough, suitable foundation for the teeth. Leaner than a German Shepherd, and longer, nose to tail, he was a perfectly designed hunter.

In the bright light his injuries were starkly grave, much worse than she had evaluated by flashlight and Alex reconsidered her decision to let him live. He was much closer to death than life. But they had struck a deal, this unconscious canine and his vet, and she would honor it. Compassion and fatigue overpowered clinical reason and briefly she succumbed to a layman's pity. She felt this wild canid's pain like a child aches for a sick pet.

Thoughts became speech and, as she had done so often in her clinic, she talked to her new patient as if he were human.

"You are a pathetic mess, my friend, that is for sure. I hope the stamina that got you to the river is still there, you're going to need it to carry you through the days and weeks ahead. You are in for one continuous throbbing session of pain." She shook her head.

"I can treat your injuries, but how you deal with that pain will determine your future," she frowned, "and if you have a future."

She knelt next to him and lifted a foreleg.

"First, let's get some fluids into you. If you dehydrate any further you won't live long enough for the pain to become an issue." By following the direction of hair growth—where there still was hair—she found the large veins in both front legs and set two intravenous needles and started drips of Ringer's solution with lactose. Then she suspended the plastic bags from a rope tied to the vertical iron bars topping the wooden stall walls. She looked at the primitive arrangement of tubing and rope, the straw beneath her patient, and shook her head.

"Pretty poor excuse for a clinic," she muttered.

But in spite of her complete exhaustion, she had come to life, energized, doing the one thing she knew better than any other. However humble the surroundings, Alex Davidson was practicing veterinary medicine again.

"Now for the burns. I guess I don't need to tell you this is gonna hurt... I'll work on the largest ones first, we'll save the feet for last." She gently soaked each patch of blanket off, flushing the burned flesh with aqueous penicillin until the dirt and ash were gone. Then she covered each burn with furacin. While carefully washing the soot from his face, she checked his eyes again, relieved to find no sign of burns or infection.

Alex winced when she started washing his paws. Small pebbles, bits of dirt, wood, and ash, had become imbedded, and the flesh had swollen around them, forcing her to patiently spread the puffy tissue and pick each speck out with tweezers. It was mind-numbing, tedious work, and took hours. She sutured the ragged wounds where toes had been torn away from both left feet and applied antiseptic. A dry dressing covered the antiseptic and one of her ski socks held the dressing in place.

"Snappy dresser!" She smiled at the white wolf, wounds cleaned and bandaged, and four bright purple ski socks stretched the length of his legs.

"I can't have you tearing at these bandages so you're gonna have to sleep for awhile." She penciled down a schedule of sedatives to keep him unconscious until the initial healing was established.

Alex settled herself in the straw near his head and tugged at the mail she had jammed into her jeans pocket. She hadn't read it since returning from the fire. All the envelopes had familiar addresses, and she smiled. You get no junk mail in the mountains.

Chapter Forty-three

Alex recognized her sister's strong handwriting and opened that envelope first, leaving the rest in the straw next to her. Outside thunder and lightning owned the night, but the stable was warm and cozy.

"Hi sis! Hope all is well in your mountain paradise. There was alot of news about those forest fires up here, but I know you were smart enough to stay away from that action..."

Right.

"... Alex, remember those picnic trips when Dad and Mom took us up to Hurricane Ridge to watch the elk? And all the hikes and pack trips in the Cascades? Well, I've always believed that you and I draw strength and perspective from the mountains. It's why I think you decided to take that job..."

Where's this going?

"... Well, sis, I'm praying with every cell of my being that those Canadian Rockies have been generous to you, and made your spirit strong, because I have some bad news. I wish I was there to tell you this in person, instead of cold words on paper..."

Alex's heart skipped a beat.

"... Yesterday, I went to Stephen's to pick up Alpha and Omega as we arranged. They weren't there. Only Carmen was home, and after some struggling interaction I deciphered that Stephen got rid of them right before he remarried. Carmen said he gave them to a family with a couple kids, a girl and a boy. But the fact is, Alex, they've been gone a long time, and were probably already gone the day you called Stephen to arrange for me to pick them up."

Alex stopped breathing.

"I know how much you love those dogs, and how much this will hurt you, and I wish I was there now. I feel your pain as you read this, Alpha and Omega were far more than pets. But please find some measure of relief in knowing they are with people that love them. You always said huskies were perfect dogs for kids, so I'm sure Alpha and Omega are happy."

The short letter ended abruptly, "I'm so sorry, Alex. Know that I love you, Danni."

It wasn't the only lie Danni had ever told her sister, but it was the kindest.

The letter slipped silently from Alex's hand and she slumped forward. The walls began to spin and the reality of Danni's words knocked the wind out of her as if she had been punched.

Her dogs were gone.

Memories of the two huskies that had shared her life so completely and loved her so unconditionally, flooded her brain. Their playfulness. Their intelligence. The smell of their fur and its softness against her skin.

When she was finally able, Alex inhaled one large gasping breath, then started to pant, as if suddenly there wasn't enough air for the three beings inside the small barn.

For several seconds she could not move from her place in the straw, but when her gaze fell on the wolf, her eyes started to blaze. She grabbed the letter, crushed it, and clenched her hands into fists so tight fingernails dug into flesh. Her jaws clamped together, and the rage her sister had felt hundreds of miles away, started to boil in Alex.

Fire and ice. Hot. Hard. Hatred.

And there were no tears.

Leaping to her feet, she reeled out through the stable doors, and lurched into the darkness, gasping as if her lungs would burst with her fury. Icy rain drenched her in seconds but she didn't notice, and if words accompanied the wrenching images tumbling through her brain, they failed to cogitate intelligently.

Exhaustion ripped away all pretense and Alex Davidson turned her face skyward, raised her clenched fists and screamed like the wounded animal she was.

"Noooo! Please! Noooo!"

In the surrounding forest, animals paused, intrigued by the mournful cries that filled the silence between claps of thunder. But none of them doubted its meaning. Alex's primal screams were as old as life itself, and they all recognized the sound of pain.

"*Damn you, Stephen*!" She cursed to the heavens as rain poured down her face, her neck, her arms. Hair hung down her back in a wild blonde mass, and her soaked clothes stuck to her body. Still, she didn't notice the wet or cold, anger warmed her blood and hot muscles tightened, rigid, poised to strike.

"Lying bastard! I will *never* cry for you again!" She gasped for breath, "Alpha and Omega were *mine*! You had no right!" She panted like an animal.

"I *hate* you, Stephen!"

All the earlier defining moments foreshadowed this single instant, and lightning flashed, illuminating a wild woman-beast, more like the wolf on the floor of her barn, than the rich man's wife she had once been. The animal inside the woman spread its wings and pain set her spirit free.

The kindred strength of every other defeated woman that had risen from the ashes of an abusive relationship surged through veins and arteries. Like Phoenix rising from the ashes, rage resurrected a survivor where a victim had languished.

Alex walked taller when she returned to the barn, and didn't change out of her wet clothes that night. They were the baptismal robes of a new life and she felt cleansed.

Reborn.

Alex stayed with the wolf that night, her treatment as much companionship as professional care. Although she would've denied it, she transferred the affection once saved for two huskies, to this, their wild ancestor. She was reluctant to leave him to bear his pain alone. That she should fear him never crossed her mind.

"It seems, my pathetic friend, that fate has not exactly dealt us the best hands."

She brushed hair from her face, and thought of Alpha and Omega. Tears threatened, but never fell. Her hand rested on the smooth fur that still clung to the wolf's ears. It was as soft as the huskies'. She focused on the wolf, side-stepping her loss.

"What was your puppyhood like? Were you part of a large litter? Obviously, you got your share at the dinner table."

And on it went through the hours, Alex's quiet voice, the barn warmed by mammal bodies, the smell of horse and straw and coffee. Calm and content at a depth unknown before, she sat with her patient, stroked him gently, and in those early hours of his care the black knot of her own wound loosened.

When her fatigue would no longer be denied she lay in the straw next to wolf, resting her hand on his neck, and slept.

Several times during the night the wolf awakened her, whining and jerking through some unconscious nightmare. Her light hand and soft voice calmed him.

Alex felt a bond through their suffering that transcended species.

The next days and nights found Alex in the stall, redressing his burns, or simply giving him the warmth of her own company. As she checked his injuries and applied medication, she talked of her life, sharing with the unconscious wolf the deepest, most humiliating betrayals that she could not share with a human. She whispered of broken trust and violated promises and, in the telling, her burden lifted.

She often brought her guitar to the stable and played and sang. They were the songs of her childhood, hiking songs, and folk songs, and ballads, learned in her life before Stephen. She had forgotten how much she enjoyed them and she had not sung them in years.

Through his deep slumber White-cub heard a soothing spirit voice and smelled a warm spirit-animal. The pain rose and fell in waves, and always when it subsided the spirit voice was there. Odd rhythmic sounds and unfamiliar melodies comforted him like the howling of his old pack, and it became a beacon through his pain.

Sedatives played games with White-cub's mind, and memories of Patriarch and his pack danced in jumbled disorder through his dreams, accompanied by the woman's sweet scent and gentle song.

White-cub recovered physically, and Alex's broken, angry heart started to mend. Woman and wolf healed one another through those early days of autumn.

Chapter Forty-four

"She has a what?" Matt's voice silenced all conversation in the Knotty Pine.

"A wolf. Alex's doctoring a wolf that she rescued after the fire." Softouch was not thrilled to be sharing the news.

"Well, she is a vet, you know."

"This isn't some blue-haired lady's poodle, Matt," the black man shook his head and lowered his voice, "and I can tell you this is doing nothing to improve her reputation in our friendly little hamlet."

"I doubt if that concerns her," he glanced around at the bar's guests, "it never did me." He slid his glass to Softouch for a refill. "How bad is he?"

"All she said on the radio is he's so severely burned that she'll have to keep him sedated for awhile." He handed Matt his beer. "Of course, half the province was listening when she said it."

"Why didn't she just put him down? She must know he could get dangerous."

Softouch leaned on the bar, "I think our pretty doctor has her own agenda." He wiped the bar where it didn't need it, and paused in front of Matt.

"I shouldn't have taken her up there to the fires, that's probably part of this problem." He frowned. "She saw some pretty awful shit, Matt. Firefighters burned like a burger too long on the grill. That plus everything else she's been through—I think she was overwhelmed. And now I think she just needs to see something live," he wiped his hands on the towel wrapped around his waist, "or maybe she needs to *help* something live."

Matt nodded. "Well, I can certainly relate to feeling powerless." He'd just returned from the latest court battle against a legalized wolf hunt in Alaska. The fight had been lost, and the hunt was under way before he was out of the state.

"Look, Matt, maybe you could convince her to quietly

put this poor beast out his misery. It doesn't take much to spook the locals, and a pain-crazed wolf running in the woods would most certainly set them to chanting."

Matt contemplated his beer and smiled, "Well, I was planning on visiting her."

"Really?" Softouch grinned, "I never would've guessed," his southern drawl eased the sarcasm. "Just tread lightly, she's not the same lady you left here last spring."

"That's the best thing you've said today," Matt muttered as he headed for the door.

Alex was humming a tune and bandaging the wolf's feet when he walked through the stable doors. She didn't hear him and he stopped behind her without making a sound, so taken was he by the sight of her on her knees, nursing the white wolf.

Her back was to him and an oversized black turtleneck sweater and black Levi's accented the shine of her hair, longer and blonder than Matt remembered.

A man could lose himself in that hair. He watched her carefully replace the last purple sock over the IV tubes.

"The socks are a nice touch." She jumped up and whirled around.

"How long have you been standing there?"

"Hours." His smile tickled some dormant internal organ south of her stomach, and Alex felt blood rising to her cheeks. She turned quickly back to the wolf so he wouldn't notice her blush.

"Yeah, he's making a real fashion statement, alright." Her mind raced for more words. Unsuccessfully.

Matt knelt in the straw so close to her that she could smell the soap he used. It was a clean man-smell, nothing like the designer soaps that Stephen collected. Matt reached out to touch the animal, then paused, hand in mid-air, "May I?"

"Of course." He lifted one 4x4 carefully to see the burn beneath it and almost winced. Scabbed over, raw flesh.

Careful, Matt, ease into this.

"Not exactly a trophy specimen you have here, Doctor."

"No, I don't expect he'd win any beauty prize, but when I found him he was barely breathing." She met Matt's gaze. *Did he see me blush?*

"Did you consider just putting him out of his misery when you found him?"

"Yes, but I just couldn't bring myself to kill the only living thing I'd seen in a whole day of charred bodies." Her hand rested on the wolf's neck defensively.

"How bad are his feet?" Matt slid one sock off, but couldn't see anything under the bandages.

"He lost the two outside toes on both left feet, and the pads are blistered on all four." Alex noticed how gently Matt replaced the sock. He weighed his next words.

"Alex, a wolf lives by his feet. If he can't run he'll starve."

"I didn't intend to cancel his room reservation tomorrow." She bristled for an argument and Matt side-stepped it.

"How long will you keep him sedated?"

"Only a few more days."

"Do you have any idea what he's going to be like when he wakes up? You could have a pain-crazed killer on your hands, Alex. What will you do then?"

"I'll put him down, of course." She knew they were dancing around this single issue—and not in the same direction.

"What are you going to do with him if he recovers? Have you planned for that?"

"I... well... I thought I'd let him go." Obviously she hadn't considered the future.

Matt took her hand and she didn't resist.

I have to make her see him the way I see him right now.

He waited until she looked at him and said gently, "Alex, I really don't think you should wake him up at all. Look at him. He's got second and third degree burns all over his body. Can you imagine that kind of pain?" They both stared at the patient. "In your clinic would you try to save a dog burned this bad?"

"This isn't a dog, Matt, and this certainly isn't my clinic."

He glimpsed her wounds, as raw and exposed as the wolf's.

"But I can't kill him now," she sighed, "I... Well... I made a deal with him."

"A deal?" He raised his eyebrows.

She nodded. "The night I found him was pretty awful. We were way out, miles from the road, there was a horrible thunderstorm. I entered the valley expecting just empty land and burned foliage. What I found was a valley full of charred carcasses." She squeezed her eyes shut to blot out the image.

"I was just so glad to find something alive that I told him if he survived til we got back here, I'd take care of him."

What made sense that night sounded silly now. "He was still alive when we got here, so..."

"I see."

Now what? A promise is a promise... he rubbed his hands together.

"You know, Alex, most wolves would go nuts just being locked in this little wooden stall. How will you know if he's just scared—which he could survive—or permanently disturbed, when you wake him up?"

Her eyes are so blue...

"Well, I don't know," she stammered, "I hadn't thought of that." She turned away from him, painfully aware of the lapses in her plan. "I've been too busy trying to just keep him alive."

She stroked the wolf for several seconds, and realized that maybe she was out of her element trying to treat this wild canine. She stood up and walked to the doorway and gazed out at the hills.

Good, she's thinking. Maybe we can resolve this yet.

She turned and faced him.

"You're right, Matt, I don't know anything about wolf

behavior. But I won't nonchalantly kill an animal that has come this far." She shook her head and a separate part of Matt's brain noticed how her skin glowed in the afternoon sunlight pouring through the doorway.

"On Friday I'm going to withhold sedatives. Why don't you come up here in the morning and we'll watch him wake up together." She took a deep breath, "And if you believe he's crazed, I'll put him down."

She walked back across the stable and faced him, suddenly defiant.

"But understand, Matt, if he lives or dies, it will be your decision. Personally, I believe any animal that can survive this might have something to contribute to the gene pool." She paused, but did not look away.

"You understand if I put him down, it will be on your head?" Matt saw the fire in her eyes and knew the challenge was a professional one.

"Fair enough," he nodded. "I'll be here Friday morning." He turned back to the sleeping animal on the floor. "You may be right, I can hardly believe he's alive now, he must've looked alot worse when you found him." And as easily as that they became colleagues instead of opponents, and it felt right to both of them.

"Why don't I fix some coffee, and you can educate me on what I have to do to set him free? That is, if he lives past Friday."

"Okay. Releasing a wolf into the wild requires approvals from the government—paperwork—a lot of planning."

This, I do understand, thought Matt.

"We'll have to move fast to have everything in place when he's ready to go."

They went into the house and were still pouring over maps, and making notes when the sun set.

"I think that's all of it. Let's see, I'll take care of the approvals, and pick up the cage if they all come through." Matt stood up and stretched, stiff from hours of sitting on the floor.

"We shouldn't have too much trouble with that location. It's very remote. No people." Alex took the coffee cups to the kitchen and started filling the sink.

"You're sure we have to collar him?" She didn't look up as she washed the mugs.

"Absolutely. It's standard practice now, and I'm sure the service would require it, considering what he's gone through. We'll want to monitor his movements for awhile." Matt grabbed the dishtowel draped over the refrigerator handle and dried the mugs as she handed them to him. It felt natural and they were comfortable with the silence that followed.

Matt asked, "Have you seen any of the wolves around here since you moved in last spring?"

Alex smiled, looking into the sink. *Have I ever...*

"Yes. Well... heard them actually, and seen tracks."

She recalled the terror of her first night and immediately decided not to share that story.

"I heard them almost every night before the fires."

"How 'bout since then?"

"Well, I've been back a couple weeks, but... no, I don't think so." She took the towel from him and their fingers touched. Skin brushed skin for the briefest electric moment, then they pulled away and looked away, surprised.

"Well," he smiled mischievously, "I think we should take a little informal survey and see if any of your canine neighbors survived."

"What?"

"Come on, I'll show you." He grabbed her elbow and pulled her toward the front door, his eyes sparkling like a child about to reveal a great secret. A sharp bite of cold greeted them outside, and while stars forbade snow that night, few nights would pass before winter would deliver it. Alex followed him to the edge of the canyon.

Matt gazed up and down the valley and Alex watched him.

What is he looking for? I can hardly see my boots.

She stood quietly while he walked to the very edge, cupped his hands around his mouth like he was going to yell, and howled. It was as close to a wolf's howl as Alex could imagine a human making.

"Won't a wolf know you're not—"

"Shh. Listen." He howled again. Silence. "You try it."

She shook her head, self-conscious. "I don't think so, I wouldn't know how."

He grinned and lowered his voice. "Just do like I did and try to sound like the howls you've heard."

Alex felt silly, but cupped her hands around her mouth like a megaphone and howled. Her first attempt was pitifully weak, but Matt encouraged her.

"Do it again. Louder."

Before she lowered her hands from her third howl, a canine voice, far distant, responded in a wild howl that raised every hair on Alex's body.

"Oh, my God, it worked!"

"Yeah, and you won't find anyone that can explain why. I've heard them respond to train whistles and ambulance sirens." The smile Matt gave her would've melted steel.

"Let's see if he's alone. Howl with me, and keep it up for a minute or so."

They did. And after a few seconds, other canine voices joined the first, and Alex was carried away by the magic of her first communication with the wolves of her valley. Matt's eyes never left her face while she howled, and when she turned back to him, the warmth of his gaze heated her from head to heels.

Matt slowly pulled her to him and lips touched, like the howl of the wolf, first tentative, then strong and confident. Her arms went easily around his neck like they had been there before, and he held her so close their bodies fused.

Alex's celibate soul responded to his kiss with a need of its own, and she surrendered to the moment. Desires, long dormant, blossomed and she devoured him like a starving refugee her first meal. They kissed with a primal drive as wild as the wolves' song.

When the wolves grew silent several minutes later Alex

dropped her head and nestled her face against Matt's chest. She felt his heart beating as fast as hers. He ran his hands through her hair and neither could find words to fill the silence. She put her arms around his waist and ran her hands up his back, exploring the hardness of his body. Her fingers elicited a soft groan and she felt his arousal, hard against her.

He pulled her face away with both hands to look into her eyes, and Alex saw her own vulnerability reflected back. Matt saw what he needed to see, liquid need and longing. He kissed her again, and again, as the desire rose for them both.

Then he hugged her close and between deep breaths he said, "I think I better be leaving, Alex." His voice was husky and she marveled at how he was so obviously moved by her. Never before had any man so openly wanted her—certainly not Stephen—and this new power gave her strength. His obvious appetite was sweet beyond words. And seductive. She pulled away from him slowly, wanting only to drag him to her bed and make love until sunrise.

"Yes, it is getting late. And it's pretty cold out here."

"I hadn't noticed." They exchanged smiles and turned to walk back to his truck. His arm fell around her waist as if it had worn a spot there from years of familiarity.

"I'll see you on Friday." She nodded, silently screaming for him to get out of the truck and stay with her.

"Be here about eight." Her smile warmed every molecule of his being, and he started the truck quickly before his sexual aching made him reach for her again.

God, I don't need this again! No woman's done that to me for years!

What Matt didn't recall was that he hadn't let a woman get close enough for years.

Alex checked on the wolf and bedded Viento who had grown accustomed to his silent canine neighbor. The tingle of her own arousal didn't fade and when she finally went to bed, sleep eluded her for hours. She ached for Matt at the core of her being, a place long barren of human touch, a place that screamed to be stroked and caressed and explored.

She replayed the unexpected evening and the inevitable questions started.

Was his kiss so good because it was Matt, or because I've been so long without a man?

Did Stephen ever move me like that? She couldn't remember.

Were we just swept away by the moment, or was there more to it?

Does Matt just think I'm needy?

It was a long night.

The hours passed no more quickly for Matt. He sat in the empty darkened bar, reluctant to climb the stairs to the room Softouch loaned him whenever he was in town.

God, I couldn't keep from kissing her! We fit so well.

He drew himself a beer, and absent-mindedly pulled a crumpled dollar bill from his pocket.

And all the rich lady stuff is gone, she seems to fit up here like a... a real wild child!

The thought appealed to him, it was a phrase his own mother called him during his boyhood. And then other memories—unpleasant and hard forgotten—returned.

But I don't need this... not again.

Two more dollars joined the first before he went upstairs to suffer his thoughts horizontally.

And wait for Friday.

Through his drug-induced sleep White-cub heard howls, some familiar, some not. And he rested.

Chapter Forty-five

Questions plagued Alex for three days, doubts about the wolf, reservations about Matt. All were unsettling, and she knew they would monopolize her brain until Friday.

How will Matt act when he gets here? Like nothing ever happened? Does he regret...? And how will my patient behave? Will Friday BE his last day?

These unresolved issues spiraled through her mind in an unending loop and shattered her calm, replacing contentment with restlessness. Each day brought her closer to resolution, and she anticipated its arrival with neither eagerness or reluctance.

The only certainty was Friday would bring change.

Thursday night Alex tranquilized the wolf for the last time. He had exhibited the remarkable healing capacity she had observed over and over with the dogs in her clinic. Burns on his chest and back were dry and scabbed over, she had left them uncovered for the last two days, and even his feet no longer oozed. Settled in the straw near him, where she had spent so many evenings, Alex stroked him with no more fear than she had petting her huskies.

"Well, my friend, tomorrow's the big day. You've been so still, it will be odd to see you open your eyes and move on your own." Her fingers played around the soft fur on his muzzle.

"I'm going to remove the rest of your bandages in the morning, you'd just rip them off when you wake up anyway. And I'm not going to tie you up, or muzzle you, so please don't tear the place apart, okay?"

Alex was reluctant to leave him that night and she sang quietly and stroked him, measuring and memorizing the feel of the wolf. A great sadness washed over her. Rationality forced her to acknowledge the end of their odd intimacy, and accept the necessity for protection from this animal she had cradled through his pain. And her own.

"I won't be able to sit with you like this," she whispered,

"not after tomorrow. And I'm going to have to lock you up, but it won't be forever."

She laid down in the straw next to him, her chest against his back like she had that first night, and draped one arm over him. His wild wolf scent overpowered the medicinal smell of antiseptics and ointment, and in her mind she was once again cuddling her husky pups. She remembered how they would fight for the closest place to her heart, curl up and sleep nestled against the only mother they had ever known. She recognized that her grief for them intensified her feelings for the wolf, and her anxiety about his future.

Reality would soon destroy the bond that had cured them both, and she would never again be able to touch him, such was the chasm that stretched between their two worlds.

"Please wake up calm, okay? Don't give Matt any reason to think you're crazy."

About midnight she left him. Two tasks remained. She pulled a venison roast from the freezer to thaw, and prepared the hypodermic she hoped she would not need. If he woke up violent there would be no time to prepare it tomorrow. Although she had terminated many dogs with the same injection, tears welled up in her eyes as she set the needle in the syringe.

"Quick and painless, my friend, I promise. No pain."

She went to bed, but her sleep was troubled by dreams that never quite materialized. Except one.

In the predawn hours she saw herself chasing the white wolf on foot, loping down a snow-covered animal track. He glanced back frequently to confirm that she was still behind him, and in her dream world, reality was skewed, her bipedal stride easily matched his four-legged speed. Her loose hair flew behind her like the wolf's tail behind him, and she sensed that miles passed under their feet, but she was not fatigued. Long legs carried her gracefully along the snow-covered path, but she felt no strike of bare foot against icy ground. Stars filled a clear winter sky, but she felt no cold.

And strangest of all, she was naked.

Suddenly her dreamself leaped over a deadfall and as her bare foot touched snow, she jerked awake, the bizarre image still vivid on her mind's eye.

Alex was a pragmatic person, she did not believe that dreams carried deep meanings, but the image of her naked self following the white wolf through the snow did not fade in the light of consciousness.

At first light she got up, and filled a mug with coffee. She had no appetite for breakfast, and wanted time with the wolf before Matt got there.

She carefully removed the tubes and needles and dismantled the IV rig overhead. Then the rest of the bandages slowly unveiled the animal.

"You're still no beauty, but you are healing." She ran her hand gently over his skin and felt the stubble of new hair growth, then along each leg to the socks over his bandaged paws. "I don't think you'll be able to stand on these feet yet, though." She sighed, "I hope you're ready for this," a huge lump rose in her throat, "...actually, I hope we're both ready for this."

In a few hours he would either be conscious, or dead.

Matt walked into the barn and heard her softly singing the song she had been humming when he saw her last.

"What's that song?" She stopped singing and looked up. His smile was better than she remembered.

"Oh, an old hiking song. I've known it for years, but I didn't know it was about these mountains until I came up here last spring. It's called, 'Ten Thousand Pine Trees'." Alex set her guitar down.

"It sounds familiar, keep singing. Please." His smile was encouraging.

"Well," she glanced at the wolf, "I sound much better to an unconscious audience."

"There are people that think I'm often unconscious... please?" *Why did I never notice her eyes?*

"Okay...

'Ten thousand pine trees, their arms open wide,
Will echo our laughter, forever after,
In the valley of the Bow.
Ten thousand pine trees are waving goodbye,
And all their teardrops, are like ten thousand raindrops,
In the valley of the Bow.
Whether ol' Rundle is shining with sun,
Whether Mt. Norguay is shrouded with snow,
You'll find me here waiting in the valley below.'"

The haunting melody drifted through the stable, touching man and wolf. When she finished, the silence hung easily.

"That's beautiful, I must have heard it when I was in Boy Scouts. How long were you in?" She set her guitar down and joined him on the step into the cabin.

"Let's see, I started as a Brownie in the second grade, did the camp counselor thing in high school, and stayed in until I went to college. Ten years, I guess. What about you?"

"Only five years. But my mom is convinced it's what sidetracked the perfect career path she had planned for me." Alex raised her eyebrows, he continued.

"I was supposed to follow in the family footsteps, straight into the family business," he winced, "and be a lawyer."

Alex's turn to grimace. "A lawyer? You're certainly not like any lawyer I've ever met," then quietly, "and I've met a few." She poured him coffee and they sat on the step where they could see the wolf through the stall's door.

Their thighs touched, but neither moved away. A physical conversation started on a silent plane that paralleled their verbal one.

Matt wondered if she would talk about her divorce, but when only silence followed, he continued, "I guess mom finally gave up when she found the bats."

"Bats?"

"Yeah, I was about fifteen—curious about everything—

and had been reading about the metabolism of bats, how some go into hibernation in the cold. So I caught three and brought them home, you know, to do an experiment. I was very serious about taking accurate data, I took their starting skin temperatures, and then the ambient temperature of my mom's refrigerator before I hung them in it."

Alex imagined the simple temperature charts and started to giggle.

"Mom failed to see the humor of three sleeping bats hanging upside down in her 'fridge when she went to get the goodies for her bridge club." Alex laughed out loud at the image.

"Thus was born the humble biologist you see today."

"What did she say?"

"You mean after she screamed? Well, not much that was coherent, but she did buy me a tiny used refrigerator for my experiments." He grinned at the memory, "and put it in the garage."

"What did your dad say?" She was still laughing, and it felt good, like the return of a familiar friend after a long absence.

"Well, he mustered up a serious reprimand and managed not to laugh until mom was out of the room."

Conversation turned to the business at hand.

"Alex, I think it will be better if I stay up here, out of sight and scent, when he starts to wake up. If it's true that animals hear and smell things when they're unconscious, it'll be better if he only hears and smells what's familiar. That's you. This place is going to be strange enough, as it is."

"What do you expect him to do?"

"Well, my experience has been he'll do one of two things. He'll either become aggressive, or silently cower back into the corner, as far away as possible. I've never been able to prove it, but my theory is the two responses are driven by whatever hierarchical position the wolf held in his pack. If he was dominant, he'll be aggressive; if submissive, frightened and timid."

"I see." She checked her watch. "Guess I'd better lock

that stall door." She placed the venison, thawed and oozing blood, in the straw near the wolf's nose, pet his face once more, and closed the door of iron bars. The latchbolt slid home with an audible ka-chunk. Then the humans took their places, Matt sitting on the step to the kitchen, and Alex on the floor outside the wolf's stall door.

And they waited.

An hour passed before there was any sign of White-cub's rising consciousness. His first jerking motions brought Alex to her feet to watch as the canine's mind climbed through thick layers of sleep. With his eyes still closed, he silently twisted his head upward. Leg muscles flinched in stiff spasms. Locked in a shallow dream state, he rolled onto his stomach and moved his head up and down, and side to side, as if to identify his surroundings by scent alone. Then he relaxed, rolled over on his side, and began to breathe deeply. He filled lungs with air and his heart rate increased, forcing the oxygen into limp muscles and clearing his brain of grogginess.

"Well, hello there, my friend. Welcome back to the world of the living. You've had quite a nap." Alex spoke very softly, hoping her voice had carried through the days of his sleep to become a reassuring element of his strange world of drugs and pain. She was not surprised that the first thing he sought was the source of that voice.

White-cub opened his eyes, lifted his head and looked directly at her. While his glazed eyes tried to focus she did not move, but continued speaking to him, hoping to stay the panic sure to occur when he realized his condition.

"Do you remember me? Of course you do, you've heard the unabbreviated story of my life."

Matt envied the wolf.

White-cub stared at Alex for several seconds. Fuzzy recollections of other hated man-smells surfaced—gun powder and airplane exhaust, Patriarch and Gentle's blood mingled with cigarette smoke—and those old memories waged war with this quiet voice. But none of those hated man-scents were here.

He lunged to his feet and yelped, as raw nerve endings sent screaming pain messages to his brain. Then he collapsed in the straw.

"Easy boy," Alex clenched and unclenched her fists anxiously, but forced her voice to be calm and quiet.

"Rest easy, those feet aren't ready to support your weight yet." He panted heavily and wolf eyes, now steady and focused, bored into hers, unblinking, to decipher whether she was responsible for his throbbing pain. But the soothing voice that had kept his sleeping spirit company was too familiar to be an enemy, and he dropped his gaze and started licking his paws.

The next time he raised his head he caught the smell of venison and sniffed at it. He smelled Alex's scent on the bloody meat and, with his first bite, the connection was made. He accepted her. She became like the grown wolves of his old pack, that had brought meat for him and his siblings when they were ravenous cubs.

"That's it, eat up. Yes, I do believe you've tasted venison before," his pink tongue licked at the blood, then teeth dug into the flesh. "probably a lot fresher, though."

Not a growl was directed against Alex, and she knew in some wordless corner of her mind that they had communicated, and the white wolf would not hurt her.

Matt observed it all from the doorway, heard her voice, and saw the wolf's gentle response to it. When the canine started to eat without so much as a snarl, or moment of fear or hesitation, he turned and walked into the cabin, puzzled, curious, and more than a little mystified. Alex joined him.

"Well, what do you think?" He looked at her in a way she had never been looked at by anybody, and it wasn't pleasant. His response was distant, coldly professional.

"In all the years I've worked with wild wolves, I've never seen anything like that. I think, Doctor, you have a unique gift. Or that wolf out there has a monumental ability to understand his situation." He shook his head, and would not meet her eyes.

"But you think he'll recover, right?" She sensed something was out of balance, but couldn't grasp what.

"Oh, yes," he glanced out the door toward the stall, "he's clearly adjusted to this place." He stared at her, "and you." He started toward the front door, almost eager to leave.

"So, I guess I'd better get that cage. How long do you think it will be before he's ready to be released?" Below the level of their conversation Alex searched her mind, analyzed her words and actions.

What's wrong here?

"At least another week or so. He'll need to be able to walk, well, run would be better. But I'd like to get him out before winter sets in and the snow gets too deep."

"I agree. Well, I'd better get busy." Almost as an afterthought, he crossed the room and gave her a perfunctory kiss, then left. Alex swallowed hard, bewildered, confused, rejected.

Did I miss something? Obviously.

As his truck rolled out of sight, she shook her head. Maybe the other night was a mistake... Her heart recognized a familiar ache and she sighed. Evidently she and Matt were still dancing in different directions.

She returned to the wolf and focused her thoughts on him, blotting out all expectations of Matt. When he didn't radio, or come by, she knew she wouldn't see him until it was time to release the wolf.

That realization was shaded with regret and stained with humiliation.

The next seven days brought healing to the wolf, and as Alex continued to pass him meat through the bars she marveled at the intelligence in his haunting gaze. She learned to read his face—curious, interested, startled—once she even thought he smiled, lips pulled back, lazy tongue draped over his fangs. He often greeted her in the morning, lazy tail flopping against his straw bed, and she had to work to remember he was a wild predator, strong enough to kill her.

She provided his physical needs separated by bars, but their spirits soared together.

Chapter Forty-six

"You back already?" Softouch noticed Matt in the bar later that afternoon. "I thought you and the lady doctor would be socializing far into the night." Matt did not return his smile.

"Well, things didn't quite go that way."

"You made her put the wolf to sleep?"

"Not exactly." His response piqued Softouch's curiosity, as well as that of Pierre Bouvier, and two other trappers seated at the far end of the bar. Matt lowered his voice.

"That wolf is no more crazy than you are."

"Then why are you here? I should think you would both be toasting to, what? Ah yes, the stamina of the spirit," he raised his eyebrows and grinned, "you know, celebrating life."

"She talked to that animal like he was human," Matt mumbled and shook his head, "and the way he listened to her I half expected to hear him respond." Softouch leaned on the bar.

"Well, Matt, like you said, she is a vet. One might expect that she learned how to communicate with animals during her career."

"This wasn't vet work. It was spooky. "

"Matt, you make Alex sound like my sweet southern grandmother, who was quite normal, until the sun set on nights with a full moon." Matt looked puzzled.

"Santeria?"

Matt shook his head, confused.

"Voodoo, my very white friend." His bar-wiping brought him close to Matt. "So, what was so strange about the good vet and her wolf?" Matt gazed into his beer, as if knowledge had taken up residence in the glass.

"The wolf didn't respond like I thought he would. Not at all. And, it gave me the creeps." Pierre planted his bulk on the next stool and Matt instantly recalled that personal hygiene was not a priority to the trapper. Some superstition about smelling like his hunting ground. The mountain man joined the conversation, uninvited.

"I thought you were gonna see that she killed that vermin, Matt. What happened?"

"Well, Pierre, from what I could see that "vermin" is at least as sane as you are. And probably a whole lot smarter."

Definitely cleaner, he thought.

"So, I figured since you're still allowed to breathe, we'd let him continue to do so, as well. Is that a problem?" Even standing Matt couldn't look the large trapper in the eye.

"Yes, mon ami, yes, it is! I thought we all made it clear that we do not want some crazy wolf hunting in our trapping area." And then as an inspirational afterthought he added, "Some of us have kids that play in those woods, and I don't want any wolf going after them." He chugged his beer and slammed the mug down on the bar.

"I knew we shouldn't have expected a biologist to take care of this!" He emphasized every syllable of 'biologist', like it was a dirty word. The other two men grumbled in agreement, finished their beers, and the door to the Knotty Pine slammed shut behind them.

"I draw great comfort from knowing those gentlemen have such a fine grasp of animal behavior, and put the well-being of their children at least second after their trapping." He slid his glass across the bar for a refill.

"Careful there, Matt, you're maligning three of my most generous patrons." Softouch opened the cash register and dropped a wad of bills in his pocket for safe-keeping. A king's fortune would be safe in that pocket.

"Are you sure you're not just jealous that Alex was able to communicate so easily with the animal? Or maybe your ego is bruised because he didn't act like you predicted?"

"No, I'm not jealous. And my ego is quite healthy, thank you."

"Well, I must say, it did this southern boy good to see that chivalry is not dead." Softouch poured himself a beer.

"What are you talking about?"

"How you stood up for Alex and her wolf."

"First, it's not Alex's wolf. I believe he belongs to the citizens of Canada. And second, I really do believe he should live." Softouch leaned across the bar facing Matt.

"Then why are you still here? I would've thought tonight would be a glorious tribute to all that is alive. A physical, human tribute, if you get my drift."

Matt shook his head, "I felt like I was intruding on something intimate—between Alex and that wolf."

"Have you ever communicated with a wolf like that?"

"No. I've read about people that have raised wolves as pets, but the wolves were conscious during the process."

"Well, I think you're just jealous. The lady doc has done something you've never done." Softouch grinned, his needling was annoying Matt, and it made his day.

"Thanks alot. I just have to think this through." Matt slid off his barstool and went upstairs.

Suddenly an old pickup truck roared past the bar and Softouch saw it from the window. It was Pierre's truck, and his two associates were jammed into the cab next to him. Three rifles were visible through the windows, and Softouch watched guns and people sway back and forth as the truck careened down the street.

Two things bothered him. Pierre was too drunk to be driving, and hunting season was over. He considered the possibilities and galloped up the stairs two at a time.

Chapter Forty-seven

Alex didn't hear the pickup skid to a stop, nor did she hear Pierre enter the barn behind her from the outside door. A rumbling growl from her patient was the first indication that she was not alone.

"Step aside, mademoiselle, I have business with that wolf." She remembered the French accent and whirled around to face a rifle barrel.

"What do you think you're doing? This wolf is under the protection of the Canadian Wildlife Service." At that moment the other two trappers walked through her kitchen door.

"He's not asking, lady."

Her temper flared. "Did you just walk into my house? I don't recall hearing you knock." She glared at them. "Since this is private Park Service property, that's at least trespassing, maybe breaking and entering. I strongly suggest you leave immediately. You have no business here."

"We came to take care of that wolf, so please move aside." Alex stood still and defiant, facing Pierre's rifle. Her voice was quiet, but intense.

"Hear me well, gentlemen," she winced at the word, the smell of alcohol blending with gamy human sweat dominated the barn. "This wolf will finish recuperating, then be relocated miles from you and your trapping. There will be no shooting here, do you understand me?" She paused. No response.

"Do you really think I will hesitate to report this? You'll be arrested."

The trapper chuckled, "Not if you're unable to make that report, eh, mon ami?" Alex exhaled and stared at Pierre, incredulous.

"You would kill me to get to him?"

"People disappear in these mountains all the time," his glassy-eyed grin chilled her. "If you stand in my way, mademoiselle, I think I might just have to do that." Her heart raced and the rifle suddenly looked like a cannon.

These men are categorically drunk and I'm going to be the object of their rage for a poor trapping season! They probably blame me for the drought and the fire, too!

Her mouth went dry, and she felt the blood drain from her upper body.

Dear God, they really could kill me and make it look like I just vanished!

While thoughts tumbled, the wolf's growling escalated behind her, which did nothing to endear him to his would-be assassins. She lowered her voice, speaking calmly. Inside, organs turned to jelly.

"Pierre, listen to me. You really don't want to do this. I'm not gonna let you kill this wolf, and I know you don't want to kill me. Think about it." She addressed her comments to Pierre, who seemed the most capable of rational thought.

He leaned close to her face, his hatred as toxic as his breath. "Your life, mademoiselle, is no more valuable to me than that of any animal—actually a lot less," he grinned, "I can't skin and sell your pretty hide." The two on the step guffawed at Pierre's drunken wit. "And, mademoiselle, we CAN dispose of you so nobody will ever find you."

One of the men spoke out from the kitchen step. "We're sick of you fancy biologists telling us how to run our forest."

The other one got brave and added, "'specially no woman." All three laughed, and Alex's anger equaled her fear. Barely.

"Murder is murder, and I really don't think you want any part of it. Do you really think nobody will look for me?"

Pierre grinned, "Of course, mon ami, but I bet even you have noticed how quickly meat vanishes in these mountains?" Alex remembered the bleached elk skull, and her stomach roiled. Drunk or sober, these men had targeted her for everything that was wrong with their world.

"*Move*! *Now*!" Pierre raised the rifle, inches from Alex's face. She could see the polished grain of the steel barrel and smell the cleaning agent he had used on it. Time stopped and its vacuum sucked the breath right out of her.

He's going to kill me.

Chapter Forty-eight

Then Alex heard it. Somewhere in the distance a helicopter approached her sky. The drunken trappers heard it too, and even though they were inside the stable, they instinctively looked up. Under other circumstances she would've laughed at the collective ignorance assembled in her barn.

The sound enraged Pierre—he sensed his advantage slipping away—but the helicopter got louder, and they all knew who was flying it. It wasn't the cavalry riding over the hill to save the day. To Alex, it was something much better.

The potential presence of witnesses confused Pierre, and he became the cornered animal. Far more dangerous. He and Alex faced each other in a tense standoff; helicopter roaring louder, descending toward the clearing behind the cabin, wolf snarling, and three rifles pointed at Alex.

Matt started yelling before he entered the stable, and his voice was the sweetest sound Alex had ever heard.

"Drop that rifle, Pierre, or I'll drop you where you stand! Do it! NOW! Assholes are NOT an endangered species!" Pierre only considered refusing for a fraction of a second, then dropped his rifle. Seconds later Softouch's voice boomed from the kitchen behind his cohorts.

"Gents, I strongly recommend you do the same. I'd truly hate to have to kill some of my best customers." They did the same.

Alex closed her eyes, and exhaled a huge sigh of relief.

"Are you alright?" It was the softstrong voice she would take to her grave. She nodded. Matt looked past her into the stall.

"Well, your patient seems okay, too," he nodded toward the wolf. "Take a look."

Alex turned to face an unfamiliar creature. Every canine muscle screamed threat. Snarling, hackles up, ears flat back, lips withdrawn to reveal pink gums and ivory-hard teeth, the wolf was poised to kill.

And he was standing.

"Now Alex, that's behavior I understand." She searched Matt's face. "He's defending his pack. You."

She turned back and knelt in the straw, and human blue eyes met canine blue eyes through the bars.

"Is that what you're doing?" Her soft voice calmed his growls, and gradually he relaxed, then plopped to the floor, panting. The exertion of his defensive performance had exhausted him.

The three trappers had not budged, still quite aware of Softouch, and the weapons at his disposal. They had seen him maintain peace in his bar, a task requiring less diplomacy than brawn, and they harbored no doubts about what he would do if they crossed him now. Softouch walked the earth like one who had killed men, and lost no sleep after the act.

"I think you boys ought to take this fine opportunity to say your farewells and make a graceful exit. It is my humble opinion that you have overstayed your welcome."

"What about our rifles?" Pierre found his voice.

"Oh, those. Well, you can pick them up at Mountie headquarters in Banff. That's where Matt and I'll drop them off after we make our report." The trapper understood the weight of his words.

"They'll arrest us!"

Matt collected the three rifles and chuckled, "That'd be my guess." Then he smiled at Alex, and she realized that whatever was broken between them, had mended. Matt faced Pierre and his voice was just above a whisper,

"Understand this, Bouvier, if you ever come near this cabin, I will kill you myself. With prejudice. Now get the hell out of here!" All three scurried out the back door like rats.

"I need to set the brake on my bird, folks, so if you will excuse me," Softouch slid past them, and abruptly Matt and Alex were alone in the barn.

"Thank you." She started to breathe normally. "They were so drunk, I really believe they'd have killed me."

"I'm sure of it. These people take any threat to their livelihood seriously, and you and I personify everything they hate. When sober they can be nasty, drunk they're easy killers. Your friend over there," he glanced at the wolf, now panting and studying them, "pushes all the wrong buttons."

Then he reached out his hand to Alex. She took it and he pulled her to him in a hug that banished all demons. Outside the engine hum subsided, then stopped.

"I think we need to get your patient out of here as soon as possible. He'll be a target as long as he's here."

Softouch returned to the barn and did not fail to see them separate quickly, self conscious as teenagers.

"And get him as far away as possible, too. I wouldn't bet on his chances in these woods." He grinned at their embarrassment. "How long until he's ready, Doc?"

"Before I saw him stand up just now, I would've thought a couple weeks, but now I think he may be ready sooner. I'd like to put some weight on him, and there are some vaccinations I want to give him—rabies and parvo—maybe a week."

"The sooner the better. Those boys may be drunk now, but even sober they'll remember how much they hate him."

"Then, Matt, let's go next Friday. Will all the paperwork be completed?"

"Should be. A hard release on Friday sounds good."

Softouch glanced toward the kitchen. "Any chance there's some coffee in there? This hero stuff can leave one truly parched."

Humans retired to the kitchen, and the barn quieted to the evening sounds of sleeping wolf and horse; dreamlocked claws scratched against straw in one stall, and hooves thumped the floor quietly in another.

Matt sprawled on the braid rug after resurrecting the fire in the wood stove, and Alex and Softouch occupied the overstuffed chairs. Softouch left no extra room in his. The smell of coffee meandered through the tiny cabin, and thoughts of the future meandered through Matt's mind. His future and Alex's.

"When will you be leaving, Alex?"

"Leaving?" She looked at him, puzzled. "What do you mean?"

"Leaving for the winter. I assume you will be going back to Seattle before winter sets in."

"Well, no, I hadn't planned on leaving. I'm working on a twelve-month census, and the twelve months won't be over until May." Softouch and Matt exchanged glances, and the black man spoke first.

"Alex, winter out here is pretty brutal. You could be snowed-in for weeks, maybe months."

"I know. I'm already preparing for it. I think I've chopped five cords of wood already, and I'm stockpiling food supplies. I've ordered three months of hay and grain for Viento and it'll be trucked in day after tomorrow. Matt groaned inwardly, but was careful not to let her hear him.

"Alex, we're talking about a whole different definition to winter than what you've probably experienced before." He didn't intend to sound condescending, but that's how the words struck her ears. Softouch knew it too.

"Thirty or forty below is not uncommon, and I've seen this cabin completely buried in snow. Did the Park Service agree to this? They hardly ever plow this road." Softouch watched the pink rise in Alex's cheeks and settled into his chair to watch the battle. Her voice took on an edge that he had come to recognize.

"The Park Service agreed to it, and said they'd try to keep the road clear." Blue eyes glared at Matt. "You think I can't handle living through a winter out here alone, right?"

This is gonna be good, Softouch thought. *Matt, ol' pal, you stepped in it this time.*

"No, Alex, that's not what I think. I'm concerned that you don't know the severity of winters in the Canadian Rockies."

"When you lived here, did you stay through the winter?"

Softouch grinned, *She's got you, Matt.* The other two people seemed to forget he was there.

"Yes, but that doesn't mean you have to."

"Only if I want to complete my work. You and I both know that animals are easier to track in the snow. And if you're worried about me going stir crazy here alone, don't. I've discovered my own company is quite enjoyable—preferable to that of some people, actually."

Threatening angry eyes kept Matt silent.

"Admit it, you just don't think I can do it."

Matt considered his response carefully, Softouch held his breath and drank his coffee. "Alex, Softouch and I know how strong you are. But isn't there any room in that gender defensiveness you wave so frantically, for friends to show real concern for your welfare?"

His words struck home. Matt took a deep breath, determined to speak his mind.

"You are so worried that someone will think you're weak, that you don't stop to consider that we already respect you for doing this. You've proven yourself, Alex, and we never asked you to. You're so damn defensive, I bet you haven't noticed that even a piece of scum like Pierre has a couple idiots that worry about him." Matt shook his head in frustration.

"Lady, you are dangerously stubborn and up here it can get you killed!" His words took the breath out of her, and echoed in her brain.

Dangerously stubborn!

She stared at the fire, remembering, and protracted seconds crawled through the silence.

"You're right," she ran her fingers through her hair, a nervous act that Matt perceived as sexy. "I'm really sorry." The fire popped and she stared into the glowing flames. Neither man spoke. Alex's next words were hushed, her demeanor subdued, and her voice had lost its edge. In the space between her words Softouch and Matt heard the cries of a battered spirit.

"The last year or so has been really, um, challenging for

me. Eighteen months ago I was a practicing vet with my own clinic. I lived in a huge house," she chuckled, "a rich husband, a designer wardrobe, multiple cars, two huskies, and Viento. My life was most women's fantasy." She looked down, studying the steam rising from her coffee.

"But I was a naive fool," she smiled nervously, "and now all I have is Viento."

"When I took this job you would've been right to doubt me; I wasn't sure I could make it by myself. But, more than my abilities, I questioned *who* I was. I'd let someone else define me in his own image for so long I lost myself. I know it's a cliche, but I really did come to the mountains to find," she shrugged, "me."

"Were you successful?" She met Matt's gaze.

"Yes, but the search has cost me a lot—physically and emotionally—so I get very defensive when you question my ability to cope. Trust me, guys, coping is one of my best things." The tension, palatable minutes earlier, dissipated. Her face glowed with confidence hardwon.

"So, if you want to be my friends, don't tell me to leave before winter, help me prepare to live through it." She smiled at them both. "Then I won't misinterpret your concern for control, okay?" They nodded. Softouch spoke first.

"Well, the first thing I think you ought to do is get a backup radio, and set up regular call times to me."

"What if she's out for a few days?" Matt looked at Alex, "You were planning on some nights out tracking—snow-camping—weren't you?" She nodded.

He accepts me as a professional! Finally.

"Then, pretty lady, just tell me when I shouldn't expect you to check in." Softouch was a large personality, even jammed into her big chair. "But, Doc, I AM going to be your old mother hen this winter. Do you have a problem with that?"

"No, I don't." She giggled, "But you don't look anything like my mother." They all laughed, and the night aged to the sound of stories of winters past.

And advice gently given, was gratefully accepted.

Chapter Forty-nine

Temperatures continued to drop during the days before the wolf's release, and although the calendar registered fall, winter threatened. His recuperation accelerated and each day Alex watched him struggle to spend more time upright. Matt had told her that a wolf lives by his feet. It was obvious the wolf in her barn knew that truth better than she.

If he couldn't run, he'd starve.

On Wednesday he started pacing inside the stall, first clockwise, then counter-clockwise, and she empathized with his restlessness. Like the cycle of tides that calls salmon to spawn, the turn of the seasons called to the wolf. It was time for him to go.

Each evening she sat outside his stall for long stretches of time, knowing she would miss him, but the approaching winter forced her to finish her own preparations. She stockpiled food for Viento and herself, a second radio now kept the first company, and eight cords of wood were stacked with military precision along the back wall of the barn.

Each morning she expected snow, but was relieved to see none. She wanted to set the wolf free before snow buried trails and scents he might need to survive.

Late Thursday night she sat outside his stall for the last time, and White-cub stopped pacing and faced her through the bars. Eye to eye. Her scent was comfortable and familiar, and he could read the woman's moods as easily as he had those of his pack. To him, her disposition was defined by body language, voice inflections, and chemical changes like altered skin temperature, increased pulse, and rising sweat. While he had no word for it, the wolf sensed her sadness.

"Well, my friend, I guess this is it. Tomorrow you're gonna be free." He tilted his head to one side, eyes and ears focused, nostrils twitching to catch each nuance of her.

"Matt said an established pack already circulates around your release site, so you may have to exercise some diplomacy." His inquisitive eyes studied her face.

"Are you any good at making friends?" His Husky-like features recalled Alpha and Omega, and she ached to reach through the bars and stroke him. Her voice was barely a whisper, and cracked when she spoke next.

"I'm really gonna miss you, you've been a good listener." Deep in his throat the wolf cooed, a sound Alex had only heard previously from her dogs, and her own throat tightened with emotion. She sighed and squeezed her eyes shut, denying tears for absent companions. Alpha. Omega. And soon the wolf.

She shook her head and combed her fingers through her hair, still wet from her shower, and he inhaled the scent of shampoo, bath soap, and Alex's earthy womanhood that no perfume could mask.

"Are you going to remember any of your time here with me?" Canine olfactory senses registered the salty smell of her tears, a mystery to the wolf, and he cooed again.

"Matt said it would be better if you forgot all of this... Listen, we need to talk about human beings. Not all homo sapiens are as open-minded about having wolves in the neighborhood as Matt and I. In case you didn't notice the other day, there are some that would like to see you dead." A scraggly white tail flopped twice against the floor.

"So when we let you go tomorrow, you need to run—run far away and avoid people. Completely. Stay away from anything that looks or smells like this place," she waved her hand encompassing the barn. "...or me."

Although eye contact was unbroken between them, Alex shook her head, frustrated. "This is ridiculous, you don't understand a word I'm saying! And all I want you to do is stay alive!"

But she was communicating. Scent and sound spoke

affection, fear, anxiety, sadness.

They stared at each other for several seconds, and Alex was intrigued by the wolf's ability to focus his attention so long in one place. He never looked away submissively like domestic dogs. For several seconds she memorized the face of her friend; alert, intelligent, curious. She would not see him like this again.

Then she slid the drug-laced venison through the bars and he fell on it immediately. She stayed with him until the drug took affect, and he licked his lips and nodded off into another deep sleep. Injections would keep him unconscious until just before his release.

Matt arrived before noon the next day, and backed his pickup truck around to the stable entrance. The cage in the back didn't resemble any dog kennel Alex had ever seen, three feet high, two feet wide, and four feet deep, front to back. It's steel structure was rugged and imposing, and once locked inside, nothing would escape.

"That's some cage." Alex's breath left frosty clouds hovering between them.

"We use the same one for cougars and wolverines, it has to be strong." The sides were smooth steel plates, perforated every few inches with holes about an inch in diameter. Across the top of the door was an open space five inches high with vertical bars, the only 'window'. Alex felt claustrophobic just looking at the box and when they hauled it into the barn she realized it was even heavier than it looked. Matt opened both front and back doors.

"I'll crawl through and pull him in, you push, okay?"

"Okay." The wolf had gained weight during his stay, and Alex realized she would never have been able to lift him now. Working together, they dragged and tugged until the wolf's entire mass was jammed unceremoniously into the cage.

Matt locked the doors and heaved a sigh, "He's definitely bigger than other wolves I've transported," he looked through the bars, "and he sure fills this cage."

"Looks kind of helpless in there." Alex gazed at the wolf, an undignified heap of fur.

"Yes, but I think he'll be just fine after we release him. Let's get him into the truck." They dragged the cage and, with no small effort, hoisted it into the flatbed of the pickup.

Matt detected Alex's melancholy. "I wonder what he weighed before the fire, he's got to be near a hundred pounds now. Bet he was quite the stud." Matt's comment encouraged her.

If he's so big, maybe he'll survive.

They pulled away from the cabin and fell into easy conversation about their work, the sharing interspersed with a banter born of familiarity. Matt caught her glance at a small box on the floor.

"That's his collar. Take a look at it." She took out the stiff collar, two inches wide, with a small box-like device attached to it.

"It's so big and heavy. You're sure this won't impact his ability to hunt or run?"

"Nope. After a couple hours he won't even notice it."

"There's no buckle, how do you attach it?"

"See the holes in the ends? When you get it sized—snug, but not too tight—you just line up the holes and screw it together."

"It *bolts* on?" An image of Frankenstein's monster with metal screws projecting from his neck flashed through her mind.

"Alex, this is a very strong animal living in a very hostile environment. It has to be durable. The batteries in that transmitter will last for two years."

She sighed. "I guess I just need to get used to the tools of your trade. I'm used to light and delicate, not heavy and durable." She fingered the collar that would deny the white wolf his privacy, and made the mental leap to the obvious. Alive with the collar was preferable to the alternative.

When Matt finally stopped the truck four hours later they had run out of road. Or deer path, as it appeared to Alex.

Highways had given way to fire roads, which had been replaced twenty minutes earlier by this trail that got narrower and less passable with each axle rotation. She had lost her bearings long before, and, had it been necessary, could not have deciphered if they were ten miles from her cabin, or a hundred. She knew they had traveled generally north, and only the pending sunset oriented her. During the drive she had not looked at a map, so engrossed was she in their conversation.

And how good she felt sitting next to Matt.

"Well, this is the spot. What do you think?" She got out of the pickup, and stretched her legs, absorbing the location. They were on a high bluff, mountains rose above them to the north, and a steep valley fell away to the south. Typical Canadian Rockies—sharp angles stretching for vertical, not a square foot of level ground. They were still below the tree line, but high enough to be above dense forests. She nodded and smiled, but had missed the eagerness in Matt's voice. He wanted her to like his choice.

"It's perfect wolf country, Alex. Lots of game, plenty of protected places to wait out winter storms, and some of his own kind cruising the neighborhood, when he's ready to breed."

"Breed?" She hadn't even considered it. *I guess that might motivate him to be diplomatic.*

"You think he's had cubs before?"

Matt dropped the tailgate. "As big as he is, I wouldn't be surprised. He'll definitely feel the urge after Christmas, though."

The image of the white wolf passing winter with a mate appealed to Alex.

"Do you want to put the collar on him?" Matt wanted to give her as much control of the wolf's release as possible. He assumed she could operate a screwdriver.

"Yes, I'll do it." She scrutinized the drugged animal through the holes in the cage. "I want to stick around until he's clear-headed, could be an hour, or so. You know, until he takes off. Is that alright?"

He nodded and glanced into the cage. At that moment a

large white paw smacked the steel wall in a drug-induced spasm and Alex and Matt jumped back.

"He's coming around so we better get on with it." They lowered the cage and opened the door closest to the wolf's nose. Matt got back in the truck.

"I'm going to back the truck a hundred yards or so around that last turn and wait for you out of sight. The fewer people around when he wakes up the better." He looked around and then pointed to a large boulder.

"After you collar him, climb up and watch him from that rock. Then just walk back to the truck when he's gone, and we'll drive back for the cage." Matt knew this was going to be hard for her, and he understood her unspoken desire to say her goodbyes alone. Her tough pride did not mask the affection she had for the wolf, or the odd relationship between them.

I don't understand it, he thought, *but I have to respect it.*

Alex slipped the collar around the wolf's neck as the truck disappeared and a hush reclaimed the ridge. A canine tongue flopped lazily across her hand while she tightened the screws, then suddenly disappeared into his mouth.

This is no place for my fingers.

But her hands didn't listen to her brain. Cradling his head, she looked into his glazed eyes, and fingers scratched the base of his ears in a manner that had reduced her huskies to sublime ecstasy. Then she walked away. The granite boulder was icy cold, but she didn't notice as she waited to observe the wolf's awakening.

As if in celebration for White-cub's homecoming, nature painted a glorious sunset that evening, washing the sky in neon pink and orange. He shook his head several times to clear the drugged fuzziness, and sniffed the wind before standing.

Then he took one deliberate step after another until all four paws touched firm ground. Radiant in sunset's fiery glow, White-cub raised his head and took his bearings. Tail high, eyes clear and searching, he stood tall, the holocaust survivor. His scars were clearly visible beneath bristling new hair, but he was not diminished by them.

That which could not kill him had made him strong. He was Survivor.

The breeze shifted and suddenly he caught the woman's scent. He faced her, uncaged, and two sets of blue eyes said silent farewells. Souls from two worlds had touched briefly and neither life would be the same.

As the sun's final rays played across the mountains he turned and bounded into the underbrush, a scrawny white tail the woman's last image of her friend. Survivor.

Chapter Fifty

"What's a hard release?" Alex tried to keep the conversation going so her mind wouldn't focus on the wolf.

Free. And alone.

"A hard release is just what we did—drive to the site and let the animal go. A soft release is where you create a large pen in the new environment to acclimate the animal to the scent of their new home, and feed it the species you hope he'll prey on, that kind of thing. When biologists released red wolves in the southeast U.S. they did it with a soft release because those animals were raised in captivity and had no hunting experience. A soft release is very expensive because humans have to manage it. Sometimes for generations until the animal re-learns what it once knew by instinct."

"So a hard release will work for this wolf because he is wild and familiar with this environment?"

"That's the theory. Also, we really didn't have much time." He glanced at her and noticed her eyes were shiny.

She's really gonna miss him...

Small spots danced in front of the headlights... and hit the windshield...

Snow.

Alex's mind riveted on the wolf.

"Do you really think he'll be alright, Matt?"

"I'm sure of it." His voice was gentle. "Alex, he's big, and at least a couple years old, so snow and winter won't be a new experience. And remember, he was smart enough to stay by the river during the fire. He understood you were trying to help him, and his natural instincts discerned Pierre and his pals were a threat. He's politically savvy. That will come in handy if he tries to integrate into the local pack."

His smile was reassuring. "Alex, whatever reasoning capabilities canis lupis has, that wolf has them in spades."

"Why would he have to be politically bright to join the

local pack?"

Keep talking, Alex, so you don't have to think about him...

The snowflakes were now larger, and Matt turned the windshield wipers up. "Most pack members are related by blood, so he'll have to be very careful about socializing. He'll need to be able to quickly recognize his enemies, and take advantage of any opportunities that come up. That's what I mean by politically savvy." The truck finally reached pavement and Alex appreciated the smoother ride.

"Are you going to be spending the winter here in Canada?" Alex hoped the question sounded nonchalant, although her interest in his response wasn't.

"No, I'm flying back to Alaska this Sunday. The November election could be pivotal for Alaskan environmental issues. Tourism dollars are starting to convince some residents that protecting what they have is an investment that will be profitable for years to come. I'm going to lend some last minute campaign help to a few of the brighter politicians that share that view."

"Sounds like a far cry from the field work you're used to."

Her mind screamed—*He's leaving Sunday?!*

"It is, but in the years I've worked up there I've made some friends and they agree there are creative solutions that can incorporate everybody's interests; the sport hunters, the subsistent hunters, as well as the animal-loving tourists with the big bank accounts. The election system isn't perfect, but it's the best option we've got."

"I would have never called you a big supporter of compromise."

He grinned and glanced across the truck at her, "In my heart of hearts, I'm not. I'd really like humans to just give nature a good, long rest for about a century. But since that's never going to happen, compromise is the only way to make any progress. And even a small success is better than no success."

Alex listened to his words with her ears, and considered

his leaving with her heart. He was unaware of her dilemma and continued talking.

"Environmentalists shoot themselves in the foot, when they abandon reason and rational discussion for hysterical rhetoric. I can't abide tree-huggers, Alex, they make my work even harder." He gulped cold coffee.

"I have a great respect for the folks that have lived out here for generations, and the most important things I ever learned about this environment I learned from them, not in college. The locals took the time to show me the secrets they've handed down for generations; how to see this environment like I'm a part of it, not just an observer."

"I never thought of it that way."

"You will by the end of this winter."

That's not the only thing I'll learn this winter, she thought wryly. The new knot in her stomach promised lessons of its own.

Silence permeated the truck as Matt drove on through the dark, both humans caught up in their own thoughts. It was a comfortable silence, and Alex was gripped by the urge to take Matt's hand, resting on the seat between them. But she had never initiated intimacy, so, while her heart screamed to do it, her timidness kept her still.

With every passing mile Alex's frustration grew. She wanted to talk to Matt, but couldn't think of anything to say. Wanted to touch him, but lacked the courage.

Matt, unaware of her internal struggle, interpreted her silence as concern for the wolf and did not intrude on it.

By the time they reached her cabin, Alex was desperate for an excuse. Then she remembered the wine.

"I have this great Gamay that someone recommended when I moved in. How about sharing it with me to toast the wolf's release?"

He grinned, and remembered that first night. "Sounds great." He needed little encouragement, he too had realized—later than Alex—that they would not see each other again for months.

He started the fire and smiled when it ignited immediately. *She really has learned to make this place her home,* he thought.

"What are you smiling about?" Alex's voice was soft and inviting—the same voice she used on the wolf—as she handed him a glass of wine.

"How well you banked the fire before we left today. It started right up."

"Thanks." They both watched sparks fly in the iron box.

"What kind of population studies are you doing? Tracking certain species?"

"No, I'm trying to document diversity, how many different species populate a given area over a year. And highlight those that are endangered."

He nodded. *God, her hair glows in the firelight!*

Their glasses emptied too soon and Matt stood to leave. "Well, Alex, promise me you'll be careful this winter, okay?" She smiled at his concern and moved closer to him.

"And you campaign hard up there, so Alaska will still be wild and wonderful when I get up to see it." Matt's arms found their way around her waist and drew her into a kiss they both needed. A smoldering ember ignited, the kiss grew more passionate, the embrace more urgent. They both felt the falling away of civilized inhibitions in the rising primal need. Suddenly Matt pushed her away and took a deep breath.

"I think I'd better leave, Alex."

"Do you really want to?" Alex heard the words come out of her mouth, but had not expected to say them.

He smiled sheepishly, "I don't think that is a question you need to ask."

"Then stay with me, Matt. Stay tonight." She was shocked by her own boldness, but did not regret it.

Matt stared at her, trying to breathe calmly and think. Both were impossible. Then his arms found their way back around her and Alex felt his strength, an embrace that melted her into him and kisses that crushed her lips. It aroused her and she responded to him with a gritty lust she had not known before.

In weeks to come when she would replay this night, she would not be able to recall how they came to be nude together in her bed. Her brain would appraise that memory insignificant among the rest.

For Matt this was his greatest fear, that he would lose control and get lost in another woman's passion. This animal intimacy had caused him the greatest pain and, more than anything else, had driven him to a solitary life. Now he felt the last vestige of control slip away as they both surrendered to the hunger.

Hands explored bodies, touching curves, learning textures. Matt caressed her breasts, alternately soft then hard and she groaned, drowning in the pleasure of it. She ran her hands up his chest, fingernails playing gently in the soft hair, raising the temperature of the fire burning in him to match the one raging in herself. Their eyes met momentarily, then continued their exploration, a new planet in each's universe.

Matt's erection grew unbearable and when he straddled Alex she grabbed his buttocks, drawing him inside her immediately. Had he wanted to go slow, she would not have allowed it. As he eased into her, the hot moist welcome nearly drove him to release instantly.

He shuddered with the initial warmth and their eyes locked as their bodies started the ancient dance. Thrust and release, thrust and release. Internal fires raged and Matt spread her arms and they clenched hands, riding the volcano. Within seconds the ecstasy would not be denied and with a final thrust they reached orgasm together, flying as one creature in a sky new to them both.

In the aftermath Matt held Alex close, and she learned the musty smell of him, he the scent of her coming. There was no conversation, just the warm glow of bodies tuned and singing the same song.

During the night they made love twice more, each mating sweeter than the previous. In her new boldness Alex mounted him, and learned a new pleasure, rising and falling with him inside her. He played with her breasts, she reached around to stroke him as he slipped in and out of her. She concentrated on his satisfaction and when it came he shuddered, yielding to her touch.

Later, he started slowly, playing in her pubic hair, caressing her, fingers sliding in and out, stroking her clitoris, almost bringing her to climax. He watched her face flush again, eyes shiny, half closed in pleasure, and learned her mating signs. Then he knelt between her legs and licked her, sucking, probing with his tongue until she squirmed beneath him for completion. Quickly he mounted her as her orgasm exploded, and came with one strong lunge that left them both exhausted. They dropped off to sleep, limbs tangled, completely spent.

When Alex awoke, she knew he was gone.

Eyes searched the cabin for any sign of him, and found nothing but a note on the table. She jumped for it and read,

"Alex, I forgot to give you this phone number last night. If you call it, the folks there will be able to send the satellite tracking data of your wolf from their computer to yours. Through something called a modem—I assume you know what that is. Respect the cold this winter. I'll write when I can."

It was signed simply, "Matt".

Not, "love, Matt", or "yours truly, Matt", or even, "sincerely, Matt".

Just "Matt".

The total lack of any acknowledgement of the previous night knotted Alex's stomach instantly. It was as if she had imagined the whole thing.

Oh, this is gonna be hard, Alex, she thought to herself. *You asked him to stay and you got what you wanted. Well, now you'll have to live with it.*

She got angry at him, then at herself. Then the inevitable thought. Does he have someone else in Alaska? Her self-confidence took another blow.

She sighed, feeling the intimate soreness in her body, the only evidence that their passionate night happened in the realm of reality. She glanced outside and in the flat white light of morning his tire tracks had already vanished under the heavy snowfall.

"It's gonna be a long winter, Alex." In the empty cabin her whisper sounded like a shout.

Chapter Fifty-one

Survivor coursed over the ground and ligaments and tendons, stiff from disuse, stretched and rediscovered their natural flowing stride. With each touch of paw to earth his body settled into its comfortable rhythmic pace. Survivor's second encounter with humans replaced the first and, while his lungs feasted on the brisk mountain air, a pleasant aftertaste of his time with the woman took up permanent residence in his memory.

Of his canine family only Guardian and Cub-bearer survived the forest fire. Hidden underground in their den the two frightened wolves had waited out the holocaust, listening to the roar of the fire, closer, and closer, until flames licked at the mouth of their refuge. For a few brief minutes it threatened to suffocate, sucking the air out of the den, filling their hiding place with smoke. The canines panted and gagged but, when the fire had finally passed, Survivor's mother and uncle were spared.

They escaped their subterranean shelter and fled their valley, two souls in search of a new home, a new life. They covered more than four hundred miles in the following days as they raced on, toward a place instinct would show them. There would be a future for these two survivors of Patriarch's pack.

For Survivor, however, there was no companion. The scent of other wolves was immediately obvious to him, but that spoor carried a strong warning. The pack that frequented this new place was large and well-established, and every sense told him he would find no welcome among them. Still recovering from his burns and weakened condition, Survivor was ill-prepared for confrontation so he avoided direct contact. He followed their trails and fed off their kills, but drew no consolation from their scent.

He was strong enough to hunt for himself within a few weeks, and with the growth of his winter coat, burn scars vanished beneath new fur. Heart and muscle strengthened and senses sharpened to the sights and sounds of his new surroundings. Each day greeted him with the pronounced bite of winter and he frisked in the first snows.

Survivor's health returned and with it his longing for social companionship. He had never been alone and the smell of wolves tortured him with fractured memories of the comfortable affection of his family. Loneliness made him bold and each day he drew closer to the local pack until he had seen each of its members and could identify the alpha pair that led them.

More than twenty wolves of three or four litters ran together, and their proud silver alpha had obviously earned his position. The respect given him by his family was offered without hesitation and he carried himself with the ease and confidence of an experienced leader.

The pack had known of Survivor's presence from the first day he crossed their trail, but since he never threatened their hierarchy they were content to let him follow from a distance. He was treated as an outcast, tolerated but ignored. The heavy snows of winter found Survivor skirting the periphery of the large pack, seen by all, but socially invisible.

This was not Survivor's family, they shared no common blood, and the closer he came to them the greater his threat to the pack's stability. For weeks he kept his appointed distance. watching and analyzing each wolf's behavior, noting strengths and weaknesses.

Survivor's life had been filled with physical interaction from Cub-bearer's first cleaning caress in the den. It was his earliest means of communication, it imparted genuine affection, and formed the foundation of his understanding of pack society, even before he had sight. Now, denied the companionship of kindred beings, life was twice cruel. As winter approached, food became difficult to obtain alone, and while he might move around the pack openly, Survivor was completely deprived of companionship. The absence of emotional interaction with his own kind threatened the spirit as seriously as hunger threatened the body. Loneliness would diminish him with the same certain end as starvation.

There was no solace for the white wolf. His misery intensified with the season's weather, and separation from his own kind within sight of them was as unbearable as any pain he'd ever known. Food became scarce, then nonexistent, as carcasses were devoured by others before he discovered them. At night he wandered the pack's trails, hungry and restless, and in his solitary howling voice rang a haunting sadness.

But one resident wolf studied him. The tan was three years old and far removed from the power in his family's hierarchy, but eager for a pack of his own.

Real or imagined, he perceived Survivor a threat.

For food. For power. And for a mate.

Chapter Fifty-two

The cougar padded along the hardpacked trail, stealthy and silent. Deep snow on both sides shielded the cat from view and her tawny coat blended with winter shadows, gray easing through gray. Her fluid grace gave no sound of her presence, back flexing side to side with a gait that rolled each foot, heelpad to toes, avoiding any crunch of snow beneath her ninety-five pound frame. The black tip of her tail hovered inches from the ground, adding stability to body design like a rudder steadies a boat.

The ghost was in her element.

The trail meandered across open spaces and through stands of hemlock and fir, and she added her spoor to those who had preceded her. Pausing at fresh animal droppings in the middle of the trail, she sniffed and growled softly. In a smaller cat the sound would've been a hiss. The tip of her tail twitched, this scent-signature was unfamiliar and she was intrigued. Grain- and grass-fed, the scat reminded her of deer and elk. Grazers. Prey. But this was not deer or elk.

Nostrils flared, she snarled again, louder, and the pain in her face sent sharp signals to her brain. The swelling was annoying, the pain briefly intense, but not intolerable. No greater than what she experienced giving birth, so she paid it no more attention. Hunger was her dominant need and she began to stalk this new alien in her territory.

The rounded hoof print was only one of many species' that marked the snow but her attention would not be distracted by the familiar. Two weeks had passed since food filled her belly and she focused on this new prey. Perhaps slower moving. Or injured. Perhaps easier to kill. The pain retreated again.

A gust of cold air blasted past Alex as she lunged into the Knotty Pine, and the heavy door slammed behind her. She stomped her Timberlands and clumps of snow plopped onto the soggy floormat as she unzipped her anorak in the smoke-filled bar.

"Greetings, Doc, what'll it be?" Softouch was at his post behind the bar, perpetual dishtowel draped over his shoulder, apron spanning his ample girth.

"Just coffee." She slid onto the barstool that had become hers over the past months and a few pairs of eyes noticed how gracefully her slender legs draped it.

"May I use the phone?"

"Absolutely. Let's see where our boy's been lately." Softouch slid the phone across the bar and Alex disconnected the cable, reconnected it to her computer, typed a few words and watched the bar graph appear that confirmed transmission had begun. Slowly it started to fill, first 3%, then 7%. Alex sighed and shook her head.

I have to get a faster modem, the last download took almost fifteen minutes.

"While you wait for that, here's your mail." Softouch watched her face fall as she thumbed through the envelopes. No return address from Alaska. He suspected that Matt and Alex had played with fire and he was looking at the one that got singed.

"I'm sure he's up to his you-know-what in election stuff, Alex." He didn't know why he felt motivated to make excuses for his friend. Her eyes never strayed from the computer screen.

"A person can be as busy as he wants to be." Her curt response didn't invite further conversation and Softouch drowned his curiosity in soapy dishwater.

When the download was complete Alex typed for awhile, and a simple topographical map appeared with two lines of different color wandering around the screen. The lines didn't overlap, but followed similar paths offset by time. She smiled immediately.

"Well, look at this, it seems he's found the local pack." Softouch leaned across the bar to see the screen.

"How can you tell?"

"The blue line is the movements of one of the wolves in the local pack that was collared a year ago. See how the red line follows the blue?"

He nodded.

"Well, that means our friend is probably eating off their kills. He seems to move whenever they move, avoiding them, but staying close." She smiled again.

"You're happy with this?" Softouch was still unsure what the lines meant.

"Absolutely!" He's probably eating, and he's looking for a way to integrate into the pack." She shut off the computer and packed it away. With her nose in the computer bag, Softouch barely heard her mumble, "Maybe he'll be more successful at the mating game than I am."

Unfinished business there, he thought.

"Oh yes, I almost forgot! I have some photos of a track I've seen a couple times and can't identify. Can you help me name this beast?" She retrieved several snapshots of an animal track about three inches long, three inches wide, showing five toes and a crescent heel pad. One photo clearly showed the complete stride in snow, with her tape measure alongside it measuring forty-five inches. Softouch glanced at them only briefly and handed them back to her with a chuckle.

"Sorry, Doc, but this is not my area of expertise. I can barely tell a tire track from a railroad track." Looking around the room he nodded toward a table with two men Alex had seen before.

"They could probably help you with it, though."

"They're trappers aren't they? Why would they want to help me? I get the feeling most of these guys think I'm barely human."

"They're outfitters. And you shouldn't be so quick to judge, not every trapper is Pierre. Go over and ask them." He grinned, "You'd be amazed at how fast a man will jump to assist a pretty lady." Alex slid off her stool, photos in hand, and headed for the table.

"Excuse me... Softouch said you might help me identify a track..."

Two faces turned toward her, late-twenties, rugged, one topped with thick black hair, the other finer brown. They had a strong resemblance and Alex suspected they were brothers. Dark hair smiled and spoke first. "Well, what kinda track did you see, um, Alex, right?"

She smiled, relieved. "Yes, Alex Davidson."

"I'm Allan and this is my brother, Terry. Can you describe it?" Terry pulled out a chair between them and she sat down and handed them the photographs.

"I've seen this track a few times... kind of like a bobcat, but that's not right 'cause the claws are clearly visible. And it's like a weasel, except it's too big and the stride's too long." She handed them the photos and they passed them between each other, and nodded. In less than a minute they returned them to her and smiled.

Terry spoke, his voice softer and lower in pitch than his brother's. "It's understandable you didn't recognize this guy. He's pretty elusive. Once we all thought he was extinct. Year's ago trappers up here used to call him pekan, an Indian word for his pelt. We call them fishers."

"What's it look like?"

"You were close when you said it looked like a large weasel. He is. Long, sleek, low to the ground, a very efficient hunter." Allan looked at the picture measuring the stride again. "This one looks like a male, maybe weighs eighteen, twenty pounds. They move through the trees about as fast as they move along the ground."

Terry spoke up, "And they're not known for their friendly disposition either, so if you see one, don't corner him. They can be as unpleasant as a wolverine."

"Have you ever seen one?" Both men nodded. Alex noticed how strong their hands looked wrapped around their beer mugs.

"Yeah, we've seen them, but just a glimpse now and

then. Seen their tracks several times."

"And, Allan, remember when we saw that bodyprint where one had jumped out of a tree?" They both chuckled.

Terry leaned toward Alex. "Yeah, that one made us slow down and keep our eyes up all day. It looked like he had just belly-flopped in the snow and took off after something."

Alex glanced from one to the other, then asked, "Do you trap them?" Both heads shook.

"No, they're so rare now there isn't really any market for their pelts anymore." Terry's voice got quieter, "Anyway, we kinda like to think they're still out there, moving through the trees, you know, doing what we do to survive."

It was a simple statement, but it opened Alex's mind to these men who make their livelihood by killing. They held in esteem the creatures they pursued. It was an attitude she didn't expect.

"If you keep an eye out, you'll probably find him near where you saw those tracks. They're creatures of habit, follow the same trails, sometimes they cache their kills in old hollowed trees."

Alex smiled and held out her hand. "Thanks alot for your help." They hesitated only for a second, then both brothers shook it.

As she walked away Allan spoke up, "Alex, have you heard any cougars up near your place? Or seen any signs of one?"

"Yes, I heard one scream a couple nights ago, but it was really distant. Why?"

"Well, we think there's an old female whose been spooking some cattle ranchers around here. If she's comfortable with cattle, she might not be afraid of humans."

"How will I know if it's a female?"

Terry chuckled, "If it screams, it's female. Looking for a mate. It's the worst time to run into one, so watch your back."

His brother spoke up, "And, Alex, they climb trees, too."

"Thanks for the warning... and the help."

On the drive home the mountain lion was forgotten amidst thoughts of an animal she'd never seen. An elusive hunter she could picture in her mind.

Alex wanted to see the fisher.

The cougar left the trees where the trail opened into a clearing and froze. Before her was a wooden structure and the scent of human was as strong as the unknown prey she was tracking.

Human was a smell that always stimulated fear. She had first scented it years ago on the carcass of an old elk, and every subsequent time she encountered it, something was dead. She never forgot it.

But the gnawing hunger in her belly wouldn't be ignored.

She waited. Watching.

For several minutes she studied the barn for any sign of movement, until experience and instinct convinced her to leave. Then the ghost glided back into the trees undetected.

Hunger unsated.

Chapter Fifty-three

Alex's resolve to track the fisher was born of multiple motives. If she could identify it as a permanent resident, its presence would strengthen her argument to protect the local area as a biodiverse environment. On a more personal level, finding the fisher would prove to herself that she was a skilled tracker, capable beyond the ignorance of her first days in the mountains.

And the challenge would keep her mind off Matt.

Viento was always frisky after a few days without exercise and horse and human went through their familiar ritual. He sashayed around the paddock, prancing in the new snow like he'd never seen it before, while Alex followed him with his saddlepad until he settled. She tolerated his performance with a mother's patience, he only exhibited an itch that infected her, as well.

"Okay, okay, can we get on with this?" Five days had passed since her talk with the trappers and her eagerness to find the fisher had intensified with each cabin-bound day, waiting out the latest snowstorm. Finally Viento tossed his head and stopped in front of her, his flesh quivering with anticipation.

"Ready for a little exercise, V.?" She tossed the pad over the mustang's back and he behaved himself through the rest of the process, swishing his tail and tossing his head.

Alex had learned from her first careless night and now the supplies for each trip were checked and double-checked. The saddlebags were always packed; a heavy-duty flashlight and collapsible shovel shared the right with waterproof matches, candles, and a headlamp, for situations that required two free hands. In the left saddlebag were extra gloves and socks, a plastic poncho, trailmix, and the black pouch. A lightweight, but strong dome tent, ground cover, and sleeping bag fit compactly, rolled and tied behind the saddle. Alex carried her computer and its spare battery in a slender backpack under her anorak, near her body to keep the hardrive from freezing. The GPS programs and information it contained could tell her in seconds exactly where she was, accurate to within a few hundred yards.

Alex did not intend to get lost again.

Hungry animals were on the move after the storm and many prints indented the trail behind the cabin, the bravest had ventured very close to the barn. But Alex was focused on the fisher and knew she wouldn't find his mark there.

So she did not see the mountain lion's print only twenty-five yards from the barn.

Alex never tired of the crisp, clear mornings that followed each snowstorm. Five days had delivered three feet of new snow, which blanketed even the smallest horizontal plane. Where the wind sculpted unbound in open areas, snowdrifts towered above Viento's withers.

Sunlight reflected off the virgin snow so bright it was painful to her eyes, and through the cloudless sky floated diamond dust, sparkling ice crystals condensed where high warm air flirted with colder ground air. Each weightless prism twisted, one of a million tiny rainbows dancing against a cerulean background. Understanding the phenomenon diminished none of the magic for Alex.

She caught her breath with the sheer beauty of the morning and patted Viento's neck with a gloved hand. He snorted, echoing her exhilaration and pranced down the trail like he was on parade.

He eventually settled into an easy walk, hoofbeats crunching snow with a steady rhythm, accompanied by the dainty song of chickadees flitting through the trees. Alex tossed birdseed on the snow and the tiny birds immediately descended on it. She laughed out loud when heavier Steller jays tried to land and sank instantly into the dry fluff, then erupted into the air squawking their great indignation.

This was snow to make her skier's heart sing, with names like 'blue smoke' and 'champagne powder', and she passed the day with sweet memories of skiing with her sister.

The cougar climbed slowly out of the rocky shelter where she had waited out the storm. Blasting wind had discovered each crack between the boulders and allowed her no rest.

And neither did the pain in her head.

Natural healing processes could not combat the infection that had spread from broken jaw into flesh, and the right side of her face was now so inflamed her right eye was swollen shut.

An instant before the moose kicked her in the head, the lioness had been in her prime; over one hundred pounds of toned muscle and fierce elegance, entering estrus, searching for a mate. Now her skeleton was clearly visible; skin sagged around ribs, shoulders, pelvis, and her coat was ungroomed and lackluster.

Sharp eyesight, a major weapon in her arsenal, was seriously impaired by the loss of one eye. Depth perception and peripheral vision were no longer available and her two-week string of hunting failures was approaching week three. Pulsing pain also robbed her of all outward signs of clear cougar thought, the patience to silently stalk and wait.

All normal instincts were replaced by the craziness of sleep deprivation, hunger, and constant, excruciating pain.

She had to eat. Soon.

She shook her head and licked her right front paw then rubbed it across her swollen face gently, a hopeless gesture to clean and heal what she could not reach with her tongue. She leaped from the boulder to the trail, an easy nine-foot bound, but landed off-balance, and the jarring detonated the pain in her head again. When her muzzle touched the ground her hunger roared afresh, triggered by the new scent from days before.

The hoofed unknown.

The spoor was recent and she collected herself and glided down the trail, head bobbing hypnotically left and right to see her surroundings with her only good eye.

☾☾☾

About noon Alex arrived at the place where she had photographed the fisher's tracks and dismounted. Two ancient spruce trees rose above her and a flattened space beneath them revealed a large animal's sleeping area. There were tracks in many directions, and she recognized deer, bobcat, squirrel and a snowshoe hare. The mass of tracks under the trees spread out into the new snow, traveling in a hurry, hungry animals looking for food after a storm.

"Wonder what slept here, V.?" The mustang looked up but continued to paw the ground in front of him. Snow under the trees was only inches deep and beneath it he found something green to nibble. Alex had watched him find browse under the snow so many times it no longer surprised her. Pacing slowly around the area, eyes down, her scrutiny was rewarded. She took out her snapshots and knelt next to tracks in the snow and compared them.

"Hey, Viento, I found him!" The horse paused, looked at her, then resumed munching. She gazed into the branches above her, but they were silent and unoccupied.

"Well, let's see where you've gone, my friend." The fisher's tracks led around the base of the trees in a tangled maze, and it took Alex almost an hour to find his exit trail thirty feet beyond the spruce trunks. She whistled for Viento, mounted, and they set out across open snow, knee-deep to the mustang, following the clear trail of the fisher.

The cougar stopped at her old bed site and snarled. Other animals had used it, and the mountain lion recognized and discarded their scent, it was the scent of human that held her interest. It defiled the place, and it was fresh. But the hammering pain in her head denied a rational response and her hunger would not be ignored. For the other scent was there also, the hoofed grazer, potential prey, and it was not far ahead.

She oozed along the horse-wide trail, confident of a meal.

☪☪☪

The fisher's trail was a three-dimensional puzzle, up and down, between trees, circling back, so tangled that twice Alex had to trace the tracks in the snow with her fingers to be sure she was following it correctly. Where more than one tree clustered together it was common for the fisher to climb one and descend from another. More than once the trick confused her, but she backtracked and sorted it out each time. Her camera draped her neck, poised and ready.

You probably won't give me very long to get a shot, will you?

In the fading light of dusk she found him. His trail had disappeared up an old fir and she discovered his long, sleek form balanced easily on a large limb, feasting on a hare he had dragged up. He ate voraciously, ripping at the flesh, oblivious to Alex.

She eased Viento closer, reined him to a stop, and lifted the camera to her eye.

Before she could squeeze off one shot, the cougar pounced into the trail behind them.

Viento whinnied and reared back and Alex barely grabbed the reins before he bolted. Her heart leaped into her throat as she spun Viento broadside, to present a larger target. This stopped the lioness, but she did not retreat. She stood her ground.

Fifty feet from horse and rider.

She looks like she's going to attack us!

Alex's mind raced. *What do I know about cougars?*

But her brain refused to retrieve any information beyond a few highly publicized human attacks.

For several seconds all animals held their position, Viento prancing, tossing his head, fighting Alex's tense restraint, the cougar crouched, paused, evaluating. Alex knew bolting through the trees in deep snow would surely trigger a chase, a race horse and rider would lose. All her strength barely held the mustang in check, hooves pounded, galloping twenty miles-an-hour in one place.

"Easy boy. Quiet down, V." The mustang would not be calmed. He recognized the mountain lion for the predator she was, and no human words would change his response.

The cougar resumed her advance one paw at a time.

Fluid, silent.

Alex glanced around her and realized they had nowhere to run. Five large trees formed a thicket and Viento had backed into it.

No escape except the trail, currently occupied by one very hungry cougar.

Come on, Alex! Think, girl! We can get out of this...

The camera! Right!

The lioness was standing in shadows so Alex raised the camera slowly until it was pointed at her and released the shutter.

The flash was brighter than she anticipated and the cougar leaped back, snarled and stopped.

Only thirty feet from Alex, and the beast she perceived as her next meal.

Alex flashed the camera again, but this time the cougar didn't move. Only then, in the light of the flash, did Alex notice the cat's misshapen head, and she scrutinized her total appearance with a vet's trained eye.

"My God, what happened to you?" She saw the swollen face, slack mouth, and starving skeletal frame, and for an instant her fear was replaced by pity. But only for an instant.

She wished she had a gun. To end the cougar's misery, more than save her own life.

"That must be excruciating..."

The cat heard the absence of fear in her soft voice and coiled. The power had shifted away from her, now she was threatened by the scent that always meant death. When she snarled Viento tossed his head, ears back, skin quivering, displaying every sign of fear.

The cat smelled Viento's fear and crouched to spring.

The black pouch! Right!

Flashing the camera repeatedly to distract her attacker, Alex transferred the reins to her right hand, and dropped her left into the saddlebag, opening the black pouch.

Her eyes never left the cougar. And vice versa. Fingers fumbled, groped, and somehow uncapped the long red tube and raised both cap and tube to eye level. She inverted the cap in her right hand and struck the end of the tube against it.

Instantly florescent red sparks crackled and shot out of the highway flare, past Viento's head.

The mustang renewed his effort to leave Alex in the snow, and the mountain lion stood and growled.

Alex waved the flare toward her and turned a reluctant Viento into the trail, facing the cat.

The cougar started to backup. Slowly.

"That's it, backup, you really don't want any part of this."

Neither did Viento, but he had no choice. One hoof hit the snow in front of the other only with Alex's urging, as the cougar backed away. After five paces Alex hurled the flare directly at her. When it landed in the snow near her face she whirled and dashed down the trail, neglecting all efforts to be silent or graceful. Alex could hear her departure, as snow-laden branches plopped their load on the ground as she brushed past. Gone in a couple heartbeats like she had never been there.

Alex pulled up Viento and sagged into the saddle, sweat-soaked, and panting. She stroked the mustang's neck for several minutes, as much to calm herself, as to calm him.

The whole incident had not filled three minutes.

Thoughts and emotions sparked and swirled. Fear, shock, near-panic. Then the blur cleared, and her mind focused on the image of the cougar. Emaciated, starving. Pity washed away her fear.

"She dying, V., and I couldn't even put her out of her misery." The cougar's distorted face floated in front of her own, and she considered the clinical reality of the bloated flesh. Infected puss. Broken bones. Throbbing pain.

A gun would've ended it.

"I should've been able to do something for her." They started back along the trail and when they reached the flare, still sizzling in the snow, Viento gave it wide berth.

Within minutes darkness fell and the snow reflected a slivered moon's light with a blue glow. Alex put on her headlamp and they made their way home in icy quiet.

After she had settled Viento for the night she turned on the radio and called The Knotty Pine.

"Softouch, this is Alex. Over." There was no response for a minute, then,

"Softouch here, Doc, over."

"Are Terry and Allan there in the bar?"

"Yes, ma'am, warming their assigned seats. Over."

"Could you get them to the radio, I need to talk to them. Over."

A longer pause this time.

"Hi, Alex, this is Terry, what's up? Find your fisher?"

Pause while Softouch told him to say, over, and switch the mike.

"Yes, I did. Found him just like you said I would. But I have a favor to ask of you two. Over."

Allan's voice came on next.

"Name it." pause, "Um, over."

Alex took a deep breath, "I found your cougar. She's in real bad shape. Her face has been kicked in, looks like a broken jaw, right eye's swollen shut..." Alex closed her eyes recalling the pitiful, "...and she's starving."

"I don't think she'll travel far. If I tell you where she is will you two go up there tomorrow and—and take care of her? She shouldn't be left like that." She sighed. "Over."

The silence at the other end of the radio swelled. Men in the bar considered this unexpected request and its unexpected source. The abyss between trappers and vet narrowed and an uncharacteristic gentleness in Terry's voice reflected her own feelings.

"We'll handle it, Alex, first thing in the morning. Where did you see her?"

She gave them the location and signed off before conflicting emotions could begin their predictable battle through heart and mind. Sadness. Regret. Impotence against circumstances beyond her control. But these feelings were old friends. It had never been easy for her to terminate an animal in her clinic, she was not surprised it was no easier to do it here.

Terry and Allan were as good at their job as she was at hers, this would be the mountain lion's last night of pain.

Chapter Fifty-four

Winter's fading sunlight drew enough moisture from the new snowfall to lift a dense afternoon fog. It rose and swirled through the trees like a ghostly phantom, fingers reaching and grabbing at all forest elements. Creature sounds, already muffled, drifted without form on the ebbing white and Survivor flowed through the mist, an ethereal canine spirit.

Driven by hunger, the wolf was blind to minute changes, a subtle shifting nuance in the mood of his environment. The translucent fog that cloaked the forest also masked a new presence, silent and stalking.

A hunter shadowed his movements.

Acute senses that would have revealed the tan wolf by scent and sound were ignored, and awareness of this approaching threat never reached Survivor's consciousness.

Hours earlier hunger had made him careless. The intoxicating scent of moose, warm and fresh-killed, seduced him into the open before the resident pack had gorged their fill and was out of sight. They saw him before a single bite passed his lips and they charged, their rage obvious, retaliation immediate.

Survivor spun away, inches ahead of their snapping jaws. He bolted for the trees, crashing through a winter obstacle course. Deadfalls snagged him from beneath the snow and branches slapped him at eye-level. Boulders offered slippery footing then dumped him into snow over his head.

Survivor's dash for survival burned precious energy he could not spare.

The sky darkened as he left the pack's territory and one by one his pursuers fell away. Survivor slowed, his pace reduced to slogging through deep, untracked snow. He had survived, but exhaustion clouded his senses.

The tan wolf followed him alone.

He had trailed the white wolf during the pursuit, behind his packmates, always downwind and now pending darkness seasoned his resolve. The tan closed to fight the interloper.

Survivor's only warning was his stalker's paw crunching through snow, and as jaws snapped shut he felt the tan's breath, a whisper against his back legs.

He spun and faced his attacker, the element of surprise lost to the tan.

The proud males carved a battleground in the snow, circling, growling, ears flat against raised hackles. Fierce snarls roared through the stillness and drawn lips exposed fangs to the gumline.

Jaws thrust out and snapped shut again and again and lesser creatures withdrew like humans before the clash of titans.

The tan feigned attack twice, then charged, dashing in low with his head cocked to one side.

Aiming for Survivor's throat.

But littermates had made this play a hundred times, and pivoting hard on his front left foot, Survivor slammed his weight into the tan. Momentum knocked the aggressor off balance and white fangs locked around a tan leg. The defining crack of broken bone echoed through the fog.

Survivor released him, assuming victory, but to his surprise, the tan did not drop to the ground, belly-up in submission. He rushed Patriarch's son again, dragging his broken leg. Survivor was unprepared for the charge and this time teeth found their mark, tearing a deep gash in his neck behind his right ear. Hot blood oozed, staining white fur, melting white snow.

Survivor's rage exploded. All the frustration of past weeks was focused on the tan. Survivor charged, body-slamming his crippled attacker before he could plant his feet, knocking him on his back.

White jaws clamped around his throat and Survivor crushed the wolf's larynx, severing his jugular vein with razor sharp precision. Survivor killed the tan before he drew another breath.

Hunger and loneliness had given him motive, and to

stay alive Survivor had killed his own kind.

Certainly these ideas did not flow structured through his wolfen mind, as they might in a human. They were the instinct imperative, and as his ancestors had before him, the white wolf obeyed.

Survivor turned away from the carcass without looking at it, and trudged into the fog. His own tongue could not reach his wound and blood continued to mark his path.

He labored through the snow for hours, without direction, ignoring familiar scents and trails. Fatigue from the fight, weakness from blood loss, and gnawing hunger compounded, and he collapsed beneath a large alpine fir, unconscious.

Blood melted the snow under him and the pain in his neck raged.

Chapter Fifty-five

Softouch could tell by the look on Alex's face that something was wrong with the wolf.

"What is it, Doc?"

"He hasn't moved for four days, and he's avoiding the local pack completely." She sighed, "I'm afraid he's sick or hurt. Whatever it is, he's obviously not eating." Her eyes met the bartender's.

"What can you do?"

She shook her head and shrugged helplessly. "Nothing."

Weary sadness overwhelmed her. Infrequent and innocuous letters from Matt that bore less affection than he would've communicated to an elderly aunt, and now the wolf—her wolf—was in trouble. Winter had suddenly become dark and cold. Softouch watched her face, read her thoughts, and poured her a beer.

"I'm sure he'll pull through. Remember he survived the fire, he's a tough guy." He changed the subject. "Cheer up, Christmas is coming, and you, pretty lady, are on the "A list" for the hottest Christmas Eve party north of the forty-ninth parallel! We do it up right, here at the Knotty Pine."

Christmas was the last thing she wanted to hear about, but Softouch didn't notice.

"Who knows, the election's over, maybe Matt will show up."

Shut up, Softouch, she thought.

"I doubt if he'll make it. He said in his last letter that he had some work to do in Denali," her eyes never left the computer screen, "some virus is spreading through the mountain goats."

"Sorry, Doc, guess I shouldn't have brought him up."

"Not your fault," her voice a feeble attempt at nonchalance. "Matt is the black hole of communication. His letters could've been written to his tax consultant, and you know how often they come." She glanced at him then back to the screen, "I'm getting used to it."

Doesn't look like you've gotten used to it from where I sit, Softouch thought.

"I need to get home and analyze this data." She disconnected her laptop and packed it away, refusing to meet the bartender's eyes.

"See you later." He watched her Jeep pull out and head toward the highway.

Three days later Survivor's red track on Alex's monitor was just a dot, and the blue line of the local pack was not even within the fifty-mile radius of the GPS data.

He hadn't moved.

Alex considered all possible explanations, none were optimistic. She hurt for her canine friend, and her distress was obvious to Softouch.

"That is not the face we like to see, pretty lady."

"He's still where he was Tuesday. I'm really getting worried." The large black man studied her for a few minutes, but he had no comforting words. Winter was hard, and he didn't need to tell Alex that.

"There has to be something I can do..." she mumbled. She watched him amble away with a tray of beer and popcorn and her eyes settled on the anorexic Christmas tree Softouch had mounted in a beer keg next to the jukebox. Tinsel and lights did little to improve it. Her melancholy deepened. How can I think about Christmas when he's alone? ...starving ...or worse.

Terry caught her attention and motioned her to join him and his brother. She sighed and left her stool.

"Why the unhappy face, Alex? Christmas is coming, where's your Yuletide cheer?"

"I think it's frozen solid."

Since the incident with the sick cougar, Terry and Allan had gained new respect for Alex, and she for them. They enjoyed each other's company and had spent hours discussing wilderness policy. Conversations got heated on occasion, but trappers and vet learned from each other and their friendship grew.

"Bad news from the eye in the sky?" Allan's voice always sounded like liquid velvet. He was intrigued by her high-tech tools and his voice had been the first raised in support of her work with the wolf.

"He hasn't moved in several days. I think he's sick, or injured." *Or worse.*

"Why don't you track him down and check?" Terry asked.

"I'm thinking about it. But I'd need to take him some meat. If he's not moving, he's not eating. You guys don't happen to have half a cow stashed somewhere, do you?"

The brothers grinned. "Oh, I think we might be able to help you out there. We drove past a roadkill this morning, a good-sized doe. I'm sure that would make a nice Christmas dinner for your friend." Allan continued, "How 'bout if we drop it by your place tomorrow?"

"That would be great. Thanks alot."

Alex's mind started churning out the list; what to take, food for herself and Viento, how much, and tracking equipment. The effort lifted her mood, mental action was better than no action at all.

"You want us to come along? We feel like we know this guy, as much as you've talked about him. You're gonna have to pack quite a bit of gear, too, and we do have some experience at that."

She shook her head, "No, but thanks for the offer. It'll be a good chance to test my own tracking skills, and with Viento, I think I can pack everything I need. I'll just tie the deer behind him and drag it."

Terry spoke up. "Alex, we think you shouldn't go out there without a gun." She opened her mouth to argue, but he cut her off. "We know how you feel, but remember the cougar? Well, there are other animals just as unsociable, or worse. Stan lost a sled dog just last week, trampled by a moose."

Allan's eyes searched hers, "And what if you find your

wolf and he's in real bad shape?" She looked down, the possibility was too painful for her to voice. "Do you want him to suffer until someone or something finishes him off? Or until he slowly starves to death?"

Alex sighed, then conceded the belief of a lifetime to their logic. "But I don't know the first thing about guns, and you know I don't own one."

The brothers were already rising from their seats. "I think we can rectify that right now." The three of them approached the bar and Allan waved at Softouch.

"We have a lady here in need of a few inanimate objects willing to make the supreme sacrifice," Softouch eyebrows shot up, "for target practice."

Softouch stared at Alex, then grinned. "Oh, I think I have some bottles that will donate their all to the cause. Shall we adjourn to the official Knotty Pine firing range, folks?"

Terry retrieved a handgun from his truck while Alex helped Softouch set up some bottles along a log behind the bar. Beyond the log was the rest of Canada. No humans, and few animals close enough to be at risk.

Terry started class. "Alex, the first item of business is gun safety..." And for the next two hours the three men drilled her in proper handling of guns in general, and specifically the .357 Magnum. Allan handed her the gun and its weight was unexpected. She nearly dropped it.

"... hold it with both hands, sight down the barrel, no, don't close one eye, Alex. And don't lock your elbows or your knees. This gun has a kick that will break your nose when you pull the trigger, so be prepared to move your head to the side."

"Like this?" She brought the gun to bear on the glass martyrs in the distance.

Softouch stood behind her, "Yes, but spread your legs shoulder width and distribute your weight evenly." He steadied her, his hands on her shoulders. "And Alex, relax. Those bottles are already dead."

His comment eased her tension and she took aim and

fired. Even with the warning she was not prepared for the revolver's kick, and almost cocked herself in the forehead. The men chuckled.

Allan grinned, "Alex, you must remain conscious to operate the equipment."

By sundown three experienced gun owners were confident she wouldn't shoot herself. Unfortunately she probably wouldn't hit anything else either, judging by the almost unbroken line of healthy bottles still standing on the log.

"Well, Alex, most animals will run if you just fire over their heads," Terry chuckled, "and you seem to have that skill nailed."

Arming her with shells, and a last serious warning to be careful, Allan handed the handgun to the devout animal-lover.

Winter solstice found her packing food and supplies in Viento's trailer and planning for a week in the Canadian woods.

Chapter Fifty-six

Survivor suffered his injury for seven days without leaving the shelter at the evergreen's base. Blood pooled beneath him and froze into a red mass of fur and needles. Around him storms blew, and calmed, but he could not have moved had he felt the urge.

Weakened from blood loss and hunger, he had no options.

Instinctively, he curled into the position of his youth, tucked his nose under his back leg, hunched up his feet beneath his stomach, and draped his eyes with his tail. He was powerless to defend himself from even the weather, and the snow buried and cleared him at whim.

Pain flared then subsided. Hunger raged, then faded. His circumstances challenged his spirit, and the will to live ebbed and dimmed.

The ping of the wolf's radio collar was faint through the headphones, but as Alex rotated the antenna it got louder, then faded. The signal was strongest northwest of the road. Dense forest rose a few hundred yards beyond a wide clearing—probably a grassy meadow in springtime—and somewhere beyond that was the wolf.

Four hours of weak sunlight remained, so Alex quickly saddled and packed Viento and set out after the electronic pulse.

Light snowfall added to the accumulated volume on the ground, two more inches and it would brush her stirrups. The deer, now sleighing on a plastic tarp with a bale of hay and some dry firewood, cut a wide swath in the fresh powder behind the mustang. Viento pushed forward through the fluff with a familiarity born of his youth on the plains of Wyoming. His basic evaluation accounted this environment preferable to the heat and flies of summer.

A roadless expanse, so vast it challenged the best

cartographer's skill, unfolded before Alex. All that her eyes could capture—millions of square acres—had evolved untouched, and unmarked by man, and most animals played out their lives without ever scenting or sighting homo sapiens. A year earlier such remote wilderness threatened Alex, now it seduced her.

The old growth forest wrapped horse and rider in a silence so complete it whispered of the sacred. Towering ancient spruce, as glorious as any cathedral spires, bore a century's mute witness to the struggles played out beneath their snowburdened arms. They offered up the only requiem for those beings who failed winter's test, as wind chanted a prayer of benediction for the weak. The unselected. Only Viento's puffing breath and hooves crunching in snow violated the quiet.

Alex was comfortable in the twenty-seven degree morning, and her only contributions to Viento's work were occasional course corrections. Her thoughts were on the wolf, and every pause to check their position against the electronic beacon brought her closer to him. By the time she stopped to pitch camp the ping was noticeably stronger.

Maybe tomorrow I'll find him...

An hour before dark, Alex reined Viento up at a stand of cedars. The trunks of three old giants, felled by lightning decades before, had fallen in a crescent, the crown of one tangled in the roots of another, backbones forming a barrier against the snow. They had been young when Caucasian foot first tracked North America, and their six-foot girths would witness many more years before rotting into dust.

A new generation sprang from their decaying remains, and this curved wall of young trunks and branches, twisted and tangled, formed a natural shelter from wind and snow. The competition for survival which would thin the young trees had not started, and Alex pitched her tent in the elbow of two of their prone ancestors. Snow was only ankle deep inside the cedar thicket, and there was plenty of shelter for her tent, Viento, and a campfire.

Minutes after sunset, Alex's tent was up, her food bag

and the deer dangled from high branches, and Viento was rubbed down and munching the supper he had hauled all day. She transformed the plastic tarp into a lean-to, protecting horse, hay, and firewood, and a warm campfire cast a yellow glow, warming body and soul of horse and human. From a stump near the fire, she watched Viento sense the heat and pivot his body, alternating which side faced the flames. She smiled at the mustang's capacity to differentiate between danger and comfort when it came packaged as fire.

Alex heated her dinner in a single pot—rice and beans—and a foil-wrapped biscuit thawed on the pot's lid. The snowfall had stopped and now a moonless sky glittered with stars. Reflections of the campfire danced along Viento's flanks, and orange light played in the snowdrifts and branches beyond her sanctuary. Alex gazed over her campsite, content with its structure and security against the elements. She smiled.

Viento isn't the only one who's trail smart.

She monitored the tracking collar one last time and drew no comfort from its stationary position.

"Please, God, don't let me find him dead tomorrow. Please?" God did not respond, and Alex drifted into a troubled sleep haunted by images of the white wolf.

Frozen stiff and hanging in a tree.

Alex's perception of time required no mechanical device, she had stopped wearing a watch months earlier. The alarm that signaled diurnal animals forth in the morning awakened her before dawn and she had breakfasted Viento and herself by the time the sun made its weak assault on the horizon. But the sky was clear blue and soon temperatures warmed to just above freezing. She would have to shed a layer of clothing before long.

The electronic signal had not moved during the night, and she set out again, northwest, dragging the deer.

"Maybe we'll find him today, V." Equine ears flicked back briefly catching her words, then forward again.

"I wonder if he'll remember us... It was only a couple

months ago, but to a wild animal..."

Through the morning the signal remained strong and unmoving, and Alex's last remnant of optimism faded then vanished. The wolf hadn't moved in two weeks.

She steeled herself to find him dead.

Survivor awoke that clear morning, alert, but stiff from days of inactivity. He yawned, then stood and shook his head. The neck pain was only modest, he'd tolerated worse. He yawned again, and stretched, toes splayed, front legs reaching far forward, rump in the air. He shook from head to tail, fluffing insulating fur. He glanced into the thicket that had protected him and then lunged away through the deep snow in search of food.

"What's this?" Alex tapped the headphones. The signal had faded. She moved the antenna and confirmed the signal was no longer northwest of them, but due west. And moving. She double-checked her compass, then the frequency on the receiver. It was correct. Swinging the antenna slowly in a 180-degree arc, she began to smile.

The wolf was moving.

"Hey, V, he's still among the living!" An invisible weight flew from her spirit and she couldn't keep from grinning. She increased the gain on her receiver to accommodate the fading signal.

Then the tracking equipment died.

"What the...?"

She switched it off and on several times. Changed the batteries. And then she slapped the receiver in frustration.

Silence through the headphones.

No beep. No signal. And no new direction.

Chapter Fifty-seven

"Oh, *great*! This is *just perfect*!"

Exasperated, Alex tore the headphones off, and they slipped from her hands into the snow. She had to dismount to retrieve them.

"High-tech junk!" she muttered as she packed the tracking equipment in the saddlebags.

"Now what am I supposed to do? I get this close, and I can't follow him!"

Viento glanced around at Alex, ears back as if he might be responsible in some way for her irritation. Satisfied he wasn't, he stood quietly.

"Okay, Alex, think. There has to be a way to salvage this." She fingered the compass hanging around her neck for a couple minutes, deep in thought. Then she looked at it.

"Wait a minute..." She concentrated, compass in front of her. "If we just go west-northwest, we should cross his trail." She nodded and stroked Viento's neck, thinking.

"Is that right? He was northwest, then west... yeah, that should work." She reined Viento to the left, and they continued through the trees.

Less than twenty minutes later they found the thicket. The frozen blood clot immediately seized Alex's attention. She dismounted and bent over it.

"Looks like you're no better at picking your affections than I am," she muttered. Removing her gloves, she poked around the icy red mass cluttered with white guard hairs, pine needles, and ground litter.

"There's a lot of blood here... what nastiness did you stumble into?" Talking to herself brought no answers as she searched the packed snow where the wolf had slept. All she deducted was that the fight had not happened there.

"But how far did you walk before you collapsed here?" This place was easily forty miles from his release site. She glanced down the wolf's new trail away from the thicket. It was fresh, and paw prints were clear in the soft snow.

Wolf prints showing only three toes on both left feet.

She had only missed him by minutes.

"Well, I guess you've recovered," she sighed, and then remembered the frozen deer, now a stiff, snowcovered mass behind Viento.

"...but I bet you're still hungry."

She returned to the mustang and stroked his face. "We'll leave the deer here, V. He might come back." She struggled to drag the carcass into the thicket, it was heavy, and now with a casing of snow frozen into its fur, it was almost more than she could budge.

By the time she finished, light was fading and she knew there was no time to follow the wolf's trail. Temperatures were plummeting, and although she was sweating inside her parka, her face and fingers were icy. It was time to return to camp.

"Well, V., at least we know he's not dead. That's good news, right? Right. Even if we don't see him, that's really good news." The mustang plodded on, the trip back to their campsite easier than the morning trip out, while Alex's thoughts stumbled, confused.

Why am I still sad? I should be happy that he's moving again, that he's recovered. I guess I just wanted to see him...

Her melancholy never clearly coagulated into loneliness, and she returned to her campsite almost as dejected as when she had left it.

Survivor worked his way through the unfamiliar territory, searching for anything to fill his belly. No fresh animal scent triggered hunting instincts, and after dark he turned back to the thicket, fatigued and starving.

The deer's scent reached him before he saw it and he loped the last hundred yards, and fell on the frozen meat ravenously. Canine teeth pierced the thick hide, premolars ripped through skin to flesh, and carnassials briefly ground the frozen meat before he swallowed it. Only two ravens had discovered Survivor's booty and they silently hopped close enough to indulge their own appetites once he had opened the feast. Survivor tolerated their company, his raging hunger the highest priority. He devoured twenty pounds of frozen venison before finally plopping down in the snow, sated.

Then he noticed Alex's scent. On the deer's skin. On the ground. And the horse's scent mingled with the woman's. Survivor raised his head and tested the wind, and faded memories returned.

Images of warmth and food. Glimpses of wood and straw. Companionship.

And the spirit-voice.

Alex brushed Viento quickly, and buckled his blanket across his back. The star-filled sky offered no protective cloud cover and temperatures plummeted, refreezing the surface snow into a glossy crust.

She refreshed the campfire and warmed her hands around the pot while her dinner – Softouch's famous moose chili—melted. The chili reminded her of Softouch's party... and the party reminded her it was Christmas Eve. She dug a frozen apple and carrot out of her food pack and offered them to Viento.

"Well, my friend," she whispered, "Merry Christmas." It was a whisper filled with longing and unhappiness as the year's events paraded before her mind's eye—her husband, her huskies, the wolf, and of course Matt, a mixed blessing of yuletide companions. Alex sighed under their burden, resting her face against the mustang's jaw. The horse's scent was peacefully comforting.

"Come on, Viento, it's Christmas. Help me think of things to be thankful for." The mustang's liquid brown eyes watched her, unblinking.

"Okay, I'll go first. Let's see... Obviously, my family. And you, of course. And Softouch," she grinned, "and his chili." She rubbed Viento's neck.

"How 'bout you? Of course, you're thankful for carrots and apples, your blanket, and," she searched Viento's liquid brown eyes, "I really think you're happier out here, than in your stall."

She returned to her stump and opened the pot. The frozen mass of meat and beans had reduced to a lumpy iceberg floating in a sea of red sauce, and the rich smell of wild meat and spices infused her nostrils. Her stomach rumbled.

"And I guess I should be thankful for Matt," she muttered, "but right now I'm not sure why..." His image marched to the front of her mental parade and she mulled over his inelegant departure. And the night that had preceded it. There was nothing to distract her, so she slogged through it again, familiar territory.

"Why did he leave me like that?... after we... like he was running away..." She shook her head and poked the fire with a stick and sparks swirled around the pot.

"...and they say women are a mystery!" She shook her head to disengage the mental madness.

"This is useless..." But with nothing to distract her the memories continued their procession, a well-worn review of all the moments she had spent with Matt, the college camaraderie, and she searched fruitlessly for any hint of the character flaw that would rise to hurt her later. As if understanding would give her peace. Then she remembered an earlier evening with him.

He had taught her to howl.

And the wolves had responded.

"I wonder..."

She gazed into the forest blackness, as unsure as she had been that first time. The frozen wild beckoned and she turned her back to the fire, and stepped into the trees. Three deep breaths of icy mountain air expanded her lungs. Cupping her hands around her mouth, she raised her head and howled, a low mournful cry that rang for several seconds, pitch rising... rising... rising... then falling away with her last expelled air. She inhaled, then howled again.

This time there was no embarrassment. Somehow the act was appropriate in this place, and it brought her unexpected calm. Wild instincts that had taken root, blossomed to full awareness with each howl. She acknowledged them proudly, testing them like an eaglet new wings.

Sharpening night vision split the undefined blackness into clear images; trees, rocks, and branches, and she easily deciphered shadows from that which cast them. Starlight intensified and organized into familiar constellations, old friends, and she welcomed them. The dominating scent of chili blended with other smells. Viento. Cold evergreens. Sweet rotting cedar.

She lost count of how many times she howled. What had started as an attempt to communicate became a declaration of her independence. Each lament climbed out of her soul, freed her spirit, and identified her as a citizen of the wild.

Then she heard him.

Hair rose on the back of her neck, a primal animal response she could not control.

And the howl came again, distant but clear.

For twenty minutes Alex and her wolf sang a duet, a discordant Christmas carol, for the private audience of God.

When silence reclaimed the night she sat by the fire, waiting for her chili to cool to eating temperature, and considered this great thing. She was not tired, but exhilarated, and minutes assembled into hours, offering their gift of profound peace in response to her profound gratitude.

She had finished her dinner and was staring dreamlike into the campfire's flames when she noticed the eyes.

White, glowing, eyes.

Watching her from the darkness.

She had no idea how long they had been there.

Her heart leaped in apprehension, but only until she glanced at Viento. Dozing beneath the plastic tarp.

Then she smiled.

"Season's greetings, my friend." Her calm whisper conveyed familiar affection.

The eyes took form and the white wolf emerged from the white background, placing one careful paw in front of another, stiff-legged. His steps were as silent as they were slow, and a full minute passed while he eased closer, then paused, then closer still. He stopped, eight feet from the campfire, and faced her through the flames.

Alex could hardly breathe, and was afraid to blink. Standing was beyond consideration.

"Nice of you to drop by," she whispered.

He lowered his head at the sound of her voice, maintaining eye contact, then raised it again.

Sight, scent, and sound confirmed this woman as friend.

"I see you had a little skirmish with one of your neighbors." Although her heart pounded, Alex controlled her voice, forcing herself into the practiced quiet that had calmed the wolf during his recuperation. It eased him now.

"...sure hope he looks worse than you do." Alex noticed fresh blood around his mouth, and smiled.

"And you found your Christmas dinner... I'll be sure to convey your appreciation to Terry and Allan." Each time she spoke Survivor tilted his head, as if he recognized the curious sound, but was as surprised as Alex to be standing in her campsite.

Then he turned and leaped into the darkness.

Gone.

Alex took a deep breath and exhaled slowly.

"Now that was a Christmas present."

Seconds later, God offered up his last gift. A curtain of iridescent green light dropped across the sky and shimmered over Alex's head. It flowed like chiffon, sparkling constellations visible through its drifting color. A single ray of blue shot in front of the green, and danced back and forth through it. The veil waved and flowed, blown on magnetic wind, then suddenly flamed from green to gold, bottom to top. Cosmic particles blasted to earth—electrons and protons charged by the sun—had circled the North Pole, invisible but save this single instant of radiant beauty.

The aurora triggered instincts Alex had only discovered hours earlier, and she freed her spirit to dance with the ancients. On rays of blue, and arcs and swirls of gold, her soul ignited and streamed across the night sky. Far removed from civilization, native myths, empowered by the night's events, gained credibility beneath the northern lights. Alex considered the possibility of things immortal.

She leaned back against the decaying log and stared into the heavens, as appreciative as she had ever been in her life.

Surface snow around her, glassy firnspiegel, mirrored the heavenly show and Alex lost herself in the reflection. Blue and green and gold, shifting and waving, below as above.

And there was no fear.

Chapter Fifty-eight

Softouch saw Matt the minute he stomped into the Knotty Pine, but continued serving other customers until the biologist had parked on a stool at the bar. The party was in full swing, beer and spiced cider were flowing as fast as Softouch could pour.

He faced Matt. "Nice of you to fit our little yuletide soiree into your busy schedule." Matt missed the sarcasm as his eyes roved the room a second time.

"Wouldn't miss it for the world." He tasted the cider Softouch put in front of him. "Is Alex coming?"

"No, she won't make it."

Matt frowned. "Is her cabin snowed-in?"

"I don't think so, the service has kept her road pretty well plowed. But she's not there, anyway. She's been out in the woods a couple days. Tracking that wolf."

"Is she alone?" Concern was obvious and Softouch marveled at Matt's ability to worry about Alex when he was geographically close to her. And not, when he wasn't.

"Of course she's not alone," he hung clean glasses from the rack over the bar, "she took that fine mustang with her."

Matt stared at him, "Do you think that was wise? Letting her go out there at this time of year, by herself?"

Softouch inhaled deeply, more to calm his rising irritation, than because he needed the air. "First, Matt, I don't think you are in any position to be criticizing how I take care of my friends." He leaned across the bar, filling Matt's field of vision. "Second, the lady's become quite accomplished at handling winter's obstacles alone since you left... what... months ago? She can take care of herself just fine."

Bewildered by the conversation, Matt changed the subject. "Why's she tracking the wolf?"

"He hadn't moved in several days, so she got worried. Terry and Allan got her roadkill, and she went to look for him."

"When did she leave? Do you know where she went?"

"She left two days ago, and no, I don't know where she went. Out there." He waved his arm in the general direction of most of Alberta. He knew where Alex was, but something kept him from telling Matt.

The noise of the party nearly drowned out his voice. "Between that wolf not trotting across her computer screen, and your mail, Matt, she was a pretty unhappy lady her last few visits to my humble establishment. And you know how I dislike unhappy customers."

"What do you mean, 'my mail'?"

"Well, unless you're also sending her letters to another address, I'm not terribly impressed by their frequency, and the content didn't exactly bring a smile to her face."

Matt was surprised by Softouch's criticism. And puzzled. He hadn't noticed the strong friendship between Alex and Softouch on his last visit. Evidently he should have.

The bartender continued, "I don't know what all happened the last time you two were together, but I do know Alex's been less happy since you left, than she was before you showed up. And the mention of your name does nothing to improve her disposition."

Terry waved from his table and Softouch left with a tray of amber-filled glasses.

When he returned to his post behind the bar Matt attempted a defense, but his words rang empty before they were even out of his mouth. "I had to go to Alaska, you know that. So did she."

"I'm not talking about your busy schedule. I'm talking about whatever unfinished business you left behind, with Alex's name on it." He polished the spotless bar and lowered his voice. "You know what I think, Matt? I think you played a round or two of 'hide-the-salami' with our fair vet, and then split when the game got too hot for you."

Matt dropped his eyes, a silent confession.

"Thought so." Softouch shook his head, "Matt, you

sincerely disappoint me—I thought you had more class than that." He glanced around the room, and his eyes paused at Terry and Allan. "Do you think you're the only man who's noticed her?"

Matt looked at the brothers for the first time as competitors. He knew other men would be attracted to Alex. That a local might interest her, however, had never crossed his mind.

Softouch saw it in his face. "Well, aren't you arrogant? In this little pissant town light years from civilization, men are especially quick to appreciate a fine looking lady. A few might even have enough sophistication to be intrigued by a bright mind." Softouch refilled a couple of glasses at the end of the bar and returned to a very subdued Matt.

"You had the inside track on that lady's affections, my friend, and you walked off the field."

Matt pulled a small leather drawstring pouch out of his pocket and set it on the bar.

"I had this made for her in Alaska. For Christmas. Will you give it to her when she comes back?"

Softouch shook his head. "No sir, I will not. Stick around and give it to her yourself." He leaned on the bar. "Matt, in this game you must be present to win."

The conversation struck a nerve, and Matt rubbed his eyes, then the back of his neck. The Knotty Pine, once his haven, had grown hostile. "When do you think she'll be back?"

"She took provisions for a week. I'm sure she'll come home before the food runs out."

Matt closed his eyes against the scene that loomed. Alex was angry and hurt, and he was responsible. To fix it, or just leave? He took a deep breath. "She's really mad?"

"I think more hurt. But considering the marital hurricane that blew her here in the first place, I don't think men are exactly scoring high in our doc's book right now." He nodded, "yes sir, now that you mention it, she's seriously pissed."

A waking grizzly is easier to deal with, Matt thought.

Softouch slid more glasses into the rack over the bar and they clinked together to the sounds of, "The Twelve Days of Christmas," booming from the jukebox.

Matt waited all twelve verses, then looked at the bartender. "Can I borrow your truck? My rental car won't make it to her cabin unless I'm towed by a snowplow."

Softouch grinned and tossed Matt a set of keys. "Take care of business, Matt. That lady deserves at least that much." Matt rose, picked up the leather pouch, and put on his coat.

Before he got to the door Softouch yelled over the party din, "By the way, Matt, she's got a gun," he grinned, "and she's a terrible shot."

"Thanks for the warning."

Softouch watched Matt and his truck vanish in the snowfall.

Alex slammed on the brakes, surprised to see Softouch's truck parked in front of her cabin. Smoke spiraled from her chimney and her heart cramped. Softouch was her emergency contact with the outside world, and since he'd left his own Christmas Eve party to be here when she returned, Alex assumed the worst. Something wrong with her parents. Or her sister. She leaped out of her Jeep and rushed through the front door, pulse racing.

When she saw Matt she froze. Door open. Mouth open. "What are you doing here?"

Matt hadn't expected a friendly welcome, but her tone was as icy as the weather. "I missed you in town and..."

She was out the door before he finished stumbling over more words he hadn't planned. He grabbed his jacket and caught up with her as she was backing Viento out of the trailer, but the set of her jaw did not invite conversation. Blue eyes focused on the mustang and she settled him in his stall as if Matt wasn't there.

"Alex, I came to apologize." She put hay in the hanging feeder and grabbed his brush. "I shouldn't have left you like that... I'm sorry."

Still no response.

"I brought you a Christmas present..."

Silence. Except for the sound of Viento chewing.

"You're not making this easy for me."

She erupted. "*Easy for you*? What am I not making easy for you, Matt? Please tell me! It was so *easy* for me, after you left me like a ten-dollar hooker! We were *friends*!" Pent-up anger powered her arm and Viento glanced around, questioning the force with which she was brushing him.

"I never meant to hurt you. Never. I just wasn't ready for that."

"How old are you, Matt? Twelve? Did you think I would just play penpal after our little night of fun and frolic? You NEVER said a word! Our night of bliss must have been life-altering, since it apparently vanished from your memory in the time it took you to dress and leave. Did you think I would just ignore that?"

She put grain in Viento's feeder, then started brushing his other side. "Well, I didn't!"

She stopped and glared at Matt.

His leaving and the time following it had aged badly—vinegar, instead of wine—and Matt was afraid to respond. He hadn't just touched a nerve, he'd severed one. He tried to change the subject. To get some breathing room and think.

"Softouch said you went after the wolf. Did you find him?"

The obvious diversion only enraged her further. He was running away again, this time from the conversation.

"Yes, I did." And suddenly the first person Alex would have shared the event with, was the last person she wanted to tell.

"You are a bastard! Even my ex-husband didn't hurt me like you did, right from the start HE wanted to fuck me! But not you, you had to be my friend, playing host and helping me release the wolf. And *then* you did me. At least with Stephen there was no pretense."

She's comparing me to her ex-husband? What if I can't fix this...?

"Alex, I apologize. I know how it must've looked."

"Looked?" Alex chuckled, a sick little laugh. "You still don't get it, do you? Well, Matt, your apology is accepted. Now goodbye."

"That's it? You're willing to just toss away any future, any relationship we might have?"

"To my knowledge the only relationship we have is penpals." She shook her head, "And I can live without that."

Matt clenched and unclenched his fists, physically grabbing at what was emotionally slipping through his fingers. "I don't want to lose you like this."

"Well, since you don't seem to know why you bolted in the first place, I can't be sure you won't do it again. And I will not be another man's victim. *I will not*!"

She finished with Viento and brushed past Matt into the house, dropping her jacket on the kitchen counter.

Matt courageously followed her and put more wood into the stove. He collapsed into one of the chairs, palms shading his eyes, thumbs rubbing his temples.

Alex watched him, and her anger eased. She was exhausted, hungry, and needed a bath. And she had no more energy for this fight.

"Alex, come and sit down. I need to talk to you." His soft voice crawled into its familiar niche, "Please?"

She dropped into the other chair, groaning with fatigue.

Matt took a couple deep breaths, and then gazed at her. "What destroyed your marriage?"

"What?" She hadn't expected a question, especially that one.

"What destroyed your marriage? What did Stephen do that chased you up here?"

She bristled, "I don't think this conversation is about my marriage."

"Just tell me. Please?" His eyes never left hers, pleading.

"Well, I guess the determining blow was finding my faithful and loving husband in bed with his secretary. In *our* bed. Why?"

"I don't think it was that. Not exactly."

"What do you mean?"

"I think it had more to do with the fact that you were totally ignorant of their affair, going on right under your nose. What Stephen destroyed, more than your marriage, was your ability to trust your judgment of human nature. You think you should've seen it." He sighed heavily. "That's what happened to me."

Alex held her breath. She realized that in all the years of their friendship Matt had never discussed the ugly breakup of his engagement only weeks before the wedding. She tried to recall that time but her own memories did not include him. Only her bright, new marriage to Stephen. And her clinic.

"You were so wrapped up with Stephen and your practice I figured you never heard what happened. And I was so humiliated… I just had to leave."

Alex held her breath, and suffered a twinge of guilt for a friendship she had neglected.

"Lisa and I were living together the last couple years of college, but you know I was gone a lot in the field." He rubbed his thighs, as if trying to knead the old pain away.

"I never thought to question anything she did. Not her friends, or how she paid for college. I wasn't really up on her Computer Science major, but I recognized she had a passion for it, so I supported her desire to make it her career." He got up, paced around the chair, clenching and unclenching his fists. Alex didn't move. Finally he sat.

"Well, one night—the last night—we were in bed when the police pounded on the door and arrested us."

Alex's eyebrows shot up. "What?"

"Lisa had been running a pornography website out of our home. They arrested us both. It was four days before they figured out I wasn't involved. Four days in jail! I couldn't convince them that I didn't even know how to turn the computer on." He rubbed his forehead as if to drive the images back into the dark. "Alex, some of the—umm, girls—were minors. And she took some of the pictures *in our house*!"

He sighed and his shoulders dropped. He seemed to shrink before Alex's eyes.

"I had no clue. I mean, I didn't even know what a website was then. I just bolted for Alaska." He shook his head. "I spent the next couple years trying to sort it out." He finally made eye contact. "Alex, I make my living interpreting complex social behavior. How could I be so good at understanding a wolf's behavior, and so ignorant of my own fiancée's twisted activity?"

Alex took a breath to reply, but synapses in her brain worked fast enough to stifle whatever she was going to say. His words finally sank in. Arrested in the middle of the night? Days in jail for something he knew nothing about? She couldn't even imagine it.

Matt stared into the iron stove.

"You are the first woman I've been with since. It's not an excuse, but it is an explanation. And I am sorry."

When Alex next looked at Matt, she saw another injured animal. His old wounds were hemorrhaging fresh blood, and she recognized some of the them. But not all.

"What do you want here, Matt," her eyes held his, "with me?"

It was the moment of truth, and Matt knew it.

He inhaled and Matt felt his own heartbeat. "I might be in love with you," he paused, "and I want to investigate the possibility that you might feel the same about me."

He had faced angry, armed ranchers, but this took more courage. The ranchers could kill his body—Alex had her fingers around his soul.

He watched orange flames reflected in her eyes flare up, down, up again, as she watched the fire. For a sign? Then her eyes pierced his. She whispered in a tone that might as well have been a shout, each word a threatening hammer blow.

"If you ever treat me like that again, I'll track you down and kill you myself."

His eyes widened, "What?"

Very slowly... she smiled. Very slowly. Then grinned. Then chuckled, and the tension vanished.

"So what did you bring me for Christmas?"

He handed her the soft leather pouch. She opened it and a small carving, about one inch long, fell into her hand.

"It's scrimshaw. Made out of petrified elk antler. The man that carved it put up a real argument when I told him the eyes had to be blue."

Alex studied the wolf carving, the blue eyes, and the creamy details highlighted by black ink. Matt took it from her and set it on his open palm.

"See, it's either free-standing, or," he reached into his pocket, "it can be put on a chain for a necklace." He threaded the gold chain through the loop on the wolf's back and timidly reached out to give it to her.

"You fasten it."

Alex felt his hands tremble as he fastened the tiny clasp behind her neck and the wolf dropped between her breasts. She fingered it while he sat down, and then looked at him.

"It's beautiful, Matt. Thank you." She studied the dainty animal, then glanced into the iron box where recent memories seemed to dance in the flames.

Her whisper graced the silence, "He walked out of the woods, Matt, right up to my campfire. I don't know how long he'd been watching me," her bright eyes caught Matt's, "but he wasn't afraid... and neither was I."

Chapter Fifty-nine

Sexual tension hung in the air like smoke after a fire. Survivor sat still, camouflaged by the snow around him, and studied the local pack from a granite outcropping above their rendezvous site. While he watched, a young male sidled up to the alpha bitch, sniffed her rump, licked her face, and rested his head across her back. Whining. Begging. From across the clearing the alpha male dashed up, grabbed him by the throat, and dragged him away from the bitch. The interloper cowered, suddenly remembering his place, slinked along the ground and then rolled over, presenting his belly in submission.

The alpha male urinated on him.

The pack had grown too large and the scent of so many females in estrus caused rising tension. While Survivor watched, the scene repeated itself again and again. Glassy-eyed males pursued the alpha bitch, and females tempted her wrath to flirt with the alpha male. Older wolves, who had been through it all before, skulked around the two alphas like sycophants around royalty, wanting to be near the action, well-aware the action would never be theirs to enjoy.

Estrus triggered an intoxicating lust, and Survivor felt its pull for the first time.

Weeks had passed since his fight with the tan, and hunger was only an occasional guest, not a constant companion. Survivor had grown accustomed to his solitary life.

Until he smelled the first blood of shewolves coming into season.

The scent triggered hormones in Patriarch's son, so strong that they drove him back to the local pack that had almost killed him. He didn't know what brought him to the overlook, he only knew that among the milling, circling wolves below him was something he needed.

He waited.

The mood below him changed. The two alphas, the dark

charcoal bitch and the silver male, romped away, youthful, light-footed over the packed snow, toward a stand of trees along the clearing's edge. Their bodies touched continually, shoulders and hips bumping as they ran. Some of the pack followed from a distance, others watched, heads bobbing, tails wagging in anticipation.

Survivor could see the couple through the trees, and he watched the male mount the female and begin the mating thrusts that would tie them together. Fangs gripped her neck, not with violence, but to hold her still. The bitch dug her claws into the snow, steeling herself against each thrust until she felt his first penetration.

They were oblivious to all around them.

Suddenly a large black female shot toward them, hackles up, and grabbed the alpha female's throat. The alpha was completely taken by surprise, and in no position to defend herself.

With raw strength, the younger female jerked her out from under her mate.

The passion of mating became the passion of combat. The older wolf twisted her head quickly, escaping the black's grasp and then lunged at the eager young bitch with the speed and grace of experience. Dodging the black muzzle, her open mouth found its target. Canine teeth dug deep into the black's shoulder, past muscle to bone, bit down and jerked hard, ripping a three-inch gash in the young flesh.

The challenger yelped in pain, as she dropped to the snow, and snarls from the alpha female kept her there.

As fast as thought forms in a wolf's mind the black knew rising would be her last act.

Her mother would kill her.

She urinated on herself and didn't move.

Soulmate was nearly two years old when Survivor appeared in her pack's territory. Born the same spring as the white wolf, her litter had numbered seven cubs, six females and one male, so competition became an immediate part of her life. Larger than the rest of her littermates, she established her superiority before they had sight.

But when nursing ceased, the fight for food included the rest of the pack and this competition defined hierarchy, as well as who would eat. To her credit she won more skirmishes than she lost, intimidating her packmates. Her narrow muzzle and large amber eyes gave her face a deceptively fragile look which she cleverly used, much to the regret of wolves that crossed her.

As the time of mating grew closer the pack's mood changed noticeably and Soulmate and her sisters' estrual blood in the snow contributed to the emotional stress.

And heightened their own lust.

The six young shewolves snapped at one another with renewed testiness and on more than one occasion drew blood. After two days of challenge and parry Soulmate again dominated her female siblings.

Buoyed by that success, she challenged the only bitch between her and the silver alpha male.

Her mother.

Soulmate's urge to mate was not tempered by wisdom or discretion. In peak condition, sleek and strong, she pranced gracefully around the silver alpha male, blatantly flirting and tempting him, as if by her passage to maturity she had achieved an elevated status in the pack.

Soulmate's mother had been challenged every year for the last four, and her experience weighed far heavier in the balance than Soulmate's eager strength. For days the black wolf harassed her mother, but the older wolf's reflexes met and exceeded Soulmate's best effort with brilliant finesse.

All previous offenses had been met with sharp fangs and increasing violence, but this attack during mating went too far.

Soulmate's mother now hovered over her, growling, daring her to get up. The alpha female did not see a daughter before her in the snow, she saw an opponent, and with snarls as serious as any Soulmate had ever heard, threatened to end the life she had created two years earlier.

Survivor heard the young female's whines of submission and pain from his perch overlooking the pack.

After several minutes—an eternity to Soulmate—the alpha bitch turned away, satisfied with her submission, shook her head and pranced back to her mate. Soulmate struggled to rise and rejoin the pack in the clearing.

But all had changed.

The rest of the wolves withdrew from her, as if on some unspoken signal, and she stood alone in the midst of her family. No one came to lick her wound as they had in the past. The young bitch tried to lick it herself, but she could not reach the gash and blood continued to run down her leg staining the snow. When she limped toward her sisters for consolation they refused to face her, resolutely ignoring her.

Soulmate had crossed some invisible line, violated some unwritten law, and now was anathema to her pack.

She slowly looked around at each of her relatives. Not one canine eye met hers. She dropped her head, resigned to her exile and staggered away, leaving a trail of red paw prints with each step.

Survivor had observed every nuance of the ritual with an objectivity born of distance. His detachment from the pack granted him perspective, but his own hormonal response to the season brought a sense of urgency to his vigil. He watched the boldness of the graceful young female and her striking resemblance to his father triggered an old memory of Patriarch.

When Soulmate limped into the woods, head down, Survivor was waiting for her.

They stared at each other for several seconds, a silent question asked, then answered. They touched noses tentatively, then he nuzzled and nibbled at her face. To the extent that wolves are capable of such feelings, Survivor felt affection for Soulmate and he licked her bleeding shoulder and caressed her gently with his nose, memorizing the scent of his new mate.

Quiet minutes passed and after the intimacy of first touch they turned and trudged deeper into the trees, Fewer scentposts marked their course and with each passing mile Soulmate's pack fell farther behind. Survivor broke trail ahead of his new mate where snow was soft, and their progress was slow. Soulmate's wound was deep and each step brought her agony.

When they collapsed under the heavy branches of a large fir Survivor and Soulmate were totally exhausted and sleep overtook them, lying together sharing body warmth in the snow.

Hours later, Survivor aroused Soulmate, who even in her pain, responded to his sexual need with a desire of her own. They smelled one another, one wolf intoxicated by the scent of the other, and they licked and nuzzled, whining as their lust intensified. Survivor rested a front paw across her back and she responded by turning her tail to him, receptive, eager to be joined.

Then Survivor mounted Soulmate and in a few thrusts they were locked together. In only minutes, the act was completed but the tie would not release them. They stood tail to tail and stars marked an hour's passage across the sky before the mating knot relaxed. Vulnerable and exposed, Survivor and Soulmate laid the foundation for one more generation.

After their passion was spent, Survivor licked Soulmate's shoulder and the enzymes unique to the saliva of canines cleaned and healed. They rested together, black fur against white, and while Soulmate slept, Survivor's blue eyes kept vigil.

Chapter Sixty

Matt watched Alex type and the GPS map with its blue and red lines came to life on the tiny screen. He was supremely uncomfortable with computers in his wilderness, but he did like Alex in his wilderness, and since she came with a computer, he resigned himself to the high-tech intrusion.

He grinned. There was information the computer couldn't tell her, and he had it. Behind him Softouch babied the friendly fire in Alex's cast-iron woodstove.

"Well, he seems to have staked out a territory for himself. He's been traveling the same sixty square miles for a few weeks, away from the other pack, and moving regularly," her voice was becoming familiar music to him, "this is good."

"Really? You can tell all that from those lines?"

I'm going to enjoy this, he thought. He caught Softouch' eye and the black man smiled. He was in on the game.

"Uh-huh. Pretty handy tools, these laptops, don't you think?"

"Maybe so, but I still believe there's no alternative for onsite observation. Radio collars just don't give you the whole picture, and that collar we put on your friend there is obsolete compared to the new ones. They provide much more information."

"Like what?"

"Well, some of the new ones can transmit pulse rate and body temperature, and tell by the angle of his neck if he's eating or sleeping, and tranquilize him with a coded firing sequence from a radio tuned to the right frequency."

"You're kidding!" She looked at him, not convinced he wasn't making it up. It wouldn't be the first time he and Softouch had amused themselves at her expense.

"Not kidding. But they're REAL expensive, and your boy there was kind of a low-budget operation."

"It would be great to have that information, though. The

ability to know that much about an animal without being invasive."

He smiled, "but even those collars wouldn't tell you he has a mate."

Her eyes were fixed on the monitor, and she almost missed what he said. Her head jerked up. "What did you say?"

"Your wolf has a girlfriend."

Softouch edged past them into her dainty kitchen that was further dwarfed by his bulk. He filled their coffee mugs, raised his in a feigned toast, and chuckled. He already knew.

"How do you know that?"

Matt grinned like a proud father. "One of our pilots spotted her while he was checking your buddy's signal. She's black as night, he actually saw her first."

Softouch chuckled, "Tom said she even turned at the sound of the plane and jumped at it. A real bitch." He grinned, "...my kind of lady."

Matt and Softouch plopped into the overstuffed chairs and Alex heard Matt's voice over her shoulder. It was serious, ominous. "There's more news."

She glanced at him, concern at full alert. Either her wolf was in trouble, or Matt was leaving again. "What?"

"You remember the project to reintroduce wolves to Yellowstone?"

She nodded.

"Well, the appeals and injunctions have finally been resolved. The first wolves will be transported to the park next month, for a soft release by February." She stared at him. "We won, Alex."

"That's great! We should celebrate!"

"Now you're talking, pretty lady." Softouch's voice boomed from his chair.

"...and your wolf will be the first."

"What?"

"... or should I say, the first and second?"

"They'll be moved to Yellowstone? Both of them?"

Matt nodded.

Alex took a deep breath and glanced out the window to the meadow behind the cabin, and memories, rich in experience and purchased with the hard currency of time, flooded back. Images of her first night and the days that followed—frostbite and terror. And fear of the wolves. Her learning had come full circle and somehow it was appropriate the white wolf—her wolf—should be one of the first wolves reintroduced to Yellowstone National Park.

"How will it happen? And what can I do? Can I be a part of it?" Her eagerness escalated with each syllable.

"Whoa, one question at a time!" Matt would never tell her how hard he lobbied to get the white wolf chosen for the reintroduction plan, and her added as a team member, but the smile on her face was worth it.

"Well, if we can drag ol' Softouch away from his exciting establishment for a couple days, he'll fly us to the wolves, we'll dart them from a helicopter, transfer to a plane, and fly them to Yellowstone."

"Makes it sound real neat and easy, doesn't he?" Softouch shook his head. "Listen to me, Doc, I'll tell you how it'll really go. We'll spend a couple weeks waiting for good weather, then we'll take off, chase our victims into the most remote hunk of real estate God glued to this rock. I'll fight updrafts, air pockets, and all manner of aeronautical nastiness, while your boyfriend there plays John Wayne and tries to shoot them in the butt with a needleful of dope." He had her undivided attention.

"And you, pretty lady, will get all the airborne excitement you could ever want."

"I don't need any more airborne excitement, thank you very much." She looked at Matt, "Won't it stress the wolves, chasing them down like that?"

"Yes, that's why we have to move fast. But I think they're good candidates. There was some concern that the male might be socialized to humans, but I think his experience with you might work to their advantage to reduce their stress. Maybe the female will relax, if she see's he's not so frightened."

He shrugged, "who knows..." His smile faded, his tone sobered. "But, Alex, you should know, it could go as bad as you can imagine."

The buoyancy of the moment vanished, stress on a wild animal in winter can kill.

"And there's more. You have to agree to some terms if you are going to be a part of this."

"What terms?"

"You taught that wolf that humans can be trusted. Now, he has to unlearn that lesson. Every second of interaction between those wolves and humans from the moment of capture must be unpleasant for them. They must learn that humans are creatures to be avoided. It's imperative."

Alex' eyes fell, she knew what he was asking her to do. Act as if she and the wolf had no history, no past. No friendship. Both men watched her face.

"We won't be cruel, Alex, but we will be professional and dispassionate. We will stab them for blood samples and tranquilizers, they'll spend time in dark, tight cages, and hopefully by the time they are released, homo sapiens will be the last things they want to see. It's for their own good. If they're going to survive in Yellowstone they have to avoid human contact." He watched her face, "You do see that, don't you?"

"Yes, of course," she nodded, subdued, "I understand." Softouch and Matt waited while she considered the terms. If she didn't agree, she would not be included.

"Can we count on you?"

She nodded, "Yes, of course."

Chapter Sixty-one

The blades of the helicopter were already rotating lazily, engine idling, when Alex parked and locked her Jeep. She noticed the cargo carriers—wolf carriers for this trip—and a gangly antenna attached to the runners. Matt hugged her and tossed her bags into the back seat. His eyes glowed with excitement.

"Ready for some fun?" This was the field biologist she had come to love and today he was in his element. Alex glanced at the noisy machine. Her words didn't quite match her voice.

"Oh yes, I'm ready."

Alex didn't notice the doors had been removed from the helicopter until it lifted off the ground, and the queasy feeling in her stomach was further aggravated by their absence. She was in the back seat monitoring the radio receiver, and quickly reached forward and tapped Softouch on the shoulder. His voice boomed in her headset.

"What is it, Doc?"

"Didn't we forget the doors?" Both men grinned.

"No, ma'am, we didn't forget the doors," Softouch chuckled, "tho't you'd appreciate the unbroken view."

"I'd appreciate the doors, actually." Her voice was weak, and she focused on the horizon line, long and unbroken through the hole where the door should be, as the churning machine accelerated its climb. Her nausea increased proportionally.

God, I hate this.

"John Wayne over here will need all the room I can give him to get a good shot at the wolves when we find them," the black man's shoulders shook with laughter, "so no doors."

I will think of some way to get even with you two...

"Be sure that seatbelt is real secure, pretty lady."

Very funny...

Softouch banked gently and turned away from town, and forty minutes later they entered the sky over the wolves' territory. Matt scanned the ground through binoculars and Alex's ears strained to hear the beep of the white wolf's radio collar. The plan was basically the simple one Matt had outlined at her cabin, but one look at the terrain below told her that Softouch probably had a better grasp of this reality.

In every direction her eyes embraced a panorama of jagged granite outcroppings and gigantic evergreens, and every spot of ground was either falling away from one peak, or rising toward the next.

Where will he land when we find the wolves? Alex's apprehension grew.

"Are you sure this is where they were last?" The humor had vanished from Softouch's voice.

"Yes, but I'm still not getting any signal."

Matt spoke up, "These outcroppings will mask the signal 'til we're right on top of them."

"Oh, perfect," Softouch muttered, "a lovely spot for an emergency landing..."

In fact, this was about the worst place to carry out their operation, the near vertical cliffs were either saber-sharp rocks or covered with dense vegetation. As the helicopter rose and fell mirroring the steep topology, all three minds focused on the challenge ahead. Matt realized all his skill would be required to get an accurate shot at the wolves. Softouch kept constant vigil for a place to land, and Alex, between waves of nausea, wondered how they would ever get the unconscious canines out of any of these ravines. They grew quiet and approached their assignment with a new level of seriousness.

Beep.

Alex's head jerked up.

Beep.

"I have him! The signal's faint, but growing stronger."

"Let me know as soon as we have a direction, doc, this is no place to waste fuel on sight-seeing."

The beeps came more frequently, and stronger as Alex guided Softouch closer to the wolves.

"They must be nearby, the signal's strong now."

Three pairs of eyes scanned the ground below for a glimpse of the canines, searching for the dark bitch, easier to spot in the snow. Matt wrapped the strap of the dart rifle around his forearm, and pointed the barrel out the gaping hole, prepared to fire. In this environment, he would not get a second chance.

Then their plan disintegrated.

Clearing a stand of trees they saw the two wolves less than fifty yards ahead and below, sleeping near the remains of a white-tailed deer. There was no time for Softouch to put distance between them before the pulsing rumble of the helicopter engines brought the wolves instantly to their feet.

Total surprise, total fright.

Matt had no chance to get either of them in his sights. Alex and Matt groaned and the expletive Softouch uttered was drowned out as he throttled up, backing away, in pursuit of the racing wolves.

The helicopter's deafening roar slammed against Survivor's eardrums, sending sound waves deep into his brain. That sound recalled another roaring flying monster, a fuzzy memory of wolf death, and Survivor's fright-flight response kicked in with the next heartbeat. Bones and muscles demanded speed, and adrenaline pumped into canine blood to deliver lightning fast reactions.

The calculating minds that could conceive an ambush for a moose were surprised by this new terror, and they sprang away from their kill without direction. Anywhere to get away from the threatening beast.

Memory cleared, sound was identified, and Survivor's anxiety was greater for it. The forgotten rage—wolf blood on ice, blasting explosions, Patriarch and Gentle still, dead, skinned—fueled Survivor's escape so that although Soulmate ran full out, she couldn't keep up. They jumped and dodged obstacles but their customary fluid grace vanished in the unpredictable flight of panic. They tripped, stumbled, fell, and raced on. Panting,

Survivor turned downhill, and in so doing sealed their fate. But he did not follow the fall line, he swerved and weaved in an effort to lose the sinister demon above them, and his canine brain challenged the pilot, as one predator pursued the other.

Using all his skill, Softouch gently directed the helicopter up and down, increasing his speed, then throttling back in an all out effort not to lose the wolves in the trees. And not crash into the trees. His mind also recalled chases of the past, and haunting memories of another time—a war in a distant jungle, gunfire and napalm, and men in green bleeding in flooded rice paddies. He did not appreciate the recollections, but he was impressed by the cunning wolf who triggered them.

Alex's heart sank. Her worst nightmare had become reality and she held her breath. All the grand sentiments that had surrounded this operation were buried under her agony for the stress they were causing the wolves.

As the vet of record she could cancel the operation if she thought the wolves were in danger, and was seriously considering doing so, when Softouch chuckled. She raised her eyes. In the distance, below them, was a dry creek bed, flat and open, and in his stampeding panic the white wolf was leading his mate directly to it. The chase had only taken a few minutes but they had dropped over twelve hundred feet in altitude to the bottom of a mountainous ravine. Alex began to breathe again.

Matt set his sights on the area in preparation for the moment the canines broke out of the trees. The male would be in front and he wanted his first shot to be dead on. He didn't want to increase Alex's anxiety over the wolves by requiring multiple shots to bring them down. The female's black coat would be harder to see through the dense brush surrounding the river bed, a clean shot at the male would leave him more time to set up for her.

Softouch changed his strategy, subtly leading them to the creek bed by making that direction appear less threatening. As the trees gave way to bushes and low shrubs, they began to see glimpses of white fur more frequently.

Matt surveyed the bank of bushes that gave way to the snow-covered riverbed in an effort to predict where the wolf would emerge. He pointed to a spot and Softouch nodded almost simultaneously. They had done this before. Matt swept the rifle back and forth over the area, waiting... waiting...

The white wolf burst from the underbrush exactly where Matt expected to see him. Softouch banked the helicopter to provide him a clean shot and the canine completed four strides before quietly dropping in the snow less than twenty-five feet from the trees.

Chapter Sixty-two

Alex watched the white wolf's chest rise and fall while the helicopter hovered overhead. Although she desperately wanted to check him, her attention shifted to his dark mate.

Minutes passed without a sign of the black bitch and the vet grew increasingly alarmed. "Where is she? I thought she was right behind him."

"So did I." Matt never took his eyes off the bushes near the clearing.

Softouch spoke up. "The last time I saw her was before we dropped over that last crag, but I was concentrating on her boyfriend." Three sets of eyes stared at the snow-covered landscape, but there was no trace of the bitch.

Softouch caressed the controls, the helicopter rose, and they began to search in ever-widening circles, squinting to see dark fur among the trees.

Alex clenched and unclenched her fists, and looked at her watch. Even if the female's fear drove her away immediately, current wisdom said she would not run far from her mate. But there was no movement of any kind along the creekbed or among the young trees at the forest's edge. The black wolf had vanished.

"Where the hell is she?" Softouch muttered, stymied.

"I don't know, but we need to find her before he wakes up." Matt continued to point the rifle into the freezing air.

Alex tapped Softouch on the shoulder, "I think we better land and track her on foot."

"The snow's pretty deep. I'm not sure it's a good idea."

"That's why we brought the snowshoes."

They all knew that the clock had started on this operation with the shot that dropped Survivor. It was imperative they find his mate soon.

"What if she's injured?"

"Well, now, there's a thought that just multiplies my

enthusiasm for tracking that lovely black bitch..." Softouch and Matt exchanged looks, and the pilot nosed the helicopter back to the clearing.

By the time he and Matt had collected their gear and strapped on snowshoes Alex was kneeling in the snow next to the wolf. Even though he was unconscious, she talked softly, hoping her voice would resonate familiar in his drugged stupor.

"Hello, my friend. How are you doing?"

Alex had admitted to no one that this was her most anxious moment.

"You're looking healthy. Feeding regularly, I can see..."

Since the wolf's recuperation in her barn and his Christmas eve visit to her campfire Alex had started to question her memories.

What exactly happened with this wolf? I know I transferred affection from my dogs to him, but beyond that...

"...your girlfriend's giving us quite a chase, you know."

During rational moments—unemotional moments—Alex doubted that they had been anything more than injured animal and attending vet. Her anger towards Stephen had found release in the wolf, and her inability to understand how, frustrated her.

She whispered and watched the wolf's chest expand and contract for several seconds. Then, with the first touch of fingers to fur Alex sighed. Her memories had not lied. What had happened between them had occurred in the realm of reality, not her imagination. The realization brought her overwhelming peace of mind.

She examined him as she would any animal patient and Matt and Softouch watching over her shoulder noticed nothing to suggest her anxiety. Alex separated fur to see the rippled scar tissue of his burns.

"Look how the fur completely covers his scars—incredible healing capacity."

"And he is one big boy!" Softouch whispered in awe. "He's huge! His feet are as big as my chili bowls! I didn't remember he was this big in your barn, Doc."

"He wasn't," she whispered softly. It was obvious the wolf belonged to the wild, it had taken good care of him.

While the healer in her touched and turned the wolf with clinical detachment, the heart of the woman felt the connection once removed, restored. She hoped there would still be a remnant of that bond lurking somewhere in the wolf's mind. The hours ahead would be easier if he remembered she was not a cause for fear.

She administered a long-term tranquilizer and they wrapped him in blankets and secured him in the cargo carrier over the left runner of the helicopter.

Matt checked his watch. "We don't have much daylight left so we better spread out." Alex and Softouch nodded.

"Keep those radios on, my friends." Softouch was the consummate mother.

The muffled stillness of dense evergreens engulfed Alex within only a few yards of the clearing. Winter sunlight battled its way to the ground in narrow knife rays stabbing through ancient trees. White silence blanketed scent and sound.

She scuffed along slowly, with little noise and less grace. In truth, slow was the fastest she could move up the steep incline in snowshoes. The silence was eerie and she shivered from it as much as the cold. It piqued her senses until they almost screamed out for any movement or sound. The voices and static from her radio squawked a harsh intrusion from another world, and she paused frequently to listen. But not even the progress of the two men she knew to be on the same hillside was audible. Their disjointed voices from her radio reflected the same edgy apprehension she felt.

Alex was about two hundred yards above the helicopter when she rounded a huge granite boulder as big as a house, tripped on a branch under the snow, and fell face first down a steep chute, sliding on her stomach.

She grabbed frantically at the branches and boulders flying past, missed, and snowplowed out of control down the curving slot like a human toboggan. Snow piled up in front of her, packing inside her parka, filling her mouth and blinding her vision. Calling for help was not an option, even breathing was difficult. Face scratched, hands torn and bleeding, she finally stopped, and sighed with relief, grateful to be alive.

Then she heard the growl and raised her head.

Three feet from the black wolf.

"Oh my God!" she gasped.

The wolf snarled and lunged. Jaws snapped shut, inches from her face.

Alex dodged her fangs again and noticed the wolf's right front leg was wedged under a large rock, buried in the same gravel and snow muck that was jammed in her parka. The bitch was stuck tight, but struggling with all her strength to get free. With each jerk her leg loosened slightly, then settled back into the gravel.

How close is she to getting free?

Rising to her knees, Alex was eye level with the wolf, and golden eyes glared at her with deadly venom. When she tried to stand a deep growl thundered from the bitch and paralyzed her in position.

On her knees.

She tried to shuffle backwards and raise her tranquilizing gun in one smooth movement, but failed. The gun caught a broken strap of her snowshoe and twisted out of her hand, vanishing beneath the snow.

"Oh no!" she whispered and snarling intensified. Alex's breath quickened. Panting like an animal. Still on her knees.

In her mind she was screaming, but only the wolf's growling broke the silence.

All action stoked the canine's ferocity and she snarled louder, fangs bared and ears flat against her head.

Struggling harder to get free.

When Alex tried again to lift the radio to her mouth, the wolf stretched her neck, snapping her jaws at Alex's throat. She could feel the wolf's hot breath on her cheeks when she lunged, and see the shine on two-inch long canine teeth.

Any human movement fueled the wolf's wrath.

Alex's blood froze like the snow she was kneeling in.

If she works herself free and attacks, I'll be dead in seconds.

Blood roared in Alex's ears. The reasoning cortex of her brain was overpowered by the ancient amygdala; instinct ruled response and her pulse raced with animal-like fright.

This was the wolf of her nightmares.

In the time traveled between two heartbeats Alex tasted her own visceral fear with the same accuracy the wolf smelled it. Trapped, in pain, the shewolf responded to that fear-scent with killing intensity, and each snapping of her jaws rang like a gunshot.

Right in front of Alex's face.

Alex's stomach cramped, her palms started to sweat, and the blood drained from her limbs. No longer the predator, she had become the prey.

Seconds crawled by. Eye to eye with the wolf.

The terror that supersedes all others froze Alex on her knees. A terror immediate, unexpected, and life-threatening. The fear of being eaten. Of becoming the flesh that nourishes another's flesh. It climbed out of her primal soul like some long forgotten piece of the evolutionary maze, refusing to respond to logic, or rational thought.

While her brain recognized her role in the dance of predator and prey, her instinct was caught up in it.

The wolf that had haunted her first nights' dreams now threatened her from inches. Alex watched her eyes focus and dilate, ears twitch, hackle hair rise, saliva moisten gums and teeth.

With the radio still at her side Alex keyed the mike button with the distress signal she had learned as a child.

Click, click, click,

Click.... click.... click....

Click, click, click,

Click.... click.... click....

Help me, her thoughts screamed inside her head.

Chapter Sixty-three

"Did you hear that?" Matt wasn't sure if he'd heard the SOS, and he didn't know who was sending it.

"Yes sir, I did, our pretty doc is in trouble."

"Where is she, can you see her?"

"No, but she must be somewhere between us if she took the hill straight up."

"Right. I'll work my way toward you, you come this way, one of us should pick up her trail." Matt paused, "What could've happened that she can't even talk?"

"Don't know, but the safety's off this man's weapon, my friend."

Heartbeats measured time for the wolf's human prey. Alex's escalating fear excited the bitch; if she could taste it, surely the wolf could smell it. With each passing minute panic multiplied, a seismic event beyond her control, driven by uncertainty... that the men even heard her signal... that the wolf might break loose... and what she would do if she got free. The canine's snapping, snarling response grew in proportion to Alex's fear and she fought an internal war to gain control.

Human mind battled human instinct and neither had the advantage.

I have to calm down! Come on, Alex, think!

She forced her mind to discipline, searching for anything that might reduce the wolf's fury.

While the wolf snapped and lunged, and she flinched and dodged, Alex recalled the structure of the pack, the hierarchy of dominance and submission.

I don't know if I can do this...

She took one slow deep breath, then another, trembling from the effort. After four deep breaths she could relax her shoulders, after five more she bowed her head.

Last and most difficult, Alex looked away from the

predator, dropping her gaze to the ground. It took every molecule of her courage. If the wolf worked herself free, Alex would not see the attack coming.

Her only defense was no defense, her only weapon, submission.

She concentrated on the patch of snow in front of her. The watermark climbing up her pant legs. The snow melting inside her shirt. The sooty color of gray gravel and white snow. Anything to avoid eye contact with the wolf.

Blood roared in her ears, and she counted her heartbeats.

After a couple hundred, the snarling diminished to a growl and the snapping fangs quieted. Although the shewolf's ears were still back, hackles still raised, her growl was softer. And she stopped struggling to free her leg.

Alex did not see the bitch shift her focus, but she heard it.

Growling stopped as canine senses detected Matt and Softouch long before human senses noticed anything, and the wolf's attention immediately shifted away from Alex. Fiery eyes stared into the trees, nostrils twitched, ears moved, redirected on this new threat.

Then she started to jerk on her leg again.

Softouch had made better progress than Matt and his was the first sound the canine heard. With her eyes searching the woods in the direction of the large black man, neither woman nor wolf saw Matt rise behind Alex and fire. The bitch collapsed like a large stuffed toy.

The three humans exchanged looks, but the only sound was their labored breathing, two from exertion, one from fear.

"Are you alright?" Matt's eyes reflected what she must look like. She could only nod while blood returned to her arms and legs.

"Thanks," she finally whispered, and Matt and Softouch nodded while they all gazed at the sleeping animal. Both men had experienced the fear they saw in Alex's eyes. It required no comment.

She took several deep breaths before reaching towards the wolf, now heaped peacefully at her knees. With each breath she forced her terror back to the dark corner from which it had escaped. An acute awareness of her own mortality overwhelmed Alex, but it slowly faded into a renewed respect for the predator. She felt no animosity, but understood more fully how they had managed to survive so long.

"I'm not sure how badly she's hurt but we have to dig her out from under that boulder."

"She must've really been hauling to fall and get wedged in so hard." Softouch shook his head and knelt to help Matt dig the snow and gravel away from the wolf's leg.

"You two push on that boulder and I'll pull her out." Alex hesitated only a second before she touched the flesh of the animal that minutes earlier wanted to kill her.

Matt and Softouch heaved on the boulder and Alex slid the black wolf out from under it. Then she examined her as closely as she had her mate. Fingers roved through black fur and gingerly, pulled her lips back to check teeth and gums—teeth and gums she had become intimately familiar with.

"Looks like her shoulder is dislocated, but other than that, she's okay." Alex panted, breathing calmly was still not possible.

"You guys will have to help me here. Hold her body very snug and still so I can get a good grip on this leg." Matt and Softouch immobilized the wolf, holding her against their own bodies as if she were a large child. Unconscious, she was like a bag of gelatin, head and legs flopping in all directions. Alex wrapped both hands around the dislocated leg near her shoulder and rotated it slowly, manipulating the strong bone back into its socket. After only a few seconds the joint slid home with a pop.

"There. Now let's get her to the helicopter." Matt unceremoniously tossed her over his shoulder in a fireman's carry and they started down the hill.

Little time had transpired since they had strapped the white male into the cargo carrier, but Alex felt as if centuries had been added to her age. With the cougar she had glimpsed the depths of her fear, now she had plunged to the bottom of that pit, and she was humbled by the knowledge she'd gained. Vulnerability had beaten dents in her courage, and shaken her confidence. Under several layers of clothing she shivered, naked before her fear.

No conversation broke the shushing of snowshoes as they trudged down to the helicopter with the sleeping wolf.

Chapter Sixty-two

An hour later they touched down at the secluded mountain airstrip where Alex and Softouch had helped fight the forest fires. It was starkly deserted and quiet, and lilac remnants of sunset tinted the buildings. Softouch gingerly settled the helicopter next to his twin-engine plane and headed for the kitchen with a large bag. Matt and Alex locked the sleeping wolves into individual cages then pushed the cages into the small hanger next to the bunkhouse.

"Something smells promising in here!" Matt declared when he walked in. His stomach cramped and he was abruptly reminded that their day had not included lunch.

"Well, I figured if I was going to eat this side of the 49th parallel, I'd have to cook it myself." Softouch nodded at Alex, the gender dig obvious.

"Isn't women's lib wonderful?!" She returned fire easily now. "So, what gourmet delight are we feasting on tonight?"

"Elk steaks, mashed potatoes and gravy. Beer and wine."

"What? No dessert?" Matt chuckled. The banter continued, warmed by beer and wine and a successful day.

They ate their dinner in front of the huge stone fireplace, and conversation returned to the wolves. Alex finally voiced the question they had all been thinking.

"Would she have attacked me if she'd worked herself loose? She convinced me she would."

Matt considered his answer while he swallowed. "I don't know. She was cornered and hurt. If she perceived you as responsible for her pain, she might've. But I think she would've just run."

The warm blaze died and wine-warmed talk quietly turned to past adventures.

"So, Doc, was this worse than the cougar?" Alex shot Softouch a sharp look. She had confided the cougar story in him, but not to Matt. She hadn't wanted a lecture then, but she expected one now.

"What cougar?" Matt demanded.

She grinned and started, "Well, I was tracking this fisher...", and was relieved to have a story to fill the space where her response to Softouch's question should've been.

Because this fear was worse. Much worse. And she didn't want to admit it.

Alex awoke with a start hours later. Panting. Heart racing. Not even Matt's deep sleep next to her could keep her mind from the day's events. And the "what-if" thoughts.

Matt didn't sound real sure she wouldn't attack me... Those jaws snapped so fast... Right at my face... I couldn't have moved to protect myself...

She tried taking deep breaths, to no effect. Finally she got up and went to the kitchen for a glass of water.

Beyond the window a smiling half moon teetered on the top of a solitary pine tree and cast a bright pathway of light across the landing strip, straight to Alex.

This fear was different than that first night with the wolves, but how?

While she watched, a large shape drifted just outside the moonlit corridor, then stopped, then moved again. Although she studied it, Alex could not identify it. After several minutes a moose stepped from the shadows onto lighted grass, easing, one step at a time, closer to the runway. Clearly visible, the large bull appeared huge even from her vantage point.

If I was out there now would I be afraid of him? She smiled. *Oh, yes.* Then she chuckled quietly to herself, *I get it. The first night I was afraid of what I could not see, and did not know. Today I was afraid of what I could see, and have learned to respect.*

She smiled and returned to bed.

It seemed like only minutes had passed when she and Matt were brought to instant consciousness by howling that quite probably could be heard for miles. She grabbed her bag and they met Softouch already bolting down the stairs.

When they turned on the hanger lights they were met by mournful blue eyes as the white wolf, now quite conscious, lustily voiced his displeasure at his circumstances. In the cage next to him his mate slept soundly, a feat which amazed the humans who found the earsplitting din verging on the painful. While Alex prepared a sedative she spoke to him calmly, but the men were convinced he couldn't possibly hear her above the cacophony echoing off the walls of the empty hanger.

"Hush now. There's no call for that. You're alright, nothing's going to hurt you. Quiet now. Shhh..."

When the injection was ready Alex walked slowly across floor. The men started to follow her but, without interrupting her speech, she shook her head and they stopped.

The powerful wolf continued to howl as Alex steadily approached him, her soothing voice reaching out to whatever memory of her still existed in his mind. Slowly his howling quieted, until finally Alex's soft voice was all that could be heard in the deserted hanger.

"That's it, quiet down, now. You're alright. There's nothing to fear here. Shhh..."

He stared at the woman through the four-inch opening in his cage until she stood next to it. Then she knelt, eye level, and placing the syringe out of his sight behind her, Alex began what could only be called a conversation with her canine friend. Two sets of blue eyes met and held fast.

"So, my friend, how have you been since Christmas? I see you've found yourself a girlfriend. Nice looking, but a real nasty attitude..." Alex spoke to him as if she were talking to another person and expected a spoken reply.

Survivor responded by cocking his head to one side and stretching his neck to sniff the air between them. Nostrils trembled to identify the colors of her scent. Ears twitched to catch the subtle nuances of her voice, and heard those sounds humans vocalize but cannot hear themselves, high frequency utterances, easily discerned by canines, that occur beyond the scope of human perception. He perceived those parts of speech that cannot lie, and in the timbre and cadence of Alex's words Survivor discerned sincerity and recognized the familiar.

Then a soft cooing sound, like the lullaby a bitch sings to her cubs, escaped Survivor's strong jaws, and he pressed his long muzzle through the cage opening to touch the woman he remembered. While the men held their breath Alex raised her hand to the white nose, palm up, allowing him to smell once again the scent he knew as kindness. As gently as a hummingbird draws nectar from a flower, Survivor's tongue licked Alex's hand through the opening, rekindling the friendship his canine brain had not forgotten.

They continued to converse, woman and wolf, for several minutes. He responded to her questions with small whining noises and an occasional slap of his tail against the floor of his cage. Their verbal intercourse was the pleasant exchange between two friends—two friends who just happen to be different species. The realm of their relationship was not defined by space or time, or constrained by gene or instinct.

The noise and excitement finally aroused Soulmate from her sleep, and by the time Survivor quieted, she was awake and silently watching the interaction between Alex and her mate. Her manner bore none of Survivor's open friendliness. Golden eyes glared at the woman.

When Alex reluctantly returned to the men waiting by the door she saw the anger in Matt's eyes and for a second she didn't understand it. Then she remembered. She'd gotten too close. Too friendly.

"Alex, you agreed not to get close to him! He's habituated to you, and it could get him killed in Yellowstone!" Matt's voice shook with anger as they packed their things to leave.

"Well, I'm sorry, I made a mistake! I got caught up in the moment..." she felt his eyes following her. "I'm sure YOU'VE never made a mistake, right, Matt?"

"Not where animals are concerned."

"Oh yes, you only screw up with people!" She paused, glaring at him. "Matt, try not to forget who and what I am. I am not a nose-counting biologist, I'm a veterinarian! A healer! Something I lost track of for a while. I touch my patients! And no demand you make—or promise I agree to—will ever change that."

He reached for her, drawing her into a hug and spoke quietly, intensely. "Alex, if he comes around people at Yellowstone, they'll have to kill him. I'll have to kill him."

"Tell me, you and Softouch have been around him, has he ever shown either of you the same affection he's shown me? Did he show Pierre and his pals the same friendship he's shown me?" Matt shook his head. "Then why do you believe he'll be chummy to total strangers?" They stacked their bags near the door where Softouch was waiting for them.

She paused for a reply, none was forthcoming.

"I attribute to this animal more of an ability to discern the beings that share his world as friend or foe, than you do. We don't know everything that's happened in his life, but he is not my pet. He's as wild today, as the day I dragged his burned body to my cabin," she rubbed Matt's arm reassuringly, "and you know it."

"Matt, my life was changed by the time I spent with him, undoubtedly his was too. But that doesn't mean he'll be chowing down around every Coleman stove in Grants Village."

Softouch chuckled at the image.

"Calm down and trust his nature. He's as much a survivor as I am," her smile was edged with strength, "and you know how tough I am."

Softouch's flight plan called for a non-stop trip to Montana. If all went as planned the wolves would be in their enclosures by the next night. Alex gazed at the predawn glow in the east and sighed.

I hope the surprises are over, this trip is proving to be

emotionally draining.

Matt had just finished securing the cages inside the plane and strapped into his seat when Softouch began his roll down the deserted airstrip. In less than twelve hours Yellowstone National Park would have its newest residents. Landing gear cleared the earth and five souls became airborne.

Chapter Sixty-five

Six thousand centuries ago, as earth's surface crust cooled, it cracked and huge plates of rock floating on a molten sea of magma stretched and shifted, seeking form and shape. Two of these plates collided and the resulting violent impact lifted a rising wall of cooling granite. It grew, spreading North and South until it divided the continent, the largest mountain range in North America.

During the earth's turbulent adolescence three massive volcanic eruptions near the center of those mountains blasted and oozed millions of tons of lava and mud. Lava flowed for centuries, raising then leveling the surrounding terrain, redefining the topology again and again.

Today the caldera formed by those three volcanos, an oval basin nearly twenty-seven miles wide and forty-five miles long, shelters over 10,000 geothermal wonders that occur no where else on the planet.

Subterranean turbulence continues to test the earth's fragile skin. Water, simmered for eons at the planet's core, explodes from geysers, or bubbles gently across the threshold between this world and the one in which it was born. Deadly gas, squeezed into fumaroles, blasts unpredictably skyward, or perks lazily up through surreal pots of glistening mud. And the smell of sulphur permeates it all, earth's amniotic scent.

The hissing and gurgling of geysers and fumaroles bears striking contrast to the stillness of the pools that incubate their subterranean life forms. Algae, rising from the bowels of the earth, thrive in their vivid blue-green or copper-brown depths. And in these mineral-rich hot springs life evolves still.

Cooling surface waters gently etch intricate scallops of white calcium carbonate and grow dramatic travertine terraces, shifting steps and ledges of green limestone.

The caldera that cradles these geological marvels wraps them in towering granite peaks, evergreen forests, and lush meadows. Great rivers, free and uncontrolled, meander lazily then plunge hundreds of feet, spectacular waterfalls roaring through canyons millenniums in the carving. And the animal life that shares this eden is as rich and diverse as its geology.

As if nature wished to leave behind a record of her planetbirth, she chose this solitary place to vouchsafe all her best works, leaving behind active clues, remnants of her labor pains.

On this clear winter day Yellowstone National Park, sacred birthright of the American people, anticipated the arrival of her newest residents.

"I really think the 18-wheeler is overkill, don't you?" Alex was tired and annoyed. And it showed.

"There will be other wolves brought in from Canada, and the livestock rig is just extra protection." Softouch drove the pickup truck that followed the huge steel trailer, empty except for the two crated wolves.

"Protection from what?"

"Who, not what. There are a lot of people around here that are about as excited to have wolves in the park as Pierre was with one in your barn."

Softouch frowned, "You mean after all the years of work there are still folks against this?"

"There were mistakes made on this project. They," Matt paused, "or I should say we, didn't show enough concern for the local residents in the beginning. A lot of bad blood has festered, and it will take years to heal."

Silence filled the cab as the small convoy wound through the Absarokas. Snow-covered pines and scrub foliage bore mute witness to the strong grip of winter.

"Do you think someone will try to kill them?" Alex's voice was small, and the question was squeezed out like one she did not want to ask, but couldn't bear not knowing.

Matt sighed, "If the local residents don't want wolves in Yellowstone, Alex, there will be no wolves in Yellowstone."

"Well, is there any support for them?" Softouch had

personally invested in this project, and he did not like to back losers.

"Only most of the population of the U.S. Even some of the locals are beginning to think this could be profitable. Outfitters, and tour leaders are already getting calls from folks who want to see the wolves in Yellowstone." Matt rubbed his eyes, sleep was a distant commodity and he was missing it. "And some of the ranchers are beginning to listen to real data that says wolves eat what they've been taught to eat."

Alex thought of the two wolves caged in the rolling fortress in front of them. "Do they ever attack livestock?"

"Rarely, but often enough to be a concern, and that's the problem. A rancher is not excited about getting a check for the value of a newborn calf that might have brought in five times as much, fullgrown." He shook his head. "We can only hope our friends will stay in the park, and stick to their diet of elk and deer, and maybe a bison or two."

The arrival of the wolves was public knowledge—so was their route—and the tension in the pickup thickened. Three minds mulled over the threat.

Softouch recalled the wolves' challenge the previous day. As hard to track as any Viet Cong. They had tested his pilot skills to the limit, and he had not told Matt and Alex how close he came to calling off the chase for human safety. Few people had earned the respect he now harbored for the wolves, and he could not rid his brain of the itchy feeling they knew more—much more—than their staring gaze revealed.

Matt's memories had a longer leash, dredged up from years earlier and the first petitions to bring the wolf back to Yellowstone. He had been in college, gushing hope and naive optimism, collecting signatures, and writing politicians. His soul was scarred with the battles fought since then. Now the optimism visited briefly and infrequently, and he could not shake the uneasy feeling the war was not over.

☪☪☪

Alex thought of her canine friend and imagined rifle barrels behind every tree and boulder. There was no niche of her gray matter capable of understanding the killing of any wolf—these two or any other—and her stomach knotted.

Although the road to the north gate of Yellowstone is usually not heavily traveled in winter, the closer they got to the park the more cars they noticed. And when the great arch at Monument came into view, clusters of people lined the road.

Then they saw the signs. And the smiles.

"Will you look at this!" Matt grinned, and read the handpainted signs:

"WELCOME BACK, CANIS LUPIS!"

"GLAD YOU'RE HOME, WOLVES!"

Alex exhaled the breath she had been holding and chuckled with relief, "This is incredible! Did you expect this, Matt?"

"Nobody expected this."

Softouch heard the lump in his friend's throat and swallowed the one in his. "Seems they already have a few friends."

The convoy passed through the arch, and wolves returned to Yellowstone.

Chapter Sixty-six

The people thinned with each mile they rolled deeper into the Lamar Valley, and each hour of darkening skies and falling temperatures. Photos of the quarter-acre chain-link acclimation pens had been front page in all the local papers, photos received with mixed reviews. But their exact locations were a well-kept secret, so when the livestock truck finally eased to a stop there was no audience to witness it, except for two mules harnessed to a heavy wooden sled. They waited with stoic indifference, each breath blasting from their nostrils like dragon smoke.

Chris Mitchell jumped down and trotted to the rear of the big rig before Softouch had even stopped the pickup. He opened the door and climbed inside, enthusiasm bubbling just below the surface, and was met by two sets of canine eyes. Glaring. He crouched on his heels, eye-level with the slot in the cages. His voice softened.

"You are a fine-looking pair. What do you think Alex? Can they handle the rest of the trip tonight?"

Alex inspected the wolves through the metal cages. And the wolves studied her. If the white male recognized her, he did not indicate it. There were too many people around, and the surroundings were unfamiliar. She stared at him, but he could've been any wolf. Alex's heart sank. He was wild, and growing more distant with each hour in the cage.

"Absolutely. I want to get them out of these cages as soon as possible."

"Hope you brought cold weather gear. The pen's quite a ride from here." He glanced at the sled and mules. "A slow ride."

Twenty minutes later Streak and Blackie plodded away from the trucks, and the sled was swallowed up by the trees. The incongruous image was not lost on Alex. On another day the mules might have been prey for the wolves, now they were transportation.

At sunset Chris locked the gate in the twelve-foot high chainlink fence and all four humans watched. And waited.

But nothing happened.

Both wolves stayed in their cages, even though the doors were open.

"What is the problem, why don't they come out?" Even Softouch was showing signs of sleep-deprived impatience.

"They probably won't leave the cages until we're gone. I recommend we retire to someplace warm and I'll buy you all a beer."

"Now you're talking!" Softouch was right behind Mitchell, Matt and Alex lingered near the pen.

"Penny for your thoughts?" Matt felt a need to stay close to Alex. Had he been observing his own behavior with a biologist's objectivity, he would've chalked it up to protecting his territory. But his mind was on another issue and he had to talk to her alone.

Alex's voice was soft, eyes still focused on the cages. "Remember when we let him go the last time? After the fire?"

"Uh-huh."

"Seems like centuries ago." She willed the white canine out of the cage. "I liked that release alot better than this one."

"I know how you feel. The wolves are in Yellowstone, but they're still not free." She nodded.

"Alex, I have to tell you something."

Her heart cramped and she held her breath.

"I've been offered a position here. With the wolf project." Moonlight highlighted her eyes and illuminated the rosy flush in her cheeks.

"Full time?"

He nodded.

"I see." Her stomach knotted. This trip really was becoming an emotional cesspool. "Well, at least someone I know will be watching out for him."

Matt took her hand and words climbed slowly. "Alex, I

want you to stay here with me. You're a good tracker, and I think we'd make a good team." Seconds crawled by. Memories crawled by. Alex took a deep breath and exhaled slowly.

"I still have two months left on my study in Canada."

"The wolves'll be in this pen at least that long."

She looked at him, appraising, weighing. "I'd like to be here when they're released. Ask me again when they're free."

It wasn't the answer he wanted, but it wasn't the worst answer she could've given him, either. He put his arm around her shoulder and they trudged back to the sled.

Chapter Sixty-seven

Alex returned to Canada before the wolves even crawled out of their cages. She knew without being told that her scent would confuse the white male, so she took it back to Alberta and resumed her work. And counted the days. What had been a welcome challenge, was now a duty to complete. She considered Matt's offer daily—hourly, if truth were told.

If he asks me again, I'll stay with him. We'll work together and see...

Survivor and Soulmate, unable to comprehend confinement, vented their frustration on their prison. Hours of biting chainlink ripped and tore sensitive lips and gums, bloodying both wolves' faces. Captivity was beyond their understanding, and they alternated chewing the fence with pacing along it, creating a deep trench in the snow farthest from the gate. Farthest from where humans brought offerings of food. It became their comfort zone, untainted by man's step and man's scent.

Survivor showed no familiarity to any of the humans when they entered the pen, but while Soulmate crouched and pressed her body against the fence near their comfort zone, Survivor stood his ground, erect, unblinking, and stared at the humans. It unnerved every human that dragged elk and deer into the pen.

"I don't get it, I thought they'd bolt out that gate when we finally opened it. Why don't they leave?" Alex was baffled by the wolves' reluctance to escape their chainlink prison. For three days they had not even acknowledged that the gate was open.

Matt and Chris exchanged looks. They were as puzzled as she, and embarrassed by their confusion. Animal behavior was their expertise, and it was obvious Alex thought they should understand it.

Matt matched Alex's hushed whisper. "We don't get it either. At first we thought it was because they knew we were up here watching them. But when we left and monitored their radio collars remotely they still didn't move."

Chris lowered his binoculars. From their surveillance point peeking over a ridge half a mile from the enclosure he couldn't see the wolves without them. But nobody believed the wolves were unaware of their presence.

"Well, this is nuts, I'm going to make some calls." If the world's foremost wolf expert couldn't explain it, nobody could. Chris crawled away from the lookout above the Alder Creek enclosure and headed for their truck. Alex and Matt continued their surveillance.

"They don't look like they've enjoyed the park's hospitality very much. You'd think they'd be anxious to leave." The bloody faces bothered Alex. She knew it was their own blood.

"And they must be getting hungry. They haven't been fed for two weeks." Matt stared at Alex while she stared at the pen through binoculars.

An hour later Chris returned, crawled up to them and peeked over the rim. Nothing had changed.

"So what's the word?" Matt's frustration hung from his words.

"He says they might just starve themselves to death before walking through that gate. Captivity is outside anything they've experienced, so he thinks the concept of open or closed is beyond them."

Matt lowered his binocs. "So, what do we do?"

"He suggested cutting the fence near their comfort zone."

"That's where the female spends most of her time." Alex was alarmed.

"I bet she moves when we start cutting. Let's go Matt, I'm ready to see them out of that pen, and tonight is going to get real cold."

Alex watched the men through her binoculars as they cut one link after another in the sturdy fence. The black bitch huddled as far away from the men as she get, and still be in her comfort zone, but the white male drifted silently around the enclosure. Every time the men looked up he was in a different place. Watching them. Constantly.

"Do you get the feeling he has something he'd like to say?" Chris had noticed his dominant stance from the first day.

Matt chuckled, "Oh yeah, and I'm real glad we aren't going to hear it."

Temperatures plummeted and stars sparkled in the cloudless sky. The light of a full moon washed the pen in blue before it even cleared the eastern hills. In its light, the men returned to the lookout. And they all focused binocs on the pen. For ninety freezing minutes they watched.

Until the wolves settled themselves in depressions in the snow and went to sleep.

"The male's out of the pen!" Chris's shout woke Matt and Alex, who were dozing on two couches in the old cabin. Grabbing parkas, binocs and snowshoes they bolted for their pickup.

When they reached the lookout only the female's ebony form was visible in the moonlight, pacing near the crude opening in the fence.

Her mate was gone.

"Wonder where he went..." No sooner were Matt's words forming steam, when a howl prickled the hair on three humans.

"Shit! He's close! Which direction was that?" Chris had heard the wolves howl only twice in the pen, and never with the wild abandon of this song. It resonated freedom, ancient wildness, and ownership. And it called a mate.

Alex pivoted, searching the trees for a familiar shadow of white.

"At least he hasn't left her." Matt watched the black

wolf's pace grow more agitated with each canine verse. "Look, I think she's about to run." Alex and Chris turned just in time to see her dash out the opening in the fence, tail tucked under her, then stretch her stride for the trees, racing toward her mate.

Suddenly another howl, louder and closer than any before, shattered the night. From a rise to their left the white wolf stared at them for several seconds, then looked away. He appraised them insignificant. Then he raised his nose and howled again. If the first howl raised gooseflesh, this one walked on their graves.

Three humans watched two wolves greet each other with exuberance, licking and prancing and pawing. Then, with tails high, they bolted away, shoulder to shoulder, a white wolf racing with his own shadow.

Chapter Sixty-eight

After their release Survivor and Soulmate did not stop to sleep, but raced along trails filled with the scent of game. They stretched cramped muscles and covered mile after mile, sometimes running side by side across open meadows, or single file through heavy snow. The joy of freedom pumped through every tendon and ligament, and their flowing grace sang of sacred wildness. For seventy years Yellowstone snow had not been marked by canis lupis, but Survivor and Soulmate wasted no time calling it their own.

They quickly learned the obstacles and features of their new home, to avoid steaming fissures and limestone holes that sprayed hot water out of the ground, and to know which bodies of water were clean and cool, or smelled of sulfur. The genetic wariness that made them survivors kept them in the high country near their release point in the Lamar Valley, where elk and deer and mountain goat waited.

And they avoided areas scented by man.

They hunted with a familiar pattern that was as successful as it needed to be. Survivor marked his territory and the wildlife of Yellowstone became more alert. An old predator had returned.

The canines journeyed great distances in the early weeks, but always returned to the Lamar Valley after each excursion. Their bond grew stronger and the lives that shared Survivor's territory recognized him as alpha.

Matt and Alex scrambled to their observation spot as predawn gray washed the eastern sky. There was no conversation while tripods were erected, cameras checked, and notebooks retrieved—both paper and electronic. Matt handed her a granola bar, and when their eyes met, smiles communicated where words weren't needed. Two souls had discovered the right path and were content to share it. At sunrise the filming and recording began.

A raven perched inches from Survivor as he stretched out to rest on a favorite granite outcropping above the meandering Lamar River. From this spot he could see miles in both directions, and the milling bison below showed no awareness of his presence. He gave the bird no notice but glanced back to watch his mate scratch lazily behind her ear before plopping nearby with a great yawn.

Three balls of fur scrambled out of the den behind her, clamored to her belly, and soon sucking sounds were audible to the raven. He surveyed the scene briefly, then took wing, there would be no leftovers here. Soulmate settled herself to her motherly task.

Survivor's life had come full circle from that first innocent glimpse of the world beyond Cub-bearer's den. Sitting next to Patriarch as a cub, his youthful ignorance allowed him to believe that all he saw belonged to him. But in the years since that day, much had been required of the young wolf and where others had failed, he had championed every challenge. Survivor had passed nature's tests and now it was true. All he surveyed was his domain.

He turned his head slowly to look out over his valley and the spirits of his ancestors gazed from regal blue eyes. There was well-deserved pride in Survivor's every breath and dignity in every step. By nature's own design he was the best of his species, cunning, strong, sentient.

The story of Survivor and his graceful Soulmate would never end. It resonated through each spring's cubs in a consecrated place where an ancient wrong had been set right.

In the summers that followed, among the recreational vehicles and tent campers, a new bedtime story was passed from campfire to campfire. Parents told their children of a blue-eyed white wolf and his ebony mate who had come to live in

Yellowstone. And as the children drifted off to sleep, two wolves—one white, one black—raced without fear through the silver moonlight of their dreams.

Long after adults grew silent and campfires faded to glowing embers, two canine voices rode the night wind. Their howling songs rose and soared, chasing one another past Old Faithful, echoing through the Grand Canyon of the Yellowstone.

The wolves had returned to a promise that never again would their song be silenced. The spirit of the wolf god, Fenryr, smiled on that wild place. Survivor and Soulmate had come home.

Author's Note

While this novel is a work of fiction, many people and organizations worked tirelessly for decades to make the actual restoration of wolves to Yellowstone National Park a reality. Their documented work with wolves, and particularly the Yellowstone restoration project, are listed below for those interested in learning more.

L. David Mech, "The Wolf", University of Minn. Press, 1970

Barry Lopez, "Of Wolves and Men", Charles Scribner's Sons, 1978

Hank Fischer, "Wolf Wars", Falcon Press, 1995

Renee Askins, "Shadow Mountain", Doubleday, 2002

Rick Bass, "The Ninemile Wolves", Clark City Press, 1992

Rick McIntyre, "War Against Wolf", Voyageur Press, 1995

Peter Steinhart, "The Company of Wolves", Alfred P. Knopf, 1995

Lois Crisler, "Arctic Wild", Harper Perennial, 1973

Michael Phillips & Douglas Smith, "The Wolves of Yellowstone", Voyager Press, 1996

R.D. Lawrence, "In Praise of Wolves", Ballantine Books, 1986
"Secret Go The Wolves", Ballantine Books, 1980
"Ghost Walker", Harper Perennial, 1991

McCall & Dutcher, "Cougar, Ghost of the Rockies", 1992

Bernd Heinrich, "Mind of the Raven", Cliff Street Books, 1999

Hogan, Metzger, Peterson, "Intimate Nature, The Bond Between Women and Animals", Fawcett Columbine, 1998

The following organizations are still working on behalf of wolves, not only in Yellowstone, but other areas of the United States as well:

Defenders of Wildlife
1101 14th Street NW, #1400
Washington, D.C. 20005
www.defenders.org

The Yellowstone Wolf Project
Yellowstone National Park
PO Box 168
Mammoth, WY 82190
www.nps.gov/yell/nature/animals/wolf

Wolf Haven America
3111 Offut-Lake Road
Tenino, Washington 98589
www.wolfhaven.org

National Resources Defense Council
40 W. 20th St.
New York, NY 10011
www.nrdc.org

International Wolf Center
Ely, MN 55731
www.wolf.org
National Wildlife Federation
8925 Leesburg Pike
Vienna, VA 22184
www.nwf.org

About the Author

Man's place in the elegant tapestry that weaves together earth's flora and fauna is the inspiration for Kathryn Madison's stories. Raised in Seattle, she discovered her passion for all creatures – fleshed and furred, feathered and finned – at an early age while hiking, backpacking, and canoeing through Washington State. Scuba diving and sea-kayaking added new dimensions to her world. Today Kathryn shares these interests with her husband and their two huskies, dividing their time between Los Gatos and Grass Valley, California.

About Windstorm Creative
and our Readers' Club

Windstorm Creative was founded in 1989 to create a publishing house with author-centric ethics and cutting-edge, risk-taking innovation. Windstorm is now a company of more than ten divisions with international distribution channels that allow us to sell our books, games, music and films both inside the traditional systems and outside these paradigms, capitalizing on more direct delivery and non-traditional markets. As a result, our books can be found in grocery superstores as well as your favorite neighborhood bookstore, and dozens of other outlets on and off the Internet.

Windstorm is an independent press with the synergy and branding of a corporate publisher and an author royalty that's easily twice their best offer. We have continued to minimize returns without decreasing sales by publishing books that are timeless, as opposed to timely, and never back-listing our books. We stand adamantly against book stripping.

Windstorm is constantly changing, improving, and growing. We are driven by the needs of our authors – hailing from ten different countries – and the vision of our critically-acclaimed staff. All of our books are created with the strictest of environmental protections in mind. Our approach to no-waste, no-hazard, in-house production, and stringent out-source scrutiny, assures that our goals are met whether books are printed at our own facility or an outside press.

Because of these precautions, our books cost more. And though we know that our readers support our efforts, we also understand that a few dollars can add up. This is why we began our Readers' Club. Visit our webcenter and take 20% off every title, every day. No strings. No fine print.

While you're at our site, feel free to preview or request the first chapter of many of our titles, completely free of charge.

Thank you for supporting an independent press.

www.windstormcreative.com and click on Shop

See next page for title recommendations.

Manual for Normal
(Rebecca McEldowney)

The Big Five-O Café
(James Wolfe)

Bones Become Flowers
(Jess Mowry)

The Broccoli Eaters
(Gregg Fedchak)

Heir Unapparent
(William Hall)

The Sitka Incident
(Walt Larson)

Visibility
(Cris DiMarco)

False Harbor
(Michael Donnelly)